WRITTEN IN BLOOD

WRITTEN IN BLOOD

LAYTON GREEN

SEVENTH STREET BOOKS®
AN IMPRINT OF PROMETHEUS BOOKS
59 JOHN GLENN DRIVE • AMHERST, NY 14228
www.seventhstreetbooks.com

Published 2017 by Seventh Street Books®, an imprint of Prometheus Books

Cover images © Alamy Stock Photo
Cover design by Jacqueline Nasso Cooke
Cover design © Prometheus Books

This is a work of fiction. Characters, organizations, products, locales, and events portrayed in this novel are either products of the author's imagination or used fictitiously.

Excerpt from Agatha Christie's *Five Little Pigs*, © Agatha Christie, 1942, and published in 1984 by Berkeley Books.

Excerpt from Fyodor Dostoevsky's *Crime and Punishment*, © David Magarshack, 1966, and this translation first published in 1951 by Penguin Books.

Excerpt from Edgar Allan Poe's *The Murders in the Rue Morgue*, published in 1999 by Barnes and Noble Books.

Inquiries should be addressed to
Seventh Street Books
59 John Glenn Drive
Amherst, New York 14228
VOICE: 716–691–0133 • FAX: 716–691–0137
WWW.SEVENTHSTREETBOOKS.COM

21 20 19 18 17   5 4 3 2 1

Library of Congress Cataloging-in-Publication Data

Names: Green, Layton, author.
Title: Written in blood / by Layton Green.
Description: Amherst, NY : Seventh Street Books, an imprint of Prometheus Books
   2017.
Identifiers: LCCN 2017024043 (print) | LCCN 2017029804 (ebook) |
   ISBN 9781633883628 (ebook) | ISBN 9781633883611 (paperback)
Subjects: LCSH: Private investigators—Fiction. | Murder—Investigation—Fiction.
   | BISAC: FICTION / Mystery & Detective / Police Procedural. | GSAFD:
   Suspense fiction. | Mystery fiction. g
Classification: LCC PS3607.R43327 (ebook) |
   LCC PS3607.R43327 W75 2017 (print) | DDC 813/.6—dc23
LC record available at https://lccn.loc.gov/2017024043

Printed in the United States of America

A literary creation can appeal to us in all sorts of ways—by its theme, subject, situations, characters. But above all it appeals to us by the presence in it of art. It is the presence of art in Crime and Punishment *that moves us deeply rather than the story of Raskolnikov's crime.*

—Boris Pasternak

1

The body was lying faceup on a sheepskin rug, the top of the head caved in like a squashed plum. Detective Joe "Preach" Everson kneeled to view the corpse. To him, the splayed limbs suggested an uninhibited fall, rather than a careful arrangement of the body.

Which didn't fit with the two miniature crosses, one wood and one copper, placed side by side on the slain man's chest.

Officer Scott Kirby eyed the battered skull and let out a slow whistle. "What did that? A sledgehammer?"

Preach replied without averting his gaze from the body. "It's blunt force trauma, for sure."

"How come the eyes are open?" Kirby asked. "I thought that was for TV."

"Gravity. The muscles relax, the lids peel back."

"Huh. Smell's not as bad as I thought," Kirby said, though Preach had seen the junior officer's brown skin blanch when they entered the living room of the fashionable townhome.

The detective knew it was Officer Kirby's first body, his first whiff of rotting flesh tinged with the sticky sweet odor of spilled blood. Kirby had been on the force for just two years, fresh out of community college and a string of dead end jobs before that, and the number of murders in Creekville, North Carolina, in the last two years was an easy one to remember.

Zero.

Preach had returned to his hometown only a month before, after a sixteen-year safari in the jungle of the human condition. Flashes from his last murder investigation, the one in Atlanta that had derailed his career, kept flooding his thoughts. He forced the past away and pressed the back of his hand to the forehead of the corpse. "Seventy-five degrees in here, not much odor . . . rough guess, I'd say we're looking at eight to twelve hours."

"That's a pretty specific guesstimation," Kirby said. "I know you worked murders before, but . . . how many you seen?"

"Too many," Preach murmured, then held up a finger for quiet as he studied the facial features: eyes the color of frost on a windshield, a goatee sprinkled with grey, tight skin around the mouth, long creases in the forehead.

Preach's gaze roved upward, to a triptych of photos hanging on the wall. The deceased was smiling in all three, but an icy arrogance in his eyes told the detective that, whoever their John Doe was, he was not an empathetic man.

A successful man, perhaps. Someone who had taken what he wanted from life.

But not a man who would see a beggar on the streets of Creekville, or a child staring out from the back of a milk carton, and take on that muted pain as his own.

Not a man who shared Preach's affliction.

The dead man looked about fifty, fleshy but not fat, the white skin a touch sallow. He wore an untucked blue dress shirt and brown cotton pants. Slip-on Merrells with gray socks. No wedding ring. White-collar hands and nails. No signs of a struggle, no visible wounds besides the head.

Kirby stepped back from the body. "He look familiar to you? I feel like I've seen him around."

"A bit, yeah."

"What do you make of those crosses? Are they from a particular kind of group or sect, whaddyacallit—"

"Denomination?"

Kirby cocked one of his signature white-toothed smiles that broadened his narrow face. He was not thick-bodied like Preach, who looked like he could play tight end for a professional football team. Kirby was tall and lean and hit the gym like Mother Teresa attended mass. "Yeah. That."

Preach folded his arms, creasing the fabric of his double-breasted, forest green overcoat he had bought during his first week as a detective. "The holes imply something was threaded through the crosses, probably a loophole for a necklace. Catholic, if I had to guess, simply because Catholics wear more crosses."

They donned evidence gloves, and Kirby extracted a leather wallet. "Our vic's name is Farley Grover Robertson, poor guy. Business card says he owns the Wandering Muse. That's the local bookstore."

Preach snapped his fingers. "That's it."

Kirby coughed a chuckle. "We've all been wondering where you go at night."

"You should give reading a try. I can help with the letters."

"Literature doesn't advance my career plan." Kirby flashed another megawatt smile. "Scotty the Body's coming to a reality show near you."

Preach held out a hand for the wallet. "Dare to dream."

"We should team up. Chicks dig that blond All-American look, plus the coffee and cream angle—they'll lap us up. *Cops* meets *The Bachelor*."

"I'd rather be waterboarded before breakfast every morning than be on a reality show."

Kirby looked relieved but nervous at the light banter, unsure if they should continue. In Preach's experience, it happened at almost every murder scene. A way of flinching at the horror without losing face.

He flipped through the wallet, finding two grand in cash, plus an array of credit cards. The driver's license claimed that Farley Robertson was born in 1964, stood five foot eleven, and weighed two-twenty. "You find a phone or a computer?"

"Yup," Kirby said. "Both password locked."

"Get IT on that."

Preach rose to take in his surroundings. They were in the living room of an upscale townhouse, nestled in the forest hovering just outside the sliding glass door. Floor-to-ceiling bookshelves on one wall, original art on the other, white leather furniture, a flat-screen television mounted above a gas fireplace, an island partitioning the stainless steel kitchen, a dead body lying on a blood-soaked rug covering half the living room floor.

An enormous cockroach climbed out of an air vent, lurching about as if some fat, drunken god of the netherworld had stumbled onto the surface. Must be a recent spray. He told Kirby to check pest control records.

They searched the two-story condo, which was a little *too* clean, *too* artsy. If Preach were back in Atlanta, he would have pegged Farley Robertson as homosexual, perhaps metro.

But in the People's Republic of Creekville, which was what everyone in the Research Triangle called the eccentric little community outside Chapel Hill, it was hard to tell. Gay or straight or bi, grad student or semi-homeless, artist, hipster, young professional, skater, brewer, doctor, yogi—the social lines were blurred in the People's Republic like nowhere Preach had ever been.

His final stop was the laundry cubby between the master and guest bedrooms. When he saw the washer and dryer, he started thinking about the amount of blood they had found downstairs. He kneeled and asked Kirby to tilt the washer.

After a moment of searching, Preach said, "Check out the grouting."

They switched positions. Kirby whistled. "Is that a spot of dried blood?"

"It's not Tabasco sauce."

Kirby eyed the bottle of liquid detergent perched atop the washer. "You think the killer smashed the vic's skull and then went upstairs to run a cycle of laundry? That takes a calculating perp. Wait—wouldn't that mean he didn't come here to kill him? Because he could have brought a change of clothes and a plastic bag."

"Maybe the killer washed the blood out in an abundance of caution, in case a cop pulled him over."

After pointing out the blood to forensics, the officers returned downstairs. "So what now?" Kirby asked. "The bookstore? Let 'em know the boss is on permanent vacation, find someone to ID the body?"

Preach snapped a photo of the corpse with his cell phone, eying the two crosses on the victim's chest while he gave a slow, uneasy nod. "I'll have Terry talk to the neighbors and search for next of kin."

"Strange how the crosses were left there," Kirby said, noticing the focus of his attention. "Like it's a message or something."

"Oh, it's a message," Preach said. "The question is for whom?"

2

Sunlight flared as Preach and Kirby stepped outside, the cloudless sear of a crisp October sky. Voices followed, a few local reporters pressing against the police tape cordoning off a tiny front lawn strewn with pine cones.

Preach could see Kirby preparing to preen for the media. "Don't talk to them," the detective said in a low voice.

"What?"

Preach lowered his head and headed straight for the Chevy Impala, forcing Kirby to keep up. As they strode past, neighbors clutched coffee cups in their front yards, staring in shock at the array of police cruisers.

The questions from the reporters came rapid fire:

"Can you confirm Creekville's first murder in ten years?"

"Is this Farley Robertson's residence? How was he killed?"

"When can we expect a—"

Preach slammed the door and saw Kirby staring at the reporters in the rearview. The naiveté in the junior officer's eyes made Preach think about the article currently headlining the front page of the Creekville Police website.

Tips for Dealing with Unwanted Deer Incursions on Your Property.

"You want to be on camera if and when you solve the case," Preach said. "Not before. Unless you want to be the guy who failed to protect and serve?"

"Yeah, sure," Kirby muttered.

"The chief can dish out the basics when she's ready."

They entered downtown on Hillsdale Street, passing a half-mile spree of lavish Southern homes with lawns shaded by hundred-year-old oaks. Creekville's Beverly Hills.

Preach still felt a pang of bittersweet emotion whenever he drove down Hillsdale. He had once been the town's golden boy, with all the unearned privilege and little cruelties that term implies. Right after high school, still reeling from a breakdown after his cousin's death, he had left home and enrolled at a two-year Bible college. The decision was part newfound faith, part a jab at his parents, and mostly a lack of direction. Ten months of preaching after that had led to a loss of faith, not in God but in the narrow interpretation of the divine.

Next came a stint as a nondenominational prison chaplain. It had been the only job he could find, a brutal job, but one he respected. A second breakdown had caused him to take refuge in a random motel in a sunbaked town in Georgia, close to the last prison where he had worked. He numbed his mind with manual labor on a pecan farm. Reflection, searching, a chance encounter with a novel that altered his worldview. He decided to read every good book that had ever been written and made a new pledge, this time to help those who could not speak for themselves.

After taking a job with the Atlanta police, he had made a rapid rise through the department. No breakdowns for a decade, his past issues firmly in the rearview.

Or so he thought.

They turned onto Main Street, the bustling farmer's market signaling the start of the small but vibrant commercial district. Preach cracked the window for some air as they passed the town hall and its unapologetic display of the rainbow flag.

"It's my first murder," Kirby said. "Chance to make a name for myself, right?"

"Someone's dead. Don't get too excited. What do we know so far? Tell me something."

Kirby flexed his fingers on the armrest. "Housekeeper called it in. Said the front door was unlocked when she arrived. No sign of forced entry, which means Robertson let him in, left the door unlocked—unlikely after midnight—or the murderer had a key."

"The vast majority of murders are committed by someone the victim knew."

Kirby whistled out a breath. "If you hurt the ones you love the most, then someone must have *really* loved Farley Robertson."

"What'd you notice about the townhome?"

"That our guy had a ten thousand dollar couch, museum quality art, and two grand in his wallet. I thought bookstores made about as much money as a travel agency in a trailer park."

"Maybe he had family money," Preach said.

He parked across the street from a long, two-story brick building that housed a line of storefronts. The building was painted Carolina blue, and whimsical street murals covered the two end walls.

The Wandering Muse was wedged between a speakeasy and a throwback barber shop. There was also a tattoo parlor and a store called Brewed Vinyl that was pretty much as advertised: a combination coffee shop and vinyl record shop.

Kirby paused with his hand on the door. "I know the chief sent us on the call cause you're the Man and I was available—"

"The chief picked you because she sees something in you."

Kirby tried to disguise his pleasure at the compliment. "Anyway, you think she'll keep us together on this? I'd like to learn a thing or two."

"You sure you want to work a homicide in Creekville? It could get ugly. No big city lights to hide behind."

Kirby's mint green eyes glowed with determination. "Oh yeah."

With its high ceilings and exposed brick walls, track lighting illuminating narrow shelves groaning with books, Preach thought the Wandering Muse resembled a microcosm of Creekville: disheveled at first glance, but *carefully* so. Educated but not studious; lively but not raucous; a welcoming, laid-back vibe ready to explode the moment someone was suspected of not conforming to the welcoming, laid-back vibe.

A thin, pale young woman was arranging a stack of hardcovers by the front door. She had short dark hair that stuck out like twigs, a wide mouth, and cappuccino eyes. Preach didn't remember seeing her before, but he had only been in a few times.

"Can I help you?" she asked, coolly eying Officer Kirby's uniform.

Her eyes were cautious, edgy. Not the shifty wariness of a criminal, but the guarded look of someone who has lived outside the candy-coated center of mainstream society.

Preach held up his badge. "I'm Detective Everson. Are you in charge this morning, ma'am?"

He could sense her gauging the power structure. "Just by default," she said, "since the owner hasn't shown up. And I've got class at eleven."

He took a closer look at the collection of sharp angles and delicate curves that defined her narrow face, quite attractive in a waifish way. Her clothing, like her hair, made a statement: a long-sleeved black fishnet top with a white camisole underneath; ripped jeans rolled at the cuffs; a layered assortment of necklaces inset with colored stones.

"Do you have someone who can watch the register?" he asked.

Realizing it was serious, she called out to a guy with blond dreadlocks named Nate. "Maybe you should just tell me? I paid that parking..."

She trailed off as Preach held up his cell phone, showing her the crime scene. "We're looking for someone who can identify the deceased."

She clamped a hand over her mouth. "That's Lee. This isn't a—ohmygod."

"Lee is Farley Robertson?"

She nodded, her hand still covering her mouth.

"Why don't we step outside?" Preach said gently.

"How... why...?"

"I'm afraid we don't know yet. Ms...."

"Hale." She moved her hand to her temple. "Ari Hale."

"I'm sorry for your loss, Ms. Hale, but I need to ask you a few questions about the deceased. Would you like some water, a chair?"

She blew out another breath. Despite her shock, she maintained her poise. "I'm okay."

Nate sauntered over, frowning at the two policemen and casting a quick, hungry look at his coworker when she wasn't looking. After a deep breath, the woman led the officers through the rear entrance, to a gravel lot littered with cigarette butts and maple leaves.

"You said you had class at eleven," Preach said. "What do you study?"

She looked surprised at the question. "I'm a 3L at UNC. Law school."

He nodded, impressed. She knew her rights and was comfortable with police. "And you work here during the week?"

"Wednesday through Sunday evenings, plus this day shift. Lucky me."

"How long have you worked here?" he asked.

"Two years."

"And how well did you know Mr. Robertson?"

Her eyes flicked to Preach's cell phone, and she bit her lip. "He paid on time and treated us fairly, but we didn't talk that much. He mostly handled the back office and author events."

"Do you happen to know his next of kin?"

"His parents have passed, and he doesn't have kids. There's a sister in California. I don't think they speak very much. I've never met her."

"What about close acquaintances?"

"No one he's mentioned to me, except for Damian Black, of course."

Preach's eyebrows lifted. "The horror writer?"

"The one and only. They were childhood friends."

Kirby scribbled the name in his notepad, and Ari raised a finger. "There is another guy who comes in more than most."

"A customer?"

"Most of the time he disappeared into the office with Lee. I'm not sure what they did back there."

"How long would he stay?" Preach asked.

"Five or ten minutes, usually. The guy always strutted out as moodily as he came in. Like a rooster with a chip on its shoulder."

"Maybe that was the appeal," Kirby said.

Ari gave Kirby an amused glance. "I don't think it was sex. Though I'm pretty sure Lee was gay."

"Was he seeing anyone?" Preach asked.

"Not that I'm aware of."

"I don't suppose you know this customer's name?"

"He's a barista at the Rabbit Hole. Look for the guy in his thirties with the beret and the moustache, puts the *hip* in hipster."

"Have you noticed a recent change in Mr. Robertson's behavior?" he asked.

She pressed her lips together as she thought. "He seemed more energetic lately."

"In a positive way, or a negative one?"

"I would characterize it as nervous energy."

"Any reason why?"

"No."

"Was there any sign of drug use?"

"Not in front of me," she said, in a way that implied the question was not unwarranted. They would see what the autopsy turned up.

"I know it sounds cliché," Preach said, "but I have to ask: did Mr. Robertson have any enemies?"

She shook her head, though her lips parted as if she were about to comment.

"Ms. Hale?"

"At the end of my Wednesday shift, he was arguing with someone in the back. I heard them shouting all the way from the register."

"A customer?"

"A writer. A *real* writer, if you know what I mean. Lonely, socially awkward . . . a weird guy."

"His name?"

She hesitated.

"We're just gathering information," Preach said.

She nudged a piece of hair out of her face. "J. T. Belker."

Preach glanced at Kirby, who made another note. "Do you know what they were arguing about?" the detective asked.

"No idea. They were still back there when I left." Ari eased off the wall and twisted one of her silver thumb rings. "Any more questions? I should get back. I'll need to call a staff meeting."

"Was Farley the sole owner?"

"As far as I know."

"Okay. Try to keep the store running for now. I hate to ask—" Preach opened his cell phone again, displaying the photo of the corpse—"but could you take a closer look at the body? We found two small crosses on Mr. Robertson's chest. Have you ever seen him with those, maybe on a necklace?"

Ari took the smartphone and enlarged the image. Her eyes widened as she brought the photo closer. "The head wound," she said, in an oddly subdued voice, "could it have been caused by the back of an axe?"

"I suppose," Preach said. "Why?"

"And those crosses . . . I don't suppose they're made of wood and copper?"

He exchanged a sharp glance with Kirby. The junior officer shifted to a more alert stance, and Preach's eyes bored into Ari. "How'd you know that?"

"So they are?" She was staring at the photo with a dazed expression.

"One wood, one copper. Does that mean something to you?"

"I don't know what it means," she said, "but the wound, the position of the body, the crosses: those are the exact details from the murder of the old pawnbroker in Dostoevsky's *Crime and Punishment*."

3

Preach was staring at Ari as if waiting for the punch line. She handed him the phone and took a step back, distancing herself from the disturbing image of the crime scene.

"You're sure?" Preach said, not sure what to make of what she said. Maybe it was a coincidence.

"I just read it again this summer." She led them back into the store, to a row of shelves marked Classics. After sliding out and rejecting two versions of the famous novel, she opted for the Magarshack translation. "Here," she said, pointing at the bottom third of page 96. He followed along as she read:

Being a small woman, the blow fell across the crown of the head. . . . It was then that he struck her again with all his strength, and then again, every time with the back of the hatchet and across the crown of the head. Blood gushed out as from an overturned tumbler, and she fell straight on her back.

"So the victim in the book is an old woman?" Preach asked. "What about the crosses?"

She held up a finger as she flipped the page:

Suddenly he noticed a ribbon round her neck ... he succeeded in cutting through the ribbon without touching the body with the hatchet, and took it off: it was a purse. There were two crosses on the ribbon, one of cypress wood and another of copper, and, in addition, a little enameled icon; and with them a small greasy chamois-leather purse with a steel ring and a little ring. The purse was full to bursting. Raskolnikov shoved it into his pocket without bothering to see what was in it, threw the crosses on the old woman's body, and, taking the hatchet with him this time, rushed back to the bedroom.

Preach took the book and read it twice more himself, his eyes lingering on the page. The inference was inescapable.

Kirby had been reading over his shoulder. "Hot damn," he muttered. "Hot buttered damn."

Before they left the bookstore, Preach and Kirby gave the back office a thorough search and found nothing of interest. Ari gave them a copy of *Crime and Punishment* and promised to contact them if anything arose. After Preach thanked her, he and Kirby walked a few streets down to a burrito joint that shared space with a Buddhist Center. In his youth, the storefront had housed a thrift shop his mother used to drag him to.

Preach ordered a sweet potato burrito, Kirby a plate of corn enchiladas. "I thought for sure those crosses meant we had a religious wacko on our hands," Kirby said, finding an open table next to the Art-O-Mat. A string of plastic red chilies hung along the wall beside them. "The Lord's Avenger come to smite Creekville for its sins."

Preach was relieved the placement of the crosses did not appear to have religious significance, nothing to do with his own past. He managed a half-smile. "Just your garden variety crime-scene-from-a-famous-novel murder."

Kirby scooped off the sour cream and most of the cheese from his enchiladas, then sat and stared at his plate.

"The bodies get easier," Preach said. "Though I'm not sure they should."

"Yeah," Kirby said, forcing down a small bite. "So what the hell's it all mean?"

Preach reached for a grimy tube of habanero sauce. "It means we have a few leads."

"Do we start with the barista or the writer?"

"The barista. Let's get a little more color before we talk to the more probable suspect. And check with Terry, see if we need to circle back with any of the neighbors."

"I thought we'd talk to them first."

"We'll get there. The neighbors aren't going to bolt; the suspects might."

Kirby nodded as he chewed. "Seems kind of obvious, you know, a writer leaving a clue from a novel."

"Most murders are creatures of the obvious."

"Oh yeah?"

Preach waved a hand. "Obvious motives, obvious clues, obvious suspects. Not many homicides possess true subtlety."

"What's obvious about this one? There's no evidence of theft, no clues besides the crosses."

"It's early. Let's talk to some people and let forensics do their thing."

Kirby took a few more bites and washed it down with a swig from a large flask. Preach looked at him askance.

"Coconut water," Kirby said. "Good for the skin."

"Gotcha."

Behind the counter, someone turned on a television showcasing a local broadcast from outside Farley Robertson's townhouse. Every customer turned to stare at the caption announcing Creekville's first murder in a decade.

"That was fast," Kirby said.

"That's how it goes. Buckle up."

Preach watched in disgust as the reporter tried to sound somber but failed to hide his excitement at catching a big story. The broadcast switched to the Wandering Muse. Ari gave a sound bite, clearly uncomfortable with the attention.

Kirby's eyes lingered on the screen. "There's something I've been meaning to ask you. What's harder, preachin' or wearin' blue?"

Preach eyed the copy of *Crime and Punishment* on the table, then flicked his gaze to a group of tattooed street kids in the corner, hunched over a basket of chips and salsa. One in particular caught his eye, a Latino boy with a pockmarked face and vacant eyes.

He felt the familiar heave of empathy, and the fingers of his free hand tightened against his jeans. "Being a preacher is harder on the mind," he said, forcing his thoughts away from another Latino boy, a candy-colored tree house in Atlanta, a case that had shattered the detective's spirit like a hammer through a pane of glass. "Being a cop is harder on the soul."

The Rabbit Hole Café was on Main Street, a few blocks from downtown and next door to the Cybrary, a public reading room that focused on eBook stations and free Wi-Fi. Creekville's version of a library.

Preach's hometown had always blended radically progressive with old school Southern, but to him, the dichotomies had become absurd. The Provence Café next door to Mami's Chicken and Waffles; the chicken feed store that rented its second floor to a start-up incubator, furnished with bean bags and living walls; the Piggly Wiggly in the same shopping plaza as a restaurant specializing in bone marrow dishes paired with growlers of local craft beer.

A collection of hybrid and electric cars, scooters covered in stickers, vintage convertibles, pedal cars, and retro cruising bicycles filled the gravel lot of the café. A pair of Segways was parked against the rear wall. Preach and Kirby entered through a side door, made their way through a lounge filled with sofas and board games, then entered a room with a stained concrete floor and brick walls painted dull orange. Patrons lined the communal wooden tables, hands gripping ceramic mugs, laptops glowing in the dim light.

Behind the register, burlap sacks displayed coffee beans from two-dozen countries. A young woman with pierced lips was taking orders. The man beside her sported a beret and a green Atari shirt with a pack of cigarettes rolled inside a sleeve. Rimless glasses, corduroy pants, and a handlebar moustache completed the uniform.

The man glanced up from steaming a cup of milk. "Been a long time, Joe."

4

The detective found the barista's small eyes and drank them in, saw the story of a man trying hard to maintain the cool edginess that had always been his calling card. His name was Wade Fee, and he had been Preach's running mate in high school. His chief lieutenant.

"About sixteen years," Preach replied. He hadn't wanted their first meeting since their senior year in high school to go down like this.

Memories oozed out of cracks in the reservoir of his forgotten youth. Long summer nights at the neighborhood pool. Sneaking girlie mags and cigarettes into their fort in the woods. Cutting school for jaunts to Surf City in Wade's convertible, a different pair of girls every time. Hitting the mountain trails with backpacks and a case of beer. The pizza joint where they all used to meet after the game to decide where to party.

Preach hadn't contacted any of his old friends because he hadn't figured out what to say. He knew Wade, especially, had felt betrayed by his sudden conversion from hard-core hell raiser to . . . someone else.

Wade poured foamed milk into the cappuccino. "I gotta say," he said, his voice a soft growl, "I never thought I'd see the day Psycho Joe walked into town with a badge and a gun. Turning into a Jesus Freak was weird enough, but a cop?" He smirked. "Or is it all penance for high school?"

"That was a long time ago," Preach said.

"Not here it isn't."

Preach folded his arms. "We need to talk."

The barista's perpetual scowl deepened. He set the finished drink on the counter and jerked his head at the girl with the pierced lips. She gave Preach a bold, flirtatious glance before taking over.

Wade wiped his hands on a towel. "Let's take it outside," he said, then led them to a sprawling outdoor area dotted with Adirondack chairs and picnic tables. Wood chips covered the ground, the smell of pine infused the air.

They found a quiet corner. After Preach introduced Kirby, Wade leaned his elbows on his knees and grunted. "So what's this about?"

"You heard what happened this morning?" Preach asked.

"Everybody heard."

"You seem pretty distraught."

Wade spread his palms, then leaned back and lit a smoke. "Man's gotta tear up every time something bad happens?"

Preach's voice remained calm. "You don't have to shed a tear to show respect for the recently deceased. Especially someone you knew."

Wade snorted and looked away. "Ask your questions, Joe. We're busy."

"This isn't an interrogation. We're just trying to flesh out the picture. How well did you know Farley Robertson?"

"I went to the bookstore every now and then."

"But did you know him personally?" Kirby asked.

"I just said I did, dude."

"You know what we mean," Kirby said. "Did you know him a bit more than *that'll be ten bucks for the book on moustache wax, please*?"

Wade flushed and stood. "We done here?"

"Did you know him?" Preach asked quietly, after giving Kirby a warning glance.

"Yeah, sure, we hung out in the office now and then, had a single-barrel and rapped about literature. He came in here as well, appreciated a good cup of tar."

"Any idea why someone wanted him dead?"

"Lee? Nah, man. None whatsoever." He rose and took a step toward the side door. "We straight now? I've got a job to do."

"I have to ask," Preach said apologetically, "where you were last night. As a matter of routine."

A nasty grin slunk onto Wade's face. "You want my alibi, Joe? He's sitting in the back office, same place I was last night. It's the door behind the pool table. Go on in."

"Thanks."

"Riiight." Wade took a deep drag on his cigarette and put it out on the wall. "So why'd you come back? After all these years?"

Preach stood and brushed pine straw off his jeans, sad at the bitterness in his old friend's voice. He handed the barista his card. "It's good to see you. I'd like to catch up sometime."

"Don't hold your breath."

"Fair enough," Preach said softly. "But if you think of anything I might need to know, call me."

"Psycho Joe?" Kirby asked, as they returned inside.

Preach shoved his hands in his coat. "Kid stuff."

Kirby chuckled. "What kind of kid were you?"

"The kind who had no idea who he was."

They walked into the game room. Preach knocked on a metal door set into the wall behind the pool table.

"Well, c'mon in!" a gravelly baritone called out.

Preach stepped into a smoky, low-ceilinged office with exposed ductwork and a floor stripped of tile. A kitschy aquarium took up half of one wall, a desk and file cabinets another. A rockabilly tune streamed from an iPad stand.

In the center of the room, four people Preach had never seen before were lounging around a wooden table. Ashtrays overflowed next to shot glasses and a bottle of rye whiskey. Underneath the table, a pit bull eyed the newcomers as it gnawed on a broom handle.

"Officer Kirby and Detective Everson," the same voice boomed. It was coming from a burly man at the head of the table, his face swallowed by a bushy black beard that cut off in a straight line with his moustache. He wore a flannel shirt underneath a motorcycle jacket, and a brown wool cap pulled low. His dark eyes possessed an unsettling mixture of deadness and energy, like twin lumps of coal still glittering in the vein. "I saw you on the news."

The door clanged when it swung shut. The pit bull growled softly, and Preach saw Kirby tense up beside him.

"Mac," Kirby said, with an uneasy edge to his voice. Preach realized his partner's introduction was meant for him. "Big Mac Dobbins."

"Welcome to my humble establishment, gentlemen. What can I do ya for?"

Preach took a look at the two men beside Mac. The man on the far left was missing a front tooth and wore a flannel vest over a long underwear shirt. The skinnier redhead had a *Walking Dead* T-shirt, pierced eyebrows, and leather wristbands with iron spikes.

Sitting next to Mac was a striking Asian American woman with fur-trimmed boots propped on the table. Tribal tattoos writhed up her crossed legs and disappeared beneath a black leather skirt.

Preach could tell at a glance that these people belonged to a different breed from Wade. All four had the kind of mean, hardscrabble eyes that told Preach that wherever they had come from, their parents hadn't met for barbecues around the neighborhood pool.

"I hope we're not disturbing you," Preach said. "We just have a few questions."

"If you're not with the IRS, you're not disturbing us. So what's on your mind, Preach? That's what they call you, isn't it?"

"My friends do," he said. As far as he knew, his nickname wasn't public knowledge. Mac had been keeping tabs. "You can call me Detective Everson."

A throaty laugh escaped the woman, and Preach noticed the hands of the other two men slip below the table. Kirby folded his arms, the woman recrossed her legs, and Mac poured himself a shot and held the bottle up. "Care for a drink? We like to welcome our neighbors right and proper 'round here."

There was a hardness to Mac's aura that went beyond that of the other three, a dangerously careless vibe, as if Mac had crossed lines in life he shouldn't have crossed.

"Wade told us you can vouch for his whereabouts last night," Preach said. "Is that true?"

Mac downed the shot. "He was playing poker with us right here at this table. All of us except Mina. Where were you last night, honey? Out causing mischief?"

"I'm a good girl, Mac," she purred. Straight black hair framed her heart-shaped face, and her arms were folded across a lavender shawl. Her mouth puckered when at rest, and she was so skinny her collarbone jutted out like a ship's mast.

Mac lowered his eyes and shook his head. "Girl, if you're good, then I don't wanna know bad. *Hell* no," he said, with a rumbling belly laugh.

"What time did Wade start playing last night?" Preach asked.

Mac eyed the other two. "What was it boys, around eleven?"

"Yup."

"That's right, Mac. Right before eleven."

Preach let his gaze rest on the other two men, who gave him defiant stares. "And when did he leave?"

"About dawn, I reckon," Mac said. "Poker night tends to get frisky."

Preach was aware he was lying. He was also aware that Mac didn't give a damn that he knew.

"Do you have video surveillance?"

Mac chuckled. "We prefer to deal with security on our own. Keeps overhead down."

"That's risky business," Preach said. "Things could get out of hand."

"Oh, they'd get out of hand all right." Mac set a fist on the table and rubbed his thumb slowly against his forefinger, eying Preach as if lancing a boil. "Real quick-like."

In the ensuing silence, the dog began to growl, and Preach resisted the urge to reach for his gun.

"Wade's a good boy," Mac said finally. "You should leave him be."

"I prefer to think of him as a grown man," Preach said, "and I'll make my own decisions. But as long as your story doesn't conflict with any other information we receive, then we're done here."

"Well, that's good," Mac said, pouring himself another shot as Preach and Kirby turned to leave. "Real good."

5

"So who are they?" Preach asked, as they walked to the car. "Local dealers?"

Kirby unwrapped a protein bar. "They're bad news is who they are. Crank and pot and pharmies, mostly, but they've got a hand in other stuff."

"Such as?"

"Breaking and entering, dogs, car boosts, gambling. Who knows what else."

"Sounds more like a mafia enterprise than a drug ring," Preach said. Then muttered, "Only in Creekville do crime lords own coffee shops."

"That's right," Kirby said, smirking. "We've got a hipster mafia."

"Why didn't you tell me Mac owns the Rabbit Hole?"

"I didn't know."

Preach stopped walking. "Why not?"

"He has lots of business interests. I guess that's one of them."

Preach sucked in a breath, reminding himself that this wasn't Atlanta. "You have to keep track of your major players. What's his history?"

"He came out of some trailer park on the South Carolina border, in the system at thirteen, swept into town like Darth Vader about three years ago. We've never pinned anything on him, and his people are too scared to roll."

"And the girl?" Preach asked, as they got into the car and headed for the station.

"Mina Hawes. Her mom's Korean or Bangladeshi or something, I forget, but they're from some shitty apartment complex right down the street. Mina's sheet's as dirty as Mac's is clean. A pair of burglaries, second degree arson, domestic violence—she beat the hell out of an ex with a tire iron. Got some legs, though, huh? Like a pair of saplings."

The police station came into view, a plain brick building with white awnings right in the middle of downtown. The station was located on the second floor, above a gluten-free bakery and an ice cream parlor. Preach grimaced every time he saw it. Who put a police station on the second floor?

"My guess is the toxicology report will show illicit substances in Farley's system," the detective said, as they parked in the rear lot.

"You're thinking Mac was his dealer, and Farley stole some stash or threatened to roll? And Wade was the point man?"

"I doubt Wade pulled the trigger, but he might have gotten someone inside the home." Preach shook his head and cursed softly, hoping his old friend wasn't involved.

"What about the crosses?" Kirby asked.

"Any chance Mac's a Dostoevsky scholar?" Preach asked.

"About the same chance he plays Ultimate Frisbee in the quad on the weekends."

Preach and Kirby briefed Chief Higgins back at the station. Officer Terry Haskins joined in, reporting that none of the neighbors had seen or heard anything suspicious. Officer Haskins was a narrow-faced thirty-year-old with a widow's peak and naturally arched eyebrows, as if he were in a constant state of perplexity. The chief told him to reach out to Farley's sister and look into the bookstore's finances.

Preach got a head start on his paperwork while Kirby looked up an address for J. T. Belker, the writer Ari had overheard arguing with the victim in the bookstore.

"J. T. lives at 725 Hager Street," Kirby said, eying his watch in embarrassment as he approached Preach's cubicle. "That's out by the tracks. Listen, I told my sister I'd watch my nephew tonight, while she takes my niece to her recital. Sis is injured and can't drive, Kayla would be heartbroken, and we don't really have anyone else—"

"Don't worry about it," Preach said. "I'll talk to the writer."

"I'll be done by nine."

"Let's regroup in the morning. Do me a favor and check with Evidence before you leave."

As Preach was leaving the station, Chief Higgins beckoned him to her office. The chief was a top-heavy redhead with oily skin and a thin, determined mouth. She had cut her teeth in Charlotte, where her former husband had died young and in the line of duty. She was the only person in the building besides Preach with homicide experience.

He updated her on progress, and she folded her oddly graceful hands on the desk, making soft *hmms* as she took in the news. Chief Higgins was full of seeming contradictions: an overweight vegan, a gun-toting liberal, and a North Carolinian who didn't care for any of the Big Three: BBQ, beer, or basketball.

"You sure you're okay to handle this?" she said.

He sat in the metal chair and fiddled with an hourglass paperweight. "The first murder in my hometown in a decade, a month after I start? Fate is a complicated thing, Chief. I believe you ignore it at your peril."

"Is that some kinda religious saying?"

"What does fate have to do with religion? Unless you're a Calvinist?"

"I dunno, I guess I'm not that deep. Fate to me is getting hit by a car. Or not."

Preach leaned back in his chair, watching the sand seep through the center of the hourglass. "I'm going to do my job."

"We can try to bring in someone from Durham or Raleigh."

"You know how that will turn out. I'll be fine. Thanks for the concern."

"It's not just about you," she said quietly.

Preach set the paperweight back on the desk. "What happened in Atlanta was different. A one-off. This is a straight murder, and I've cleared dozens of them."

"Therapy?"

"I start in two days," he said evenly. "We both know it's just a rubber stamp."

She took a sip of masala chai and folded her hands on the desk. "We'll do our best to give you what you need."

"What about Kirby? He expressed an interest, and I think he shows promise."

"An interest in what, being on TV? I'll give him some rope."

"Why don't I know about Mac Dobbins yet?" Preach asked.

She nodded. "He's an up and comer, all right. Smarter than the rest of the yahoos trying to deal drugs around here. Kept his nose clean so far, but I agree—he's dangerous."

Her phone rang. When Preach rose to leave, she said, "I know it's Creekville, but keep your wits about you. Things have changed around here. Hell, small town America has changed."

The lights of Creekville sparkled in the headlamps of Preach's car. Downtown consisted of a few blocks of two- and three-story brick buildings, but the hustle and bustle was frenetic for such a tiny town. Part of it was the nearby university, part of it was the starry-eyed bohemian vibe that attracted wanderers and artistic types from all over.

He cranked the heater. The temperature had gone into free fall. As he drove, he thought about the two crosses and the anomaly they presented. He had told Kirby that most homicides were creatures of the obvious, and they were.

Easy motives, easy chain of evidence. Murder by numbers.

What he hadn't told the younger officer was that when it came to some crimes, some *psyches*, statistics were worthless. He had learned that not only on the force, but as a chaplain in some of the worst prisons in the country. Listening to the confessions of minds so bankrupt his skin prickled from the toxic energy seeping through the glass barrier. Dealing with moral compasses so skewed from the norm that he wondered if he were talking to a human being at all, and not some other lifeform that had evolved on a separate evolutionary track, irrational to the rest of humanity.

He passed the turn to his mother's house and remembered they were supposed to have dinner. Since her house was three minutes away, he decided to let her down in person.

Virginia Everson still taught sociology at UNC, but Preach's father had died of a heart attack three years before. His mother had stayed in the house, a sparkling white midcentury modern with a wall of windows overlooking the forest. The home was a substantial upgrade from the rustic wood bungalow in which Preach had been raised.

He parked, and his mother met him at the door. Tall and long-limbed, her hair was a mass of tawny spirals parted in the middle and streaked with gray. She was wearing reading glasses, loose cotton pants, and a beige blouse. None of the piercings, henna tattoos, headbands, and sloganed T-shirts Preach remembered from his youth.

"I've seen the news," she said. Polite but removed as always. "I take it we're off tonight?"

"I'm sorry."

"Does it have to be you?"

"It's my job," he said.

"I just thought, after Atlanta, that maybe . . ." Her words faded away, and she averted her eyes.

"Thanks for the concern."

They swam in the unasked questions concerning his career. He didn't want to discuss it, and his mother wouldn't probe. She recoiled from displaying emotion, public or private. She had always been far more aligned with the aloof hipster crowd, even before it was a thing, than with the *finger on the throbbing love pulse of the universe* set. That had been his father.

"Farley Robertson and I went to high school together, you know," she said.

"Did you keep up?"

"We hadn't spoken in years. We were never close."

"What was he like?"

"Lee was popular but not well-liked, if you know what I mean. In high school, he had a talent for making people feel small. Honestly, he was rather mean." She rolled her eyes. "God, what a terror teenagers can be. You remember what you put us through, don't you?"

"How could I forget?" He checked his watch. He wanted to catch Belker at a reasonable hour. "Look, I have to go."

"Son . . ."

He knew she was worried about him and struggling to voice her emotions, to say something real.

Just once, he wished she would win the battle.

"Yeah, Mom?"

"Thanks for coming by to tell me," she said finally.

Preach slowed as he pulled onto Hager Street, a ribbon of age-spotted pavement crowded by row houses with cheap siding. Not the worst part of town, but far from the best. A light was on inside Belker's place. In the yard next door, a neighbor had erected three fake graves for Halloween and labeled the headstones *Stalin*, *Ayn Rand*, and *Rush Limbaugh*.

Preach and his old crew had often walked the railroad tracks across the street, following them to the trestle in the woods and tossing beer cans into the gushing creek below. The memory felt like a tangible thing, both warped by time and achingly familiar.

Someone inside Belker's house peered through the drapes. Preach rang the bell, his hand on his gun. One never knew how a murder suspect would respond, what panicked thoughts might be running through his mind.

Especially if he was guilty.

A heavyset man in his late forties opened the door wearing thick glasses, baggy gray sweatpants, and a food-stained T-shirt. His head was bulbous, his hair stringy and balding.

"Can I help you?"

Preach displayed his badge and told Belker about the murder. The writer's uneven mouth contorted into a shocked expression. "Farley's *dead*?"

Preach saw glimmers of something else behind the surprise, something the writer was trying to keep hidden. "You didn't see it on the news? Talk to anyone in town?"

"I've been home all day. And I don't watch the news." He led Preach into a kitchen piled with pizza boxes and crusty dishes, then shook two pills out of a prescription bottle. He downed them with a glass of water.

"So you're a full-time writer?" Preach asked.

Belker spluttered water into his glass. "No, Detective. I am not."

"What else do you do for a living?"

"I'm a freelance editor. With an odd job here and there," he muttered, "depending on the month." He paused as if coming to a realization. "Why are you here?"

"I'd like to ask you a few questions. Shall we sit?"

Belker's stoop became almost a hunchback as he grabbed a thermos and led Preach to two sagging armchairs in a living room heaped with uneven stacks of books. Next to Belker's chair was a clunky laptop on a rolling TV table.

Preach watched the writer's eyes bob to and fro, landing everywhere except on him. "What was your relationship to Farley Robertson?"

"Customer and capitalist."

"That's it?"

"He was also, I'm sorry to say, my publisher."

Preach's eyebrows lifted. He had to get Farley's laptop unlocked.

"He co-owned a small press with Damian Black," Belker continued. "Pen Oak Press."

"So you write horror?"

"I write *novels*."

"Implying that Damian doesn't?"

Belker snorted. "Damian's a businessman who churns out swill for the lowest common denominator. And of course I'm jealous, before you ask. I'd kill for success like that."

Belker stopped talking with his mouth hanging open, realizing what he had said. A vein pulsed on his neck as his hands shifted from his lap to the arms of the chair.

Preach smiled to disarm him. "Many people would."

Belker ran a hand through an oily clump of hair. "I was, of course, speaking metaphorically. Being a successful author is like finding true love: it happens to only a handful of writers in the world, while the rest of us slave away in obscurity."

"So why do it?" Preach asked, trying to put him back at ease.

"Because we writers are called to fail en masse, bash our pens against the jagged rocks of greatness so the flame stays alive until one of us becomes a Proust, a Shakespeare, a Chekhov." The ugly little man cackled and swept a hand down his chest. "At least, that's what people want to hear. Do I look suited to anything else to you? My only skill in life is the ability to see how people tick, the hidden gears with all the pooled grease and hidden, dark compartments. I've been cursed with the compulsion to share—as if anyone wants to listen. Today's readers want vampires who look like, well, you."

Preach's eyes flicked across the frayed brown carpet. Books, books, and more books. "What about Dostoevsky? Are you a fan?"

Belker took a swig from the thermos, wary of the question. "Of course. He was a genius."

"What's your favorite of his?"

"*Notes from the Underground*. Wh-why?"

Preach showed him the photo of the crime scene, enlarging it so

Belker could see the crosses. The writer made a choking sound, and his limbs contracted, like a hermit crab retreating into its shell. "Is this a joke?"

"I'm afraid not. Those were found on the body. I assume you know the significance?"

"Of course. Wait, you don't think that I—"

Belker started cackling, and Preach's instincts told him that this sad recluse could never stand behind someone with an axe and mercilessly cut him down.

Then again, it was the outliers—the ones who could swing an axe and then lie about it so well a detective's instincts spun like a compass at true north—that kept Preach in his chair and asking questions.

He pressed the writer to keep him off guard. "Where were you last night?"

"Here, writing. I almost never go out."

"All night? Alone?"

"I save my drafts at fifteen minute intervals," the writer said.

"Laptops are mobile devices."

"Surely an IP address could establish my presence?"

"It can't establish that your fingers were on the keyboard."

Belker fell silent.

"Tell me more about your relationship with Farley."

The writer looked away. "Lee wouldn't buy my next book. My last novel didn't earn out."

"What do you mean, didn't earn out?"

"We're paid an advance. The publisher fronts us money, and we don't see another penny until the book earns out the advance."

"How much was your last advance?"

"Nine hundred dollars," he mumbled.

Preach knew writers struggled, but now that Creekville had become a fashionable place to live, nine hundred dollars was barely a month's rent. "What about Damian? He had no say?"

"Damian's the money man. He enjoys the prestige of funding a literary press. Lee ran the nuts and bolts of the company. They only did four or five books a year, mostly local authors. E-books with a miniscule print run. I doubt they paid the electric bill."

Preach made a mental note to talk to Damian Black as soon as possible. "Have you found another publisher?"

His attempt at a sardonic grin came across as a leer. "I couldn't earn out on nine hundred dollars. I'm tainted goods."

"I see. So you were pretty upset with Farley?"

Belker sniffed a few times before responding. "I . . . maybe I should call a lawyer."

"That's your right. They're awful expensive."

Preach stared at him, until the writer jumped up and started pacing. "I'm sure someone at the bookstore told you about our fight. Of course I was furious. Wouldn't you be, if your dreams were shattered? I might never be published again." He lifted his flabby arms above his head. "But the sad truth is that if I tried to swing an axe at someone I'd probably miss and chop off my own foot."

While his arms were raised, Preach glimpsed a long white scar on the inside of his left wrist, like an X-ray image of a worm. He decided to switch gears for his final few questions. He didn't have enough on Belker to search his house. "Do you have any thoughts on the significance of the crime scene?"

Belker returned to his seat, idly plucking at his hair as he considered the question. "You do know the premise of the novel?"

"I'm afraid I haven't read it in some time." Preach knew the gist, but he wanted to hear what Belker had to say.

"It's a novel about many things, Detective. One of the greatest novels of all time. But the central crime, the one that was," he swallowed, "apparently replayed in Lee's house, is perpetrated by someone with no clear motive other than an existential one. Raskolnikov, the main character, wanted to see if he had the guts to commit a murder—and the brains to get away with it."

6

Darkness pressed against the tall windows of the bookstore. After the last customer filed out, Ari finished straightening and restocking. She didn't know what would become of the store, but she felt an obligation to keep it running smoothly until she found out.

The death of her employer had left her in a state of disbelief. She kept expecting him to walk out of the back room, run his eyes over the store while he shrugged into his newest sport coat, and bid her good night.

She supposed that was why people went to funerals, suffered through the body lying in the coffin like some macabre wax effigy. Not just to say goodbye, but to ensure that some terrible mistake had not been made.

To make it real.

She gave the store a final walkthrough, her eyes lingering on the comforting stacks. She worked because she needed the money, but she worked at a bookstore because it meant she would not have to suffer, at least not as much, that feeling of being parched without a good novel to quench her thirst. Ari craved not just any novel, but one that left her feeling weightless because the prose was so sharp and true, the story so moving, the characters living in the same room as her, breathing the same air.

Her law school class load often left her too exhausted to read for pleasure, which she resented. But even a chapter here and there could see her through.

A noise from the front of the store caught her attention. It sounded like someone trying the front door. Couldn't they read the store hours?

An image of Lee's corpse popped into her mind. The crushed skull and sticky crimson stain, the two crosses lying primly on his chest. Maybe it *had* been a robbery, and the murderer was still searching for something.

Maybe he thought it was here.

The thought gained currency in her mind, and she took a step toward the rear entrance. A moment later she heard another sound from the front door. Not a wild pounding, but a deliberate rapping of knuckles on glass.

Once she saw who it was, she released her tension with a self-effacing chuckle. Maybe she needed to lay off the serial-killer novels.

Standing at the door was the blond detective from earlier, the one with the white teeth, All-American haircut, and creased but pretty face. He'd seemed sincere when he was questioning her, but it had to be an act. He was clearly a former jock as well as a cop. He wore violence and intimidation as a jacket.

She opened the door, and Detective Everson stepped inside, his hands tucked into the pockets of his rumpled overcoat. His navy blue eyes flicked around the store, then rested on Ari with unsettling poise.

"I was driving by and saw the light on. I thought I'd ask a few follow-up questions. If you don't mind?"

He was nice and polite, a good Southern boy. Which was strange. The defining characteristic of the cops with whom she had dealt had been arrogance. Maybe he hid his true nature to keep his witnesses and suspects off-balance, ready to whip it out and turn the screws when needed, a magician conjuring a vicious little rabbit from a hat.

Or maybe he'd just stopped by to hit on her.

"Go right ahead," she said.

"Given the nature of the murder . . . I was wondering if there were any other local authors who had a relationship with Mr. Robertson?"

"He knew lots of authors. Plenty of them local." The detective was looking at her with that sincere expression of his, and it was making her blush. Which irritated her. "I'll make a list, if you like."

"I would appreciate that." He leaned a shoulder against the counter.

"I'll need to read *Crime and Punishment* again. From what I remember, it's not a quick read."

"It's quicker than you might think," she said, thinking he had probably read the CliffsNotes in high school. "Dostoevsky is a surprisingly accessible writer."

"Is he?" the detective said mildly. "Are we talking accessibility of prose or accessibility of ideas?" He waved a hand. "It's been a long time. I'm sure you're right."

Ari curled into an armchair a few feet from the counter. "No, you have a point," she said grudgingly. "You could read that novel in a few days, or you could ponder it for years. I was just—" She bit back what she was about to say.

"Surprised that a cop with a Southern accent has actually read Dostoevsky?"

"Your accent isn't *that* Southern."

He gave a faint smile. "I was wondering if anything else about the novel struck you as potentially germane to the crime."

"I . . . no, not really."

"Have you had time to think about it?" he asked. "I'm sure it's been a trying day for you."

She twisted her thumb ring. "It's not as if I can remember every detail—"

He smiled again as he interrupted her. "Don't get bogged down in the details; I'll look out for those. Was the book of any particular significance to Mr. Robertson?"

"I can't recall seeing him reading it."

"What about anyone else? His author acquaintances? A frequent customer?"

She stopped fiddling with her ring and felt the need for a cigarette, though she didn't smoke anymore. It had been a long day. "I can see if anyone's ordered a copy recently."

"Please do. Though only someone who's taunting us would do something as foolish as that. And what criminal would try to toy with a detective?"

At first she thought his arrogance was emerging, and then she got the reference. Raskolnikov, the protagonist-murderer of *Crime and Punishment*, had fancied himself superior to the police and had at times goaded them.

"Maybe the crosses on Lee's body," she said, chewing on her lip as she thought, "were a reflection of the murderer himself. His mindset."

"Someone who lives in squalor and barely takes the time to wash, thinks of himself as intellectually superior but is a failure by his own high standards."

Their eyes met. While he could have been describing Raskolnikov, she had a feeling he had paid a visit to J. T. Belker.

Could the local author with meek, haunted eyes, she wondered . . . could he be capable of something like that?

"Someone who maybe wanted to make a statement," Preach continued, "beneath the surface of the crime itself."

The detective's gaze flicked to the petite tattoos facing each other on the insides of Ari's wrists. *Half hope* and *half agony*. "I'm curious, have you ever tried your hand at writing?" he asked. "Since you work in a bookstore and clearly love literature?"

Did this guy actually realize her tattoo was a Jane Austen quote?

Then she grew cold as she realized what he was getting at. Cold and pissed off. "You don't have to be a writer to love books. And no, *Detective*, I don't write anything these days that's not related to the study of law. Did you come here to ask about *Crime and Punishment* or to question me?" She crossed her arms, eyes sparking.

"It could also have been someone trying to *frame* a writer," he mused, as if the previous exchange had never occurred. "Why do you think there were two crosses?"

The question caught her off guard; she had expected a response to her challenge. Now he was looking at her with a frank, almost intimate expression. She had always written off his type—guys that classically good-looking were never interesting—but she had to admit there was a depth to those eyes.

Depth and sadness.

"Sorry?" she said. It occurred to her that this detective used his appearance to his advantage.

"A single cross could symbolize a communion in blood between Raskolnikov and the pawnbroker, or the suffering he'd have to undergo before salvation, or something else beyond my limited powers of thematic interpretation. But Dostoevsky used two crosses—that strikes me as odd."

"I . . . don't know," she said. "I suppose I hadn't thought about it."

"Why don't you, then?" he asked, pushing off from the counter.

"Isn't there a literature professor you can talk to about this?"

He let his gaze linger, his eyes unreadable. "Not one who knew the victim," he said, then thanked her for her time.

After Detective Everson left, Ari sent him a text with the names of the three students with whom she had pulled an all-night study session the night of Farley's murder. They had been preparing a simulated jury trial for Trial Advocacy.

She finished her closing tasks and locked the front door behind her, hand lingering on the knob, trying to wrap her mind around the terrible events of the day. When she turned to leave, she noticed someone in a beige overcoat and a bowler hat leaning against a wall across the street.

It was dark and she couldn't make out a face, but from the hefty build and the way the figure reclined against the wall, nonchalantly but with an aura of physical menace, Ari assumed it was a man.

She hesitated, wondering if she should go back inside. The figure appeared to be looking at her, but she couldn't tell for sure.

And what if he was? Watching someone leave a store isn't a crime. He's probably just waiting on a ride.

Still, Farley's murder had spooked her, and her fears from earlier crawled back into her head. She found herself wishing the detective were still around, or that she had not walked to work.

Then she berated herself. She was not some silly sorority girl, born and raised in the privileged bubble of Chapel Hill. During her twenty-seven years she had already traipsed through dodgy cities on six continents, often alone. She could take care of herself.

She pulled her leather jacket tight and started down the sidewalk. A few cars whisked by. The bar next door was noisy and well-lit. She debated ducking inside but pressed on, knowing she had at least two hours of cases to read.

The only thing that worried her was the greenway, which was two blocks away. Her apartment was just on the other side of it. But the greenway—one of a dozen paved, vehicle-free walkways that connected the main streets of Creekville like spokes on a wheel—would be isolated at night.

On the other hand, this was Creekville. There was more danger of being verbally abused for a non-PC remark than being the victim of a crime.

At least before last night.

As she approached the mouth of the greenway, its narrow path lit by streetlamps but the wooded sides cloaked in darkness, she risked a glance back. The man in the overcoat was leaning against the wall in the same position, still facing the bookstore.

Just in case, she pulled out her cell phone and feigned a conversation as she stepped onto the path. A few yards down the walkway, she pocketed the phone and hurried forward. The sudden and powerful urge to break into a run overcame her, but she settled for a brisk walk instead, refusing to have the mindset of a victim.

The greenway was the equivalent of a three-block walk, and when she reached the midway point she glanced over her shoulder.

Nothing. No one.

Her pace slackened on the second half of the walk. Once she saw the lights of her apartment complex gleaming across the street she forgot about the figure in the overcoat. Her mind returned to her class load, the shocking death of her boss, and the dull ache of her breakup with Trevor.

Where was he tonight, she wondered? Preparing the night's tracks as he lay shirtless on the couch, brown locks spilling halfway to his jeans, eyes lit with an internal fire as he nodded in time?

It was the music, he had said, and not her. Maybe things would change when the band was established and he had more time.

She left the greenway. Her single-story apartment complex waited across the road, the wings of the U-shaped building extended as if reaching for a hug. A dirt-cheap rent, peeling paint, creepy-neighbors-in-the-common-space sort of hug.

Still, it was home. She was ready for a bowl of noodles, some cheap Shiraz, and a night curled on the sofa, finishing her reading and then drifting to sleep to a late-night talk show.

Out of an abundance of caution, or perhaps the irresistible pull of curiosity, she took a final look back—and saw the man in the overcoat standing in the middle of the greenway, hands shoved in his pockets, staring right at her.

Ari's peace of mind melted into a slushy puddle at her feet. Heart thumping against her chest, she hurried inside and locked the door, her cell phone gripped in the palm of her hand.

7

After Preach had left the station, Chief Higgins stopped by Kirby's desk. "You're on, kid."

"Chief?"

"The murder. You're helping Preach. An extra shift a week okay with you?"

Kirby sat up straight. "You know it. Thanks, Chief. I'll..." He trailed off as Chief Higgins walked away. She wasn't one for empty promises, so it was better not to make one.

He gave both his wrists a flick, snapping his fingers. He hoped they had their hands on the weirdest, sickest, flashiest case in the country. Something that would hit YouTube from day one, land him a book deal and a string of guest appearances.

They were off to a good start with the literary angle. Yet despite the eerie correlations between the crime scene and the passage in the novel, he couldn't help thinking the two crosses had simply fallen out of the killer's pocket. That the winning lottery ticket couldn't possibly be his.

Tapping his pen against the stack of reports, he leaned back and eyed the *Playboy* calendar he kept pinned to the inside of a cabinet door. After his babysitting duties, Kirby had a date with a hot little waitress he'd met at Diamond Dave's in Greensboro. His plan had been to stay the night in G-town, but now he wasn't so sure.

What kind of hours did homicide cops work, anyway? Was he expected to mainline coffee until they broke the case, like on TV?

He reached for his phone. One of his relatives was a patrol officer for the Atlanta Police Department, and now that Kirby and Preach were partners, he wanted to see if he could gain some insight into the mysterious arrival of Detective Joe Everson.

"Franklin here."

Jesse Franklin was a second cousin on Kirby's mother's side. Kirby knew almost nothing about his dad's family, except they were white and poor and hated black people.

"It's Kirb."

"Cuz! About time ya holla'd at ya boy."

"Last I checked, you weren't blowing me up either."

"It's the big city. I've got a lot goin' on these days. What's your excuse? Cow-tipping pickin' up?"

"Nah," Kirby said. "Just can't get away from the crib. Someone's always pulling me back inside."

Franklin laughed. "Is that how it is? So what's up?"

"Just caught my first murder."

"Yeah? Good for you, man."

Kirby caught the undertone of envy. Franklin had joined the force two years before Kirby and was still on patrol.

Then again, Atlanta was a much harder ladder to climb.

"Listen," Kirby said, "I was wondering if you'd heard of a guy named Joe Everson. Goes by Preach, used to be APD."

"I know *of* him. He's a bit out of my league."

"I didn't ask if you were trying to nail him."

"Hey, I'm not the one who drinks beet juice and trims his eyebrows. I just meant he was a hotshot homicide guy, and I'm, well, you know how it is. Knights in armor don't mingle with the serfs."

"Any idea why he left?" Kirby asked.

"He was working the Candyland Murders, had some kind of breakdown. Didn't know he'd landed up your way."

"Candyland—wasn't that the guy who lured kids into a Willy Wonka tree house and then, well, yeah. Guy was twisted," Kirby muttered, and found himself thinking that maybe he didn't want *the* sickest case out there.

"It was bad. Never caught the guy, either."

"Preach didn't handle failure too well?"

"Nah, man—he broke down *during* the case. Not when they found one of the bodies, but when they found one of the kids alive up in that tree house. I don't know the details, but it seemed strange for a guy who's seen it all."

Kirby remembered the detective squatting at the crime scene, staring into the eyes of the corpse. "Maybe that's the point, you know? That you've never seen it all."

"What would I know? I'm just a patrol guy. Preach is a legend, though. The word around here was that if things got too sticky, he'd get on a call with the man upstairs, find out some things no one else could."

"What are you saying?" Kirby asked, pressing the phone tighter.

"He had this little prayer room at the station that glowed white as Gwyneth Paltrow when he went inside, and when he came back out he always had a fresh piece of evidence and knew the score of the night's game."

Kirby relaxed his grip and rolled his eyes. "Bite me, cuz."

Franklin guffawed. "We need to get you out of Mayberry."

Kirby walked down the hall to check with forensics. Their evidence guru was a tall, skinny guy named Dax who was based in Chapel Hill. He had flaky pink skin and an elongated neck. Whenever he bent over his clipboard, he reminded Kirby of a flamingo.

"Any word on the prints?" Kirby asked.

"We found a partial that wasn't the vic's in the laundry room, but it wasn't enough to ID."

"Damn. Anything else?"

"We had to send the phone and laptop out to Division, so that will take a few days, depending on the level of encryption. But we found marijuana, meth, and alcohol in his system. Oh, and I believe I've identified the cause of the blunt force trauma."

"You can tell the type of weapon?"

"It's impossible to be certain, but the contours of the wound are consistent with the shape of the common hatchet. I'd say at least five blows, probably more."

"A hatchet? Like an axe?"

"They're different, actually. The ax head is larger but tapers only slightly from the blade to the back. True axes aren't designed for pounding. The hatchet, on the other hand, has a full hammer head on the rear side of the blade."

It was then that he struck her again with all his strength, and then again, every time with the back of the hatchet and across the crown of the head.

Kirby felt the skin on his arms prickle. "What about the crosses?"

"The wooden one is cypress. Hand cut, not manufactured. The copper cross looks factory-made, we're not sure where. It's almost impossible to tell. Oh, and we found microscopic ribbon fibers on both crosses. My guess is they were attached to a string and cut loose."

Suddenly he noticed a ribbon round her neck ... he succeeded in cutting through the ribbon without touching the body with the hatchet, and took it off ... there were two crosses on the ribbon, one of cypress wood and another of copper ...

"Good work," Kirby said weakly.

After hitting the gym, Kirby drove to his sister's trailer to babysit his nephew, his good vibes from landing the new case evaporating the closer he got. It wasn't terrible as trailer parks went. Plenty of pine trees around, a few extra feet between the lots, no ungoverned trash heaps stinking up the place. In the spirit of Creekville, there was even a communal vegetable garden.

But it was still a single-wide. And as anyone who had grown up in a mobile home knew, as Kirby did, the social stigma attached to living in such an undistinguished crib was more destructive than a direct hit from a tornado. And his sister Jalene still hadn't escaped.

An eleven-year-old girl with light brown skin and freckles, all limbs and hair, threw herself into his arms. She was a clone of her mother at that age. "Uncle Scotty! Cool jacket."

"Hey there, beautiful. You ready for tonight?"

"Yep!"

He squeezed her shoulder. "Where's the mom-ster?"

"Right here," said Jalene. She stepped gingerly into the room, wincing with each step. His sister had aged well, still thin and gorgeous despite the stress of raising two kids by herself.

Kirby hurried over to support her. "How's the hernia?"

"A little better than yesterday. It's supposed to work itself out in a few weeks."

He lowered his voice as Kayla twirled away. "Who says? The rent-a-nurse at the clinic?"

"There's all kinds of different hernias. This isn't one of the bad ones."

"It looks pretty bad to me," he said. "You're sure you don't need surgery?"

She sucked in a breath and reached up to pat him on the cheek. "And who's gonna pay for that, hon? The hernia fairy?"

Kirby gritted his teeth and looked away. His sister was an office assistant, but the attorney she worked for had let her go three months before, after he had gotten a divorce and had to cut back on expenses. Kirby hated the fact that he couldn't provide more support. He had a solid job and benefits, but a junior cop's salary sure as hell wouldn't cover a second rent check or uninsured medical expenses. His sister was eking by on welfare, living in fear of a medical disaster.

His eight-year-old nephew shuffled into the room, head bowed, a serious little boy with the opposite energy of his niece. Kirby scooped him up and kissed him on the forehead. "How's my number-one guy? Still leaving ladies in the dust like Speed Racer?"

Jared squirmed out of his arms. Kirby's pulse spiked as he watched his nephew, who used to greet him with a huge smile and some arcane fact about the insect world, sit cross-legged and sullen in front of the TV, as if some parasite were siphoning off his vitality.

A bright and bookish kid, vibrant and sensitive to the world, Jared had retreated into a shell once the bullying started. Kirby had gone with his sister to the principal's office, only to be told that until a teacher witnessed the mistreatment, there was nothing anyone could do.

Nothing they could do, Kirby had wanted to know, about the five pounds his nephew had lost from having his lunch repeatedly stolen? Or the bruises on his arms and chest? Or the fact that his sister's baby boy wouldn't look him in the eye anymore?

Jared went to a school with a ninety percent free or reduced lunch rate, a severely undermanned staff, and elementary school kids who didn't have discipline problems, they had *criminal* problems.

Jalene leaned on Kirby as she limped to the car, her face taut from the strain. He pleaded in vain with her to let him go in her place. After she drove off with Kayla, he stood in the driveway with slumped shoulders, terrified of his sister's condition and not ready to deal with his nephew's dull stare, hating the incessant trailer park babble of tires on gravel and flimsy doors banging shut. He struggled to corral the feeling of helpless fury that, beneath his cheery disposition, had always defined him.

Later that night, after Jalene and Kayla had returned, Kirby went to Greensboro and partied away his tension. He managed to put everything out of his mind, including the case, until he got a text from Preach at three a.m. asking him to meet first thing in the morning.

Kirby knocked back one last beer as the waitress slept beside him. He couldn't shake the weird premonition that something worse than usual was headed his way.

8

Preach's rented cabin was perched on the edge of a small tract of wilderness filled with deer, red-tailed hawk, muskrat, and coyote. Now and again a bear or a bobcat wandered through. He had fallen asleep on the hammock on the screened-in porch, drifting off to the orchestra of insects. He liked to soak in the world and not feel stuck in a manufactured environment.

The sun nudged him awake. Instead of brewing a pot of coffee, he decided to change clothes and stumble straight to Jimmy's Corner Store, a local provisions market and café that doubled as his second office. On his way out the door, Preach stopped to straighten his one piece of art: a wooden Jesus figurine, melancholy and thoughtful, sitting lotus-style on a pointed spear precariously attached to the wooden base.

More than ever, the figurine reflected his state of mind. One more day until therapy, he thought. One day closer—or further—from knowing whether he could have his old life back.

"Mornin', partner," Kirby said, when he arrived at the café. He flashed his signature smile as he slid into the seat across from Preach. "I gotta say, I like the sound of that."

Preach lifted his mug. "Congratulations."

The café smelled like roasted coffee tinged with honey. Despite the fact that it now drew the type of crowd who demanded small-batch coffee beans and a careful pour-over, much of the store remained unchanged from his youth: the blue clapboard walls, the refrigerator selling eggs and bacon and dairy products from local farms, the dry goods shelves that stocked regional specialties like spiced pepper relish, Cackalacky marinade, and elderberry preserves.

His father used to take him to Jimmy's after elementary school on warm Friday afternoons, when they had free homemade ice cream for kids. Often, his father would bring his dulcimer and join impromptu jam sessions on the patio while Preach played on the lawn. He cherished the memories of his parents from before he was old enough for them to impose their ideologies on him.

Kirby stirred a packet of honey into his mug, which looked like it contained some type of fruity, green-tea concoction. "Late night, my man?" Kirby asked. "Your text came in at three a.m."

"I was up reading."

"Russian literature?"

Preach nodded.

"Anything useful?" Kirby asked.

"I'm starting to wonder if the details of the murder aren't secondary."

Kirby waited for him to continue, then spread his hands. "You gonna kill a brother with suspense?"

A thought had broken Preach's concentration—if recreating Dostoevsky's crime was so important, why had Farley's killer chosen to murder a man instead of a woman? Was it the killer's signature on the crime—a truly random act?

If Farley was specifically chosen, however, then it meant the crime scene was a setup—or that there was another, deeper, meaning.

"Hmm? Sorry. The psychological state of the killer, that's the thrust of the novel. Why he does what he does, and how he deals with it."

"Why'd he do it in the novel?" Kirby asked.

"Because he could."

"Come again?"

"Raskolnikov believed in the idea that certain men, he calls them Napoleons, are justified in whatever actions they take—including murder—if it allows them to break out of their circumstances and achieve great things in life. Similar to Nietzsche's idea of the Superman. Or joining a reality show."

Kirby rolled up his sleeves. "I'm not that edu-ma-cated, but do you mean he killed someone because he thought he was *entitled* to?"

"Sort of. He was broke and powerless but thought he was destined for greatness. In his mind, the only way to be sure was to kill and rob a random old woman."

"So he could find out if he really was a Napoleon."

"Yeah," Preach said. "That's my take so far."

"That's whack."

Kirby stopped to eye an athletic woman wearing yoga pants and a hijab wind her way to a tattered armchair in the corner, next to a grizzled old man strumming a folk tune. "The blood under the washer at Farley's house—did that happen in the book? The killer stick around like that?"

"The opposite. He ended up killing two people, almost got caught, and had to sneak away. All of his planning went out the window in the heat of the moment."

"So whatever the murders might have in common," Kirby said, "Farley's killer was smoother than the guy in the book."

"Calmer, more careful," Preach murmured. "Not subject to the same doubts."

Kirby ran his thumb nervously along his teacup, then gave an update on the forensic report. Preach caught Kirby up on the interview with Belker, then pushed away from the table. "Let's go visit the neighbors."

It was a clear and frigid morning, unseasonably cold for late October. Preach donned his wool cap and gloves. Kirby was wearing jeans and a brown leather jacket, blowing on his hands to keep warm.

"Feel good to be in plainclothes?" Preach asked.

"Yeah, except for the polar vortex. Since when do those cross the Mason-Dixon line? I don't care about politics, but people need to chill with the nitrogen emissions so black people don't freeze to death in the South."

Preach chuckled. "Don't you drive an SUV?"

"It's a Jeep, Preach. An old Cherokee. That's different."

"How's that?"

"Because I look fly driving it to the gym."

They spent the bulk of the day re-questioning the residents of Farley Robertson's townhouse complex nestled in the Creekville woods. The interviews turned out to be a waste. Early forensic results confirmed the murder had occurred late Tuesday night, probably between two and three a.m. Farley owned an end unit, and his sole neighbor was a spinster who sat by her window most of the day and went to bed at midnight. She claimed Farley had arrived home just before she turned in, and no one else had entered his condo. At least while she was awake.

According to his neighbors, Farley Robertson was a polite and fastidious man who put out his recycling on time, petted the neighborhood dogs, and waved at the babies in the strollers. A budding author in the complex, a waitress with a PhD in East Asian religions, heralded Farley as a champion of local artists who promised her a signing at his bookstore when she was published.

A set of French doors in the rear of Farley's townhouse opened onto a small wooden porch. Through the half-naked trees, Preach could make out the backs of single-family residences poking out from an adjoining neighborhood.

Preach stepped into the woods. Beds of colored leaves glittered like gemstones in the rays of sunlight that reached the forest floor. A woodpecker hammered in the distance, and the tops of hundred-foot pines swayed as if made of rubber.

Ten paces inside the woods, he spotted a beaten-down path paralleling the line of townhomes. He cocked his head at Kirby, and they followed the trail past Farley's complex to where it adjoined a nature trail.

"Pretty good escape route," Kirby said. "Killer could have used a dirt bike, since no one saw a strange car."

Preach kept walking, though he knew the trail could lead all the way to Chapel Hill. The air was fresh and dry, leaves crackled underfoot. A family of deer eyed them as they walked. A hundred yards in, he paused when the trail passed behind the small office complex where his aunt worked, and then paralleled a wide creek. Stone supports buttressed a trestle high above the water.

"I feel you," Kirby said, when Preach didn't move. "This could take all day."

Preach pointed to their left, at a steep side path that led up the incline, right to the railroad tracks.

Tracks that Preach knew, from his own childhood jaunts and from his visit the previous evening, passed right by J. T. Belker's house.

He told his partner.

"That's awfully convenient," Kirby said. "Pay him another visit?"

"Let's talk to Damian Black first. He just flew back from New York."

"So he was gone the night of the murder?"

"No, he was here. He flew out yesterday for a one-day writing convention."

"We have any reason to suspect him? Business dispute? Lover's quarrel?"

Preach checked his watch. Damian should be home by now. "We're about to find out."

9

Less than five minutes outside Creekville, the houses and businesses disappeared, replaced by narrow country lanes and corridors of trees. Preach lowered his visor as they drove west, straight into a setting sun that lit the road with a radioactive glow.

Ten minutes later they turned onto a driveway that wound through a dense pine forest for a quarter mile before ending at a house that brought to mind a Faulkner setting crossed with the Brothers Grimm. It was a white, two-story farmhouse manor, encircled by a wraparound porch supported by ornate pillars. Atop the third story was a pyramidal tower that jutted upward like a wizard's hat, complete with gargoyles cavorting on the downspouts.

Mature oaks dotted the lawn, their muscular branches scraping at the eaves. Giant faux cobwebs had been stretched between the trees for Halloween. As Preach pulled into the circular drive, two huge dogs bounded out of the house, followed by a man in his fifties wearing plaid dress pants and a velvet smoking jacket.

"Bela! Boris! Heel!"

The dogs looked like black and white teddy bears with curled tails. They halted at the sound of their owner's voice, then slunk back to the front porch.

Preach stepped out of the car. "Mr. Black?"

"Just Damian, please. Grown men don't need to call each other by their last names."

The author delivered the soft rebuke with a smile. His bland but affable face, combined with his curly brown hair, reminded Preach of the grownup version of a kid on a cereal box. He was of medium height and build, and Preach noticed a black and silver signet ring on his left index finger.

"I'm sorry for your loss," Preach said.

"Me, too," he said. A wave of genuine sadness crashed over his face. "Lee was a dear friend."

"You live out here all alone?" Preach asked.

"Don't forget Bela Lugosi and Boris Karloff," he said, sweeping a hand at the two canines, who wagged their tails at the attention.

"Akitas make good guard dogs."

"You know your breeds," he said in approval. "Handsome, aren't they? Come in, gentlemen. Let's chat in the parlor."

They followed the author inside. Kirby kept a wary eye on the dogs as they padded along behind them. Damian led the officers past a foyer where two gleaming, full-sized suits of armor stood at attention, then down a hallway decorated with framed posters of classic horror films.

The paneled sitting room was furnished with high-backed leather chairs, a baby grand piano, a liquor cabinet built into the wall beside the fireplace, and standing glass cases that housed a cornucopia of bizarre objects and horror memorabilia.

Preach examined the contents of the glass cases while Damian poured himself a drink. Among the items on display were an Incan child mummy, the fused skeletons of Siamese twins, a pair of shriveled hands covered in fur, and copies of early horror novels so old he guessed they were first editions. *Dracula*, *The Picture of Dorian Grey*, *Carmilla*, *The Castle of Otranto*, and *Frankenstein* were all in the collection.

"I see you bring your work home," Preach said.

"I've always had a taste for the macabre," Damian replied, waving them into chairs.

Kirby was standing next to a ghost-white lamp shaped like an upside down lotus flower. "You seem like a pretty normal guy."

"I hear that a lot. How does a regular guy from Creekville, who looks like a Boy Scout leader, come up with the stuff I write? It fascinates people. And my response to them is, why do you *read* what I write? But isn't that the beauty and mystery of human nature? How we're all so different, and you can never tell what's lurking about on the inside? Take that lamp next to Officer Kirby. It's the most innocuous item in the room, yet it's supposed to steal your soul if you linger near it for too long."

Kirby flinched, and Damian laughed. "The fact is, gentlemen, that I *am* a normal guy. Plain as toast. I write to escape my banality. Forgive my manners—can I get you something? Sweet tea, water, scotch?"

"We're fine, thank you," Preach said.

"Just let me know. I assume you're here about Farley?" His voice softened. "What a terrible, terrible tragedy. Supernatural creatures perpetrate the murders in my novels, but human beings always remind us who the real monsters are."

The fire had warmed the room. Preach unbuttoned his coat and forced his eyes away from the display cases, whose morbid contents possessed a magnetic pull. "How well did you know Mr. Robertson?"

"We grew up together in Creekville, and remained close. Damian Black is a pen name, though I've taken to using it with most people."

Preach knew about the pseudonym. According to public records, the author's real name was Evan Shanks. He owned a second house in Key West, four cars, and a private plane, which he kept in a hangar at Horace Williams Airport in Chapel Hill. No kids, never married, parents who were public schoolteachers. He was one of the mayor's principal donors, and also the founder of Second Chance, a charity for street kids.

"Lee was a huge supporter of mine, even before I was successful. We were quite close." Preach noticed him taking a longer sip than usual.

"Did he have any enemies?"

He thought for a moment. "No, not like that."

"You mean no one with a motive for murder?" Preach said.

"Yes."

"You paused."

"I hate to mention it. It's nothing serious."

Preach clasped his fingers. "Indulge us."

Damian hesitated, then gave a wry smile. "You probably know that

Lee and I started a publishing house together. Just a small endeavor, a way to showcase local talent. We have a writer named J. T. Belker whose recent proposal was . . . not what we were looking for."

"It wasn't up to par?" Kirby asked.

"Oh, it was good. Brilliant, in fact. J. T. has true talent. His prose, depth of thought, intricate characterizations . . . my writing is childish and one-dimensional in comparison."

Quite a departure from what Belker said about him, Preach thought.

"Isn't popularity a form of genius?" Preach asked. "You're touching a nerve with a lot of people."

The sadness returned to Damian's eyes, and he clinked the ice cubes in his Scotch. "You're kind, Detective, but my work is trite and I know it. Still, I *am* a real writer, which has nothing to do with talent, and everything to do with compulsion." He laughed and raised his glass. "When else in life do you actually get to tell the truth in public?"

"If Belker's new work is so good," Preach said, "why didn't you publish it?"

"Partly because his first novel didn't earn out, though frankly, many of our novels don't. But in J. T.'s case, his submission was . . . how do I say this? It was ahead of its time. Too abstract even for us. His characters were unsympathetic, sadistic even. As if they were trying to crawl out of their own skins. Did you know he's being treated for depression?"

"I did not," Preach said.

"There's also the subject matter of the submission." Damian swirled his Scotch. "His new novel concerns an unpublished writer who snaps after his previous novel fails to sell. He kills one of the publishers who wrote a rude rejection letter, writes a roman à clef about the murder, posts the novel on social media along with pictures of the actual crime scene, and then hangs himself in prison."

Kirby and Preach exchanged a disbelieving look. Preach didn't think the author was lying—these were easy things to verify. But the revelations about Belker felt almost . . . calculated.

Damian continued, "As I said, it's brilliant. The themes of identity and loss in a modern world are expertly explored. And for what it's worth, Belker is excitable, but I've never seen his temper escalate beyond words."

Neither do the tempers of lots of criminals, Preach thought, *right until they snap.*

He showed Damian the photo of the crime scene. Unlike Belker, Damian appeared not to get the reference. Preach filled him in, then watched him carefully.

"My God . . . do you really think . . ." He looked up and shook his head. "I haven't read that novel since high school."

"Did Farley have any particular connection to that work?" Preach asked.

"Not of which I'm aware. From what I remember, the protagonist was—" He cut off and gave Preach a sharp look, grasping the similarities with Belker.

"I need to ask you something else," Preach said, "and I apologize if it's upsetting."

"What's upsetting is Lee's murder. I'll help any way I can."

"Did Farley have a drug habit?"

Damian pursed his lips and glanced away. "I'm not sure I should be talking about that."

"We're not concerned with arresting you for possession," Preach said. "Do you know where he might have procured his narcotics?"

"I'm afraid not."

Kirby leaned forward. "How about a guess? Maybe you two used the same hook up?" He glanced at Preach to see if he was overstepping. The detective let it go.

Damian took a long sip of Scotch. "I don't use drugs. And I'd prefer not to speculate on Lee's activities."

Preach gave a sympathetic smile. "It's fine. We'll look into that for now."

Damian averted his eyes. Preach wondered if he knew that Mac Dobbins supplied Farley and was afraid of naming him. Also, while the author seemed genuinely distressed by his friend's death, Preach could tell he was holding something back.

He asked a few more questions and learned nothing new. Wanting to search Farley's emails before he pressed Damian any harder, Preach stood to leave, but Kirby put his elbows on his knees and leaned forward, eyes gleaming. "I gotta ask. What's it like being famous?"

Damian looked amused. "Am I famous? I wouldn't know."

"You know for sure if you're *not* famous," Kirby said. "Trust me."

The author looked down as he clinked his ice cubes again. "In that case, I live alone, my best friend was just murdered, and my life's work is, by all accounts, pedestrian. So I guess your answer is that it can be just as shitty as anything else."

Preach and Kirby returned to the station to finish their paperwork. When Kirby left for home, Preach could hear his footsteps padding across the deserted office. It was strange, after the hustle and bustle of the APD, to experience the hush of the Creekville station at night.

While the cicadas chirped their arias in the trees outside, Preach stuck around to read the last few chapters of *Crime and Punishment*. He'd barely slept the night before, trying to finish. He poured a fresh cup of coffee and bent over the novel.

Not long after he turned the last page, fingers tapping as he contemplated the ending, his cell rang. He glanced at the unfamiliar number. "Detective Everson."

"Hi, it's Ari Hale. From the bookstore." Her voice sounded rushed. "You said to contact you if anything came up, and I think someone's stalking me. A man followed me home from the bookstore last night, and I just saw him again, in the parking lot outside my window. I wasn't sure what—"

"Ms. Hale, where do you live?"

She gave him the address. It was less than a mile from the station.

"Lock the doors and windows and stay put," he said. "I'll be right there."

10

Ari opened the door in a pair of black leggings and a long sweat-shirt bearing a color-spattered, impressionistic drawing of the Eiffel Tower. A moody pop song played softly in the background as she eyed Preach with a mixture of gratitude and wariness.

"I've never reported a stalker before," she said. "Just so you know."

"You did the right thing."

"I haven't seen him since I called, but . . ."

"Why don't I come in? It wouldn't hurt to keep the cruiser in the parking lot for a few minutes."

She nodded in relief, then ushered him inside and hung his coat by the door, next to a black concert T-shirt slung over a peg.

"I finished the novel," he said, as she led him into the combination living and dining room.

Her eyebrows lifted, and he took a seat in a faux-leather reading chair. She curled up on the couch, feet tucked under her legs. A text-book titled *International Human Rights Law* was open on the coffee table, a closed laptop and a glass of wine beside it. He thought her place smelled like violets and coffee.

"But let's hear about the stalker," he said, settling into the chair and pushing up the sleeves of his gray sweater.

She told him about the figure in the overcoat who had followed her home from the bookstore, and how she had just seen someone similar, in the same hat and overcoat, standing on the edge of her parking lot and staring right at her window.

"You couldn't make out any features?" he asked.

"The hat concealed his face."

"Was he standing by a particular car? I took down license plates before I came in."

"The green Corolla that looks like it should be in a museum. It's mine."

Preach pursed his lips. "If you see him again, don't engage under any circumstance."

"I wasn't planning on it."

"It's unfortunate, and I hate to say this, but there's not a lot we can do at the moment. Try not to put yourself in vulnerable situations. Avoid walking alone, especially at night, and don't answer unfamiliar knocks or calls. Keep everything locked. You might consider an alarm system, or a dog. Come to the station tomorrow and get a formal complaint on record."

She chewed on her bottom lip. "Thanks for believing me."

He looked at her askance. "Why wouldn't I?"

"I've been upset about the murder, and nerves can do funny things to the mind—but I know what I saw. And you know, women get stalked a lot, and the police have a tendency not to take it seriously."

He frowned. "Which police?"

She gave a throaty laugh. "Creekville's such a nice place," she said, and then her laugh faltered. "Usually. So am I still a suspect?"

"You never were. But I verified your alibi. Your friends vouched for you."

She nodded and rose to refill her wine glass. Unlike most attractive women, neither her movements nor her clothing were calculated to draw attention. Preach guessed her looks had appeared later in life.

"Shiraz?" she asked. "I don't have much else."

"That's fine."

She brought him a glass and returned to the couch. "You continue to surprise me."

"Because I drink something other than Budweiser?" He flashed a smile that both chastised and charmed, his preacher's smile.

A smirk touched the corners of her lips.

He said, "Maybe it'd be easier if you went ahead and got the rest of your assumptions off your chest?"

"It's probably better if I don't."

"No, please. Impress me with your powers of observation."

She swirled her wine and didn't respond.

"I insist," he said.

After a moment, realizing he was serious, she met his gaze and leaned back into the sofa. "Okay, then. You're from Creekville, which, despite its quirks, is still a Friday Night Lights town for the high school set. I'm guessing you were the star quarterback and could have any girl you wanted, and did, and everyone in town treated you like, well, a little blond god. After high school, you . . ." She sat back with a guilty look.

"What's wrong?"

"You seem like a nice enough guy. You came to help me tonight. This isn't fair."

"It's okay," he said softly. "I appreciate the honesty. For the record, I wrestled instead of playing football. I can't throw straight."

She looked doubtful.

"Go on," he said.

"I was finished."

"No, you weren't."

"Look, I'm sorry if I've misjudged you."

"You're not off base, but you're still looking at me like you have something to say. Why don't I finish for you, so I can carry on with my investigation?"

She took another sip and eyed him coolly. "Whatever you want."

He rested his forearms on the chair. "Because I was all brawn and no brains, with even less vision in life, I was stuck in Creekville and eventually became a cop. I needed an outlet for my frustration and physical aggression, and it was either become a cop or join the army, and I'm far too much of an entitled pretty boy to shave my head and take orders all day. After a decade of paying my dues, and because Creekville is a one-horse town with low crime, I somehow became a detective. Now I live a petty, insular life harassing Yankees and hippies and grad students." He smiled, and could tell from the way she averted her eyes that his assessment had hit home.

Looking uncomfortable, she shifted to cross her legs under her again, on the other side. "So tell me who you really are, then."

"Words are cheap, Ms. Hale. I'll let you judge for yourself."

She rolled her eyes. "That's unfair. Now I'm embarrassed and I don't even get a chance to—"

"It's okay," he said. "As I said, I just wanted that out of the way. Now you can look at me like a human being, and not a member of genus *blondus footballus starus*. So let's talk about the novel. I want to run a few theories by you and see how they might apply to your employer."

She opened a palm. "Let the judging begin."

Preach began tapping on the arm of the chair, debating how much to discuss with her. She already knew about the crosses and had led him to Dostoevsky, so he saw no harm in exploring that angle. He wasn't convinced the staging of the crime scene was anything more than a diversion, but he would be remiss not to consider other implications.

He said, "I'm wondering if the two crosses had nothing to do with Farley—and everything to do with the murderer. A statement."

"That's rather terrifying, given the nihilistic nature of the crime."

"Exactly. Raskolnikov wanted to be some kind of superior being who had the right to take what he wanted from life, even committing murder."

"But he failed," she said, guessing where he was going. "Raskolnikov was a slave to his moral conscience. A true Napoleon would have no guilt, no remorse, no doubts as to whether he was a Napoleon. He would simply kill and get on with it."

"That's right," Preach said. "At first I thought the killer was telling us that, unlike Dostoevsky's character, *he* had no remorse. *He* could kill without conscience. But now I'm not so sure. There's so much more to the novel. Themes of isolation, sacrifice, redemption, the guilt associated with immoral actions and the question of where that guilt comes from. If the novel is taken at face value, Dostoevsky seemed to be saying that there are real and powerful consequences to our actions."

"You've lost me," Ari said. She was looking at him strangely. "I don't disagree with the analysis, but how do you think it might apply to the mindset of the murderer?"

"I said I became convinced the crosses—the reference to *Crime and Punishment*—had nothing to do with Farley. But I've rethought that. I still don't think it was a direct reference, meaning I don't think Farley stole someone's favorite first edition copy. But neither do I think some random nihilistic killer decided to pull a Raskolnikov in Creekville, North Carolina. Not that this wouldn't be the place for someone to implement a radical philosophical theory."

She chuckled in agreement. He rubbed at his two-day's growth of stubble and said, "What I do think is that something in the novel, maybe one of the themes, is the reason Farley was murdered."

She took a moment to absorb his words. "So maybe it's even simpler than it appears. Maybe Farley did something awful, and the killer felt like he needed to pay for it. Crime and punishment."

"Yeah, maybe." He glanced out the window, at the murky shadows of the pines looming over the parking lot. "If the clue is simply the title, then I could have saved a lot of hours over the last few days. I feel as if I've run a marathon in my mind."

"But your life wouldn't have been forever enriched by the wisdom of a timeless work of genius. What did you think of it, by the way? I am, of course, now going to assume that you're widely read."

"Why make assumptions at all?" he asked.

"Why don't you just answer my question? You're worse than my law professors."

He gave a faint smile and finished the last of his wine.

"Care for another?" she asked.

"Not tonight."

She sank deeper into her chair and wrapped her fingers around the stem of her glass. "You liked the book, didn't you?"

"I did."

"So you enjoyed the story of a quasi-sociopath who commits murder and spends the rest of the book whining and trying to justify his actions?"

Preach started to say he didn't see it that way, that he had a very different view of the main character and his motivations, a view he hadn't seen mentioned in any of the commentaries. But he stopped himself.

"I know it's heresy," she continued, "but that's the beauty of litera-ture. It's all in the eye of the beholder. I don't have to love the voice that speaks to you, just the one that speaks to *me*."

They shared a moment of silence Preach thought would be awkward but wasn't, as if they had dozens of silent pauses under their belts.

The room felt warm, too warm, and Preach pushed to his feet. "Thanks for the drink."

"You can't leave yet." The ends of Ari's mouth curled upward, like the stretch of a jungle cat. "I haven't heard your assumptions about me."

"I find that actions are the best judge of character."

"C'mon, I've already made a fool of myself. And you have to promise to be completely honest."

Preach had already glanced around the apartment. The living room walls were unadorned and painted a soft blue. On a mantle above the gas fireplace, a line of framed photos depicted street scenes from foreign cities, never with Ari in them. More photographs graced the hallway, none of them family except for one that Preach guessed was Ari as a little girl. She was sitting on a low, snow-topped stone wall, her parents standing beside her. A smiling older man with Ari's eyes hugged her from behind, their rosy cheeks touching.

Through the half-open bedroom door, Preach glimpsed candles, cheap shelving overflowing with books, a jewelry box, and more books atop an Indonesian-style trunk. A pair of concert posters from bands Preach didn't recognize was pinned to the far wall.

"I'll give you a little help," she said. "Privileged rich girl from the suburbs goes to high school in Charlotte and then a private liberal arts college. She joins a sorority and goes straight to law school after gradua-tion, and that's about the sum of her life experience. Her grand plan is to marry rich in law school, move back to the suburbs, and repeat the cycle."

Preach gave a soft chuckle and moved for the door. As he reached for his coat, she called out to him.

"Play fair," she said. "Impress me with your powers of observation."

He gave a rueful smile, realizing she had thrown his words back at him. A useful skill for the courtroom.

He was going to leave anyway, but he saw something in her eyes that told him she was yearning for someone to tell her something about herself. Something that hadn't been said a hundred times already from a bar stool or on a stilted first date, something that spoke to *her* and not a shallow image of her passed around in the minds of hopeful suitors, like a baton in some never-ending, Darwinian relay race.

Preach held her gaze as he shrugged on his coat. "Okay, then, Ms. Hale. I think you're an only child, and I don't think you grew up anywhere near a suburb. You didn't stay put in the same state or even the same country. Maybe your parents were military or worked for an NGO, but you were always on the outside looking in, and you never had a place to call home. In high school you were at the top of your class, far more worldly than the other girls your age—not to mention the boys. That might have made you cool, except you hadn't grown into your looks and didn't speak or think like anyone else. Your precociousness made you even more of a misfit, so you rebelled, I'm guessing as a Goth or a punk. And instead of protecting you from the world, your parents left you to drown in it."

Ari's face had drained of color, giving her white skin and red lips an ethereal pallor, like a wounded ghost. Something inside him was drawn not just to her intelligence but to her chaotic hair and restless slouch, her lack of focus on herself.

"Go on," she said from the couch, her voice so low he could barely hear her.

He looked her in the eye. "You chose to go to college in a big city, studied literature, and explored everything you could. You found that adult life, as you suspected, was incredibly multifaceted—but none of those facets made the world make any more sense. You grew into your looks and started to receive a lot of attention from guys, which you weren't sure what to do with. You would rather have eaten a bag full of spiders than join a sorority. After graduation, you missed traveling, so you backpacked for a year around the world, all by yourself. Because you're smart and realized you had to do something with your life, you decided to go to law school. You traveled enough to witness the terrible injustices of the world, so you're studying to be a human rights lawyer. Your parents don't give you much, if any, financial support, but you have a beloved grandfather from North Carolina who allowed you to establish residency, and you chose UNC Law. You work in a bookstore and live in Creekville because you need the money and because the people in Chapel Hill remind you too much of high school. You still don't have a city, a state, a tribe, a home—books are your country."

He stopped to take a drink. Her face had grown as still as a cave pool. "My parents were teachers at international schools," she said softly. "We moved every two years my entire childhood, which is a social death sentence for a kid. They were far more into traveling and each other than to me." Her smirk looked forced. "I guess you're better at this than I am. And my love life? Would you care to expound on that eternal mystery?"

He heard the resentment in her voice and remembered the long T-shirt hanging by the door, like a lost relic from summer vacation. He answered not to be cruel, but because, again, he thought she wanted someone to tell her the truth.

"You had a breakup recently," he said. "The guy is tall and aloof, good-looking, maybe an artist or a musician. But even though he liked what he saw, he doesn't yet know how to love anyone besides himself. So you let him go, and he didn't protest very hard."

She gave a bitter laugh and said, "Strike one, Detective. *He* broke it off. And since we're being honest, you're not talking to me about Dostoevsky just because I work at the bookstore and knew the victim, are you?"

His lips parted in a faint smile as he opened the door. "You called in an incident tonight, ma'am. I just responded."

11

When Preach arrived at the station the next morning, Officer Haskins told him he had finally heard from Farley's sister, a dentist in Los Angeles. She had helped finance the bookstore and still owned a stake. Though she had no interest in keeping it, she promoted Nate, the dreadlocked fulltime employee, to manager until a buyer was found.

Preach talked to the sister himself but gained no useful insight. She and Farley had not been close in years, and a quick check confirmed her claim that she was in LA the night of the murder.

Soon after, he got an email from Evidence. Farley's laptop and phone had been unlocked.

He had sent the two items to Durham PD, which was large enough to employ Rance Crowley, a full time IT guy who also helped with cybercrime. Rance was a Silicon Valley transplant, smart but glib, an avid computer gamer and trail running enthusiast who fit in with the cops in rough-and-tumble Durham about as well as a rye whiskey drinker in Napa Valley.

In the evidence room, atop Farley's laptop, Preach found a handwritten note:

Easy-Peasy. Standard four-digit pin on the phone, and un-encrypted installation of Windows.

Preach had Kirby check Farley's texts and phone messages. Preach worked the laptop, starting with a Gmail account that opened with a stored password. He found a slew of work-related emails from book distributors, authors, publicists, and Farley's accountant. Preach noted with interest that the bookstore was losing money.

The browsing history was personal. Website after website of gay porn. Preach clicked on the first dozen, saw nothing underage or criminal, and made a mental note to have a PO dig deeper, check for an escort service that might have sent someone to the townhouse. He had seen no evidence of a jilted lover, but he had learned never to discount jealousy as a motive.

The first keyword search he tried was "Belker." He got dozens of hits, most sequestered in a Pen Oak Press folder. The emails pertained largely to the publication of Belker's first novel. The final correspondence was the rejection: a rote email informing the author that, regrettably, Pen Oak Press would not be publishing *Refractions of a Murder*.

He searched for Damian's name next, and got another slew of hits. Curiously, the last entry was six weeks old. Before that, the two men had corresponded on a daily basis, everything from political rants to book tips to plans to get together on the weekend.

Why had the two men, close friends since high school, stopped writing?

"Yo, Preach!" Kirby called out from his cubicle. "You need to see this."

"See what, a new body lotion?" another officer yelled, followed by hoots of laughter. "Is it mango-beet-papaya?"

"Give us a pose, Scotty the Body!"

Kirby stood on a stool with his hands behind his head, flexing his biceps. The troops cheered. He jumped down and walked over to show Preach a text on Farley's cellphone that Wade Fee, the Rabbit Hole Café barista, had sent to Farley at 11:45 p.m. the night of the murder.

-Will b there in 30-

Below that was the initial text from Farley, sent at 11:37 p.m.:

-Up late tonight, can you swing by with some groceries?-

Preach ran a hand through his hair and released a deep sigh.

"I don't think your boy was swinging by with a lasagna," Kirby said.

"No."

"So he shows up fifteen minutes after the neighbor goes to sleep, sells Farley some crib, and the drop goes bad. But what about all the other stuff, the crosses?"

"Maybe the drop didn't go bad. Maybe there was another reason they wanted him killed, and they left the crosses to muddy the waters or to frame someone like Belker."

"Seems a bit, I don't know, *weird* for Wade and Big Mac Dobbins to use a famous novel at a crime scene."

"Yeah. It does." Preach handed the phone back to Kirby. "Do me a quick favor and run a DMV report, find out what kind of car Wade drives."

He decided to go alone to pick up Wade, thinking his old friend might be more forthcoming in private. A squall had passed through, and Preach inhaled the loamy smell of rain-soaked pine needles as he strolled to the side door of the Rabbit Hole Café. He had seen Wade's restored Chrysler in the parking lot, so he knew he was working.

Mac and his crew were shooting pool, and Mac gave him an ironic salute. "Afternoon, Detective," the café owner bellowed. "You should try the butternut squash empanadas, wash them down with a pint of our new milk stout. If you need to do some detectin' after that, we'll set you up with a nice pour over, give those brain cells a jolt."

Preach ignored him. When Wade saw him, the barista's face soured like he'd bitten into a lemon. "What now, man? It's the afternoon rush."

"I hate to do this," Preach said, "but you'll need to come with me."

"Huh? Why?"

Preach lowered his voice and said, "Because we found the texts you exchanged with Farley the night of the murder."

Wade looked dazed. He asked the younger man working the espresso machine to take over.

"We'll cover for ya," Mac said to Wade as he left with Preach, but the café owner was looking at Preach when he spoke, his mouth fixed in a rictus above his beard, eyes hard and unblinking as they followed the two men out the door.

"It's not what you think," Wade said from the passenger seat. He was wearing his rimless glasses and brown beret, and the day's T-shirt of choice read *Rubik, The Amazing Cube*. He had recovered his gruff tone, but his right knee pistoned silently in place as Preach drove.

"That's good," Preach said. "Because what I think is that we have a text suggesting you were at Farley Robertson's condo at the time of the murder. And that's what a grand jury will think, too."

"Like I told you, I was playing poker with Mac and the others."

In response, Preach made a sharp left, off Main Street and onto Goodson Drive, away from the station.

Wade straightened. "Where're you going?"

Preach took a two-lane road that passed by the high school, a field of dead cornstalks, and then the dairy farm where, long before keg parties and cliques and angst-ridden crushes, their parents used to take them for ice cream, chatting on the rocking chair front porch while their kids chased each other through the meadow.

"How's your life been, Wade?"

"Peachy."

"Wife and kids?"

"Nope."

They passed the park where Preach used to play Little League. His dad had attended all his ball games, despite the fact that he hated competitive sports.

"You gonna hit all our old spots?" Wade said. "We can stop the car and make out if you want."

"I'm sorry I handled things like I did. We were just kids."

Wade snorted. "You think I've been pining about it all these years?"

"I just wanted to say it."

"Well, you have."

Preach gripped the wheel. "You really want to go down for those guys? I know you ran drugs to Farley, but I don't think you pulled the trigger. Which could be a whole different ball game in a court of law."

Wade took a cigarette out of the pack he kept rolled inside his shirt cuff. It took him three swipes of his thumb to light it. "I wasn't there."

"If you never showed, how come you didn't send a text to Farley telling him you weren't coming?"

"I mean I wasn't there for the *murder*, man."

Preach gave Wade a tight-lipped glance. "So what, you made a delivery sometime after midnight, left, and someone else waltzed in and murdered him? What was it, a revolving door of vice? Tell me what you know, Wade. Did you leave the door unlocked? What do the crosses mean? How much was Lee into Mac for?"

"I've got no idea who killed him," he muttered. "That's all I have to say."

"We're off the record here. I wanted to chat with you, man to man, before the interrogation room. Give you a chance to come clean."

Wade sneered as they crossed the tracks next to a hardware store where Preach had stacked lumber for a summer. "Why? For *old time's sake*? What happened to you, man? You just dropped us like . . . like you were better than we were."

Wade had never been an athlete, or the cleverest kid in class, or the best-looking. His popularity had stemmed from his aloof attitude and his ability to befriend the cool kids. He always had his finger on the pulse of the scene, knew where to score the best weed, how to get into college parties.

When Preach flipped the switch during their senior year, Wade saw it as a betrayal of the highest order, an attack on their way of life.

"It wasn't like that," Preach said.

"Then what the hell was it? Your cousin? I know that was rough, but none of us believed the church stuff was real. And a *cop*? I know you, man. People don't just change like that."

"Maybe, maybe not. But people do conceal who they are."

Wade shook his head.

"This isn't about my life, it's about yours. And you do not want to go to prison, Wade. Trust me on that one. You think you're hard, but you're not."

Wade kept shaking his head and fiddling with the ends of his moustache, his knee bouncing faster.

Preach killed the engine as they pulled into the station. "Let me talk to the DA and get a wire on you. Maybe they'll overlook the drug charges."

Wade gave an ugly little laugh. "You don't have anything. And you sure as hell don't know anything about Mac, or you wouldn't mention a wire. Off the record?"

"Yeah. Off the record."

"Between you and me, a little birdie told me that over the last few months the recently deceased had developed a three-G habit."

"Per month?" Preach said.

"Per *week*."

Preach stared at him.

"Hooked something fierce," Wade said, "and probably supplying his johns, too. But like I said, he was straight with us. No debt. So how's a strung-out bookstore owner keep up an account like that? Why don't you detect *that*, Joe?"

12

As soon as Preach walked Wade into the station, a tall and trim man in his fifties approached them. A crown of sandy hair rimmed his comb-over, and his bespoke brown suit with a red-and-white-checkered tie screamed *attorney*.

"Why, exactly, are you driving my client around town without his consent? Maybe this is how things are done in Atlanta, but not here. Not unless you want a civil suit with your morning coffee."

Despite the challenge, the attorney's voice remained polite. His rural North Carolina accent, as rich and smooth as oak-aged chardonnay, sounded a touch overdone to Preach.

"It's fine," Wade said. "We were just talking."

Preach saw Chief Higgins standing off to the side, watching the exchange with folded arms. Kirby hovered behind her.

The attorney gave Wade a piercing stare. "They have no reason to hold you." He turned back to the detective, as if daring him to challenge the statement.

Preach spread his hands. Maybe they had enough for an arrest, maybe they didn't. Either way, this attorney was going to stonewall further questioning. Preach decided it was better to let Wade walk—for now.

"Believe it or not," he said, "I have your client's best interests in mind."

"I'll choose skepticism in this instance." The lawyer curled a finger at Wade. "Let's go."

Preach called out to his old friend as they left. It was depressing to see how his life had turned out, a lackey for a local drug dealer. "Do you really want us to start digging? Are they worth it?"

Wade sniffed and reached for another cigarette. "Do what you have to. Great seeing you again, Joe."

After Wade waltzed out with his attorney, Chief Higgins stopped by Preach's desk. "That was Elliott Fenton, Creekville's best defense attorney. Mac called him."

"Must be a peach of a guy, if Mac Dobbins has him on retainer," Preach said.

"Elliott's not known for his client selectivity."

"Which lawyer is? Atticus Finch?"

Chief Higgins snorted and crossed her meaty arms. Her red curls looked oilier than usual, the color of a low-grade grease fire. "Be careful. Elliott's connected, and this town is so focused on doing the politically correct thing they've cut off their own balls."

She looked not in the slightest bit abashed about her gender-specific reference. Preach knew the chief drank herbal tea and practiced yoga and shopped at the co-op, but she'd also told him about growing up poor in a small town outside Fayetteville. She belonged to that class of scrappy Southern women far removed from the debutante set: nurturing, but tough as a cast-iron skillet. Trailer parks instead of subdivisions, Folger's instead of Starbucks, pork rinds instead of sweet potato soufflé.

She lowered her voice. "My point is you can't take the gloves off around here, and my other officers are as green as unripe figs. Most of them have never fired their guns."

"What about bringing in a few people with some experience?"

"You think I haven't tried? I only got you because someone retired."

Preach and Kirby spent the rest of the afternoon digging through Farley Robertson's emails, searching for connections. The elements of the case swirled in Preach's mind like an inchoate chemistry experiment, the materials scattered in dark places around Creekville, waiting to be unearthed and combined into a combustible form.

Thermos in hand, Kirby appeared at Preach's cubicle. "My eyes are bugging from all this screen time. What's the next play? Shake Mac down?"

"His attorney would just handcuff us. Let's get a forensic accountant on Farley's finances." He rose and shrugged into his jacket. "An expensive drug habit and a bookstore losing money? I want to know where the money came from."

"Going somewhere?" Kirby asked.

"I've got an appointment."

As he brushed past, Kirby stepped aside and eyed him with raised eyebrows, waiting for a longer explanation that never came.

The nighttime streets were glossy, slick with the yellow glow of headlamps as Preach cruised through downtown during what passed for rush hour in Creekville: a brief flurry of commuters returning home from Durham and Raleigh.

The chief, and no one else at the station, knew where Preach had to go. After his breakdown in Atlanta, despite his stellar record, he had been forced to transfer out of the department. Reeling, he had applied to a few cities, but no one had an opening. Or maybe they'd gotten a whiff of what happened in Atlanta and decided to pass. He'd widened his search and discovered the opening in Creekville. At first he'd recoiled, unwilling to deal with a past he'd left behind like a discarded snakeskin, but then his inner voice started urging him to return: hole up someplace calm, handle some minor crimes while he figured out if he was fit to be a murder cop again.

So much for that idea.

The chief was thrilled to take on someone with his experience, but she had mandated therapy as a condition of employment. Preach had not been happy. A negative psychiatric mark could ruin a career.

Still, the chief just wanted to tick a box, and she didn't care what form the therapy took or who Preach saw. He knew colleagues who had seen a friend or relative when they needed an easy sign off, and his Aunt Janice happened to be a brilliant psychologist. She'd reluctantly agreed to see him, free of charge, for a few sessions.

He was praying that was all it would take.

He swung into the parking lot of the office complex and parked beside his aunt's Passat. She had a purple lambda bumper sticker, and a flag-shaped decal that read *At Least The War on the Environment Is Going Well*. In the passenger seat, he saw a red wig that made him smile: serious Aunt Janice liked to moonlight as a clown at the pediatric cancer ward.

Aunt Janice was his favorite relative. His parents had been early adopters in Creekville, professors at the University of Chapel Hill who had helped establish the nearby town as a bastion of extreme liberalism. "Greenwich Village with BBQ," it was called. "San Francisco of the South."

Young Joey had run with the kind of Orange County crowd they abhorred: the popular kids, the lemmings of the mainstream, the kinds of kids who judged each other based on looks and how much alcohol they could consume at keggers.

That was okay, though. Joey would go to Berkeley or NYU and realize the pettiness of his ways, discover the joys of the counterculture. Hit the used bookstores, see a few shows, drop some acid. Then he would take up the family mantle and fight the good fight against evil corporations, the war-mongering government, and the scourge of organized religion.

His parents could deal with his teenage rebellion, but they had not been able to abide his sudden adoption of Christianity or his decision to become a cop.

Aunt Janice was a big part of the reason Preach had returned. She was the only person who had visited him during his ill-fated stint as a junior pastor in a West Virginia town so provincial they didn't even have a physician. Yet his mother and aunt had not seen each other since Janice had moved back to Creekville the year before. His mother always deflected Preach's questions about the source of the animosity. Janice was gay, so it wasn't jealousy over a lover. Preach assumed his mother had offended her in some way. He hoped it wasn't due to jealousy over his fondness for his aunt.

The ravenous chirp of insects echoed from the surrounding woods. Preach stood with a hand on the door, lost in the past, unsure of his decision. Baring his soul in front of his aunt would be embarrassing. And what if there was truly something wrong with him?

He took a deep breath and reached for the door.

13

Her nametag read Dr. Allen, but Preach could think of her only as Aunt Janice. He remembered her as a handsome woman, but middle age had grayed her hair, thickened her limbs, and broadened her midsection. Her ash-colored locks bobbed on either side of her chin, framing crinkly eyes and a mouth whose lips always seemed slightly parted, as if in perpetual knowledge of a secret.

With her hefty build, dowdy sweater, and down-to-earth mannerisms, she didn't look too much like a psychologist.

Which was probably why she was a good one.

"Here's the deal, Joey. It's not an ethical violation for me to see you, but it's frowned upon. I'll see you for a handful of sessions, and if I think a real issue might be present, I'm sending you to someone else. No favors. No special treatment."

"I understand," Preach said, working not to show his disappointment. Special treatment had been exactly what he was hoping for.

They moved to the green-walled therapy room that overlooked the forest. After a few minutes of lightly probing questions, warm but clinical, she said, "I'd like to discuss the past."

"You mean Atlanta?"

"Not the recent past. Not yet."

"I don't understand."

"With law enforcement officers, an incident such as yours is often a reaction to an accumulation of stress. It can happen to the best of us. True trauma, however, is typically rooted in a past event." She clasped her hands. "Has anything similar to Atlanta ever happened to you before?"

He hesitated. This was part of the reason he had chosen his aunt:

she already knew what he was about to tell her and had never mentioned it as a potential problem.

Then again, he supposed she had never had a reason.

"Cousin Ricky," he said. "But you know that already."

"I think you should tell me."

He shrugged. "I was at his house when it happened. I went to the hospital with him." Preach was a seasoned interviewer himself, so he was aware of how telling it was when he spoke in monotone and stared into the woods. "We were seventeen."

"They were mostly third-degree burns, weren't they?"

"Yes."

"On his face?"

"His face, his arms, his legs, his chest, his genitals."

"Do you feel responsible for the accident?"

"He was working on his car. I was just watching."

"That's not what I asked," she said.

He looked away. "Of course I wonder what I could have done. But the truth is, probably nothing."

"Did you know he was going to die? At the hospital?"

"Probably. That wasn't the issue, never has been. I can accept death."

"Then what is the issue?" she asked in surprise.

His eyes flicked back to regard her. "Suffering."

She paused a beat before she spoke, expressionless. "I see. What about before Ricky? Had you felt that way at other times?"

He moved his hands into his lap, rubbed at the callouses on his palms from the weight room. "Before that, for all of my life, I struggled to express emotion. As if there were something alien bottled up inside me, which I couldn't even put a name to. Do you understand? I'm not even sure I do. For example, at granddad's funeral when I was twelve, I just . . . shut down. I sat there and stared at the body and then started doodling random shapes in my notebook. There was so much going on inside, so much that didn't manifest in a relatable form like grief or rage or sadness, that I just turned off. Everyone thought I was cold-hearted, and that's what I thought, too."

"You didn't recognize the emotions for what they were?"

"Everyone was crying, and I didn't feel like crying at all. I felt something, as I always did, but it was cold and hard and vast, not soft and human. To be honest, it made me feel like a monster. And that's the way I acted for most of my youth. Like a monster."

"And you figured it out when you saw Ricky in the burn ward?"

"I didn't figure anything out. For whatever reason, when I saw my cousin in agony on that hospital bed, his body shaking with pain, his eyes shining with it, an avalanche of sadness overwhelmed me. I cried for the first time since grade school, and I didn't stop until I went catatonic. As you know, they put me in the same hospital. I was home the next day, but after that, for weeks, I got emotional at the slightest provocation. Everything affected me, sent me spinning."

He stopped speaking, but he could tell she noticed something in his eyes.

"Is that all?" she asked.

His gaze landed on a wall calendar displaying a bonsai tree garden with a view of Mount Fuji. "Every time I was in that room with Ricky . . . it was as if I could feel it myself."

"The burn?"

"Not the physical sensation, but his mental anguish. His pain." Preach waved a hand, as if to say, *it's all in the past.*

"Mirror-touch synesthesia," she said, after a long pause. "Have you heard of that?"

"No."

"Hyperactive mirror neurons that fire when others are in pain, causing tangible physical sensations in the sufferer."

"If I had that, I couldn't be a cop. I've never felt physical pain in response to someone else's suffering, not anywhere on the spectrum."

"Then where?" she asked.

"I don't know. I guess that depends on one's belief system."

"And what do you believe?"

He laughed. "Auntie—"

"Not in here."

He looked at her. She was dead serious. "Sorry—Doctor. And you know what I believe."

"You've kept your faith."

"As well as my doubts," he said.

"I'm curious; how did you cope for all those years? I would think no one has seen more suffering and extreme emotion than a police officer."

"Isn't it better to look the world in the face than ignore it? For me it is. And I've never had another . . . incident. Well, not like that." He paused and looked down. "Not until Atlanta."

"We'll get there," she said.

He pressed his hands together. The blood was starting to pound in his head at the memory. He didn't want to look up and see his aunt's face, deal with the horrors of the past or the shame of the present.

A buzz from his phone saved him. He dug it out of his pocket and saw a text from Ari.

-I found something in Farley's office you need to see. Can u come?-

Preach looked up. "I'm sorry, but I have to go. It's work."

She put her hands on her knees. "That's enough for tonight, anyway."

"How many times do we have to meet?"

"As many times as it takes."

"I know we have to do this, but I'm okay, really. There's nothing going on that will affect my job."

"I'm afraid I'll have to be the judge of that for myself." They left the room and she embraced him at the door, compassion warming her eyes, a beloved aunt once again. "Take care, Joey. Come see me at home soon."

Preach parked on the street outside the bookstore. The evening was cool and foggy, the buildings a smudge in the early darkness.

Ari unlocked the door. "Thanks for coming so quickly," she said, her eyes scanning the street as she pulled her cropped denim jacket tight over a lacy emerald shirt. "I was getting nervous."

He stepped inside, wary. "Did something happen?"

"No, but after what I found . . . Let me show you."

She led him to a walnut bookshelf in the interior office that Preach and Kirby had searched on their first visit. "I put it back so you could see." She pulled out a weathered, hardbound copy of *Great Expectations*. The cover bore a picture of Pip and Estella creeping through the old Victorian manor.

"Farley's favorite author," she said, opening the book to reveal a hollowed-out center. A folded manila envelope was tucked inside the artificial pocket.

Preach opened the envelope. Inside was a plain metal key, about the size of a post office box key. It possessed no numbers or other identifying marks. He whistled. "Any idea what this unlocks?"

"No, but it got me thinking." One by one, she moved around the bookshelf and pulled out a series of hardback Dickens novels. She stacked them on the desk and opened the one on top. *The Pickwick Papers*.

Inside was another hidden pocket. This one contained a roll of hundred dollar bills, bound by a rubber band.

Preach flipped through the wad. "That's got to be five grand." He opened the six other Dickens novels and found similar stacks of cash.

His gaze met Ari's. He could tell by her eyes that she was seeing her employer in a whole new light.

"You know, Dickens was a contemporary of Dostoevsky," she said. "He was born about a decade earlier. You think that means anything?"

"I was hoping you could tell me. Have you looked through the rest of the books?"

"Just a few," she said.

"Do you mind waiting while I finish?"

"Sure. I've got some studying to do."

She started to walk away, and he asked, "Any more stalker sightings?"

"No. But thanks for asking."

After she left, he pulled out the rest of the books one by one, raising a cloud of dust. Farley had shelved his personal collection by topic: classics, modern lit, poetry, modern architecture, travel guides to Napa and the North Carolina coast.

He found nothing else. After giving the entire office another once-over, he placed the money and the Dickens novels in evidence bags. He found Ari perched on a chair by the front door, reading *Night Film* by Marisha Pessl.

He eyed the novel. "Law and Literature class?"

"One can only study for so long."

"Give you a lift home?"

She closed the novel and stood. "I took your advice and drove."

"I'll walk you out."

He followed her out the rear entrance. A trace of her perfume, citrus and rose and cinnamon, drifted to his nose.

She unlocked her car, then turned. "How's the case going?"

"We have a few leads," he said evasively.

"Any more headway with Dostoevsky?"

"I've come to an agreement with my existential angst, if that's what you mean."

Her eyebrows arched.

"I won't question its existence," he said, "as long as it doesn't question mine."

Her smile was quick and devilish. "If you'd like to discuss the novel any further, tonight's a good night. I've got a light study load."

He hefted the canvas bag full of books. "I have to get this into evidence. And I've got someplace to go after that." When he saw her flinch, just barely, he added, "For the case."

He opened her door, and she slid inside. A jolt of attraction arced through him when she looked back and their eyes met. Something else seemed to pass between them as well, a glimmer of newfound knowledge, as if they had both just realized they might be reading the same book.

After Ari pulled away, the feeling of attraction blossomed further, spreading through him as he got into his car and swerved into the street. He took a deep breath to shake it off.

Working a case did that to you sometimes: heightened emotions, made everything feel sharper and more intense. He knew he wasn't her type, and she clearly wasn't over her ex.

More importantly, he had a case to work, someone to find that evening.

Someone who drove a restored, maroon-and-white '57 Chrysler New Yorker and who had made regular visits to Farley's back office. Someone who Preach would bet his last dollar knew something about the stacks of bills stashed inside the Dickens novels.

14

As Preach drove around Creekville, searching the parking lots of the weekend haunts for Wade's car, he thought about the key Ari had found. The obvious conclusion was a post office or safe-deposit box.

He knew Farley had maintained an account with the Creekville branch of PNC Bank. Some states required banks to microstamp routing numbers on their keys, though Preach wasn't sure about North Carolina. When he returned to the office, he would check the key with a magnifier.

If that didn't pan out, he would have Kirby call the rest of the local banks to see if Farley had set up a second account, then watch Farley's mail for incoming statements. Keeping a key secret meant someone else had a reason to desire it—and that Farley was afraid of that person.

Yet how did it relate to the stacks of cash, the murder, the two crosses?

He needed more pieces to the puzzle, and it was time the person who possessed them coughed them up—whether he liked it or not.

After swinging by the Rabbit Hole and Wade's apartment, Preach widened his search. It was Friday night, and his old friend was sure to be out on the town. Some of the places he checked for Wade's car had been their old stomping grounds. The slew of college dives on the east end of Main Street, unchanged over the years. A pool hall turned wine bar that catered to single professors, the honky-tonk bar at the edge of town that still catered to single rednecks.

He even tried the lookout spot by the lake, a forested picnic area where bald eagles sometimes soared over the water in the dying light of the day. The night of Ricky's accident, Preach had been at the lake with Lisa Welsh, a statuesque redhead Preach had dated for most of his senior year. The night before that, he'd been with Carly Vezzani, captain of the cheerleading team, the kind of girl who had been comfortable in her sexuality since the seventh grade.

No sign of Wade's car. Memories pressed against Preach like trapped spirits. The midnight call from Ricky to come drink beer and help him with his car, a 1967 Mustang Fastback. God, how his cousin loved that car.

Get us a couple more beers, he had said to Preach, lifting the container of gasoline to pour into the carburetor. *I'll have it started by the time you get back.*

You sure that's safe?

Ricky had laughed. *I do it all the time.*

His parents were out of town. Preach went inside, popped two Budweisers, then heard the engine backfire and the first scream.

Preach ran outside just in time to watch his cousin's face melt.

Shuddering even after all these years, he would never forget the sound of Ricky's screams, not long and drawn out but ragged bursts of sound, involuntary, as if they were being ripped out of him.

After another half hour of driving, Preach finally spotted Wade's Chrysler wedged into the crowded dirt parking lot behind the String Shack, a popular live music venue. Preach parked and went inside.

The long, scruffy bar was just inside the entrance, along with a pair of pool tables. Just past the bar, the club opened into a cavernous space packed with people clapping and stomping to a loud Americana band jamming onstage at the far end of the club. The floor was sticky, and the place smelled of sweat and cheap beer.

The String Shack had been around since Preach was a kid, and as far as he could tell, not much had changed—including the three people shooting pool near the bar who were staring at him as if he were some mythical creature made real.

A hulking slab of aging football-player flesh named Eric Danforth slammed his beer bottle on an oak barrel serving as a cocktail table. "By Gawd, if it ain't Psycho Joe himself, boots and all!"

Eric was from the sticks and had been one of the chief officers in Preach's high school "army," the kind of raw-boned country kid who would smash a couple of heads without asking questions. He wasn't stupid or even mean, he just preferred that someone else told him what to do.

"I heard you were back," Dennie White said, his voice bloated with festering anger, "though I got no idea why." A good-looking kid, slim and tough, Dennie had been a star pitcher who boxed on the side. He was the mean one and had hated blond Joe Everson until, on the last day of ninth grade, Preach had confronted him behind the school and beat him senseless, then offered him his hand.

That was a language Dennie spoke.

The third, Lisa Welsh, said nothing. Her face looked sallow, as if Preach's presence made her ill. He had broken up with her on an answering machine two days after he returned from the hospital.

Though they looked different—Eric with a shaved head and tattoos wrapping his biceps, Dennie with a Van Dyke beard and thirty extra pounds, Lisa with more makeup and wider hips and modern clothes—they also looked the same, as if Preach had stepped into a time machine and walked into the String Shack after winning another wrestling tournament, ready to shoot a few games of pool and sneak beer in plastic cups from the bartender, who happened to be Carly Vezzani's older brother.

All three made subtle shifts away from Preach as he approached. The band had switched to playing an Irish jig, and two silky-smooth fiddlers were battling onstage, chins gripping their instruments.

"It's good to see you all," Preach said. "I wish I could catch up, but I'm looking for Wade."

Preach caught Dennie's eyes darting to the side, toward the hallway Preach knew ran behind the bar. The glance was so quick he probably wasn't aware of it. "Who?" Dennie asked.

"Funny," Preach said.

"I'm surprised you remember our names."

"Don't," Lisa said.

"Don't?" Dennie said. "You're the last person that should be telling me to stop. He drops us all like a bad habit, fifteen years without a word, and then strolls in here and asks for Wade? Good to see you, too, old buddy."

"I'm sorry," Preach said. "I was a dumb kid. I handled it poorly. All of it," he said, looking at Lisa.

"Yeah, you did," Dennie said.

"Let's grab a beer soon, and you can give me hell about it," Preach said. "Listen, about Wade. I know he's here. I saw his car."

Eric gripped Preach's elbow. "Maybe it was someone else's, you know?"

Preach looked down at Eric's hand on his elbow, then slowly back up, until his gaze locked onto the face of the larger man. Eric jerked his hand away, then lowered his eyes and took a step back.

"God, you're still afraid of him," Dennie said, then stepped into Preach's face. "What are you today, Joe, a cop or a preacher? Or did you finally realize what a two-faced dick you are, and it's back to being a hell-raising ladies' man? Is that it? We gonna start up the old crew again?"

Dennie shoved him in disgust, but Preach didn't so much as wobble. Dennie cursed and picked up his pool stick, then leaned down and took a shot. "What do I care about Wade? He's probably in the back office, drinking Scotch and smoking it up with one of his new *friends*. He's too good for us, too, these days. Or maybe it's just that we don't cook meth."

"Dennie!" Lisa snapped. "Shut your mouth."

"It's not like they don't know."

On his way past the pool table, Preach stopped beside Lisa. He didn't know what he was going to say, but she didn't give him a chance to say anything, refusing to meet his gaze and stepping behind Eric, who folded his arms and glared at him.

Mouth tight, he continued walking, past a line of club kids posing along the back wall, then through a swinging door and into a hallway. Behind the last door on the left, he found Wade sitting in an overstuffed chair and sharing a joint with an emaciated older man wearing a blue silk shirt and leather pants.

Wade's companion jumped to his feet.

"You need to leave," Preach said, before the aging rocker could speak.

"Excuse the hell outta me? This is my brother's club. I—"

Preach flashed his badge. "Now."

The man swallowed whatever he was about to say. "You got a warrant to come back here?"

"You really want me to get one? I doubt your brother would be too happy about that."

The man sputtered a few curses, put out his joint, and glared at Preach on his way out of the room. The muffled sounds of the band floated through the walls.

"My attorney will have you for breakfast," Wade said, his loathing for his old friend sparking in his eyes.

"And who's paying that bill?" Preach grabbed an empty chair. "Looks to me like Mac's the one living large, while you do his dirty work. Running drugs and working a cash register at thirty-five?"

Wade stubbed his joint in an ashtray and picked up a beer. "Look man, what's your beef? I've told you everything I know."

"Have you? I found thirty grand in Farley's office. You used to disappear in there with him. What's the money for, Wade? Was he dealing, too?"

Wade smirked and reached for his cell. "You just don't listen, do you? Never did. I'm calling my—"

Preach smacked the cell phone out of his hand. It clanged and settled on the tile. Wade jerked back, his mouth hanging open. "Still the same old Joe, huh? Roughing someone up when you don't get your way?"

The detective leaned forward. "You think this is a game, Wade, because you haven't been caught. I know you—you've got attitude and you're a little selfish, but you're not a bad seed. Mac and his boys, they're from a whole different world. A different universe. Did you know I was a prison chaplain for a few years before I was a cop? When I was at the Cummins Unit in Arkansas, there was a guy on suicide watch who reminded me of you. Lionel Simmons. Small town guy, same age, same aloof demeanor. Lionel was found with twelve ounces of pot during a traffic stop, caught a bad judge, and got sent away for six months."

Wade wasn't looking at him, so Preach snapped his fingers in his face. "Lionel was raped at knifepoint his first week in prison and nine more times over the next five months, usually by a gang of cons, sometimes by guards. Lionel finally snapped and stabbed a guy in the neck with a fork, which resulted in the first extension of his sentence. By the time I got to him, he'd been in jail for eleven years. Three months after I left, he committed suicide by stuffing toilet paper down his throat."

Wade was staring at the far wall. He hadn't touched his beer during the story.

"Where'd Farley's money come from? Did you bring it in?"

Wade sniffed and finally took a drink, then wiped a trickle of beer off his moustache.

"Lionel wasn't an outlier, Wade. Hate me if you like, but I don't want to see you fall."

Wade jumped up and started pacing the room. "I told you what I know about that night. We both know why I went there. But that's *it*, man. I swear to God."

Preach softened his tone. "If you think you're protecting Mac, you're not. He'll leave you to the wolves without a second thought."

"You're *not listening*. If something else went down that night, I didn't know about it." His voice lowered to a whisper. "Even if I did, I can't cross him, man."

"The books full of money?"

Wade plopped back into his chair, threw his beret on the floor, and plucked at his short, cowlick-laden, thinning black hair. His voice sounded defeated. "I carried the money, yeah, but not for Mac."

Preach sat back in surprise. "Then who?"

Wade pressed his lips together. "This didn't come from me."

"You have my word."

The barista looked from side to side, then down at his hands. "Damian Black," he muttered.

Preach's surprise grew. "I don't understand."

"We had a . . . business relationship. Over the last few months, he asked me to carry a manila envelope now and then to Farley. He never told me what was inside, swear to God."

"We also found a key in Farley's office."

"What?"

"A small key, maybe to a safe deposit box."

"So?"

"So what was it for?"

Wade's face flushed red. "Bust me if you have to, but I've told you everything I know. On my honor, on whatever we had between us in the past, on my mother's damn grave—I didn't have anything to do with Farley's murder, I have no idea what that money was about, and I don't know a goddamn thing about any key."

15

Preach felt on edge as he drove away from the String Shack. Jittery with nervous energy over the case, restless with worry for Wade. He had seen no deception skittering in his old friend's eyes, and he could only hope, for his sake, that he was telling the truth.

A front had blown in, stirring up the fog and resulting in a luke-warm fall night, pregnant with clouds and static electricity. The giant oaks along Hillsdale loomed on either side of the street, and he felt as if Creekville had disappeared and he were driving through an ancient forest, in a time before cities and towns and villages, before swarms of people had invaded the earth.

A mile from the city limits he pulled into the parking lot of his gym. Preach was not a workout fanatic, but sometimes tossing around large plates of iron for an hour was the only way to clear his head.

At this time of night, the gym would be deserted, which suited Preach just fine. It was a relic from another era, a single-room shack with rusty iron weights, no mirrors, and hard rubber mats covered with a layer of dust and dried sweat. The members all had keys, paid a nominal monthly fee, and used it whenever they liked. The owner was Ray Logan, Preach's old wrestling coach. A devout Christian, Ray had taken Preach to his church after Ricky's death, when he saw him strug-gling to cope. They had remained close over the years.

The first drops of rain spattered the windows as Preach slid the plates onto the bench press bar. His mind roved elsewhere during the workout.

The news about Damian had muddied the waters. Preach drew the only reasonable conclusion: Farley was blackmailing his old friend.

It would explain the bookseller's sudden enrichment, the clandestine nature of the payments, and the abrupt cessation of contact.

But what did Farley have on Damian?

Unlike most murder cases, Preach now had an abundance of suspects. He finished a set and threw on more weight, loading the barbell down with three forty-five pound plates on each side. Lightning backlit the trees outside the window as he slid onto the bench. He gripped the bar and knocked out six hard reps, paused to take a few quick breaths, then prepared to push out one more.

After a deep breath, he lowered the bar to his chest as a crash of thunder rocked the gym. Just as he began to push, four men in black ski masks poured through the doorway.

The entrance was twenty feet away. Preach had locked the door behind him, and he didn't have time to ponder how the men had gotten inside. All he knew was that if they reached him before he got that weight off his chest, he would be at their mercy.

He blew out a breath and thrust as hard as could, channeling a burst of adrenaline.

Push, he urged himself. *Push*.

The intruders' muddy work boots swished over the mats. The first was halfway there. Preach's gun was on the bench behind him, within arm's reach if he could just rack the bar and free his hands.

He thrust his heels against the ground and lifted his butt off the bench, arching his back as he pushed. If he had used a lighter weight, he could have thrown off the bar or risked sliding out from under it. But this was three hundred and fifteen pounds of solid cast iron. He had to rack it.

The first man reached the foot of the bench, a worn military jacket flapping behind him. Preach felt his elbows lock, and he braced to throw the bar back. Just before it fell into place, the man grabbed the bar and leaned on it, forcing it down.

Preach's arms buckled as the bar fell against his chest. He spent his final ounce of energy making sure the bar's descent didn't crush his sternum.

All four men hovered over him, reeking of whiskey, greasy hair hanging beneath the ski masks. Preach knew the flinty stares leering from the eyeholes belonged to men who had either served hard time or weren't afraid to.

It took two of them to force the bar higher on Preach's chest and onto his neck, but once they got it there, he started to panic. He was choking, and the bar was too high for him to engage his major muscle groups. Even if these men left now, he might not be able to get the bar off by himself.

"I'm a cop," he managed to whisper. It felt like an elephant was crouched on his throat.

"Ain't helping you much right now, is it?" rasped the first one who had reached him. His harsh, rural Southern accent was tires crunching over gravel.

Preach couldn't breathe. He was already light-headed. He tried to kick at one of them, but they slapped his legs away.

The lead assailant spit in Preach's face, and he caught a glimpse of a jagged cleft-lip scar above his mouth.

"You're poking around in the wrong shed with that murder. Don't stick your nose where it don't belong."

The man's spittle trickled down Preach's cheek. He tried to croak out a reply, but he couldn't get the words out, and bright spots filled his vision in staccato bursts.

Fear morphed into rage, and he got a final burst of adrenaline. He struggled to lift the weight off his throat, but his assailant held the bar down as his deadened eyes bored into the detective's, easily overpowering the effort.

Preach's fingers quivered and slipped off the bar.

Just after nine p.m., Kirby knocked and then pushed open the door of his sister's trailer, late for their weekly dinner. Kayla, his niece, greeted him with a pirouette. "Guess what? We're having Domino's tonight!"

He whistled. "Wowza, high roller. What kind?"

"Cheese and onion and pepperoni. Just how you like it."

He squeezed her shoulder, then crossed the room to hug an unresponsive Jared. His nephew had become a falling leaf in the forest, his buoyant spirit fluttering unheard to the ground. It was breaking his heart.

His sister winced as she rose off the couch to greet him. He hurried over to help her. "Sorry I'm late."

"It's okay. We snacked."

"No better?" he asked, in a low voice.

"A little," she said, smiling.

He wasn't convinced.

They chatted until the doorbell rang. Kirby saw the Domino's car through the window. As he rose to pay, his sister pressed a twenty into his hand. He tried to push it away, but she insisted. "My treat tonight."

"Oh yeah?" he said. On the phone, she had dropped a mysterious hint that they had something to celebrate.

Her smile widened, larger than he had seen in months. Years. "I'll tell you at the table," she said.

They sat down to eat, Jalene fussing over the kids' manners. When everyone was situated, she raised her glass of Coke and said, "I have some great news." She looked at Jared, her amber eyes bright with pride. "We've always known we have a little Einstein in the family, and I'm so proud to tell everybody—" her voice trembled as tears sprang to her eyes—"that my baby boy has just been accepted into the Chapel Hill Academy."

Jared looked confused. His mom came up behind him and wrapped him in her arms. "Baby—baby, you're going to a new school now. A *good* one."

Kirby's slice of pizza stopped halfway to his mouth. "A good one? That's the best private school in the Triangle. Jalene . . ."

He trailed off because he didn't want to ask the question in front of the kids. The question being, how in the world could his sister afford a two grand a month private school?

"Not just accepted," Jalene continued, her sly glance telling him she knew exactly what he was thinking. "A scholarship. He got a full scholarship."

Kirby flew to his feet and pounded the table. "Are you kidding me? For real? Hell yeah—I mean, heck, yes!" He lifted his nephew into the air, pressing him up and down as he carried him into the living room. For the first time in months, Jared giggled, and when Kirby brought him down to hug him, his nephew squeezed him back.

Kayla grabbed Jared and started twirling with him. Jalene came up behind Kirby and put her hands on his hips, and they paraded around the narrow living room in a conga line, whooping and kicking their feet like Russian folk dancers.

The sound of breaking glass broke the spell. "What was that?" Jalene asked, her hands falling off his hips.

Kirby heard the front door open, and he reached for his gun before remembering that he never carried inside his sister's trailer. He jerked a lamp off the table as four men in black ski masks poured through the door.

Jalene and Kayla screamed, and Kirby stepped in front of them. "Call for help!" he said, then broke the lamp on the table and advanced on the men with the jagged ceramic handle. The man in front pulled a gun and aimed it at Kirby's head. "Back it up, nigger."

The racial epithet was delivered fast and harsh, like the crack of a whip. Kirby felt as if he had been punched in the gut. He lowered the lamp and took a step back, his arms spread wide to protect his family. "I'm a cop," he said. "Now just—"

"We know exactly who you are," the man said. He was tall and built like a bull. A tattoo of the Confederate flag, with skulls in place of stars, wrapped his left forearm. He swung the gun toward Kayla and then Jalene. "This is our town, and you best lay off our people if you know what's good for yours."

Kirby snarled and raised the lamp. "You touch a hair on their heads, and I swear to God I'll—"

The intruder shoved the gun into his cheek, leaning in so close

Kirby could smell the bacon fat and cigarette smoke stinking up his breath. He cocked the gun. "Give me a reason!" he roared.

Kirby stood very still, adrenaline and fury pumping through him in shuddering waves. He had never wanted so much to put a gun to someone's face and pull the trigger.

But he had no weapon, no leverage, and no choice. These men were crazy enough to attack a cop's family. He balled his fists at his sides and didn't take a breath as the man stared him down. At last the thug eased his gun away, but then he reversed the motion, slamming the weapon into the side of Kirby's head.

His ear exploded in pain, and the sound of rainfall disappeared, replaced by a metallic ringing. Kirby stumbled to a knee and grabbed his head, blood dripping onto his fingers.

The intruders backed toward the door. "You remember what I said, now."

Just before they left the trailer, one of the men lit a cloth-wrapped torch, and then threw it into the living room. It hissed and burst into flame, emitting a foul odor that stunk like rotten eggs and cat urine.

Kirby scooped the kids up and rushed them outside. Through the window, he could see his sister smothering the fire with a wet blanket, choking on the foul smoke coating the room.

The men sped away in a black Dodge Charger. The neighbors had fled inside, and for once the trailer park was quiet. Shaking, Kirby called 911 with a voice so thick with rage he didn't recognize it as his own.

16

Preach was lying on the floor of a one-room, timber-frame house. A raging inferno consumed his body from the inside. Time had blurred into a flat line of pain, broken only by his meditations on death and the nightly rattle of the death cart. The gruesome wagon had paused outside his dwelling, long enough for him to weakly lift his hand. After it passed, Preach coughed up blood and melted back into the floor.

The smell of decay had seeped into his rags, the walls, the floor. Thirst scratched at his throat like someone buried alive, fingers clawing at the dirt. He tried to scream at God, but the words left his mouth in a trickle of muted sound. *Why are you killing us like this? Your creation? Why?*

A stream of water hit him full in the face. He tried to slap it away, but it poured down, clogging his nose and throat, drowning him—

"Joey! Wake up, son. Wake up!"

Preach blinked and saw his old coach, Ray Logan, standing over him with a pitcher of water. He was about to toss it again when Preach raised a hand. Instead of a plague-ridden medieval village, he realized he was lying on his back on a workout bench, the loaded-down barbell on the floor beside him.

He remembered.

Water dripped off his hair and chin as a siren whined in the distance. Ray leaned over him, his bald head shining under the cheap fluorescent lights. "A neighbor saw some suspicious men at the door and called me. Thank God you're okay, son, but what were you thinking? Pressing that much without a spotter?"

Preach gingerly touched the front of his neck. It felt as if he had been worked over with a baseball bat. "Not too smart, huh?"

"Didn't I teach you anything?"

Preach blew out a long breath. "I guess I never was a fast learner."

Chief Higgins met Preach at the hospital. His stomach clenched when she told him about the attack on Kirby's family.

"Was it Mac's boys who attacked you?" she asked grimly.

"I think that was the message," Preach said, his voice raw from the injury. "They were smart enough to keep it anonymous."

"This isn't like him. He's never come after a cop before."

Preach's face darkened. "He has now."

"I guess we've got to assume he's got a murder rap stuck in his craw."

"If so, that was a dumb move."

The chief looked away for a moment, which surprised him, but then he understood. Mac Dobbins thought he could get away with murder in Creekville—and she was worried that maybe he could.

"I'm calling the mayor in the morning," Chief Higgins said. "You need help on this."

"Do what you need to."

It was well after midnight by the time Preach was released from the hospital. After driving home, he set the painkillers aside and picked up a beer instead.

An attack like that would never have happened in Atlanta. Criminals didn't taunt cops in the big city. The more he thought about the night's events, the more he came to the conclusion that his shakedown of Wade had triggered the attack. Either the String Shack had cameras, or Wade had come clean.

But that entirely didn't ring true to Preach. Wade was just a pawn.

So what didn't Mac want them to find? If he was so concerned with someone poking around his business, why not make Farley disappear, throw the body in a quarry? Why draw attention to the murder with the bizarre reference to a nineteenth-century novel?

His hand paused on the refrigerator door with sudden knowledge. What had they learned from Wade? They had learned about Damian. About the blackmail.

Had Damian grown tired of making payouts, and hired Mac to take care of the problem?

Preach changed his mind about the beer and poured a tumbler of bourbon instead. The solitude of the forest enveloped him as he threw on his jacket and stepped onto the back porch. A barn owl eyed him from its perch above the woodpile.

He made a fire in the potbelly stove squatting in the center of the porch, then sat on a stump of wood and thought about the violence that men do and the darkness bubbling in his own soul. A darkness that coexisted with the thing inside him that had gone catatonic at the sight of Ricky's suffering. That had suffered a system failure inside that tree house in Atlanta.

He had once asked Aunt Janice why she decided to become a psychologist. Her answer had stuck with him. *Have you ever tried to look inside yourself, Joey? Really figure it out? It's like trying to solve a billion-piece jigsaw puzzle where all the pieces are solid black. It's frightening and disconcerting, as if you're looking at someone or some*thing *else. Only when we disengage do we feel whole again. Real.*

And I want to know what that means.

A young woman with spunky eyes and scattered dark hair drifted into his thoughts, and he traced her lips and cheekbones in his mind, remembered the soft wisps of hair that feathered her neck. He thought about how little he knew of Ari, how little she knew of him—and how little it mattered.

The owl hooted, and the pines whispered, asking about the two crosses, wondering why he hadn't told Ari the rest of his thoughts on *Crime and Punishment.*

For regardless of what the commentaries said, Preach knew what Dostoevsky was really writing about. He could see it flashing like a neon billboard throughout the novel, behind the clever rhetoric and symbolism. At the quiet center of it all was a human being—Raskolnikov—who was in pain. Deeply afflicted. A lost, lonely little boy who had wandered far from his village home and wanted so much for the universe to make sense, for something to *matter*, that he planned and committed a murder for the sole purpose of trying to shake that sleeping colossus awake. Offered himself up as a sacrificial lamb in order to discover whether his crime would be punished, not by the authorities or Sonia or even himself, but by a higher power.

Since Raskolnikov realized he had a soul and understood the import of what he had done, he knew he had found his answer. And that would have been fine—a great victory, in fact—except it wasn't enough, not for someone like him. It would never be enough. He cared and he didn't know why and he knew he never would.

And *that* was the knowledge that destroyed him.

Preach poked the fire and chuckled away his thoughts. Moral of the story: leave murder to the sociopaths.

He leaned his elbows on his knees as the bourbon warmed his belly, easing his aches and pains. Theme or no theme, he knew he had to stay on his toes in the morning, when he paid Damian Black a visit in his fancy country manor and asked him if he had murdered his best friend with a hatchet.

17

The morning sky was a violet haze as Preach strode through the door of the police station, his neck purple with bruises and stiff as a piece of frozen cloth. He could tell by the drawn faces of the other officers that they had heard what happened.

Kirby was waiting on him, a bandage covering the left side of his head. "You okay?" Preach asked.

"Not even close. Who's first?"

"Damian." Preach lowered his voice. "We'll deal with Mac tonight."

"What time you think a writer gets out of bed?"

"I don't care."

It was only eight a.m., but Preach and Kirby were already too late. As they parked outside Damian Black's residence, to a soundtrack of chirping birds and two furiously barking Akitas, the door to the Southern Gothic manor opened, and the author stepped onto the porch in a monogrammed white bathrobe, accompanied by Elliott Fenton.

Kirby cursed under his breath, and Preach thought about how convenient it was that Elliott represented everyone associated with Mac Dobbins.

He also noticed how Damian had a shot glass of amber liquid pinched between two fingers, how both men looked sleep-deprived and agitated, and how Elliott's lavender necktie was loose and off-center under his pinstriped gray suit coat.

"Can I help you, officers?" Damian asked evenly.

"I was in the area," Preach said, looking straight at the author, "and thought you might want to grab a cup of coffee."

"Breakfast is over," Elliott said. "Sorry you missed it." He had a handful of coffee beans, and popped one in his mouth.

"The invitation was for Damian," Preach said, still eying the author. "And it might not be there tomorrow."

He didn't have enough to bring the writer in, but he was getting closer, and he wanted Damian to know it.

Elliott stepped forward, as if in physical defense of his client. The attorney had an angular face with calculating hazel eyes, and a mouth that tilted to one side when he spoke. "Did you come to arrest my client?" he asked.

Kirby started to speak, but Preach laid a hand on his arm. "We're just here to ask Mr. Black about some large cash payments he might have made to Farley Robertson," he said, causing Damian's eyes to whisk away from his.

Elliott popped another coffee bean in his mouth. "Detective, you seem to be making a habit of harassing my clients without due cause. I'd advise you to rethink your strategy."

"Rethink *my* strategy? The only thing you're doing for your clients is increasing my interest in them."

Damian's eyes disappeared into his tumbler. A dismissive smile appeared on Elliott's face. "Good-day, gentlemen. Don't let me find you near my client again without my knowledge."

The attorney ushered the writer inside. The dogs continued barking as Preach and Kirby returned to their car.

Chief Higgins beckoned Preach and Kirby into her office. On her desk, photos of her three Yorkies shared space with a quartet of bowling trophies. She had never remarried and had not discussed her social life with Preach.

"I just got a call from the mayor's office, asking why we were harassing one of her largest donors."

"I guess Creekville's just a cliché after all," Preach said.

"Yeah," Kirby muttered, fiddling with one of the trophies. "Like the one about how the rich get away with murder."

"Not on my watch, they don't," she said. "So you'd best get to finding something solid."

"We'll hit the laptop and the phone today," Preach said. "Hard."

"The mayor also denied my request for more officers. Or at least put it off until the next budget meeting. Hang in there until the fifteenth, and I might be able to get you some help."

Preach pursed his lips as the chief reached into a bag of honey and lemon lozenges and popped one into her mouth. "Trust me, if we find a smoking gun, the mayor will cut the line with Damian faster than a fisherman who's hooked a turd." She turned to Preach. "We responded to a call this morning at the Cedar Street Apartments. Wade Fee was beat half to death with a monkey wrench. Couple of broken ribs, bashed up his face something good. He was unconscious when we found him, no prints on the weapon." She looked at Preach. "Your card was sticking out of his pocket."

Preach's face flushed, and he stared down at the carpet. "Who called it in?"

"Anonymous tip."

Though his head stayed lowered, his eyes moved upward to meet Chief Higgins's.

A look that spoke volumes.

"Oh, and guys, one more thing." She handed them each a plastic pumpkin from a bag beside her desk. The pumpkins were filled with candy and a gift card from the local bakery. Preach realized he had forgotten the date.

"Creekville Elementary thanks you for your service," she said. "Happy Halloween."

Rance Crowley swung by to help Preach scour Farley's hard drive, Kirby handled the phone records, and Preach enlisted Terry and another patrol officer to sift through the deleted emails. The afternoon came and went, but they had nothing to show for their efforts except a pile of grease-stained Chinese take-out boxes.

By six p.m., the POs were off duty, and Kirby had left to take his sister's kids trick or treating. Frustrated with the lack of progress, Preach rose for a cup of coffee. Outside the station window, he could see costumed revelers cavorting around downtown, children swinging their containers of loot as they tried to outdistance their parents. Across the street, a food truck decorated to look like a giant hearse was serving Piña Ghouladas and gourmet Halloween cookies.

"Detective!" Rance called out, a note of excitement in his voice.

Preach rushed over to find the IT expert holding Farley's cell phone, grinning at a photo of Damian entwined with two Asian teenagers, a boy and a girl, on a four-poster bed with silk netting. All three were naked.

"That looks like a fun game of Twister," Rance said. His wispy goatee and weak chin gave his face a rat-like appearance. "We have a few more of these." he flipped through more photos of the same three people in flagrante delicto. "Five, to be exact."

The phone was attached to a laptop with a USB cord; Rance was running recovery software to restore the deleted files.

Preach felt a growing excitement that the pieces of the puzzle might be fitting together. "Can you tell when these were taken?"

"Six months ago, buried in a pile of random shots. Something else: there's a lack of metadata from a single day, about six weeks ago."

The time period rang like a fire alarm in Preach's head. That was the same time communications had ceased between Farley and Damian. "Scrubbed?"

"Yep. My guess is he downloaded a file shredder. Pretty simple stuff, even for a muggle." His Adam's apple bobbed as he chirped a laugh. "Sorry—even for someone with no tech background."

Farley must have made hard copies of whatever he was using to blackmail Damian, Preach thought, and then deleted the images.

"Great work," Preach said. "Can you run this photo through facial recognition software?"

"Easy-peasy."

Preach paced the room as Rance did his thing, hurrying back over when he called out. "Got a hit," Rance said, pointing at the mug shots onscreen. "Tram and Kim Vu, eighteen- and nineteen–year-old siblings, both with rap sheets for drugs and prostitution."

"Of age," Preach murmured. Still, the fact that they were prostitutes strengthened the case against Damian. But were the photos enough, he wondered, for the author to pay money to keep them hidden and orchestrate a murder? Or was there something worse out there?

One thing was certain: it was enough to bring Damian in for questioning.

Preach knew the author was scheduled to be the keynote speaker at another writing conference, two days away, this time in Los Angeles. Damian would probably fly out in the morning, if he hadn't left already.

He texted Kirby.

-I found something. On my way to pick up Damian. I know you're with family but let me know if you want to ride along-

Kirby's reply hit before Preach could pocket his phone.

-wait on me-

18

Preach and Kirby flew past the old Southern homes on Hillsdale. The oaks were festooned with hanging skeletons and battalions of orange and black lights. As they left town and hit the back roads, the Halloween decorations grew sparser and more sinister. Zombie scarecrows standing sentinel over cornfields, porch stoops lit by candles glowing inside rotting pumpkins, ragdoll witches propped up in the scraggly front yards of country shacks.

"You think Damian will bolt?" Kirby asked.

"Not from us. I think he's praying he gets out of town before we circumvent his lawyer."

"You use big words sometimes."

"That's only three syllables. Try exegesis, or anthropomorphic, or amillennialism."

"Do those have anything to do with this case?" Kirby asked.

"No."

"Then shut up."

Preach was grinning in the darkness, eager to arrest the author, pleased that Kirby felt comfortable enough to banter with him. "I am a detective, you know. A sergeant."

"Then why haven't you detected what that key fits? I've tried all the banks in town, local storage units, the post office, and shipping companies. A locksmith told me his best guess is a padlock or some kind of locker. Which could be anywhere."

"Anywhere in the vic's world, yes. I have a feeling we may need whatever that key opens. We've got enough to bring Damian in, but not to convict."

"You think it's really him, huh?"

"He's smart, he was being blackmailed, and the literary angle fits. I don't think he's a stone-cold killer, but maybe he's a warm cheese dip one. Someone who'd pay Mac and his boys to get their hands dirty."

"They're the same in my book."

"Mine, too."

They pulled onto Damian's long drive, the trunks of the hundred-foot pines hedging them in like the bars of some giant prison. They parked beside Damian's BMW X5. The faux spider webs stretched between the oaks on the front lawn glistened eerily in the moonlight, and a pair of life-sized grim reapers had been added to the front porch. As Kirby climbed onto the first step, the reapers raised their scythes and cackled, a red glow flashing from their eye sockets.

Kirby jerked back, almost falling off the porch. "Dammit," he muttered.

Preach stopped moving and held up a finger. "What don't you hear?"

"Huh?"

Preach waited in the near silence. Only crickets broke the spell. After a few moments, he said, "No dogs."

Kirby gave the front door an uneasy glance, then followed Preach's lead by easing his handgun out of its holster. Preach rang the doorbell.

No reply.

"Maybe he left town early and boarded them," Kirby said.

"Maybe."

Preach rang the bell a few more times. He could hear it, so he knew it was working. He tried the doorknob.

Unlocked.

"That's just weird," Kirby said, glancing around nervously.

Preach placed both hands on his gun and raised it to chest level, then eased the door open with his foot. It swung silently inward. "Mr. Black! Are you home?"

Still no response. Creekville was a friendly place, but not friendly enough to leave one's door unlocked at night.

The two suits of armor stood sentinel in the foyer, and there was a faint smell of booze as Preach crept down the horror-poster lined hallway and into the parlor, where the smell was much stronger, probably due to the dozens of liquor bottles that had been smashed on the floor. He drew a sharp breath as he scanned the destruction with his firearm raised.

It wasn't just the bottles: the crystal candelabra had crash-landed atop the baby grand, and glass from the shattered cases of horror memorabilia glittered on the moss-green carpet. The child mummy, the Siamese-twin skeletons, and the other grotesqueries were strewn about the room, the splayed limbs making them look even more sinister, as if they had acquired a spark of life and leapt to the floor.

"Preach," Kirby said, his voice grim and a touch hoarse. "The fireplace."

The detective's gaze shifted to the enormous stone hearth heaped with ash. Buried head down in the gray flakes, the rest of the body angling upward into the fireplace, was the corpse of Damian Black.

Enough of the face was visible to make an ID. The deceased author was still clad in his velvet smoking jacket, his face and clothes smeared with blood.

Preach stepped over an upturned leather chair to reach the body, landing on a shriveled hand that crunched underfoot like a desiccated tarantula. At the base of the fireplace, he found an odd arrangement of objects: three large silver spoons and three whitish, smaller ones; a topaz earring; four plastic gold coins that looked like they had come from a toy pirate chest; and two canvas bags full of the same coins.

Next to the hearth, placed upright in the armchair like an evil puppet master in charge of the other bizarre objects scattered about the room, was a bloodstained straight razor.

Preach leaned down to examine the corpse. Bruises covered the writer's face and neck. After reporting the crime to headquarters, Preach hovered over his phone and searched Google for "hearth corpse upside down bloodstained straight razor." He had to scratch an uncomfortable itch that was growing inside his head.

He scanned the results.

Nothing.

He added "silver spoons" to the field. Three results down, a Shmoop article told him that these search terms all appeared in *The Murders in the Rue Morgue* by Edgar Allan Poe.

He pulled up the article and, once convinced it was a fit, he stared at the corpse of Damian Black stuffed upside down in the fireplace, a pocket of coldness spreading and then settling inside his chest.

19

Police sirens whined in the distance as Preach showed Kirby the article he had found.

Kirby gave the Google results a disbelieving stare. "What the hell?"

"Yeah." Preach ran a hand through his hair as he eyed the glass case full of rare novels, noting uneasily that it was the only untouched item of value in the room.

As the evidence team dissected the parlor, Preach and Kirby explored the white country kitchen, the wainscoted dining room, and then a living room with judges paneling and built-in bookshelves. They found the two Akitas slumped by a fireplace in the den. Preach radioed for someone to call a vet, then leaned down to check the dogs' vitals. "Pulse is slow but steady. Probably a tranquilizer."

"Have to be a good shot to get 'em both," Kirby said.

"Maybe there was an accomplice. Or a poisoned piece of meat. Let the drug go to work on the dogs, and then deal with Damian."

"Implying the perp was in the house before the murder."

"Did you see any signs of forced entry? I didn't. Which, unless we're missing something, greatly narrows the suspect pool."

"To someone who knew both Damian and Farley," Kirby said.

Preach's answer was a set of pursed lips.

The master and guest bedrooms comprised the second story. Preach and Kirby gave it a thorough search and found nothing unusual. A spiral staircase wound upward into the tower, where they found Damian's writing studio overlooking the dense woods behind the house—though the studio looked more like a stage set for a Vincent Price flick.

Carved in the likeness of a black widow, Damian's desk had eight grasping legs and a glossy onyx writing surface with a red hourglass in the center. The chair was a throne-like contraption with an assortment of actual bones worked into the high-backed frame. Built-in bookcases climbed the walls, and a wooden sarcophagus stood upright in the corner.

Preach gave the chair of bones an uneasy glance. The whole setup would have been laughable except for the quality of the materials and the craftsmanship. Instead of coming off as cartoonish, the room possessed an eerie, lifelike feel.

Just like a good horror novel.

"White people," Kirby muttered.

"Detective!" Terry's voice called out from below. "You need to see this."

Preach and Kirby descended to find Officer Haskins waving them toward the living room, where a flokati rug had been moved aside to reveal a trap door. The door was hinged open. Preach climbed down a folding ladder and into a spacious, open basement with leopard-print carpet covering the floors and three of the walls. The ceiling was a giant mirror, and the fourth wall was given over to a collection of erotic artwork depicting half-human, half-animal figures engaged in a variety of sex acts.

A giant four-poster bed with silk netting, which Preach recognized from the photos on Farley's cell phone, dominated the center. A number of BDSM contraptions dotted the rest of the room: swings, harnesses, bondage racks, a human-sized cage suspended from the ceiling, and something that looked like a giant X with cuffs attached.

Even before they had found Farley's photos and Damian's hidden dungeon, Preach had thought of the author as someone who wasn't what he seemed. Looking back on it, Preach should have known better. The author had been too agitated, too obviously distressed, to be the killer. Had Damian's anxiety stemmed from the blackmail and the secret life he knew an investigation would uncover?

Or was it something else?

Two forensic techs scurried about the room like a pair of curious ferrets. The place must be a petri dish of DNA, Preach thought.

Kirby was staring at a painting of a satyr erotically entwined with a mermaid. "Whatever this was about, it must be something big, to off someone famous like that."

"You think fame and fortune affords you some kind of immunity? The statistics say otherwise. The bigger they are . . ."

Kirby started toward the bed, but Preach put a hand on his elbow. "Prepare yourself."

"For what?" Kirby asked, and Preach read his confused expression to mean, *how could it get any worse than what we found inside this house?*

If you only but knew, Preach thought. "For what happens after a second victim is found," he said.

20

P reach woke bleary-eyed the next morning. They had processed Damian's house until four a.m., finding nothing else of interest. Local reporters had eventually swarmed the scene, and while the chief decided not to release details, the connections between Farley and Damian were easy to make. Speculation of a common murderer would soon follow.

He stumbled into his kitchen and made enough coffee to safely operate a motor vehicle. After picking up a copy of *The Complete Short Stories of Edgar Allan Poe* at the Wandering Muse—Ari wasn't in that morning—he took the book to Jimmy's Corner Store, holed up in a corner, and turned to the beginning of *The Murders in the Rue Morgue*.

After giving the thirty-page classic a careful read, he reread the passage that paralleled Damian Black's murder:

> The apartment was in the wildest disorder—the furniture broken and thrown about in all directions . . . on the chair lay a razor, besmeared with blood . . . upon the floor were found four Napoleans, an earring of topaz, three large silver spoons, three smaller of metal d'Alger, and two bags, containing nearly four thousand francs in gold . . . an unusual quality of soot being observed in the fireplace, a search was made in the chimney, and (horrible to relate!) the corpse of the daughter, head downward, was dragged therefrom.

He browsed through a few online critiques on his phone, got a third cup of coffee to go, tried to visit Wade in the hospital but was told to get the hell out, and then headed into work.

"Maybe we should release the details," Kirby said, after Preach told everyone about the Poe reference. "You know, see if some mad genius out there can figure this out."

Preach and his partner were sitting in a bland conference room with Chief Higgins, Officer Haskins, and Officer Wright. Terry Haskins was married with two young kids. Officer Bill Wright was an unmarried older officer, but he had transferred in from a sleepy hamlet near the coast. No homicide experience. He had cropped white hair and a beer gut, and Preach knew he was counting the days to retirement.

Chief Higgins folded her forearms on the table. "What's more likely to happen is that the crazies will come out of the woodwork, weigh us down with false leads, and stall the investigation. We'll become ground zero for every journalist and half-baked online news outlet in the country. Which is what you want, isn't it, Kirby?"

"Nah, Chief, I just thought—"

She pointed a finger at him. "No leaks. I mean it."

Kirby lowered his eyes and slid his morning smoothie closer to his chest.

"You're right," Preach said to Chief Higgins, "but so is Kirby. Something like this is bound to get out. Better to be in front of the storm than behind it."

The other two officers hadn't said a word. They were staring with deer-in-the-headlights eyes at Preach and at the reporters clamoring in the street outside the window.

"So what's your suggestion?" the chief asked.

"Give us some rope for a week or so," Preach replied. "I've got an expert lined up. I doubt the average literature professor can help us, but you never know. If there's no progress, I suggest we start thinking about a public statement."

The chief rapped her knuckles on the table and bobbed her head like a chicken in slow motion. "Have you talked to the coroner?"

"The cause of death on Damian was strangulation," Preach said. "Bruises all along the neck, fractured hyoid."

She drew back in surprise. "What about the razor?"

"It was used to make a few cuts, nothing more." Preach's mouth tightened. "Just like in the story."

The chief took an angry sip of her chai, as if the beverage had offended her.

"No bruises on the body, no skin under the fingernails," Preach continued, "which is strange with such a close-quarter kill. Damian was a grown man. He would have put up a fight. Toxicology isn't back yet, but I'm wondering if our author didn't unwillingly partake—"

"Big words again," Kirby muttered, and Preach knew he was just trying to deal with the gravity of the moment. The other two officers worked hard not to snicker. Chief Higgins gave them a look that would have cowed Vladimir Putin.

"Of the same incapacitating substance that put the dogs to sleep," Preach finished. "Terry and Bill are searching for common acquaintances between the victims. Especially other authors signed by Pen Oak Press. Kirby and I will continue investigating the main suspects."

"Remind me?"

"Belker and Mac Dobbins. Oh, and Forensics is working Damian's computer."

"What about the gym?" Terry asked. "How'd they get a key?"

Preach waved a hand in dismissal. "I know the owner, and trust me, he's not involved. The other members have keys, but a metal shank sheathed in modeling clay is Breaking and Entering 101."

"Trace the hatchet, the razor, the tranquilizer, the spoons, and the plastic coins," the chief added. "Anything that might relate back. Find out who inherits Damian's money. What about his neighbors?"

"We talked to them," Preach said. "Anyone awake was too far away to be of use."

"This might be a stupid question," Kirby said, "but should we notify the FBI?"

"It's way too early," Preach said. "They won't look twice until it's an established serial killer or the case has national implications. Even then, maybe we'd get a profiler for a day and a few database searches. They've got bigger things than this on their plate, sad to say."

"What about Chapel Hill or Durham?" Terry asked.

Chief Higgins scoffed. "They've got their own problems, and far more of a backlog than we do. The mayor pushed aside my request for more people, so stop worrying about getting help and start solving this case."

The chief dismissed everyone except Preach. "There's another reason I don't want to go public."

"Me."

She nodded. "I'll do my best to protect you, but if things get out . . . you know what those vultures are like."

"Don't worry about me," he said. "I've been in the limelight before."

She nodded, unconvinced, and then steepled her fingers. "It seems like you're doing all the right things. What's your gut on this?"

He took a moment to respond. "Most of the circumstantial evidence points to Mac, and the evidence usually doesn't lie. Usually. But the literary angle . . . I see three possible explanations. Whoever's behind this is trying to throw us off, they're toying with us for some reason—or they're trying to tell us something."

Preach felt frazzled as he left the chief's office. This case was blowing up in all the wrong ways. Atlanta had chipped away at his confidence, and though he didn't want to admit it, he had the feeling he wouldn't feel right until his aunt cleared him.

And if she didn't . . .

Kirby caught up with him in the hall. "You want some company with the expert?"

"Why don't you spearhead the physical evidence," Preach said. "Make sure Bill and Terry get off on the right foot. And stay on that laptop."

"Sure." Kirby shot Preach a sly look. "Word on the street is Mac Dobbins's favorite band, the Twisted Goosenecks, are playing at the Gorgon tonight."

Preach cocked his head, jaw tight. "That right?"

Kirby drew a concert flyer with shredded edges out of his coat pocket, and set it on the conference table. His lips were upturned at the ends, but his eyes were glittery and hard.

21

Driving through the stately quads and tidy stacked stone walls delineating the University of North Carolina at Chapel Hill was like entering a cozy womb. The campus was so close to Creekville it was practically a backyard playground. Preach had a vivid flash of lazy spring days from his youth, skipping school with his friends to watch the coeds stroll by, the smell of honeysuckle and freshly cut grass, nothing on the agenda except deciding which of the town's oak-floored pubs to sneak into.

What would his younger self have thought, he wondered, of Psycho Joe's disgraceful exit from his job, visits to a therapist, and an interview with a literature professor?

His younger self would have stared in disbelief, punched his future self in the face, and then cracked a beer.

Preach allowed himself a wry grin. Younger Self did have a certain rough-edged charm.

He parked outside the Department of English, then asked directions to the green carpeted, diploma-lined office of Dr. Glen Marcy, professor of Early American Literature.

The professor was a fortyish man with horn-rimmed glasses, curly black hair, and a doughy, feminine face. He gave a nervous chuckle at Preach's presence. "I'm not in any trouble, am I?"

Preach warned him of the confidential nature of their conversation, described the murder of Damian Black, and passed him a photo of the crime scene.

Dr. Marcy deflated when he saw the image. "I saw the murder on the news, of course, but—" He looked up with a strangled expression, jabbing a finger at the photo. "That wasn't reported—that's—Oh Jesus."

"Your bio states you've published works on Poe. Is there any reason you can think of why someone might use this particular short story?"

He held the photo as if it were contaminated. "Detective, I'm only ... I don't know how ..."

"Take a deep breath," Preach said. "I just thought that due to the nature of the crime, it would be prudent to consult someone like yourself."

Dr. Marcy swallowed and started bobbing his head. "Yes, yes, of course. You've read the story, I assume?"

"And some commentary."

Dr. Marcy grimaced as he stared at the photo. "*The Murders in the Rue Morgue* was published in 1841 ... Poe was paid $56 dollars for it ... he changed the title to better invoke the theme of violent death, believing readers would respond. As you probably know, the story concerns a brilliant loner named Monsieur Auguste Dupin—widely acknowledged as the first literary detective—who investigates a murder that has the Parisian police stumped. It was a new kind of puzzle story at the time, a 'tale of ratiocination.' The clear prototype for characters such as Sherlock Holmes and Hercules Poirot."

The professor's face looked pained, as if he was trying to come up with something useful to say. Preach stayed quiet, let him work it out.

"Poe had a very clever mind, Detective," he said finally. "He was an extremely original thinker—most would say twisted—and virtually invented a number of genres. He believed in challenging his audience, and *The Murders in the Rue Morgue* was the ultimate test, both for the reader and for Poe's fictional sleuth."

"What do you make of the evidence at the scene? The spoons, the gold coins, the overturned furniture, the razor? Are they just literary references?"

Dr. Marcy adjusted his glasses. "Remember, this was one of, if not *the* first tale of its kind. There were no genre rules in place. The gold coins, the spoons—as far as I or any other critic has posited, these have no veiled meaning. They were red herrings placed in the story to draw attention from the true clues. Pieces of an ingenious literary puzzle."

Preach recalled Poe's story. A number of witnesses had come forth after the murder, each claiming to have heard a voice in a different language emanating from inside the victims' house. In reality, the voice had been the animalistic cries of the murderer—an enraged orangutan.

The differing accounts of the voice, along with the unnatural strength and ferocity required of the crime, had been the true clues.

None of which had occurred in the parlor of Damian Black.

"Maybe the killer left the coins and spoons at the author's house for the same reason," Preach mused. "To draw attention to the story, but also to throw us off the trail with red herrings. Waste our resources. Toy with us."

The professor mumbled a reply and avoided looking at the photo.

"Do you see anything different about the crime scene in our case?" Preach asked.

The professor's eyes crept downward. "I suppose the body was found at the base of the chimney, rather than stuffed halfway up it. There were no clumps of hair found, no iron safe. I—" He gave Preach a helpless look.

"You're doing fine," Preach said.

"It makes you think . . . what kind of a person . . ."

Preach slid another enlarged photo in front of the professor, this one taken at Farley's Robertson's townhome. Dr. Marcy flinched at the sight of another corpse, but it was obvious he didn't recognize the parallel to *Crime and Punishment*.

So Preach told him.

Dr. Marcy paled. "So there is . . . there are . . ."

"How familiar are you with Dostoevsky?"

"Not very. As you can see, I didn't even recognize the—" He glanced down again, and his shoulders slumped.

Preach retrieved the photo of Farley, leaving the first one in place. "Any final impressions?"

Dr. Marcy wiped his glasses on his sleeve, then sat back as if physically exhausted. "Have you read the last line of the novel? Or shall I say have you seen it translated—you don't speak French, do you?"

"I'm afraid I don't," Preach said, ignoring the offhand condescension in the professor's voice.

"I quote Monsieur Dupin, the detective in the story: 'I mean the way he has *de nier ce qui est, et d'expliquer ce qui n'est pas*.'" The professor's eyes flicked to the photo. "Monsieur Dupin was talking about the Parisian Chief of Police, who failed to solve the case. The translation of the French phrase is: 'to deny what is, and explain what isn't.'"

Before Preach could ponder the translation, the professor continued, "Poe is alluding to an earlier discussion in which Monsieur Dupin described how imagination is more important than intelligence in solving crimes. He makes an analogy between chess and whist, a card game with strategies similar to poker. A man of pure reason, Poe argues—for example, a world-class chess player—will always be confined by the strict rules of the game, however convoluted they may be. A master of whist is a different breed and must deduce *what the other players are thinking*. Poe's point is that a man of imagination can think outside the box. Combine analytical thinking with creative deduction."

"Meaning the Parisian police failed because they took the evidence at face value," Preach said with a grimace. "They didn't have the vision to figure out the big picture. The meaning of the clues."

"Exactly," Dr. Marcy said, looking dazed as he realized the parallels. "The superiority of imaginative deduction to pure reason is perhaps the principal theme in Poe's story."

Rance entered Kirby's cubicle carrying Damian's MacBook Pro. "I thought I'd swing this over myself. Save you some time."

"Thanks. What's up?" Kirby asked, trying to act nonchalant while his hand slipped over the business card on his desk.

The IT expert set the laptop down, then clicked on a folder marked

GL. Inside was a slew of Word documents. Rance opened the first, a manuscript entitled *Centaur Love* by Griffin Long.

"Our famous author has a pen name," Rance said. "Or I should say another pen name."

Kirby skimmed the first few paragraphs of *Centaur Love*. His eyebrows rose.

"Pretty sick, right?" Rance said, grinning. "The whole folder's full of shape-shifter porn. You know, werewolves and other lycanthropes, people who can—"

"Yeah, I get it. It's whack and all, but we need something solid."

Rance set down a small stack of printer paper. In the middle of each page was the rectangular image of a deposit slip. "He used his birthday and street address for all his passwords. I've already cracked his bank account." He rapped a knuckle on the stack of papers. "These are cash withdrawals for fifteen hundred dollars, twice a week for five weeks. Fifteen grand in total."

Kirby had been looking down at the papers, but his head jerked up. "That's only half the amount we found in Farley's office."

Rance shrugged, and Kirby laced his fingers behind his head, getting a whiff of his own toxin-free deodorant. "Anything else?"

"Not yet," Rance said, fingering his chin hairs.

"Thanks. Keep at it."

Kirby waited until Rance was out of sight, then uncovered the business card he had been hiding.

Monica Hutchinson
Freelance Reporter

Creekville was a popular stump stop for the Left, and Kirby had met the reporter during the run-up to the last election. He and Monica had hit it off at a bar, screwed like college kids, traded numbers and empty promises.

They had only exchanged a few emails since, but that wouldn't matter if his call involved business.

And Monica worked national gigs.

National.

One call and the Literary Killer, as Kirby had dubbed him in his mind, would be plastered all over the news and the tabloids—with Preach and Kirby as the star detectives in pursuit.

Kirby had even named his future memoir that reflected on the crimes: *A Theme of Murder*. On point, catchy, and it sounded like one of those old British mystery novels that would sell a gazillion copies.

It was perfect.

He stared down at the card. The telephone number below Monica's name called out to him like a siren from Greek mythology, beckoning him toward the rocky shore of fame.

Jared might have a reprieve from the bullying, but Kirby's sister still didn't have health insurance or a real house or a reliable car. No savings, no money for college, no safety net for emergencies.

One phone call could change all of that.

It could also end his career and put him on the street.

Kirby picked up Monica's card and flipped it over, twice and then a third time, weighing the risks as his stomach churned with anxiety.

22

Ari closed her *Immigration Law* textbook after reading the same sentence four times in a row. The problem wasn't the assignment; it was her nerves. Two murders in Creekville in one week, one of whom was her former employer. Her overwhelming class load, the stress of keeping the bookstore running, her *stalker*, an impending meeting with a detective with whom she had no idea what was going on—if there was anything at all.

At least her locale was soothing. She was at Cup of Nirvana, an East Asian–themed teashop. The place was quintessential Creekville, ensconced in the corner of a converted brick cotton mill, shielded from reality with silk curtains and potted banana trees, wallpapered with multilimbed Hindu goddesses sporting naked breasts and matronly smiles. There was even a gas fireplace shaped like a volcano.

She checked her watch and cupped her hands around her jasmine tea. On the table was a copy of *Edgar Allan Poe: Complete Tales and Stories*. Detective Everson had asked to meet *her*, and he was thirty minutes late.

A dark-haired guy across the teashop smiled at her. Panama hat, tattooed forearms, keffiyeh scarf over a V-neck sweater. Using a tattered novel he wasn't reading to draw attention. Poser.

Deep breaths, Ari. Channel some of that Ganges-soaked Creekville Zen.

Detective Everson finally walked in, wearing jeans, a fitted gray sweater, and that musty green overcoat he favored. She almost gasped when she saw the ugly bruise covering the bottom of his throat.

"Sorry," he mouthed at her, then cased the teashop with a bemused but accepting expression that mirrored her own thoughts on the yogurt-soft version of the world that Creekville offered.

"Would you care for a sample of flavored tea?" the barista with glasses and tattooed forearms asked the detective. "We have vanilla, banana, and soy pineapple today."

"Um, just a cup of coffee, please."

Ari watched the exchange in amusement. The detective's raised eyebrows implied he would rather drink his coffee under a cold shower than replace it with a cup of soy pineapple tea.

"Would you like to drink the husk water?"

"What? I—no, thanks."

After paying for his coffee, the detective slipped off his shoes and coat and joined her on the carpet. All the tables in the café were one foot high and surrounded by embroidered pillows.

"Sorry I'm late," he said. "Husk water?"

"It's a thing. Of which, thankfully, you're unaware."

He offered a small, distracted smile.

She wanted to ask about his neck but assumed it had to do with the job. She wondered what it was like to investigate murders, to wade through the muck of humanity on a daily basis. How it must affect the hunter as much as the hunted.

He said, "Were you able to look into what I asked?"

"In the last six months there were no pre-orders for either author, and only eight receipts—two for collected works by Poe, six for *Crime and Punishment*. Five of those were cash."

"And the credit cards?"

She handed him three receipts. "My guess is parents buying required reading for school."

"What about the staff?"

"No one remembers anyone buying those two together, or anyone suspicious buying either of them. But this was just you covering all your bases, right? Because even a killer with half a brain wouldn't buy those books from that bookstore." Ari leaned forward and put her hands on the Poe collection. "I could have told you all this on the phone. The press didn't release details of Damian's murder—he was killed like one of the victims in Poe's story, wasn't he?"

"I'm not in a position to disclose those details. But," the detective said, with a glint in his eye, "supposing there was a connection between the two works, I wouldn't mind your hypothetical opinion on what it might mean. In confidence, of course."

She swallowed at the implication, though she felt a thrill of excitement that he was trusting her. She sensed it hadn't been an easy decision. She also sensed it meant the investigation wasn't going very well. "Do you think it's a . . . serial killer?"

"That's a term of art," he said, and Ari thought she saw something shadowy pass across his eyes, quick as a pulse beat, as if some terrible memory had clawed its way to the surface before he shoved it back down. "We're not ready to go there yet."

She pursed her lips as she thought. "You're aware Poe used the ape as an allegory for humanity? The animal within us all?"

The detective nodded, his eyes gummy with exhaustion.

"Have you thought about the detective in the story? Monsieur Dupin?"

"What about him?"

"Well, he's . . . not really a detective. He's a brilliant guy, but not someone who fights crime for a living. And that's kind of Poe's point—in the story, his 'detective' solves the case not out of any sense of justice, but because it's a puzzle to him, an intellectual challenge. A game."

He looked at her sharply. "A game the killer might be inviting me to play."

"It's just a thought."

"I take it you've read some commentary?" he asked.

"And majored in Comparative Lit."

The detective continued his finger tapping, the nascent crow's feet around his eyes taut with concentration. Ari wasn't used to seeing age lines on a guy she was attracted to, but they made the hardened detective seem more approachable.

"I can't say why exactly," he said, gazing at the volcano, "but this doesn't have the feel of a game. A lesson, perhaps, or a smokescreen, but not a game."

"Most critics think Poe's detective—a loner, an outcast from society—was supposed to mirror the plight of the orangutan, an interloper from an exotic land loose on the streets of Paris."

"And that helps us how?" he asked mildly.

"Maybe the focus shouldn't be on the killer or the victim but on the detective. Maybe the killer chose this particular story because he's establishing a bond with you. Not that I think you're an outcast," she said hastily. "I'm a law student, not a detective. I don't have a very good mind for this."

"On the contrary," he murmured, "I think you have excellent instincts."

Ari had lied; she was beginning to harbor a suspicion that the detective, despite his All-American looks, was an outsider like her. Ari shied away from the crowd like a recovering alcoholic from happy hour, and she had always been drawn to men with a different perspective on the world. Someone on the edge of society, someone with something to say.

And she was far from convinced about the detective. People who looked like him were *never* outsiders.

Not unless something had happened.

The detective started reading from his copy of Poe's work: "'He found the beast occupying his own bedroom, into which it had broken from a closet adjoining, where it had been, as was thought, securely confined. Razor in hand, and fully lathered, it was sitting before a looking glass, attempting the operation of shaving, in which it had no doubt previously watched its master through the keyhole of the closet.'"

He looked up. "The orangutan is trying to be human. Maybe someone is doing the same."

"By killing people?"

He opened his palms. "I've seen stranger, believe me."

She wasn't sure she wanted to.

He drained the last of his coffee, though his eyes looked even more tired than when he had arrived. Not just from lack of sleep, but from the weight of discussing the mind of a killer.

Which she again found strange. Weren't detectives supposed to be immune to that sort of thing, jaded to the point of nihilism?

"Let's talk about a possible connection between the two stories," he said. "I haven't gotten very far on my own."

She shifted to stretch her legs on the carpet, noticing when the detective's eyes traveled, quick and subtle, down the length of her calves. She was wearing a long black sweater over green leggings. *La Vie Bohème* was printed in yellow cursive on the sweater.

"How about a change of venue?" she asked. "I could use a drink."

He opened his mouth as if to protest, then checked his watch and shrugged. "Sure. The pub next door?"

"I was thinking my place."

Their eyes met, and the space between them seemed to soften and contract. *What am I doing?* she thought.

"The drinks are free there," she said. "Though I only have wine."

Some of the tension around his eyes relaxed. "I still drink it."

A light rain began on the way to Ari's apartment. The smell of charred toast wafted off the pavement as she led the detective inside. When he hung his coat by the door, she wondered if he had noticed the absence of Trevor's black T-shirt.

Probably. He didn't seem to miss very much.

She uncorked a bottle of zinfandel, put on a Pandora station seeded with Lorde and Soko, and joined Preach on the couch.

"Where were we?" she asked.

"About to discuss potential common ground between *Crime and Punishment* and *The Murders in the Rue Morgue*."

She was glad he had taken his jacket off; it meant the elimination of that faint odor of thrift shop. Without it he smelled like cedar and caramel, with a hint of good soap.

"What are your thoughts so far?" she asked.

"They were written in a similar time period, both involve murder investigations, both are meditations on the application of reason and the nature of man. But the plots and characters vary wildly." Preach's eyes flicked to the window and then returned. "Dostoevsky is focused on the state of mind of the murderer, while Poe's killer is an orangutan. The Parisian police officer who flubbed the case is a buffoon; Detective Porfiry is the star of the show."

He stretched an arm across the top of the sofa, his fingertips resting an inch from her shoulder. "Two women were murdered in each story, both times an old woman and her daughter."

"Maybe the gender is irrelevant—how very Creekville!—and it's the *nature* of the victims that are important. The two older women were a bit sketchy."

"Surely there are better targets if punishment for sins is the point?" Preach said. "Rapists, child molesters?"

"Maybe," she swallowed, "he was one."

"Maybe," Preach said slowly, casually brushing a wisp of Ari's hair from her eyes. When he met her gaze, she found his dark blue eyes solid and comforting, if a little shopworn. Like a favorite pair of old jeans.

She reclined deeper into the couch, the nape of her neck falling into Preach's hand. He didn't react, and the contact of their skin caused a tingle of warmth to spread through her.

She hadn't eaten all day and was heady from the wine. When she shifted to face him, his arm moved with her, slipping around her back. She leaned into the embrace.

"Maybe we should discuss something besides murder," he said in a low voice.

"Maybe we shouldn't discuss anything at all."

The touch of his lips sent a jolt through her. She set her wine glass down and cupped his face with her hands. He pulled her into his lap, and the kiss grew in intensity faster than she expected.

She slipped a hand under his shirt, curling her fingers into the firmness of his chest, and then they were startled by a knock at the door.

It took an effort of will for her to pull away, as if they were conjoined forces caught in a magnetic field. She grinned and pressed a finger to her lips for silence.

The knocking came again, insistent, and she could see the tension and worry flow back into the detective's eyes. His hand slipped to his gun, and she had a stab of memory, like a splash of cold water, as to the nature of his profession, her stalker, the double murder.

He started to rise when her cell chirped from the kitchen counter. After getting a nod from Preach, she pushed off the couch to check her phone.

-I know you're home, Ari. C'mon, open up. I just want to talk-

She stared at the text, and then her eyes slipped to the detective. Conflicting emotions writhed inside her. "It's Trevor. My ex."

She could have added, "He'll go away," or "Give me a minute."

But she didn't. She couldn't deny the thrill that had gone through her when she saw Trevor's name pop up. She didn't like it, and she didn't understand it, but pretending it didn't exist wasn't fair to anyone.

The detective got the hint. He rose off the couch in one smooth motion and gave her a lopsided smile as he handed her his wine glass. "Thanks for the drink. I haven't had its equal in some time."

Her voice was almost a whisper. "This is something I need to do. I'm sorry."

"It's fine. I have a concert to attend. Just do me a favor and keep our hypothetical conversation to yourself."

"Of course. A concert?"

He flashed a grin and retrieved his coat. The knocking resumed, and Ari watched in mild horror as Preach ushered Trevor inside with a sweep of his arm and then disappeared into the night.

Trevor closed the door. He smelled like cigarettes, and she could tell he was drunk by the slump of his shoulders.

Despite the lingering feel of Preach's strong hands around her waist, seeing her ex brought back a rush of attraction. Dark haired and thin, Trevor was a gorgeous but self-absorbed musician. His spunky confidence had always attracted her, but for the first time she saw how incomplete it was. Inconsistent with the harsh realities of the world.

"A little steroidal for you, isn't he?" Trevor said. He was wearing his typical: black T-shirt, holey jeans, earrings, a collection of leather necklaces and wristbands.

"You can crash here," she said, a little coldly, "but I'm turning in."

He took her hand. "I've been doing some thinking. About us."

She pulled away, irritated. She knew exactly what he wanted.

"Is this guy turning you into a soccer mom?"

"I'm a law student, Trevor, not to mention everything else that's going on."

Instead of inquiring further, he moved closer and hooked his thumbs into her jeans. "At least you still don't wear underwear," he said with a grin.

He leaned in to kiss her, but she held him off. "Sleep tight, Trevor."

For the first time in a long while, she fell asleep thinking not about Trevor but about someone else, worried about the mysterious concert the detective was attending. Despite his parting grin, there had been a darkness in his eyes when he had mentioned the evening's destination.

Darkness and violence.

23

The lights of Creekville disappeared, leaving the highway a smear of gray chalk between the trees. Preach drove in silence while Kirby seethed beside him.

They passed two gas stations, a lumber store, and a trailer park before easing into the gravel parking lot of the Gorgon. The bar was an old log cabin fronted by a fire pit and a row of shriveled tobacco plants. Motorcycles, pickup trucks, and a few battered sedans filled the lot. How quickly, Preach thought, the quirks of Creekville gave way to the traditional South.

"There's Mac's Harley," Kirby said, cracking his knuckles.

"Good," Preach said. "Recognize any others?"

"Not offhand."

Stars filled the sky like a box of jacks tossed onto black velvet. A clapboard sign with block lettering read "The Twisted Goosenecks—$5 Cover."

Ten p.m. No sounds spilled out from the bar. Just before they stepped inside, Preach put a hand on Kirby's elbow. "I know how angry you are, but keep your head. We're police officers."

Kirby's handsome face twisted with wounded pride. "Angry doesn't quite do it, cuz. They went after my family."

"I know. We'll get him. Just not tonight."

"Then what's this about?"

"I want to look into Mac's eyes, without his lawyer around, and ask a few questions. And sometimes you have to send a message."

Preach locked eyes with his partner until he saw the self-control he needed to see. Then he stepped into the low-ceilinged bar.

Scuffed tile floor, blinking Michelob sign, a wooden booth filled
with pot-bellied older men with thick gray beards. All four were
wearing black leather vests and motorcycle chaps over jeans. They
stared at Preach and Kirby with the kind of pinched, callous eyes that
Preach would know anywhere, eyes of men who had frittered away
their lives in hot tobacco fields or decaying country towns, eyes with no
tolerance for outsiders.

Kirby handed their cover charge to a brunette in a cowboy hat,
and the two officers stepped through a pair of swinging doors into a
much longer room with concrete walls painted red. An old stoplight
was propped up beside the doors. Black speakers crouched like beetles
in the corners.

An assortment of people filled the room, mostly men with
unkempt hair and scruffy beards and shit-kicker boots, but also a few
women with yellow nails and mouths that were harder than the men's.
Preach scanned the space for exits. A hallway led to the bathroom, and
a pair of stained glass windows were the only link to the outside. Far
too claustrophobic for his liking.

"Why, Detective Everson! C'mon over!"

Preach turned to find Mac Dobbins, mouth spread wide and eyes
gleaming above his beard, waving them over to his booth. Mina and
the two men from the back room at the Rabbit Hole were with him.
Preach heard Kirby suck in a breath.

Preach surveyed the room as he walked over. Mounted deer heads
and a few lackluster Halloween decorations hung from the walls. His
gaze moved from face to face, searching for a cleft-lip scar.

No dice.

Mac clicked his tongue and jerked his head to the side. The two
men across from him slid out of the booth, eying Preach and Kirby like
pit vipers. The stale air hummed with the threat of violence.

Preach let Kirby in first, so he could take the outside. Mina had an
arm looped through Mac's, and she was sipping on a pink cocktail. Mac
had a shot glass full of whiskey and a bottle of Heresy Brown Ale.

"So how's Creekville treating you, Detective?" Mac boomed.

"Didn't somebody say that leaving and coming home again ain't the same as never having left?" He winked at Mina. "Hard lesson to learn, ain't it, darling?"

"Oh, you know it," she said.

Preach kept his gaze fixed on Mac. Despite the warmth of the bar, the café owner was wearing a plaid flannel shirt beneath an unbuttoned shearling coat.

"To what do we owe the rare pleasure of your company?" Mac asked, his slapped-on smile still in place.

"I think you know," Preach said.

Mac's face turned quizzical, and he turned to his girlfriend. "Do we, hon?"

Mina was wearing a miniskirt and a red, long-sleeved lace shirt that exposed a black bra. She shifted to kick her heels up on the booth, revealing twin ribbons of slim brown leg. "They must have come for the band."

Mac slapped the table. "That it? You two officers a fan of good tunes? I have to warn you, this ain't your momma's bluegrass."

Kirby leaned toward Mina. "My sister's place still smells like rotten eggs."

She eyed Kirby with a flat stare and took another drink. "You know what he's talking about, baby?"

"Nope," Mac said. "Though it sounds like it's none of our business. And when something's none of my business," he looked right at Preach, "I keep my nose out of it."

"Maybe your sister's place just stinks," Mina said. "Trailers don't ventilate so well, especially if there's trash inside."

Kirby snarled. "You better value this foot of space between us like your little sister at a frat party. I swear to God, if you ever come near my family again—"

Preach silenced him with a hand on the arm. "Serious infractions were committed two nights ago," he said to Mac, "against myself and Officer Kirby and his family. So by definition, both professionally and personally, the events of that evening are very much our business."

"I think you're confusing cause and effect, there, Detective. When one thing flows from another, that don't mean they're one and the same—if you catch my drift."

"And I think you're confusing past and present realities," Preach said.

"Oh? How say?"

"In the past, you've gotten away with whatever you wanted in this town. That's no longer the case."

After a pause, Mac gave a low chuckle and knocked back his Scotch, then signaled one of his men, standing with folded arms by the hallway, to bring him another. "I'm curious as to what's changed?" he said. "Your arrival?"

"You crossed the line the other night, and you know it."

Mac's massive hand curled around his beer like it was a pencil. His expression turned amiable so quickly it unnerved Preach, as if the man had a split personality he could access at will. "Over at the café, we just got a batch of Kopi Luwak in from Bali. Best liquid gold you'll ever drink. You know how the growers harvest their beans over there in Bali, what makes the coffee so special? They use beans that pass through the digestive system of a civet. That's a kind of jungle cat that eats the pulp of the coffee cherry, digests it, and defecates the bean. The enzymes inside the cat's stomach remove the bitterness. Now ain't that some shit, Detective?" He roared with laughter at his joke, then slapped the table and leaned forward. "We're considering implementing their methods in our own operation. Taking out the bitterness, that is."

"I didn't know you roasted your own coffee," Preach said calmly.

Mac slowly wiped his mouth with the back of his hand. "We don't."

"I have to say," Preach said, "you're full of surprises. Are you always so fond of allusion? Of literary devices in general?"

A smile parted Mac's lips above his beard. "Oh, you're a clever one, ain't you?" He winked at Kirby, who had both fists clenched atop the table. "A world above the rest of the yokels they've got looking out for our safety here in Creekville. Do you know the kinds of criminals that run around town these days, Detective? I mean, *murderers*? Who's supposed to protect us all? Denzel wannabe over here?"

The band had been warming up onstage, and it started to play: a violent, electric guitar-infused version of North Carolina folk music. The crowd started stamping in time with the tune.

"Watch your mouth, you stupid hillbilly," Kirby said over the music. "You don't get it, do you? You're finished."

Mac's deadened eyes sparked at the insult, like a corpse lurching to life. Mina lit a napkin with a lighter, watching it burn as she smirked at Kirby. Mac stood. "G'night, gentlemen. It's past my bedtime. I hope you enjoy the band."

Preach grabbed Mac's thick wrist, bristly with dark hair. "I didn't say we were finished." He put his business card on the table, the one they had found in Wade's pocket. "I believe you left this behind."

Mac tried to jerk his arm away. Preach held him fast. "Leave Wade alone," he said, then let Mac go with a long, stony look. "I mean it."

The café owner lowered his chin, face quivering in fury. "Boy, don't you *ever* lay a hand on me again. You mentioned an attempt at murder, but you should know that I don't attempt anything. I either do or I don't."

He backed away with Mina by his side. A number of men pushed off the wall nearest their booth. For a moment, Preach thought they were crazy enough to assault two cops in public, but the men backed off when he flashed his badge.

As Preach and Kirby passed through the front room, one of the older men at the lone booth spit loudly into an empty glass. "Coon-ass cop," he muttered.

Preach whirled, picked up a beer bottle, and smashed it on the table. Beer sloshed over the man's beard and vest. He spluttered and tried to rise, but Preach put a hand on his shoulder, forcing him down. "Why don't you sit."

"Ain't you ever heard of free speech? I ain't committed no crime."

"It's a crime to be a racist, xenophobic, militia-joining asshole," Preach said, recognizing a few of the tattoos on his arms.

The man started to speak, then looked in Preach's eyes and thought twice about it. Outside, the two officers found that someone had slashed the tires on their car. Preach called a tow.

Kirby paced back and forth as they waited for another car to arrive, clenching his fists. "Thanks for what you did in there, at the end. I know it wasn't your style. But you don't have to fight my battles for me."

Preach's arms were folded, and he was watching the bar for signs of trouble. "Who said I did it for you?"

Back at the station, after they wrote up the slashed tires, Kirby stopped Preach as he was leaving.

"You think Mac knows about the connection to the books?"

"Definitely," Preach said. He had caught the look of recognition in the crime boss's eyes.

"So he's our guy?"

"It doesn't all fit, but he's in the middle of something."

Kirby finished his carton of coconut water and tossed it in the trash. "If Mac's behind the murders, wouldn't it have been better to lay low and go after the evidence? Catch him off-guard?"

Preach opened the rear door of the station, letting in a rush of cool night air. "You might be right if we knew what was going on. But we don't, and I want him to feel like he's being watched." He shrugged into his overcoat. "At the moment, I'm more worried about future victims than past ones."

24

A phalanx of white vans and grasping reporters greeted Preach outside the station the next morning.

"Detective Everson, can you give me a statement on the Literary Killer? Are there any suspects?"

"Can you confirm there have only been two victims?"

"Is this the work of a serial killer?"

Preach lowered his head and barreled through, repeating "No comment" a dozen times before he entered the station. He swept past reception to find a group of officers clustered in the briefing room, all of them eyeing the chief's closed door with nervous eyes. Through the glass window, Preach could see a tall, sandy-haired woman in her fifties, dressed in a sharp gray business suit, pointing her finger at Chief Higgins.

Kirby was standing by the coffee machine. The other officers were hunched over their desks, fielding calls. His face grim, Preach shrugged out of his jacket as he approached his partner. "The Literary Killer?"

Kirby took a sip of coffee. "Some blond chick broke the story this morning."

"How'd she get it? How much does she know?"

"No idea, and pretty much everything."

Preach took in the news with compressed lips. "Who's giving it to the chief?"

"The mayor." Kirby's eyes met Preach's for a brief instant, then slid away.

"You okay?" Preach asked.

"Just thinking about the spotlight, like you said."

Before Preach could respond, the door to Chief Higgins's office burst open, and a tall, stylish woman with elegant bone structure stormed out, followed by two aides. The mayor leaned forward when she walked, as if fighting against the wind. Her thin lips looked stitched together.

Chief Higgins appeared in the doorway, hooked a finger at Preach and then Kirby. They hurried over.

The chief shut the door behind them. Elbows planted on the desk, she interlocked her fingers and tapped them against the backs of her hands, like the flapping of a butterfly's wings.

"Anger gets us nowhere, and I'm not a person who believes in jumping to conclusions," she said in a tone of careful neutrality that spoke far louder than a shout. "So I will say this only once. If either of you was the source of the leak and you come forward now, I'll only suspend you."

Preach didn't respond. He had nothing to say.

Kirby beamed a smile at Chief Higgins. "Hey, if it was me, I'd be on TV already."

"There's nothing funny about this. You saw the mayor's face. Not to mention this might drive the killer underground, or move him to destroy evidence."

Preach waved a hand. "When you leave crime scenes like these, you have to know there'll be press."

With her palms flat on the desk, Chief Higgins took a deep yoga breath that started in her stomach and fluttered through her chest. "We got a match for a set of prints in Damian's parlor, off the drinks cabinet."

Preach leaned forward. "Someone we know?"

"Elliott Fenton."

"So it's probably nothing. Still, he might have been the last person to see Damian alive. We'll talk to him."

"*Politely*," Chief Higgins said. "I've already had a call from him this morning, too. It's been a peach of a day, lemme tell you." Her expression hardened. "I assume you two went off-duty to a bar owned by Mac Dobbins in retaliation for the other night?"

"Not retaliation," Preach said. "Just a message of our own."

She looked back and forth between the two. "The second we find something concrete, we'll haul his ass in. I don't care if Johnny Cochrane rises from the grave to defend him. Until that time, if you want to avoid a civil suit and an internal investigation, keep your messages and lessons more discreet."

"Duly noted," Preach said.

"Kirby?" the chief said sharply.

"Yeah, sure," he said, though his voice lacked conviction. Preach knew the wound from the attack on his partner's family had gone deep, deeper even than Preach had realized.

"Listen," the chief said with a sigh. "We fielded a call from some weirdo this morning—we can't keep up with the calls—in response to the news story. But this guy sounds legit in a *can't make this up* kind of way. He lives behind Farley Robertson's place and says he saw someone walking through the woods before Farley's murder. Apparently the hiker stopped to admire his condo." She took a sip of tea. "He did it every day for a week."

Preach crossed his arms. "Does he have a description? Why call it in now?"

"You'll have to ask him—our caller's demanding to see someone in person." She smirked. "Says he doesn't trust cell phones, or any technology invented in the last five hundred years, besides the telescope. His words, not mine."

"You should get your family somewhere safe, at least for a while," Preach said to Kirby as they drove through one of the scruffy neighborhoods near downtown. Instead of Bermuda grass and trimmed hedges—bourgeoisie affectations—the residents of Creekville seemed to be having a contest as to who could accumulate the most pine cones, rocks, sticks, and sweet gum pods.

No answer. Preach glanced at the passenger seat and saw a mixture of pride and frustration on his partner's face.

"What about a relative?" Preach asked. "Uncle, grandparent?"

"Nope."

They passed a series of modernist homes with boulders randomly dotting the front yards, like the remains of some prehistoric creek bed. Preach tapped an index finger on the wheel and then rang the station and asked for Chief Higgins.

"You got something?" she asked.

"I'd like an officer posted to Kirby's sister's house whenever he's not there. At least for a few days."

"We don't have that kind of manpower—"

"She has two kids, Chief. Pull someone off patrol."

Chief Higgins hung up.

"She'll do it," Preach said. "She knows you won't have your head in the game otherwise. Plus she's a softie."

"Thanks," Kirby mumbled. "Pretty sad, huh? Living paycheck to paycheck, can't even afford a hotel?"

"There's nothing sad about doing your best."

"Sometimes your best doesn't cut it. The world sure doesn't give a damn about it." Kirby turned to look out the window. "Did you know they say all cops want to write a book, Preach? You know why solving crimes isn't enough for us? Same reason all men want to be Hugh Hefner or Derek Jeter. So they can get paid, laid, front the parade. That's the only way to take care of you and yours in this world for sure. The law of the jungle."

"Is that where you want to live? A jungle?"

"It's where I was born."

"So leave."

"Like I said. Nowhere to go."

"You can take your mind wherever you want, Kirby. That's what sets us apart. Oh, and you're right."

"About what?"

"I want to write a book, too. Doesn't everyone? We just don't all have the desire to publish." Preach kept his eyes on the road. "I don't think you were the leak. But if you were, you should tell the chief before she finds out on her own."

"Good advice. I'll pass it on."

A few miles from downtown, Preach turned onto a gravel drive that serviced a cluster of homes in the forest. Following directions provided by the witness, his hand on his firearm in case it was a setup, Preach parked in a grassy cul-de-sac at the end of the gravel drive.

Twenty yards down a dirt footpath, shoes crunching on leaves and dead locusts, they spotted a geodesic dome in a clearing. It looked like a gigantic white thimble with solar panels, a telescope, and an anarchist flag planted on top.

An older man in green camouflage emerged from the trees, brandishing a bow and arrow pointed at the ground. "What the hell you doing on my property?"

"Whoa," Kirby said. "We're police officers, pal. Ease up."

Instead of raising his gun, Preach merely tightened his grip on his weapon. He could already tell that cooperation, rather than a show of force, would win this battle. "Will Bradford? You called in a witness report this morning?"

"Your hand's still on your gun," the old man said.

"Your hand's still on your crossbow," Kirby shot back.

"It's a longbow, and I've got a right to protect my property. Now let's see some ID."

Preach held out his badge, and the old man moved to meet him. He had a ponytail of white hair underneath a brown military cap, and his droopy facial features were squished together, like a bulldog's.

"I'm Detective Joe Everson. That's my partner, Officer Kirby."

The old man peered at Preach's badge, then turned it over and held it up to the light. After handing it back, he said, "Name's Willard

Bradford. Friends call me Will." He started walking toward the dome. "C'mon, then."

He led them to the rear, or Preach supposed it could have been the front, of the dome. In a clearing strewn with pine needles, there was a large stack of firewood, a hammock, and a fire pit. Off to the right, a wire cage enclosed a henhouse and a vegetable garden.

Will pushed on the smooth surface of the dome, causing it to hinge open.

"Where do you keep your car?" Kirby asked.

"Don't have one."

"Um, groceries?"

"Look around, son. The land has all you need."

They stepped into a small kitchen containing a wood stove, a wall of door-less cabinets filled with homemade jars and cans, and an oval breakfast table. A box of Pop-Tarts and a glass bottle of Mountain Dew sat atop the table.

Will shot the Mountain Dew an embarrassed glance. "My niece brings me a few things from time to time," he mumbled. "Lemme get another stool."

When he left the room, Kirby said in a low voice, "You think we can trust him?"

"He's just a little weird. He probably has two PhDs. Let's hear him out."

Will walked back in with a third stool, as well as a cell phone with a row of antennas attached to a bolt running lengthwise across the top.

"Y'all believe in aliens, right?" He set the strange contraption on the table. "I mean, Creekville being an energy vortex and all. More human beings believe in aliens than in God these days, if you trust the polls—which I don't. But that's a different conversation. Alone in a universe this big? Don't think so. Maybe they all died in the old universe, before the Big Bang. Ever think about that?"

Preach gave Kirby a chagrined glance. "About that call to the station," Preach said. "I hate to be rude, but we've got a murder investigation to conduct."

Will slurped on his Mountain Dew and offered them each a Pop-Tart, which they declined. "He came through on the trail. The first day he stopped, I thought it was no big deal. Could have been a deer. Some people like to stare at those nasty things. But then he did the same thing the day after that, and the next, and the next. Thought no one could see him."

"So how did you?"

"I was in my tree stand."

"How long did he stop?" Preach asked.

"Usually about fifteen minutes. Staring through the forest right at that condo across the way. The one where the murder took place."

"You're sure about that?"

"He walked right up to it, to the edge of the woods. Ten feet from the back door."

"Did he do anything else?" Preach asked. "Make a phone call, write something down?"

Will wagged a finger. "He did take notes a few times, when he was done staring. In a journal."

"You could see him that closely?"

"High-powered binoculars."

"Anything else?"

Will took another drink and smacked his lips. "He always walked back faster than he came in. Like he was excited about something."

Kirby leaned forward. "Can you describe him? Man, woman, old, young?"

"Oh, it was a man. Middle-aged, I suppose. It all looks the same before sixty. Balding, glasses, kind of squirrely. Walked through the woods like he was stepping on tacks."

"Why didn't you call it in earlier?" Kirby asked.

"I didn't think much about it until my niece stopped by and told me about the murders. I don't watch TV or get out much. When I realized he'd been staring at the home of a victim, I thought someone should know."

"You did the right thing," Preach said. Stomach twisting with anticipation, he took a small stack of suspect photos from his inside jacket pocket, all of which he had printed off the Internet. They were all random except the author photo of J. T. Belker.

Will squinted as he flipped through the stack, then stopped and jabbed a gnarled finger at the photo of Belker. "That's him all right."

25

Belker opened the door in a pair of sweatpants and another grubby T-shirt. A few graying chest hairs poked out of the V-neck. He appeared to be in some kind of hypnagogic state, barely aware of his surroundings.

Was he a writer caught in the vortex of his imagination, Preach wondered, or was it the sort of detached behavior he had seen in suspects with guilty consciences? Someone who knew the game was up?

Preach had berated himself the entire morning, during his efforts to procure a warrant to search J. T. Belker's residence. Mac Dobbins was the more conspicuous suspect, but Preach's job was not to be distracted by the obvious. He had let himself be swayed by Belker's gimpy appearance, his pathetic living conditions, and the faded scar on his wrist.

What if he had kept a closer on eye on Belker? Might Damian Black still be alive?

"Can we come in?" Preach asked.

The writer blinked, then pushed his glasses further up his nose. "I, um, yes, of course."

Preach caught a whiff of stale sweat and discarded pizza boxes as Belker sank into one of the sagging armchairs. Preach took the other armchair, leaving Kirby with a green rocker.

On a folding table beside Belker's chair was his laptop, a thermos, and a copy of *City of Glass* by Paul Auster. Preach scanned the stacks of books on the floor and noticed a pile of Edgar Allan Poe's work.

Preach crossed his legs. "How's the writing going?"

Belker snapped back to full consciousness, offering a bitter smile. "How do you think? I'm a writer without a contract."

"Damian Black said you had true talent, you know. In fact, he said he'd give anything to write like you."

"Then he should have published me. Have you considered the fact that he might be lying?"

"Have you considered the fact that he's dead?"

Belker gave a start. "Still playing with straw men, are we?" He swept a hand down his pudgy body. "Am I the best you can do?"

Kirby leaned forward. "Murderers come in all shapes and sizes."

"Maybe I'd sell a few books if I murdered someone," Belker muttered.

"Maybe you would," Preach said.

The writer looked back and forth between the two officers. "You're serious. I'm actually a suspect."

Preach showed him the photo of the crime scene in Damian's parlor. Belker blanched and tugged on an oily strand of hair. "Good God."

"You recognize it?" Preach asked.

He gave a slow nod. "*The Murders in the Rue Morgue*. Very clever."

"Someone thinks they're clever," Preach said. "Someone literary."

"Or someone trying to *frame* someone literary."

Preach gave a single nod, acknowledging the point. "Damian was right, you know. At least in my opinion. Though I'm hardly qualified to judge."

"About?"

"Your literary talent. I found a copy of *Refractions of a Murder* in his library."

Belker's eyes slid away at the mention of his novel.

"Though I have to say," Preach said, "I found the subject matter unusually timely. You really have your finger on the zeitgeist. At least in Creekville."

Belker sneered. "Who would actually kill their publishers after *writing* about killing them?"

Preach let his eyes drift to the scar on the writer's wrist. "Someone who isn't afraid of the consequences?"

Belker's gaze followed Preach's. "I'm afraid you've mistaken me for someone decisive and proactive."

"I'd say finishing a novel qualifies as both."

"Mistaken me for a man of action, then." He let out a wheezing laugh. "This is a ridiculous conversation."

"Where were you on Halloween night?" Preach asked quietly.

Belker stared down his nose at him. "Here."

"Can anyone verify that?"

Belker looked away.

"Someone saw you in the woods, Mr. Belker," Kirby said. "Staring at Farley's condo. We know the tracks outside your house lead right to the murder scene."

Belker's supercilious expression faded, replaced by a haunted one. His eyes darted to the kitchen window, as if debating his escape options.

"We know you argued with Farley Robertson before his death," Preach pressed. "Literary clues were left at both murder scenes. The two publishers who rejected your novel—cruelly, judging from the email string—are both dead. You have no alibi. You wrote a *book* about it."

Belker slumped in his chair and drew his arms tight against his body, curled in the fetal position. "I'd ask for a lawyer, but having a public defender would probably be worse than representing myself."

The writer fell silent, balling his hands into the folds of his sweatpants. Kirby started to speak, and Preach gave him a warning glance to hold tight.

"Lee took advantage of me, you know," Belker said finally. "Of all of us writers. Paid us nothing. Forced contract terms on us that would make Don Corleone blush. But it was more than that. It was the way he looked at us, treating us like indigent serfs. Children. Party favors to bring out on release day, a quick *pop* for his friends and then shredded wrappers on the floor. It's what he did. All of that psychological abuse. How he operated."

Preach thought Belker was going to disappear into the armchair, but then his face twisted into a snarl, and he slammed his forearms on the cushioned sides.

"I didn't *kill* anyone!" He stood and started to pace the tattered carpet, waving his arms. "Yes, I hated them. Damian was almost the worse of the two, with his watery horror novels and Faustian success and his Raphael face. But Lee, he had a special gift for cruelty. For making another man feel inferior. He should have been born in eighteenth-century Louisiana, whip in hand. And you're right, I snuck right up to his condo, multiple times, and thought about it. I *yearned* to. Just like in the novel! Just exactly like it! Is this what you wanted to hear, Detective? I'll tell you a secret, though. I was going to do it with a gun, not an axe. Killing him just like that rascally Raskolnikov—now *that's* a bold and brilliant idea! That's what a *true* Napoleon would do, not some impotent louse like myself. And the second murder, the nod to Poe—on Halloween no less—what a brilliant piece of work! It's as if someone plumbed the depths of my soul and fulfilled my fondest desires! Good God, what a lightning stroke of karma has struck our little town!"

He started cackling, doubling over with ugly bursts of laughter. Kirby's eyebrows had risen higher and higher during the rant. Belker wiped his eyes, then pointed a stubby finger at Preach, his mouth cocked with an uneven grin. "The real killer, a true Napoleon, is no doubt escaping to Canada, or plotting his next crime. You're outclassed, I'm afraid to say."

"Maybe I am," Preach said calmly. The writer's burst of temper had been a convincing display of outrage. Too convincing. "Or maybe you've been playing us for fools, and you're taking as much pleasure in stringing us along as you are from leaving literary clues at murder scenes."

Belker clapped, slowly. "Genius—sheer, unadulterated genius—you've got me pegged."

"Did you kill them yourself, or hire someone?"

"Hiring a professional assassin of such skill—with all of my spare funds! Yes, you've really nailed it!"

Preach took the signed and sealed piece of legalese out of his coat. "We have a warrant to search your premises, including the laptop. Tech support is on its way. I trust you won't interfere."

"You'll find nothing but broken promises in this palace."

"We'll see."

26

The deeper Preach delved into the life of J. T. Belker, the sadder he grew. Roaches skittered over crusty dishes in the author's kitchen. Stacks of food stamps and unopened medical bills shared drawer space with heaps of plastic utensils. The refrigerator was stocked with Diet Coke, a box of Velveeta cheese, and packets of bologna.

Belker remained slumped in his armchair during the search. The bathroom yielded a moldy tub and a stocked medicine cabinet. Preach dropped a pair of unmarked pill bottles in an evidence bag. Leaning towers of books lined the bedroom walls, even more precipitous than the stacks in the living room. Preach could detect no discernible arrangement; he noticed works of literary fiction both modern and classic, peppered with poetry, literary critiques, and philosophy.

Next to Belker's bed was a pile of *Hustler* magazines, a box of tissue, an alarm clock, a book of *New York Times* crossword puzzles, dog-eared copies of *Ulysses* and *2666* and *Gravity's Rainbow*, and a blood pressure monitor.

Kirby opened the top drawer of the bedside table and pulled out a cluster of stenographer's notepads. "What about these?"

"Set them aside," Preach said. "We'll have to look through them."

"Detective!"

The high-pitched voice had come from the kitchen table, where Rance Crowley was poring over Belker's laptop. Kirby and Preach crowded around. Rance's spindly fingers repositioned a fifteen-inch Toshiba so the officers could see the bank account statement displayed onscreen. It was Belker's.

"What are we looking at?" Preach asked.

Rance pointed the cursor at a counter withdrawal on August 22, almost two months prior. "This."

The amount of the withdrawal was twenty thousand dollars.

Kirby snapped his fingers, leaving his thumb and forefinger in the shape of a gun, pointing at the screen. "Bagged and tagged." In a less confident voice, low enough so that Belker couldn't hear him, he said, "Is that enough? To put two contracts out?"

Preach turned to look at Belker, who was staring at the wall, chin against his chest. "You can hire a killer off the street for a dime bag. For a double murder in this market, but with subtlety involved . . ." He shrugged. "It's enough."

"Wait—what about the fact that the vics likely knew the killer?"

"Belker could have gotten the killer inside, then let him work."

Kirby cocked his head inquisitively in the direction of the writer.

"Go ahead," Preach said.

When Kirby pointed out the withdrawal to Belker, an ugly little smile, slow and sure, spread across the writer's face. He started cackling again. "The irony—it's too much! Oh, it's . . . it's . . . *poetic*."

"Where'd you get the money?" Kirby asked. "Did you kill someone else first, and then rob them?"

Belker threw back his head and howled in delight. "My life's savings—it's too much, I tell you! Too much!"

"So you admit it?" Kirby pressed. "You hired someone to kill Farley Robertson and Damian Black?"

"I gave that money away."

"To who?"

Belker convulsed with laughter, tears streaming from his eyes. "I don't even know her name."

"Where is she?"

Belker stopped laughing and looked as if he were going to say something, then thought better of it.

Kirby was looking to Preach for guidance. If the murder charge didn't stick, a drug charge for unmarked pills might. "Read him his rights and take him in," Preach said. "Bring the laptop."

Back at the station, Preach decided to sweat Belker before talking to him. It could take up to forty-eight hours in North Carolina before a public defender was appointed. Maybe iron bars and jail food would loosen the writer up.

It was three in the afternoon, and the appointment with Elliott Fenton was in one hour. Preach was starving. He talked Kirby into ordering takeout from a Vietnamese joint that operated out of a clapboard shack sandwiched between a dog park and a retro style arcade. Kirby hesitantly pointed to the plainest-looking noodle bowl on the menu. Preach ordered a skewer with chicken gizzards, beef intestines, and spicy shrimp.

They carried the food two blocks over to the local co-op, an organic grocery store with picnic tables set on a sprawling lawn covered in wood chips. After grabbing drinks from the co-op, the two officers sat as far from the crowd as they could. It was a pleasant day, and a hodgepodge of people filled the tables: students, professors, tattooed drifters, crunchy types in yoga pants and old sweatshirts, a group of stay-at-home dads clustered beside their baby strollers.

Preach popped his ginger beer and held up a chopstick. "Care for a bite?"

"Uh, no thanks, cuz. You can keep that creepy stuff to yourself."

Preach peeled off one of the gizzards. "You did good back there. At Belker's house."

"For real?"

"If you're not careful, you might become a murder cop."

Inside the co-op, the cashier had been so nervous at seeing Preach that she'd dropped his change. He had overheard three separate groups of people discussing the murders, eyes alight with a titillating excitement.

Eyes that, if Preach and Kirby failed to catch the monster plaguing their community, would soon turn sticky with fear. That fear would morph into panic, and then anger, and then blind accusation.

Preach had meant what he said to Kirby, and while the junior officer had a ways to go, he wanted him to have the confidence to withstand the storm.

Especially if Preach couldn't.

Kirby preened and took a sip of his probiotic. "What're you thinking about Belker?"

Preach thought about the author's acerbic wit, his mood swings, the range of emotions in his eyes. Empathy. Sadness. Pain. Jealousy and kindness. Compassion and anger. All of it trapped beneath the scab of resentment the writer's life had become.

And then there was the sentiment Belker possessed in spades: pity. For himself and for others. Pity was a dangerous thing, a dehumanizing emotion.

"I think he's a very complex man," Preach said.

"You're not convinced it's him? Because there's no connection to Mac, and we know that bastard's involved?"

"That's one. What's really bothering me, though, is that hiring someone to commit the murders isn't very Raskolnikov-esque. Somehow, I think Belker would consider such a thing beneath him."

"You really think that weasel could kill two people in cold blood?"

"No," Preach said slowly, "though I'm not sure he'd hire someone, either."

He pulled the last shrimp off the skewer and eyed a wiry, shirtless black man with waist-length dreadlocks performing Tai Chi by the road, oblivious to passing traffic. An instrument out of tune with the rest of the orchestra. An outlier. "But the twenty grand is a problem," he said, "and you never know."

Before they left to see Elliott, Preach stepped away to call Ari. She answered on the first ring.

"I'm glad it's you," she said.

"Are you?"

A pause. "I was too embarrassed to call. I thought I might never hear from you again. Look, I'm really sorry about last night."

"It's okay," Preach said.

There was a silence in which she could have said something more but didn't. Preach respected her for that.

"I called to check on you," he said. "Any sign of the stalker?"

"No, thank God."

"You're taking the precautions we talked about?"

"Most of the time," she said.

"Make it all of the time."

"How are you holding up? You're famous right now, you know. At least in Creekville."

"That's unfortunate."

"You look good on camera," she said. "America's detective."

"I just do what they tell me, ma'am. Protect and serve apple pie."

She groaned, and another silence ensued.

"Listen, Joe—" he braced for the news that she had reunited with her ex-boyfriend. "I know you're busy, but I'd like to see you again. Tonight, maybe? Just a drink?"

He stopped to lean against one of the oaks. Getting involved with someone connected to an investigation, even someone on the periphery, was never a good idea. But in addition to his desire to see her, he had begun to value Ari's insight into the murders. She knew books, and more importantly, in line with Poe's measure of a good detective, she had imagination. Insight. She was a *thinker*.

"Sure," he said, "as long as nothing comes up. Maybe around eight? Someplace we can grab a bite?"

"How about the Railway? It's right on the tracks, close to the mill."

He glanced to his left. He could see the entrance across the parking lot. "I know it."

They hung up, and Preach checked his watch.

It was time for a very unpleasant conversation.

At four p.m. sharp, Preach and Kirby entered the downtown law office of Elliott Fenton. The attorney's receptionist, a woman with chin-length black hair and a body shaped like a swizzle stick, greeted them with a condescending smile.

"I'm Detective Everson, and this is Officer Kirby. We have an appointment."

The woman rose to knock on a mahogany door. Elliott's syrupy drawl issued forth. "Come on in, gentlemen."

The attorney's office had the feel of a well-appointed hunting lodge, replete with bearskin rug, framed diplomas, and a montage of portraits of Elliott's bird dogs. The desk was a mess of folders and papers.

Elliott swiveled to reach into a glass container full of coffee beans. He was wearing another brown suit, this one with a blue-and-yellow tie. His jacket was on. Preach wondered if he took it off to sleep.

"Please, have a seat," Elliott said.

Preach and Kirby settled onto a buttery couch. "You're from Creekville?" Preach asked.

"Born and bred. Daddy was a tobacco farmer, momma taught school."

Preach again had the feeling that the attorney's accent and his persona, the contents of his office, were somewhat contrived. Necessities of doing business in small-town North Carolina.

"Me, too," Preach said.

"What brought ya back?" he asked, with a slight smirk that hinted he already knew.

"I needed a change of pace."

"Don't we all, sometimes. Now what can I do for you, gentlemen? Have you caught the bastard who killed Damian?"

"Unfortunately, no," Preach said.

Elliott leaned forward, his hazel eyes small and intense. "Suspects? Theories?"

"That's what we came to discuss."

The attorney's left eye twitched, as quick and subtle as the first blossom of spring. Was it grief, Preach wondered? Anticipation? Knowledge?

Elliott's tone possessed a carefully controlled ardor. "Care to elaborate?"

"I'm not at liberty to disclose details at this time," Preach said.

Elliott gave him a flat stare and reached for another coffee bean. "In that case, I assume you're here to request permission to badger one of my clients."

"Accepting someone as a client does not render them immune to the law."

Kirby snorted in approval.

Elliott glanced at his stainless steel watch. "I have an appointment in fifteen minutes."

"Then we should start," Kirby snapped, "by discussing your finger-prints that forensics found on Damian Black's liquor cabinet the night of the murder."

Elliott stopped chewing. "Congratulations, officer. You just proved that I spent time at the house of one of my best friends, as well as my client."

Preach put a palm out to quiet Kirby. The junior officer wasn't ready for a pro like Elliott. Keeping his voice calm and his expression neutral, Preach said, "As far as we know, you were the last person to see Mr. Black alive. We're simply here to better understand the course of events."

The attorney gave Preach a long, contemptuous stare. "I'll do what-ever I can to help apprehend whoever killed my friend."

"Were you with Damian the night of his death?"

"I was."

"What were you discussing?"

"That's confidential."

"So your conversation involved solely legal advice?"

"Damian and I have known each other since high school. There were pleasantries exchanged. I won't say what else."

"Didn't Farley Robertson attend Creekville High around that time?"

"The three of us were classmates. I'm afraid it's quite the small town."

Preach noticed Kirby sitting up straighter in his chair. "Were you and Farley close in high school, too?" Preach asked.

"I don't see what relevance that bears, but yes, we were friends. I had other friends as well."

Preach let his eyes roam the office. His gaze alighted on a bookshelf by the window. Legal tomes took up most of the space, but the top shelf was given over to Faulkner, Styron, Pat Conroy, and John Hart. The coffee table held stacks of literary journals and *National Geographic*, as well as the *Triangle Business News*.

"You're a fan of literature?" Preach asked.

"The law is a harsh mistress. I don't have much time for anything else. But yes, I pick up a novel from time to time."

"And a literary journal."

The attorney opened his palms. "This is starting to feel like an interrogation." He checked his watch again. "I'll give you five more minutes."

Preach paused long enough to convey the fact that should he need more time, he would take it. "Did you know about Damian's involvement with Mac Dobbins?"

"His involvement?"

Preach didn't respond; the question had been self-evident.

"Mr. Dobbins is a present client, so I won't be able to join you in your far-reaching speculations."

"Did you see or hear anything unusual at Mr. Black's house that night?"

"No."

"What time did you leave?"

"Right before nine."

"His dogs were present?" Preach asked.

"As always."

"Do you know if the door was locked behind you?"

"I assume so," Elliott said. "I've no idea."

"What about potential suspects—you knew the deceased well, were there any recent arguments?"

"Damian was very well-liked in the community," Elliott said. "I don't know of a single person with whom he was at odds."

"Are you familiar with a writer named J. T. Belker?"

The attorney leveled his gaze on Preach. "I know Damian felt bad about not publishing him. Is there something else I should know?"

"Did Damian ever mention that he might be afraid of Belker?"

The attorney's eyes narrowed even further, a look Preach took for interest in the topic. "No."

Preach considered his next question as a train whistled in the distance. "Was Damian a happy man?"

Elliott looked surprised at the question, then pensive. "We've all thought about it, haven't we? Being a writer, an artist. There's a certain romanticism involved. But it takes a toll on you. My friend was like a new pack of baseball cards, Detective: you never knew what you'd get. He was complicated, both the saddest and the happiest man I ever knew."

"Thank you for your candor," Preach said. "I always find it helpful to understand the victim." He pressed his lips together. "I apologize, but I've got to ask, since your fingerprints were found at the scene. Do you have an alibi for the rest of that evening, after you left Mr. Black's house?"

"I thought I wasn't a suspect?"

"We're just ruling out possibilities."

"Of course you are. We wouldn't want this case to become any more of a fiasco than it already is, would we? How about you let me know when I'm officially a suspect, and then we'll talk about an alibi."

Preach locked eyes with Kirby, a signal meant for Elliott, and then stood. "That's all for now," he said. "We appreciate your time."

The attorney saw them to the door, his tone obliging once again. "I knew both men. Let me know if anything comes to light; maybe I can be of assistance."

Preach turned. "Let me know, too, please. If anything comes to light."

"What was that about?" Kirby asked as they returned to their car. "You think he might know something?"

"I don't know what I think about this case," Preach said. He ran a hand through his hair and unlocked the car. "But I can't shake the feeling we're on the outside looking in."

27

"Tell me about being a prison chaplain," his aunt said. Her office was wood-paneled and hushed, a chapel of manufactured calm.

After the interview with Elliot Fenton, Preach had dropped Kirby off at the station and driven straight to his aunt's office. It was a difficult transition. "What do you want to know?"

"Why did you stop preaching after only one year?"

Preach made eye contact with his aunt. She knew this already. She was the one who had helped him realize that becoming a preacher had been a kneejerk reaction, an attempt to make himself into something he was not. "I had a crisis of faith."

"Of belief in God?"

"Of my place in the church. I just didn't feel like I was helping anyone."

"Did you have any breakdowns during this year?"

"No."

She waited, and he waved a hand. "There were plenty of moments when I felt saddened beyond belief, almost to the point of paralysis, at the amount of pain in the world. But nothing like what happened earlier."

"So the other incidents happened during your time as a chaplain? You mentioned there were others, just 'not like Ricky.'"

Preach's hand twitched. He knew letting that slip had been a mistake. "It was just one, and it was minor." He waved a hand. "Nothing I couldn't deal with."

She wrote something down. It made him uncomfortable. "So you left the church and signed up to be a prison chaplain?"

"That's right," he said.

"I'd like you to talk about it. Your state of mind during this time."

Preach's eyes roamed the room, seeking a reprieve. Besides the desk and the loveseat, the only other furniture was a grand piano.

Nothing hung on the walls except two framed prints, one of which depicted a pair of lotus flowers. It looked like a Monet. The other was also Impressionist and showcased a dark-haired young woman in a white-washed Middle Eastern city. Her head was tilted to the side, regarding the onlooker with an introspective gaze. Two bright red ibises, one standing on her hand and one perched on a wall, seemed both integral and strangely alien to the scene. He wondered why his aunt had chosen it. Knowing her, there was a therapeutic reason.

"For starters," he said, with the sudden desire to meet the mysterious woman who had inspired the painting, "there's the crimes these prisoners committed. The worst of humanity. I had to listen to confessions that . . . let's just say that if I hadn't believed in the existence of evil before I heard them, I did after."

She gave a gentle, encouraging nod. "What else?"

He blew out a long breath. "The questions raised, I suppose. Concerning the ultimate nature of man and God. How did humanity come to this? Why did God let us? If free will is the answer, but God created everything, then what does that say about God? I struggled daily with these questions."

"What triggered the incident?"

"I wouldn't call it an incident. Just a . . . tragedy."

"Okay."

She waited for him to continue. He felt himself start to disassociate, his mind working to stuff the memory in a tidy, out-of-sight corner of his psyche.

"I think it would be helpful to talk about it," she said.

He refrained from looking at the paintings again, tried to appear as detached and in control as possible. "There was an inmate who got pregnant. Raped by a guard. She managed to hide the pregnancy by staying in isolation until she started to show."

"Why would she do that?"

"Just listen. It seems impossible, but she delivered the baby herself, in isolation. The first mealtime after the birth, somehow keeping the baby quiet, she asked for a guard when food was shoved through the slit in the door. Not just any guard, but the man who had raped her, the father of the child. She knew he would come, expecting to trade sex in exchange for release from isolation. And he did come. He opened the door and saw the floor soaked in blood, a tiny baby cradled in the prisoner's arms. She told him about his son. And then, before the guard could react," Preach's voice grew barren and distant, like a sliver of cracked gray asphalt running through the desert, "the mother stabbed the baby to death with a pen."

Whatever words his aunt had been about to utter were cut off as if bitten in half by a shark. He could see her jaw working back and forth in minute increments, controlling her reaction in front of her patient.

"I lost my voice and couldn't finish the session," Preach said. "I went home and didn't leave my couch for two days. It felt as if anchors were holding down my limbs."

"Did you recover on your own?"

"Yes."

"What happened after you did?"

"I had another crisis of faith, which led to my resignation."

"In God this time?"

"In my ability to objectively serve the prisoners."

"You felt you had done that prisoner harm? Shaken her faith in someone she looked to for redemption after committing such an abominable act?"

He felt his hands clenching at his sides. He had been hoping his aunt wouldn't go there. "Not her. Him. The father. As soon as I went back, I visited with the guard. He had killed the mother with his bare hands in that cell. He was in custody now, of course." Preach swallowed. His throat felt coated with glue. "After he killed her, another guard found him in the cell, rocking the dead baby in his arms. When I went to see him, I assumed he wanted to talk about what he had done and God's forgiveness. But all he wanted to know was why they had taken his son away and when he could see him."

Preach drove away from his aunt's office in silence. It did not help to talk about such things. It only hurt.

Though she didn't show it, he knew it was hard for her as well, and that pained him. He should have gone to a stranger.

Or to no one at all. He could tell Aunt Janice thought something was wrong with him and was going to send him to someone else for further evaluation. He had no idea what he would do if he couldn't be a cop.

The streets were quiet, damp from a light rain. Moonlight glossed the sides of the buildings as he passed through downtown Creekville and continued into Chapel Hill. Before he met with Ari, there was a stop he had to make. Questions about the past he needed to ask, from someone who had been there.

Preach's mother opened the door with a glass of white wine in her hand. "It's good to see you, son."

"You, too."

As Preach watched the delicate way she held the glass, he had a flashback to his twelfth birthday, when his mother had reached up to hang a piñata for him and his friends, colored bangles slipping down her wrists, the smell of reefer and coconut shampoo mingling in her hair.

Back then she never drank wine. She drank beer straight from the bottle.

She led him to a low gray sofa in the living room. A gas fire flickered inside a brick column. "What an unexpected pleasure. Can you stay for dinner?"

"I'm sorry, I can't. I have to meet someone."

"Will you at least have some tea? A beer?"

"Water's fine. I can get it."

When he returned to the sofa, her hands were in her lap, cradling the wine. "I can't . . . I can't believe there was another murder."

"It's why I'm here. I mean it's always good to see you, but I have a few questions."

"For me?" she asked in surprise.

"About Farley Robertson and Damian Black. I'm trying to get a better understanding of their relationship. I thought I'd start with you."

"What could high school possibly have to do with why they were murdered?"

"I don't know. Probably nothing."

She sat back. "We were never close. And don't you think they might have changed over the years?"

"Maybe, maybe not. You've told me about Farley. What was Damian like?"

She was quiet, as if reflecting on the gravity of his murder. "Shy, polite, almost demure. Silver-tongued with the girls, though. One of those guys who doesn't stand out in a crowd, but when they get you alone, they whisper sweet nothings in your ear. A friend of a friend dated him."

"How did that end?"

"I can't remember, honestly." Her gaze went distant, searching for memories. "Oh, honey, this was all so long ago!"

"You're doing great. It's helpful. What about Elliott Fenton? Wasn't he in their class as well?"

"The attorney? I believe he was."

"What do you remember about him?"

The question prompted a strangely superior smile from his mother. It was a smile sparked by memories, one he knew she must have unleashed on unlucky suitors, dazzling the boys—his father—with her distant blue eyes and striking good looks.

"He was about the same as he is now," she said. "Arrogant, privileged, Southern. He was everything your father and I resented about the Old South."

"He said his dad was a tobacco farmer."

"That he was. He farmed about half the county."

"Anything else you remember about them? Unusual stories, rumors?"

She curled her hands around her wine glass. "I . . . not offhand, no."

"What about common interests or hobbies?"

"Evan and Lee were involved in the school paper. Maybe Elliott, too."

"I don't suppose you have any old issues?"

"Hardly."

Preach tapped the edge of the couch. "Were there any tragedies that happened around that time? At school or in town?"

Another pause. "Not involving them. There was a suicide our senior year, a girl named Deirdre Hollings. And one of the teachers died of a heart attack."

A suicide and a heart attack were not uncommon occurrences, but he made a note to check them out. See if there was some bizarre connection to Belker or Mac Dobbins. "Anything else?"

"Not that I recall."

Preach checked his watch and rose. Time to meet Ari. "I've got to run. Thanks for the chat."

"You know," his mother said, as he was moving toward the door, "there was something . . . God, it's just been so long . . . some kind of secret club that posted anonymous love poems and stories in the school paper. Innocuous on the surface, but the students all knew they were code for the social scene."

He stopped moving. "This secret club—do you remember the name?"

Her trill of laughter was sharp, judging. "Something incredibly pretentious. What was it . . . the Byron, the Byronic forest—" She snapped her fingers. "The Byronic Wilderness Society. That was it. I can't believe I actually remembered."

"And Damian, Lee—they were part of this?"

She swatted a tendril of hair out of her face. "I don't think anyone ever knew for sure who was behind it. But those two were probably good candidates."

"What about Elliott?"

"I just don't know. Why don't you ask my sister about the past?" she asked, failing to conceal her bitterness. "I assume you've seen her?"

"Aunt Janice was six years ahead of you," Preach said. "Why would she know anything?"

"During grad school she interned as a guidance counselor at the high school. I resented it greatly. But maybe she heard something."

"Even if she did, it was confidential," Preach said. "But I'll ask her. Why don't you come with me?"

"She knows where to find me."

"And you know where to find her."

She rolled her eyes. "My sister isn't the saint you think she is." She looked as if she were going to say something else, something cruel, then buried her face in her wine.

"I don't think she'd claim to be."

Preach was so tired of their feud. He got nothing else useful from his mother, but as he drove away he couldn't stop thinking about the Byronic Wilderness Society.

28

Ari loved fall in the South. The clarity of the sky, the wind whipping piles of leaves into a colorful flurry of miniature whirling dervishes, the delicious spookiness of grasping oaks and moss-covered cemeteries and shriveled cornfields. Fall was brisk walks in the Carolina woods, patio nights with an old sweater and a bottle of wine, curling up at her favorite haunts with a cappuccino and a good book.

She was studying at Caffè Driade, an eclectic little coffee shop nestled in the forest. The interior was warm and cozy, a jazz note trapped in amber walls and a low wood ceiling. French doors led to pebbled paths and a terraced patio where Ari was sitting. Metal folk art was sprinkled among the trees.

Despite the sublime setting, she felt jittery. She was falling behind in her classes. Finances were tight. Two employees of the Wandering Muse had just quit, anticipating bankruptcy or a fire sale, despite the fact that business was booming. Especially sale of Damian's novels.

Most of all, she couldn't shake her dread stemming from the two murders that had poked a hole into the cocoon of her quirky little town.

At dusk, a reminder bubble floated onto her refurbished MacBook Air. It was almost time to meet with Detective Everson.

Joe. Preach.

Which name did she prefer? He seemed to be all and none of the things his different monikers implied.

A complicated man, for sure. An exciting change from Trevor, who wore his rebellious personality like a billboard.

She didn't understand the detective's interest. She got that some men were drawn to her, but Preach was very good-looking, and, in her mind, Ari would always be the frighteningly skinny girl in the dark makeup and cool-but-not-sexy clothes. The one who watched other lives unfold.

Unable to read another word about jurisdictional authority or motions for summary judgment, she stuffed her laptop into her backpack next to a steampunk novel she couldn't find the time to finish.

When she looked up, a man with greasy hair spilling out of an old Texaco cap was walking toward her. Her table was halfway down a wooded slope, in an isolated corner of the terrace.

Before she had time to react, he sat across from her and slammed his elbows on the table. He leaned in, a cruel grin drawing attention to a scar that made the top of his lip look caught in a fishhook.

"Evenin'," he said. His voice was raspy, poor, rural. The cap was pulled low over his face.

Her gaze locked onto his hard green eyes and the bushy sideburns curving across his cheeks. Though not a big man, he had a rough, wiry physicality to him that reeked of violence.

"Do you want the table?" she asked. "I was just—"

"I want you to shut the hell up and listen."

The statement shocked her into silence. His faded army jacket was spattered with white paint, and underneath the jacket, the hilt of a hunting knife poked out. The sight of it caused tendrils of fear to slither down her arms.

"We gave your new boyfriend a warning. Pretty boy don't listen."

Her hands trembling, she realized she had to say or do something. Anything. She stood and grabbed her backpack. Inside was a canister of mace she had bought because of her stalker. "I don't know what you think—"

He grabbed her wrist and jerked, forcing her back into her seat. His grin turned into a snarl. "Don't you dare scream, bitch."

The fact that he had approached her so brazenly in a café had somehow paralyzed her. *We're in a public place*, her subconscious screamed. *You can't do this.*

He tightened his grip on her wrist, causing her to wince. His other hand touched his scar. "I see you starin'. You tell your boyfriend he gets in our face again, pokes his nose into our business, then you and me, we're gonna have something in common."

Her shock passed, replaced by rage and terror. Underneath the table, she put her foot on the edge of his chair and kicked as hard as she could, causing him to jerk backward and release his grip on her wrist.

"Get away from me!" she shouted. "Help!"

Heads turned on the terrace above. A man in a designer hoodie jumped to his feet. "Are you okay? What's going on?"

The man in the army jacket held Ari's gaze, eyes burning into hers like he was cauterizing a wound. "I told you not to scream."

She backed away. "Fuck you."

He traced a finger along his scar and smiled, then turned and strode through the woods, toward the parking lot.

She watched him climb into a battered red pickup with no hubcaps and rusted fenders. The truck churned up gravel as it sped away.

"Can I help with something?" the onlooker asked, nervously eyeing the parking lot as he walked down to check on Ari.

The forest surrounding the café had turned threatening, sentient. Ari was shaking like it was twenty degrees outside. "You can walk me to my car."

Detective Everson was already at the Railway when Ari arrived. The bar was situated right beside the railroad tracks that bisected Creekville, and the establishment was comprised of four original railcars retouched in red and green paint, arranged in a square around a raucous biergarten covered with vinyl tarp. Kitschy Southern memorabilia provided the decor, including a vintage racing motorcycle suspended above the bar.

Unlike most places in town, the Railway didn't cater to one particular group; it served fifteen-dollar high-gravity beers as well as pitchers of Miller Lite and happy hour margaritas. Gouda cheeseburgers alongside BBQ slaw dogs and fried pickles.

Ari elbowed her way between a group of grizzled old-timers at the bar. She ordered a double shot of Jameson and a beer, downing the shot on the way to Preach's table. He was sitting at a quiet window seat in the car beside the tracks. He took one glance at her face and jumped to his feet.

She laid a hand on his forearm, expelling a shuddery breath. When she steadied, she sat across from him and told him about the encounter.

He listened with a grave expression, nodding along carefully until she finished. When she described the man's scar, Preach's face darkened.

"You know him?" she asked.

"We've had a run-in."

"Who is he?"

"He was wearing a ski mask when I saw him. Do you think you could come to the station tomorrow morning and give a description?"

She swallowed, then reached out and gently touched the bruise still covering the bottom of Preach's neck. "Did he do this?"

"Him and his friends. They're in desperate need of a lesson in manners."

She felt a surge of anger. "I'd *love* to give a description."

"You're brave. Most people would worry they'd be in danger."

"I want him caught. And apparently I'm already in danger."

He squeezed her hand across the table. A tingle of warmth spread through her. She felt safe with him, better already. "You're a good listener," she said.

"I've had lots of practice."

The corners of her lips curled upward. "With women? Or with witnesses?"

"With people who need to be heard."

Her eyes slid away. "I never thought I'd be one of them."

"We all are. Trust me."

She touched her forefinger to the place on her lip she had once pierced, a nervous habit she thought she'd left behind. "The guy with the scar . . ." she said, trailing off. "I don't think he reads Dostoevsky."

"No."

"I heard on the news that J. T. Belker was arrested for the murders."

Preach grimaced as he took a swig of beer. She gathered he was less than pleased with the publicity.

"If you've arrested someone," she said, "why was I assaulted? Does that mean J. T. is innocent?"

"He's still a person of interest," he said, and she could see him struggling to decide how much to tell her. "I wish I had more answers for you."

A waiter approached, and they both ordered the Carolina Burger, a menu item most restaurants in the area claimed to have perfected, and which generally came with chili, coleslaw, mustard, and onions. The music changed to a bluegrass tune full of fiddles and aching voices, a mournful, pure lament of the people of the land.

She said, "What if you've been looking at it wrong—what if it's the authors themselves, not the protagonists, who have parallels to the victims?"

"I've thought about that. Poe and Damian Black were both horror writers who wanted to be taken more seriously—easy link. But Dostoevsky and Farley . . . what's the connection?"

"Some people think Dostoevsky identified strongly with Raskolnikov," she said. "Maybe the killer knows more about Farley than we do."

The burgers arrived. Preach took a bite and wiped ketchup off his mouth. "It's an interesting theory. But I'm not sure where it gets us."

"Because it would be impossible to predict the next combination of author and victim."

"That's right."

She devoured a third of her burger; she hadn't realized how hungry she was. "*Mmm*, this is good."

They chewed in silence for a while, and then Preach said, "What if *both* books describe the murderer? The penniless, frustrated intellect of Dostoevsky combined with the devious imagination of Poe. Wait— wasn't Poe a drug addict? Opium?"

"That's mostly been discredited," Ari said. "He had an archrival who hated his guts and vilified him after his death. He was actually quite handsome and athletic. Vibrant, even. Except for the attempted suicide."

Preach had been reaching for a French fry, and his head jerked upward. "He tried to kill himself?"

"He overdosed on laudanum and nearly died."

"I thought he wasn't an addict," Preach said.

"Most biographers think he took just enough laudanum to gain the attention of a woman he was pursuing. Poe was never afraid of a little drama."

Preach pushed his plate away, thinking of Poe, the scar on Belker's wrist, and the suicide his mother had mentioned. Interesting, but it seemed tenuous.

"I need another drink," Ari said finally. "I've got a bottle of wine at home, and you probably need to get going."

Preach's eyes shifted to meet hers. Sometimes the directness of his gaze and the depth of the experiences reflected within made her feel out of her depth.

"You shouldn't be alone tonight," he said. "Not after what happened."

"I'm a big girl. And where would I go?"

"My place."

She started. His gaze was kind and warm, but also cop-like, protective. She wasn't sure how to take his offer.

"It's not protocol, but it's the only solution I like," he said. "At least for tonight. I'll see if I can get a detail assigned to you tomorrow, until we can sort this out."

She knew there was no assurance that anything would be sorted. "What about my drink?"

"If you can take your whiskey a bit sweeter, I've got plenty of bourbon."

"I can handle that," she said, thinking *it's you I'm not sure about.*

They paid and left, and when they stepped into the shadows of the parking lot, she rubbed her wrists where the man had grabbed her. The memory of the encounter washed over her again, a bucket of filthy dishwater to the face.

29

They stopped at Ari's condo so she could grab some clothes and her laptop. She followed in her car to his secluded cabin. A lacy veil of fog draped the trees.

Preach ushered her into an open living space filled with track lighting and furniture made of reclaimed wood. There was a bedroom loft, built-in bookshelves, a fireplace, and a wall of exposed brick.

Ari liked the space. It was cozy and smelled of pine.

He pointed at the loft. "Take the bed. I sleep on the hammock most nights."

"Outside?"

He jerked his thumb. "On the screen porch."

She noticed he didn't have a television. Or much of anything. No photos, no knickknacks, no reminder notes on the refrigerator door.

Just books.

Like her.

He went to the kitchen to fix drinks, and she eyed the coffee table, noticing copies of *Crime and Punishment* and *The Complete Short Stories of Edgar Allan Poe*. Next to the novels was a leather-bound journal and a stack of take-out menus.

She sidled to one of the bookshelves. Old magazines stuffed the bottom shelves, mostly about hiking, food, and travel. Thank God there were none of those pathetic men's magazines.

The top shelves were full of theology and philosophy. Classic and modern fiction took up the middle. A large portion was devoted to international writers.

He brought her a glass of bourbon. "I've got some reading to do on the porch, if you want to join me. I'll make a fire."

"Sure," she said. "Nice pad."

He shrugged. "It's a furnished rental. I needed a dose of nature."

"Are these your books?"

"Yep."

"You have good taste," she murmured. "They take you there, don't they? The great novels? Even if you haven't been for yourself."

"I like what Kafka said. 'A book is the axe for the frozen sea inside us.'"

She felt as if he had just cupped her face in his hands and kissed her. She took a long sip of bourbon. "I have to ask—where's the television? Everyone owns a television. Even the hipsters who pretend they don't."

He gave a small smile. "It's in the loft."

"Good to know. I thought for a minute this was some kind of staged encounter."

He chuckled, then grabbed a brown case file from the kitchen and led her to the screen porch. It was a beautiful night, calm and starry and mild, the moon a silver bauble above.

The detective stacked wood inside the potbelly stove while Ari curled up on the hammock, soothed by the hum of cicadas.

"Why does your partner call you Preach?" she asked.

"I used to be a preacher."

That was not what she expected to hear.

"A real one? Sorry—I mean, I . . . that just seems so different from being a detective."

"I can't argue with that."

"Why did you . . . are you okay to talk about it?"

"I don't mind," he said, with a lack of interest.

"Why did you leave?"

He paused with a log in his hand. "It's a difficult thing, to feel responsible for the spiritual guidance of others. People see it as a form of moral authority, when for me that was the furthest thing from my mind."

"Do you still . . . believe?"

He reached for a book of matches. She sensed it was a question everyone asked him. "Don't we all have that nagging sense that God is real, even if we know that all isn't right with our religion? I've met very few true atheists over the years, and the agnostics—" He waved a hand, his back still to her. "To me, believing that the creator of nanotechnology and coral reefs and a hundred billion galaxies isn't a personal God is a bit like believing Da Vinci didn't care about the Mona Lisa."

"Maybe Da Vinci loved her when he painted her, then moved on to other things," she said. "It isn't the existence of God that bothers me. It's whether or not he still cares."

"Because a god who doesn't care is worse than none at all," he said softly, turning back from the lit fire. "Like having a parent who doesn't love you."

She felt the darkness settling on her back, as if it were a tangible thing. "That's right," she whispered back.

He met her gaze, his eyes sad and knowing. She rose and went to him, pressing her mouth against his. He took her by the arms. They kissed as if they had something to prove, to themselves and to the night sky, an affirmation of human existence.

She pressed her hands into his back. Her palms felt small and insignificant against the contours of his muscles. He eased her onto the hammock, and their legs intertwined like pieces of a puzzle locking into place.

His hand moved under her shirt, caressing her stomach as their kiss deepened. Her pulse quickened when his fingers slid upward, sliding over her breasts. She arched and moaned, and then a rustle in the forest startled them. The sound was heavy, methodical. Like footsteps crunching on leaves.

Preach peeled off her. "Inside!" he said in a harsh whisper. "Stay low."

Panic surged into her throat. Heat pulsed from the stove as she crawled toward the door on her hands and knees.

Was it the Literary Killer? Or the man with the scar, coming to fulfill his promise?

Were they one and the same?

She tumbled inside, the detective right behind her. He pointed at the couch. "Behind there. Stay down."

She obeyed. He pressed his back against the wall as he rose to switch off the lights, leaving a faint glow of moonlight seeping through the windows.

Peering out from behind the couch, she watched him move in a swift crouch for the kitchen table. After grabbing his cell phone and gun, his fingers flicked over the keypad, but then he snarled and swung his gun toward the screen porch. "Signal's terrible."

More rustling emanated from the forest. The detective had left the door to the porch open, she assumed so he could hear outside. He kept his gun trained on the small clearing behind the house while he continued trying the phone.

He finally got through. "Anne, it's Detective Everson. I may have a situation at my house. Can you stay on the line and alert whoever's on duty?"

The crackling of leaves grew louder, until it seemed like it was right outside. Ari's heart thumped against her chest. Adrenaline surged through her, until her nerve endings crackled with electricity.

Preach was kneeling beside the door to the screen porch, watching the forest with both hands gripping his gun, his phone squeezed against his ear.

More swishing and crunching from the woods. The sounds seemed fainter. Finally they ceased altogether, and a few minutes later Preach lowered his weapon.

"Could it have been a family of deer?" Ari asked, forcing her voice to obey.

"Too loud for deer. Those were footsteps. Multiple ones."

She heard the whirr of a siren, then tires on gravel. The detective asked her to stay out of sight as he stepped outside to converse with the driver of the police cruiser. After a few minutes, the car pulled away.

Preach came back inside. There was a look of barely restrained violence in his eyes that both disturbed and relieved her. "Whoever it was, they won't be back tonight," he said. "That was just a message, or they wouldn't have been so loud."

She peered up at him. "How many more messages will there be?"

Instead of answering, he locked the door to the screen porch and made sure all the windows were secured. After that, he picked up the leather bound journal on the coffee table and sat beside her on the couch. The sexual tension was still there, but it felt out of place in the midst of all the danger.

"I shouldn't have been so lax," he said, setting his gun on the table beside him and opening the journal. "Feel free to read or watch TV. I need to get through this tonight."

She snuck a glance at the first page, thinking it was another case file.

The journal was J. T. Belker's.

30

Hours later, Preach closed the journal and sank into the couch. For the thousandth time, his gaze flicked across the room, out each of the windows and into the woods.

Nothing stirring in the trees.

His gun and bourbon and cell phone were parked on a chair to his left. Ari was asleep beside him, her hair a dark halo on the pillow. He reached to trace a finger across her cheek, then stopped. This physical infatuation between them was becoming dangerous, and not just because of the ethical considerations.

He was putting her in danger. Mac Dobbin's men knew they could lean on her to get to him, and he had to stay focused and protect her. Solve the case. He and Ari could sort out whatever it was between them when this was over.

He also suspected she wasn't over her ex, and that he was a diversion for her. An exotic and temporary entertainment. As for himself, part of him was still . . . in a dark place.

He pushed those thoughts away and stared at the leather-bound journal he had just finished reading.

Belker.

A troubled and complex man. But was he a killer?

Preach revisited the passages he had marked. According to the journal, they all came from the current year.

Jan. 10—Wind, rain, the cold a stinging slap to the face. I lie in bed and the novel lies unfinished, wallowing in a state of entropy, anchored by self-delusion.

I am never at rest. Filled with discontent that rises inside me like bile. What will happen, I wonder, when the acid spills in bright green drops and forms rivulets and then a river, a burning river, that scorches the green and fertile earth around me?

I am awed by the vast unrealized potential of my actions. Of the power of sheer human will.

We cannot control the amount of good we do to others in this life. We are limited by means, circumstance.

But we can control the evil.

May 1—Query: is the entire human race an afterthought, a mistake, a failed experiment by God? Virus-ridden puddles of DNA given too much free will and abandoned to a cosmic junkyard? Our brains swimming in bacteria like an ocean bottom, devising calculus and poetry while preyed upon by hordes of invisible, mindless things? I understand the evil of man, but not the capriciousness of God.

July 23—We can only take so much before we burst. Yes, all of us. It is a certainty of the human condition that we all possess a breaking point.

Today, I have found mine.

August 23—I've done it!! Taken that first all-important step on my journey. Rasky would be so proud. How do I feel on my mensi-versary, I ask myself? How did Alexander the Great feel when he crossed the Hellespont? Napoleon at Alexandria? Mankind when he latched onto the gray and bloated moon, trod on its lifeless, pock-marked surface as a child first grasps its mother's nipple?

Hopeful, fulfilled.

Anxious for more.

October 28—Farley Robertson has finally been put in his place. I hope he fucking burns.

Preach set down the journal with a chill.

But we can control the evil.

His chill turned into prickly little bumps of unease when he confirmed a few suspicions about the dates.

July 23 was the same date Belker had received the email from Farley Robertson stating he was rejecting Belker's novel.

A mensiversary, Preach discovered, was a term signifying a commemoration one month after a significant event. August 23 mentioned an all-important step. What had Belker done?

And October 28, the shortest and last entry in the journal, was the day Farley Robertson was murdered.

Kirby lay on his back in a king-size bed at a ritzy hotel in Chapel Hill. Monica Hutchinson collapsed on his chest, shuddering through her orgasm.

She eased off him, bare hips swaying as she strutted to the marble-tiled bathroom, straight blond hair falling down her back like a spool of golden thread.

Kirby wasn't one of those black men who fantasized about snagging a white girl. Maybe it was because his dad was white and the novelty factor was low, but he had yet to meet a white woman who could be with him and not be self-conscious about it. They were either ashamed or trying too hard not to be.

The über-liberal locals were almost worse than the racists back home: sleeping with him was a badge of honor in Creekville's socially conscious circles. Even better if they held hands at the farmer's market on Sunday mornings. The last white girl Kirby had dated, an anthropology PhD candidate at UNC, had wanted to adopt a Nepalese orphan with him. She had probably been fantasizing about the social cachet—a black baby daddy and a little brown baby, not from Africa or some other cliché place, but from Nepal, no less! It might even be the next Dalai Lama.

Kirby had told her that if she wanted a baby from Nepal, she should marry a Sherpa. And buy a big furry coat made of slaughtered baby minks, because it was butt-ass cold there, and everyone was too poor to be PC.

At least Monica was straightforward. She just wanted a good lay and information on the case.

She reclined next to him. "You know how to keep a girl happy," she purred.

"It's one of my many talents I feel will translate to the big screen."

The reporter put her chin on her hands and looked at him. Her eyes were as clear and pale blue as a glacier. "Do you have anything new?"

"Jeopardizing my career so you could break the story wasn't enough?"

"No one will ever know." Her tongue flicked into his ear. "I don't kiss and tell."

"The truth always comes out at the worst time. Haven't you heard of Shakespeare?"

"This is real life, darling, not a story. Politicians lie, businessmen cheat, people do whatever it takes to get famous."

"Yeah," he said. "Sure."

He glanced at the clock. Less than an hour remained before the patrol officer parked at his sister's trailer expected him to return. Kirby was supposed to be running down a lead.

Monica's voice turned to maple syrup as her thigh slid over his leg. "You're not sure about Belker, are you? You still think it might be Mac Dobbins." Her eyebrows lifted. "Or is there a new suspect?"

The meeting with Elliott Fenton ran through his mind. If Kirby even hinted at the attorney's involvement and it came back on him, Elliott would have Kirby's badge stapled to his forehead. "Nah," he said. "You know everything I do."

"Where did Detective Everson go tonight?" she asked.

"I don't know."

"A detective not telling his partner where he's going during a major investigation?"

Kirby shifted to look at her. "We've got personal lives. Do you think he knows where *I* am right now?"

"No, I just think you lied to him."

He moved her leg off him. "Preach is good people."

"He's also a disgraced detective heading up a double murder."

"I mean it, Monica. Leave him out of this. If there were any problems with his record they'd handle it internally."

She stroked the insides of his thighs until he hardened again. "You said this is the second time he's gone off the grid."

It wasn't as if Kirby was trading sex for information; they had hooked up long before that was in play. His dilemma was with his own conscience. Leaking a story was one thing, keeping tabs on his partner another.

She climbed on top of him, breasts swaying against his chest, hair spilling into his face. "If it's not us, it'll be someone else."

Kirby knew he wasn't athletic enough to be a pro, smart enough for a top degree, lucky enough for anything to change. He had a flash of his sister, barefoot and pregnant in their trailer when she was seventeen, bawling on his shoulder after her boyfriend left her. Spreading his seed and drifting to the next town just like their father had done, pollen floating on the warm southern breeze.

"Find out where he goes," Monica said, purring as they fell into rhythm. "We'll break this case together."

Kayla handing food stamps to the cashier. Jared bullied by poor white trash in that cow patty of a school. Jalene hunching as she walked, cradling her hernia, living every single day on the edge of a thousand-foot cliff.

Monica rocked with him. "You'll look great on camera."

His voice was husky when he spoke, and she mistook it for desire.

Preach woke to rays of weak yellow light slanting through the trees. He had fallen asleep upright on the couch, his left hand on his gun. Beside him, Ari's chest fluttered with the soft breath of sleep.

He felt tired and uneven, saddled with tension. He had dreamt of dark things, of damp cellars and bare prison walls, of a tree house full of horrors hidden deep in the Georgia woods.

He gently extricated himself from Ari and padded to the kitchen. The aroma of fresh coffee helped him relax, and he took his mug to the hammock. The air was thick and smelled of wet leaves.

His pulse quickened as he pondered the investigation, which was starting to feel like a jigsaw puzzle with a missing piece right in the center. A collection of spokes with no hub.

It was possible the novels were just an ingenious diversion. But that didn't ring true. He still believed the crime scenes were a message, but to whom? To anyone who dared inhibit the desires of a megalomaniacal writer? To literature-loving interlopers in the affairs of Mac Dobbins?

Preach had found no mention of the Byronic Wilderness Society on the Internet or in the police database. Even if Damian, Farley, and Elliott had all been members of the same club all those years ago, so what? They liked literature and had formed a silly, trite clique in high school. So had millions of other people.

Except not all cliques had two key members who turned up dead within a week of each other.

Maybe he was grasping. Creekville was a small town, its long-time citizens bound to be connected in various ways. Belker was years younger than Damian and Farley and had been raised near Charlotte. Mac hadn't even grown up in North Carolina.

He paced the screen porch in disgust. Any cop could work the clues, the physical evidence. What had always set Preach apart was that he understood *people*.

But he was failing. Had the return to his hometown thrown a veil of familiarity over his eyes? Had his last case damaged his ability to see behind the curtain?

His cell buzzed. Chief Higgins.

"I need you here," she said.

He glanced at Ari, still asleep on the couch, limbs tucked into her chest as if forming a protective shell. "What's up?"

"Belker wants to talk."

31

Preach woke Ari and followed her to a popular café on campus. He told her to stay inside and stick to crowds of people. He would work on getting someone assigned to watch her at night.

Their parting had been awkward, two people who knew something had started but didn't know what.

Maybe it was better they kept getting interrupted, he thought.

Maybe it was a sign.

When he pulled into the station, a group of reporters descended on his car like seagulls on a discarded piece of bread. He put his head down and waded through them.

Kirby was at his desk, eyes grim and haggard. Preach nodded at him and went straight to the chief. She was sitting in her office with a steaming cup of tea, kneading a stress ball with a yin-yang symbol painted on the surface.

"Belker's ready to see me?" Preach asked.

"Yep."

"Any idea why?"

"Said he'll only tell you." She stopped kneading the ball. "How are you holding up?"

"What do you mean?"

"Do I need to say it?" she asked softly. "You're seeing your therapist?"

"I am," he said evenly.

Chief Higgins glanced out the window, at the media milling about the parking lot and the bucolic backdrop of oaks and historic brick buildings. "The mayor's pressing us hard to wrap this up with the suspect in custody."

"You tell the mayor that Mac Dobbins is out of control and we need more men. I can't protect my people."

"I did. Her hands are tied until the budget meeting."

"That's because they're not her people."

Chief Higgins pressed her fingers deeper into the ball, then released one of her deep, therapeutic sighs. "Go see Belker. Nail this down before this circus gets any wilder."

"Good morning, Detective," Belker said, with his typical acerbic tone.

The writer was sequestered in the basement of the building housing the police station, in a low-ceilinged cell with white cement walls. A metal, diamond-patterned cage separated detective and prisoner.

Preach waited, but the writer just stood there, grinning at him.

"You want me to believe you think this is a game," Preach said, "but you're posturing. What did you mean when you wrote that you could control the evil in your life? That you'd taken 'that first all-important step'?"

"You read my journal?" Belker asked in surprise.

"I did."

"Then what do you think I meant?"

"It doesn't matter what I think. It matters what a jury will think."

"It matters to me."

Preach looked him in the eye. "I think, without a doubt, that you wanted to kill Farley Robertson and Damian Black."

Belker's grin turned lopsided and ugly. "But you're not sure if I did."

"There doesn't have to be certainty. Just lack of reasonable doubt."

"Ah, yes. Our vaunted justice system. The one that has served our society so diligently and left a third of us saddled with a criminal record. Or is it just that human nature is that irrepressible?"

Preach walked slowly over to stand in front of him, his footsteps echoing in the silence of the hall. "Why'd you ask for me?"

"You want to know where my money went, Detective? 2881 Prospect Street. Your answer is there. I give you my word."

"The anonymous woman?"

"She was living at that address. That's all I know."

"Why'd you give the money to her?"

Belker remained silent.

"Why the games? Why not give me the address at your house?"

"Would it have kept me out of jail?"

"No," Preach said.

"As I thought. I was going to consult an attorney but changed my mind."

Preach's face tightened in frustration. He didn't know what game Belker was playing, and he was far from ready to discount what he had read in the journal.

On the other hand, he wasn't comfortable with the possibility of having the wrong person behind bars. Especially if it meant Mac Dobbins went free.

"What do you know about the literary references at the crime scenes?"

"Less than you, I suspect."

Preach took a stab. "What about the Byronic Wilderness Society?"

"The what?" Belker's perplexed stare looked genuine.

Preach's next words came low and hard. "If you're wasting my time, I'll make sure your unpublished novel, the one that might benefit from a sudden surge of notoriety from this case, never sees the light of day."

Belker's forced joviality melted like plastic on a hot stove.

"I'll tie it up as evidence," Preach said, turning on his heel to leave, "and bury it in a hole."

Silence followed him up the stairs.

Preach stopped by his desk to check his calendar. He thought he had two more days before his next appointment with Aunt Janice, but he wanted to make sure.

Just before he sat in his squeaky black office chair, he noticed the seat was pushed out and facing to the right.

When it came to certain things, Preach was a very careful man, almost obsessive. He always pushed his chair straight underneath the desk, facing the computer. Always.

He stood in front of his desk, still as stone. The department employed a janitorial service, but they only cleaned the floors once a week. And they had never left his chair in a different position.

He checked the rest of his work area but noticed nothing else out of place. Maybe a new janitor had taken over, someone careless. Maybe, just this once, Preach had left in a hurry and forgotten to replace his chair in the same position.

Or maybe someone had been at his desk.

He quietly took his emergency fingerprint kit out of a drawer, dusted for prints, lifted a few that were probably his own, and put the kit in his jacket pocket. He could drop it off with evidence later.

Kirby walked over. Preach caught him up on the night before, as well as the conversation with Belker. His partner may or may not have talked to the press, but he knew everything Preach did, and he didn't think Kirby was dirty. And he sure as hell wasn't working with Mac Dobbins, not after what had happened to his family.

Before they left, Preach found Terry at his cubicle. "How's it coming with the Pen Oak Press authors? Anyone I need to follow up with?"

"There's only three besides Belker, and none of them have a beef."

"Did you dig deep? Check their contracts, financial situations?"

"They all have solid day jobs. Two are under contract for another book, the other's a poet who was shocked he was published in the first place. He dedicated the book to Damian and Farley. Oh, and most of Damian's inheritance goes to his mother. She lives in a nursing home in Wilmington."

Preach gave a slow nod. "You got some more time?"

Terry swallowed his last bite of breakfast sandwich. "Yeah, of course."

"Good. I need you to go to Creekville High and find copies of the literary journal printed while Damian Black and Farley Robertson were in attendance. I also need old yearbooks. And while you're there, see if anyone's heard of the Byronic Wilderness Society."

"The what?"

Preach spelled it out for him.

"And if someone has?"

"Let me know."

Terry scribbled everything down. Kirby came back over, holding his coat and a cup of coffee.

Preach set the GPS on his phone for 2881 Prospect Street.

32

The address Belker had given them was a homeless shelter.

Preach shut the car door and slowly approached the converted Queen Anne. The building was a block off Main Street, a tidy property with a wraparound porch, shaded by pine and magnolia. A gravel walkway wound past a vegetable garden and a bird bath.

The Nondenominational Center for Social Services, a handsome stone sign proclaimed. A woman in a flannel shirt and stained blue trousers was sitting on the front porch, staring slack-jawed into the garden.

What is Belker playing at?

The officers moved inside, through a hallway smelling of ammonia and into a tired director's office filled with file cabinets and wooden plaques showcasing the center's public service awards.

A toned Native American woman in her thirties sat behind a drafting desk. Her hair was cropped close on the sides, and an eagle-shaped medallion rested against the hollow of her throat.

Preach took a seat and flashed his badge, causing her eyebrows to rise. He told her the basics and showed her the photo of Belker.

"He doesn't look familiar," she said. "You think he spent time here, as a guest?"

"It's possible," Preach said. "According to his rental history, he's only been in his current house for two months, with a blank period before that."

"I think I'd recognize him if he'd been here for any length of time."

"Do you mind if I ask around?" Preach asked.

"Actually," she clasped her hands, "I do. Many of our guests have had unpleasant experiences with law enforcement, especially men, and further contact might . . . upset a delicate balance." Her smile was tight-lipped. "I'd be happy to place a blown-up image on the front door for a few days."

Kirby snorted and started to respond, but Preach laid a hand on his arm. This woman, if he got her on board, could reach far more people than they could.

"I've worked with at-risk individuals myself," Preach said calmly, "as a prison chaplain. I know what it's like to try to reach someone and have your progress impeded by callous authority figures."

She had looked ready for a fight, but his words softened her stance.

"I've got a homicide investigation to conduct," he continued, "and the photo needs to be shown around. In person. But I don't mind passing the torch to someone the residents trust."

He pushed the photo toward her. She hesitated but took it.

"If anyone has seen this man, or you think they might have, please let me know as soon as possible. I'll be happy to conduct further interviews here, with you present."

"I . . . guess that's acceptable."

"Thank you. Do you keep a list of your guests' names?"

"Only those who stay the night. We don't require verification, so as you can imagine, those identities might not be accurate."

"I hate to ask, but I'll need you to compile a list of every guest on file in the last year."

"I suppose I can do that."

"What about photos? Does the center take any?"

"No."

He pursed his lips and thought for a second, then stood. "I didn't catch your name."

"Deborah. Deborah Kingfisher."

Preach slid his card onto the desk. "We appreciate your cooperation and understanding, Ms. Kingfisher. It's very important that you show the photo to anyone who might have seen this man. Your guests, your staff, cleaning crews—anyone on the premises. It could save lives."

She gave a curt nod. "I'll do my best."

"You're slick," Kirby said, as they returned to the car. "Is Belker buying time by running us around Creekville, or is this for real? You thinking there's someone who can verify that he blew his savings on blow, women, the track?"

"My theory after seeing this place?" Preach said, his voice grim. "If this is for real, I don't think he spent the money on himself."

Kirby stopped with a hand on the roof. "You think the killer might have stayed at the shelter. Belker either met him while he was homeless or came here to hire him."

Preach locked eyes with his partner across the roof of the car.

"Why not just tell us?" Kirby asked. "If he wants us to track someone down and then confess, why delay?"

"Why re-enact the crime scenes of famous novels?"

Kirby's hand pressed into the thin layer of dirt on the roof. "As you've said, someone's sending a message."

"Someone who wants to be heard," Preach said.

They returned to the station. As he eyed the cubicles around him, Preach kept thinking about the placement of his desk chair and how brazenly Mac and his thugs were acting. The crime boss always seemed a step ahead of the police.

The more Preach thought about it, the more uncomfortable he grew. The office was too quiet for the middle of a workday. It was starting to feel as if he were caught behind enemy lines.

He thought about it further, and one name kept coming to the forefront, linking everything together. He grabbed a pair of mug shots off his desk, then strode to Kirby's cubicle.

"You ready to go?" Preach asked, keeping his voice low.

"I was born ready, cuz. Say the word."

"I have something important for you."

"You mean us?"

"I mean you." He handed Kirby the mug shots of the two prostitutes captured on camera with Damian. "Think you can find them?"

"I'll beat the bushes till they're flat."

"Find out what they know, and, more importantly, who they've seen. See if there was anyone else who liked to party with Farley and Damian."

"I'm on it. You've got something else lined up?"

"We'll talk later."

Preach felt Kirby's eyes on his back as he walked away. It wasn't his partner that worried him; it was the station itself.

And he didn't want a sharp-eared mole or a listening device informing Elliott Fenton that Preach was about to tail him.

33

Ari's professor's voice seemed muted, her classmates cardboard cutouts of people, the entire tree-lined campus a pale imitation of the real world of murder investigations and monsters in broad daylight and sad-eyed, brooding detectives.

Class ended, and she shuffled down the hall in a daze. Exams were coming up, but she couldn't focus on anything except the case that had turned her life into a thriller novel.

Or was it horror? Real life had a way of blurring genres.

Trevor kept texting her, but she had yet to respond. A waning infatuation was a strange thing, when something fades that you never thought would. It was like the removal of a veil she hadn't even realized had been covering her eyes.

She felt flushed at the memory of her latest encounter with Preach. Desire mingled with fear, and it felt strange, incongruous. Was that all it was with the detective? Passion heightened by the thrill of the chase? The quite literal chase that had her looking over her shoulder and down every hallway, afraid to go home alone, terrified of seeing a man with a scar on his lip and eyes that burned like hot coals?

She left the law school and took a high-traffic path toward the nearest cafeteria. She'd been living on coffee and air.

There was something else about the detective. She sensed something holding him back, not just with her but with life. When she saw him next, she would—*ohmygod*.

A man, standing on the other side of the leaf-strewn quad, in front of a low stone wall. Hunched shoulders, beige overcoat, bowler hat. Too thick to be the man with the scar.

Her stalker. Tracking her in broad daylight.

Ari's stomach jackknifed. She took three steps backward, hands open and shaking, and then stopped.

Class had just let out. There were dozens of people around.

What was he going to do, attack her in front of the entire campus? *Enough.*

She left the paved path and made for the street, walking straight through the quad toward her stalker. One hand grasped her canister of mace, the other dialed 911.

Her stalker watched her approach, arms crossed and face shielded by the hat.

"Emergency 911."

"I need police assistance," Ari said.

She walked faster, wading through the people milling about on the quad, laughing and talking, unaware of the scene unfolding. Cardboard cutouts.

"Ma'am? Where are you? What's going on?"

Ari was halfway across the quad when her stalker slipped over the wall and into a cluster of evergreens. Ari kept moving forward, secure in the crowd.

"Ma'am? Are you okay? Can you speak?"

She lost sight of her tormentor in the foliage. Panting from adrenaline and the rapid walk, Ari strained for a glimpse of the beige overcoat.

There was nothing but green.

She hung up and backed away, her breath returning in long and tattered inhalations. She was struck with the knowledge that none of this was about her. Not really. She was only leverage.

Her stalker had just wanted her to see him. Let her know that he was there. A warning that they were watching her all the time and could get to her anywhere. Even at school.

She also had the sudden certainty that if Preach didn't back down, there wouldn't be many more warnings.

If there were any at all.

34

At four p.m., Preach parked in a small public lot a block away from Elliott Fenton's office. Three hours later, the attorney still hadn't left, leaving Preach simmering in anticipation inside his car.

Earlier, he had fielded a call from a slightly hysterical Ari. Instead of trying to calm her, he escalated her fears about her stalker. He wanted her worried, cautious.

When he asked her to leave town for a while, she said that would kill her semester. He didn't respond, letting her imagination take over. The best thing he could do for her was work harder and faster.

Elliott finally left in a late-model, forest-green Jaguar. Preach let him get almost out of sight before trailing him in the baby-blue Prius he had rented for the stakeout. He couldn't afford to have Elliott make him, and a blue Prius was a common sight in Creekville.

The attorney drove less than a mile before parking in front of the Tar Heel Inn, a mahogany-walled gentlemen's club full of cracked leather and heated debates on college basketball, the best style of barbecue, and the price of flue-cured tobacco. The place had been around since before the cotton gin.

Preach would love to know who Elliott was meeting, but the club was too small to enter unnoticed.

Two hours passed. Night fell cold and hard around him. He wished he was inside the lounge, drinking a single batch bourbon on the rocks and eating a bone-in rib eye as rare as a blue diamond. Instead he was drinking bottled water and staving off his hunger with snack crackers.

Thirty minutes later, Elliott exited alone. He stumbled and then righted himself on the curb. The Jaguar lurched onto the road, and Preach grimaced at the flagrant display of intoxication.

He let it pass. He was hunting for bigger game.

The Jaguar flew past the huge house on Hillsdale that Preach knew was Elliott's home address. A few miles later, the attorney turned into a gated upscale development signposted as the Mediterranean Village.

Elliott stopped at a guard shack and rolled through when the gate opened. Preach took a risk and pulled quickly to the gate, afraid the Jaguar might disappear into a garage. After the guard eyed his badge and shooed him through, Preach asked, "Any idea where that Jag's headed?"

The guard hesitated and then lowered his eyes in deference to greater authority. "Try the second left, last house on the right. You didn't hear it from me."

Preach gave a curt nod. "Thanks."

Inside the development, stucco mansions hunched side by side on treeless lots, like ogres squatting on lily pads. Wide curving streets, rotundas, and backlit stone fountains in the front yards.

It was exactly like the Mediterranean, Preach mused, minus the landscaping, architectural restraint, culture, and good taste.

He followed the guard's directions and saw the door of a triple-car garage closing on the Jag. The garage belonged to a particularly garish house, a turquoise Italianate with a barrel-tile roof and French balconies that looked tacked on. Preach returned to the guard shack and parked in a visitor spot, then took his gun and binoculars and backtracked to the house on foot.

Thankfully, whoever lived there didn't keep a dog outside, and believed in foliage. After checking for watchful eyes, Preach hopped the wooden fence and slunk into the jungly depths of a young magnolia.

No sign of movement on the first story. No lights, either. That told him this was a social visit, probably a romantic rendezvous.

A light winked on in the second story, then went out again. Preach climbed until he had a better view. Braced himself on a limb as he swung the binoculars around.

Shadows of bodies entwined on a bed. The two figures grasped and clutched, and then Elliott's face became visible through the window.

He was behind someone, one hand pressed into a mass of long blond hair, the other clutching a slender waist.

Seconds later they were finished. After lying on their backs for a spell, the woman rolled over and flicked on a light, revealing aging but attractive features, and lips that were still slack with pleasure, a far cry from the rigid expression Preach had noticed the last time he had seen her.

Her name was Rebecca Worthington, and she was married with two children.

She was also the mayor of Creekville.

After an unsuccessful afternoon rousting junkies and petty thieves, Kirby decided to talk to a bartender—always a great source of information—at the Striped Coyote, a local vegan bar. Organic beer, organic fruits and vegetables, organic tablecloths.

Which Kirby was all about. The body was a temple, and he was down with keeping it free of chemicals manufactured in some lab in New Jersey.

Unfortunately, eating the way God intended had a price, and it was about triple that of the local Food Lion. So Kirby did the best he could.

He slid onto a stool at the bar. A tall, slim bartender with almond-colored eyes ambled over. She was pale, her long brown hair tied back in a bandanna imprinted with the Jamaican flag.

"A little early for you, isn't it?" she asked in a British accent. "Or did you pop in for a veggie shake?"

Her name was Maggie, and she was one of a recent influx of European wanderers and artists who had come to Creekville because they couldn't afford to live in Brooklyn or Santa Cruz. Kirby knew she sold handmade puppets at the Farmer's Market, and hung with the drifter crowd. He was hoping she had run across Tram and Kim.

Kirby placed mug shots of the two prostitutes photographed

with Damian Black on the bar. "I'm on duty." He flashed a grin. "Plainclothes."

Her eyebrows rose. "Look at you."

"Yeah, right? You can still make me a veggie shake. Hey, and take a look at these photos. You seen these two around? Kim and Tram Vu, brother and sister team?"

She stopped wiping her hands on a towel. "You never bring work in here." Her eyes flicked to her other customers before glancing down at the photos. "What's in it for me? If I've seen them."

"The best karma ever. Bob Marley level. A karmic orgasm."

She gave him a wry smirk and left to serve her other customers. Kirby tapped his foot on the bar stool, trying to expel his nervous energy. He wanted to show Preach he had something to add.

That, and his guilt was eating him like a cancer.

Maggie returned five minutes later with Kirby's veggie shake. He slid her a twenty. She looked down at it. "You'll tell your rich hookups to buy my art?"

"Every single one."

She wiped her hands on the towel again. "This didn't come from me."

"I swear," he said, sincerity and charm rolled up in his smile like a pita wrap of trust.

She lowered her voice. "You know a Cuban guy named Donnie? Short, built like a bull, always wears those poncey tank tops? He comes in now and again. I think he works out at the gym."

There was only one commercial gym in town, the same one Kirby used. The Fitness Zone. Kirby got a mental image of a short, swarthy, cocksure guy in his twenties, with thick arms and a square face, preening around the gym. Kirby had seen him around, usually in the evening. "I know him."

"He comes in at night and takes up a booth in his girlfriend's section."

"He's straight?" Kirby asked, surprised.

She shrugged. "I only said he had a girlfriend."

Kirby tapped one of the photos with a finger. "You think he knows where to find these two?"

"I assume so. He's their pimp."

Later that day, Kirby pumped out another set of biceps curls at the Fitness Zone. He had already ridden ten miles on the stationary bike, and he figured he might as well get a workout in while he waited.

Just as he was beginning to wonder if today was Donnie's rest day, he walked through the door flanked by two women who resembled steroid-infused power lifters from behind the Iron Curtain. The Amazons had on tie-dye Lycra workout gear, and Donnie came as advertised: five foot five, stomping in like a buffalo, George Michael stubble, rocking a Rainbow Brite tank top over black sweats.

Kirby waited until they were warming up at one of the bench-press stations, then walked over. The rest of the benches were occupied. "Mind if I work in?"

The two women glared at him. Donnie grunted as he slid onto the bench. His swollen muscles looked cartoonish. "Yeah. We do."

Is this guy for real? Kirby thought. *He's living in an Eighties movie.* "It's a free gym."

"So?"

"So I'd like to work in."

Donnie clapped his hands and then rubbed them together as if trying to start a fire. "The three of us, we go one at a time. Bam bam bam. No time to rest." He took a few quick breaths, pushed the bar off the rack and knocked out ten reps.

As soon as he stood, one of the women pushed past Kirby and lowered herself onto the bench.

Kirby slid his badge out of his pocket. "I was trying to be polite."

Donnie eyed the badge, then put his palms up. "So what you want?"

Kirby showed him the two mug shots. "I need to talk with these two. I'm not looking to bust them—or you. Just a little chat."

Donnie put his hands on his hips, his chest puffing out like rising dough. "Oh yeah? Bust me for what?"

Kirby scrambled to think of something to say. The two women were smirking at him. "Listen, I thought we could talk, man to man, without taking this somewhere less pleasant. You feel me?"

Donnie's eyes lowered, and he seemed to deflate. "Okay, okay." He flung a wrist at the bench. "Let me finish my set. Give me a spot?"

"Sure."

Donnie stretched his shoulders, and Kirby stepped behind the bench. Donnie positioned himself under the bar and took a series of short quick breaths to get ready. As Kirby bent over to help with the lift, he realized one of the women was missing. He whipped his head around and saw her hustling someone in a gray hoodie out of the gym.

Kirby cursed, grabbed his sweatshirt, and sprinted for the door.

35

Kirby caught a glimpse of a gray hoodie disappearing into a tract of woods on the other side of the gym parking lot. He dashed after the figure, beeping his car door and stopping only to yank out his gun.

Dusk had fallen. Shadows rippled through the trees as spindly vines and branches whipped into Kirby's face. After a hundred yards, the forest spilled into the rear of an apartment complex.

A flash of gray slipped around a corner. Kirby followed, gun raised, stepping over a pile of trash overflowing from a pair of dumpsters. He gave chase through the center of the complex, sprinting past pickup trucks and aging imports, praying his quarry had not ducked into one of the apartments.

Heads turned as he ran, wary eyes tracking his movements. A young black man sprinting through a working-class apartment complex with a gun? Someone was probably calling the cops on *him*.

Kirby could call for backup, but that would mean handcuffs, police cars, a trip downtown.

Preach wanted answers, not more red tape.

At the end of the apartment complex, Kirby spotted the gray hoodie fleeing down a narrow country lane. He assumed he was chasing Kim Vu, but whoever it was, he was fast.

Vines poked out of scraggly bushes and stretched onto the road like sleeping snakes. Trailers and ramshackle houses dotted the sides of the blacktop, cars and toys littered the lawns. This was the poor side of Creekville, and it only got worse.

A pit bull barked and lunged for him. Kirby shouted as he jumped into the middle of the road. The dog was frothing at the mouth, trying to pull its tether out of the ground. Kirby swallowed and kept running. The gray hoodie had turned at the sound of the dog, then fled down a gravel road.

Kirby topped a small knoll, sprinted down a steep incline, turned right on an even narrower gravel road. He slowed as the road dead-ended at a low-lying cul-de-sac surrounded by an unruly mass of weeds, sickly oaks, and overgrown bushes. Interspersed among the vegetation was a loose circle of shacks made from cement blocks and topped by corrugated iron. Rusting vehicles were parked haphazardly in the weeds.

The cul-de-sac had the stink of sewage water. Kirby scanned the shacks and saw broken windows, moss-covered woodpiles, and broken furniture lying in the grass.

The cul-de-sac was eerily quiet. He peered around in vain for a glimpse of the gray hoodie. The only sign of life was a young child poking at a bird's nest with a skateboard that had lost its wheels. The light had almost failed, but Kirby could see far enough down the gravel road to know that no one was on it.

His quarry was here somewhere. Hiding.

Kirby gave the shacks a nervous glance. He had his badge, and could go door to door if needed, but he doubted it would help. It could even be dangerous, if the runner had holed up with someone familiar.

Kirby stood with his hands clenched, debating what to do. He glanced at the little boy, who had stopped poking at the nest and was staring at a rotting barn tucked between a dying oak and a thicket of bamboo. Bag worms hung grotesquely from the desiccated branches of the oak.

Why was the kid staring at that barn?

Kirby decided to report his location, in case something went south. By the time he finished his call, the kid had run into one of the shacks. Kirby raised his gun and waded through knee-high grass toward the barn, his head on a swivel.

The barn door was half off its hinges. A crow cawed, causing him to jump. This was the diciest thing he had done as a cop. Hands down.

He berated himself for his cowardice. Preach would already be inside that barn.

Preach might also be on his knees, retching at the memory of whatever he had seen in that tree house in Atlanta.

The door creaked as Kirby pulled it open. Huddled against the back of the barn was a boy in his late teens, wearing gray track pants and a matching hoodie. A quick glance revealed mildewing bales of hay and spider webs feathering the eaves, grimy with trapped debris.

Kim Vu—Kirby recognized him from the mug shot—had the dark hair and smooth features of a teen model, though his eyes were harder and shrewder than any kid on a billboard.

He was staring at Kirby with a sullen expression. The teen's slender, effeminate hands were empty. Kirby breathed an internal sigh of relief.

"It's okay," Kirby said, dialing up a smile as he lowered his gun. "I'm a pol—"

A starburst of pain exploded in Kirby's head. He dropped the gun and reeled, dimly aware of the sound of shattered glass, trying to stay on his feet. Something wet and sticky ran down his neck.

A voice, a female voice, shrieked in a foreign tongue as Kirby toppled backward. His vision was blurry, but he saw Kim racing toward the barn door, leaping into the air to clear Kirby's prone form.

Kirby mustered the strength to snare an ankle, jerking Kim on top of him. The impact hurt like hell. Someone kicked Kirby in the ribs. A girl. Tram. The sister.

Kim went for the gun, but Kirby punched him in the side and ripped it out of his grasp. Kirby's vision started to clear as the girl came at with him a pitchfork. It grazed him as he twisted to the side, ripping his shirt. The lunge overextended her, and he rushed forward, tackling her before she could regain her balance. He twisted her arm behind her back and pointed the gun at Kim. He didn't want to hurt either one of them, but the situation was spiraling.

He nudged the gun toward the rear of the barn. "Back there," he yelled at Kim. "*Now.*"

Kim didn't move, and Kirby wrenched the sister's arm higher up her back. Tram yelped, and Kim limped backward to the rear of the barn, hands holding his stomach, eyes spilling hate.

"I just want to talk," Kirby said. Moving carefully, he used his gun hand to lift his sweatshirt and reveal the badge clipped to his belt.

Kim gave a high-pitched laugh. "Cop just want to talk. Right. So what you want, a freebie sandwich?"

"You think I chased you all this way for a lay? I'm looking for information."

"We don't know nothing. And we don't snitch."

Kirby softened his expression and stepped to the side, still holding Tram. "My bad, then. There's the door. You can go ahead and leave."

Kim took a step toward his sister, eyes mistrustful. Kirby put a hand out. "I said *you're* free to go. Your sister, she just assaulted a police officer with a deadly weapon."

Kim stopped moving.

"You know how quickly she'll move through the system for that?" Kirby said. "I'd have to look it up, but I'd say that goes for ten, maybe fifteen years."

Tram squirmed. Kirby held her tight. "I'll pretend I never caught you," he said. "I won't say a word about this, and Donnie will never know. Neither will Mac Dobbins."

Kim's coffee-colored face paled at the mention of Mac's name. "You think people haven't seen us? You one stupid cop."

"I need to talk to you about Damian Black and Farley Robertson. That's it. I don't care about anything else."

Kim looked around the barn, searching for a way out. He locked eyes with his sister, and some telepathic message seemed to pass between them. After balling his fists, he slumped to the ground, his back against the wall. "You give us money for bus ticket out of town. I tired of this place anyway. This place crazier than Hanoi." He turned to his sister, said something in Vietnamese, and she nodded. He turned back to Kirby and held out his hand.

Kirby took out his wallet and gave him fifty-five dollars. It was all he had. *This better be worth it*, he thought.

"Did Donnie send you to Damian's house?" Kirby asked.

Kim nodded.

"How many times?"

The teen inclined his head toward his sister. "At first it just her. Then he find out about me and pay to watch us together. Then he pay to join."

Kirby struggled to contain his revulsion. "Where was this? At Damian's house?"

"Yeah. In that weird basement."

"What about Farley Robertson? Was he there from the beginning?"

Kim shook his head. "He come later. First for videos, then for me. My sister not his type."

Kirby gritted his teeth. "Did Farley and Damian . . . did they ever participate together?"

"Sure. But never with each other. Side by side, sometimes."

"Was there ever anyone else?"

Kim thought for a moment. "A few times. Another man. I don't know his name."

"How did you know Damian's and Farley's names?"

"Farley owns bookstore. I buy books to practice English. And Damian, he famous."

"This other man, was he balding? Tall, thin face, probably arrived in a good suit?"

"That sound right."

Kirby pulled up Elliott Fenton's website on his phone, stomach churning as he enlarged a photo of the attorney and showed it to the siblings.

Kim stepped closer, and Kirby kept a firm lock on Tram's elbow. "That him," Kim said, and then chortled. "An attorney? How come he no pay us better?"

"Were there ever any other prostitutes involved?"

"Sure. He have reputation on the street. An *appetite*."

"Who? Farley?"

"Damian."

Kirby started. "What do you mean, an appetite? Were there minors involved?"

"Why not? People like him, they always need different. I know he love sushi."

"Sushi? What's that?"

"People who don't hook but need the money. Amateurs. One-timers. Fresh fish."

Kirby's opinion of the deceased was sinking lower and lower. "When was the last time you were with them?"

"Damian?" Kim said. "Maybe a week before he die."

"What about Farley and Elliott?"

Kim pondered the question again. "Been some time."

Alarm bells started ringing in Kirby's head. "Were all three of them together the last time you saw Farley or Elliott? About six weeks ago?"

"That sound right."

Kirby swallowed and tried to think of other angles. "Have you heard anything on the street about who might have killed Damian or Farley?"

"That your job, not mine."

"It's your sister's future," Kirby said grimly, "not mine."

Kim's expression turned sullen, warping the silky contours of his face. "We answer your questions. Let us go."

"Look at me, Kim." Kirby waited until he was looking him in the eye. Tram squirmed again, and he gripped her elbow harder. "What's the word on the street? Who took them out? J. T. Belker? Mac? Who?"

"The only word on the street is that cops asking too many questions, and Mac not happy." He pointed at Kirby. "The word is that you next."

36

Preach woke to a stiff neck from sleeping in his car. Officer Haskins had agreed to watch Ari's apartment until two a.m., and Preach spelled him around midnight, right after leaving the mayor's house. Elliott had still been inside when Preach left, but he didn't want to risk being seen. Ari's lights were turned off when he arrived, and he had fallen asleep with his hand on his gun.

Silvery predawn light slunk through the windshield. He debated waking Ari and decided against it. She needed to rest. Instead he drove to Jimmy's Corner Store as the case churned through the fog in his brain.

Elliott and Damian and Farley, friends since high school.

Elliott at Damian's house the night before the murder. A murder that was committed by someone who most likely knew the victim.

Elliott's connections to Wade and Mac Dobbins. Elliott sleeping with the mayor, protected at the highest levels.

Elliott, Elliott, Elliott.

Sipping a coffee, he drove down Main Street, passing the station. His aunt had agreed to see him early, before the day began. It was his fifth session, and she said she was close to making a decision.

His stomach fluttered thinking about which way she might go.

After greeting her, Preach asked his aunt about the Byronic Wilderness Society. She barely remembered it and gave him the names of a few teachers who had been more clued in to the social scene, Preach thanked her and then hesitated. "Once this case calms down, I'd like to get you and mom together for dinner. I'll host."

His aunt gave him a sad smile, and then surprised him by nodding.

"You will?" he said.

"If Virginia agrees."

She squeezed his hand, then resumed her professional demeanor as they entered the therapy room. As always, the abruptness of the change unsettled him.

"It's time to talk about Atlanta," she said, after they sat.

A knot of tension formed in Preach's stomach. He had known the time would come and that he wouldn't be prepared. When he shifted, the movement felt wooden.

"During your time as a homicide detective, before your last case in Atlanta, did you have any other incidents? Even minor ones?"

"No. Nothing."

"Why do you think that was?"

"I don't know why it triggers, unless it's a buildup of emotion that has to release. Or when something happens that..." he trailed off, unsure how to finish.

"It's so terrible your mind can't accept it?" she offered. "Was it something you hadn't dealt with before?"

"I saw plenty of terrible things in Atlanta. Daily."

"As bad as the incident at the prison?"

"Maybe not," he mumbled. "But close."

"Were you afraid it would happen again, as a police officer?"

"Of course I was. And it did."

"But not for a long time. Almost a decade."

Preach lifted his palms. There was nothing much to say.

"You're a brave man for facing your issues head on, in the line of duty."

"Was it brave? Or selfish and stupid?"

She looked confused, and he gave her a grim smile. "You don't know the details of the case."

"I was going to ask you to tell me, when you were ready."

He looked down. He had never admitted his lack of ability to discuss that day, not to anyone but himself.

Whenever his mind edged closer to the events of that night, his thoughts got fuzzy and it felt hard to draw a breath. Yet he knew the memory was there, hiding inside him like some crouching gargoyle.

What if he let the memories in and he had another breakdown in front of his aunt? She would be forced to turn in a negative report. He would probably lose his job.

"Joe?" she asked, as carefully as if trimming a bonsai tree. "Can we talk about the tree house?"

When she said those two words, *tree house*, the tension in his body hardened into a point, a dagger of repressed memory.

Her voice softened, a warm compress settling over the pain. "Why don't we work our way there?"

He blew out a breath. "Sure."

"What can you tell me about the case?"

"I had never dealt with a child murderer before. At first, we thought it was just one body, a missing runaway we found at the bottom of a pond. Then we found three more in a field nearby and realized we could have a serial killer on our hands."

"The children had been molested?"

His jaw tightened. "Yes."

"And how did that knowledge affect you?"

"How do you think?" he snapped. "It's the worst crime of all. The betrayal of innocence. An abomination of what it means to be human."

"But you were able to carry on."

He fidgeted in his chair. "When I read the coroner's reports on the bodies, I had a rough night. Lots of soul searching. But not an episode. I thought the worst was over. Maybe I should have backed off, but it would have been extremely awkward to explain to my captain. And also, I don't mean to be arrogant . . . but I was good. Very good."

"*Are* very good," she said.

He waved a hand. He wasn't so sure about that. "I wanted the bastard caught. Put in a hole. And I knew I was the one with the best chance of doing it."

"What happened next?"

"I found him," he said simply. "A local schoolteacher. Third grade. The year before, he had won a teaching award. His MO was following kids around homeless shelters at night, then luring them into his car."

"How did you find him?"

"I discovered a pattern in the victims, a certain type, and I interviewed street kids all over Atlanta. Eventually I found one who had seen a suspicious man prowling the streets near one of the shelters. The kid was able to give a description. Another confirmed it, said the same man had tried to lure him into his car. I won't bore you with the details, but I found the guy in the system, a convicted pedophile from California who had changed his identity and gotten a job as a school teacher."

His aunt's eyes briefly lowered.

"Yeah. Exactly. It was two a.m. the night I made the connection. I couldn't bear to wait another second. I called my partner and told him to meet me at the address, but he was groggy and lived thirty minutes away. I grabbed a random patrolman and went to the teacher's house. I left the patrolman to guard the door and, on a hunch, explored the property. Pedophiles who kidnap victims often keep them in a basement or a separate structure. In the backyard I found a path leading into a tract of woods. A hundred feet inside I found . . ."

He trailed off, and when he failed to continue his aunt laid a hand on his arm. "Don't do it for the job, do it for you. Or it will weigh you down forever."

Preach's tongue felt coated in glue. He took a long drink of water, then kept swallowing until his tongue didn't feel so thick.

Maybe his aunt was right, and maybe she wasn't. He had to try something, because he knew what the memories were doing to him. He knew their vicious power.

"I found a . . . tree house . . . that looked like something out of a fairytale. A miniature castle painted in bright colors, with gingerbread trim and plastic candy canes all around it. Any child in the world would have loved it." He paused to collect himself again. "The tree house was completely hidden. There was a kid in there, I could feel it. And that child wasn't staying in there for one more second. I called for backup, radioed the patrolman to keep an eye on both the house and the back-yard, then climbed the ladder and tried the door." He cradled his glass of water as he croaked out the words. The memories were an oncoming train and he was tied to the tracks. "There was a deadbolt. I had to use my shoulder. I remember feeling enraged but calm enough to do my job. I was a professional. I opened the door and—"

A mental image overcame him, a flash of remembrance previously buried in his mind. The memory came as swift and sure as the snap of a lion's jaws.

Shelves stuffed with children's books and jars of candy. A bean bag on the floor. Dolls and action figures. The limbs of stuffed animals poking out of toy chests. Walls painted with colorful jungle murals. Two windows in the ceiling, duct taped and reinforced with iron bars.

And in the center of the room, a young boy.

God, no.

Naked and gagged. Handcuffed to a red-and-white striped pole, like the ones at the old-time barber's shops.

Wh—what is this? What. Is. This.

Preach stilled. Couldn't seem to make himself move. Though he had read the coroner's reports and seen the aftereffects of child abuse before, nothing had prepared him for this child, nine or ten at most, covered in bruises and whimpering as he looked at Preach with the eyes of a cornered animal, a human animal, a little boy, one whose lost inno-cence and terror washed over Preach like he was standing at the bottom of Niagara Falls, millions of tons of water cascading down on top of him. Drowning him in the boy's eyes.

Those eyes, he thought. They were at the root of his blocked mem-ories. *Those eyes those eyes those eyes.*

Preach felt his entire body start to convulse, now back in the present, shaking with rage and loathing at the world. He groaned as his gaze moved to the window, and then to the painting of the girl with the ibises, somewhere, anywhere to escape the memories of that night. A deep, shuddering breath rolled through him. He tried to stand and felt dizzy.

"You're almost there," his aunt said softly.

His heart was pounding so hard it scared him, and his balance felt off, as if the room was tilted at an impossible angle. He felt for his chair with the jerky movements of a marionette.

"When I saw the boy," he said finally, pushing through tar for the words, "when I looked in his eyes and saw what was inside, the pain and brokenness, I froze."

"What do you mean?"

"I . . . for a split second, I couldn't move. Couldn't breathe, couldn't do anything. I heard sirens and knew that backup had arrived, but the only thing I remember was feeling a crushing pain in the side of my head. The next thing I knew I was in the hospital."

After a moment she said, "Anyone could have frozen under those circumstances."

He slowly shook his head. "Not a cop. Not a good one."

"The killer hit you?"

"With an aluminum bat."

"Thank God he didn't kill you," she said.

"He did something worse."

She drew back in confusion. "Worse?"

"He got away."

37

Preach drove away from his aunt's office with both hands loosely holding the wheel. He felt empty, drained of emotion.

After the session, Aunt Janice had hugged him tight but said nothing about the outcome. He no longer cared. He did not *deserve* to care.

By the time backup had reached the tree house, the Candyland Killer was nowhere to be seen. The teacher had kept a dirt bike stashed nearby, and a search uncovered a maze of paths that wound through the forest behind the house and came out miles away, on a nest of different roads.

They had put out APBs, used dogs and helicopters and roadblocks, called the airports and bus stations. None of it mattered. Defying the odds, their quarry had disappeared into the night.

Gone. Thrown back into the world, a shark released into a pool full of guppies. Free to find a new home and repeat his unspeakable actions.

And for that, Preach would never forgive himself.

He had done what he could, given the chase everything he had, but after a few weeks passed without a trace, they had known it was futile. It was too easy to hide in this country.

Preach had told the truth during his debrief. Admitted he had frozen. He wasn't about to compound his terrible failure with a lie.

Choking under pressure was not necessarily a firing offense but, because of the high profile nature of the case, the department needed a scapegoat. After the suspension, there were only two reasons Preach had allowed himself to consider working as a police officer again, risking the chance of a repeat performance.

The first was because there was still good for him to do in the world. Perhaps not enough for his own atonement, but enough to make a difference in someone else's life.

The second was because he thought he had seen the worst humanity had to offer—the ultimate suffering of a child—and didn't know what else could catch him off guard.

He felt numb by the time he parked at the station. An unusually large number of newspeople had accumulated outside, stirring with restless energy. It was early; had something happened?

He checked the local news on his phone and grew cold when he saw the headline.

Breaking News: Lead Detective on Literary Killer Case
Seeing Local Psychologist.

He parked the car. His skin turned from cold to warm, and then flushed with heat, as he made his way through the phalanx of reporters. Their voices rose in a desperate crescendo, inquiring if he had mental problems, questioning his ability to work the case, begging for a sound bite.

Preach walked through them in a daze, numb by the time he entered the station. What did it matter, anyway? Let them discover what had happened. Let them know.

Conversations ceased when he entered the station. Coffee cups remained poised in midair, and dozens of eyes flicked to the side at once, as if following instructions from a conductor. He walked straight to the chief's office.

She folded her hands atop the desk. "I'm sorry."

"How long do I have?"

"The mayor's already giving me heat. I can buy you a few days, but..."

"What?"

"I'm worried that if you stay on and things go south on another high-profile case, it might be worse for your career than stepping aside. Joe ... you might not find another job."

He stared at her. "And who would work it, if I bowed out?"

"Kirby, until the mayor brings someone in."

"He's not ready."

She spread her hands. "At a minimum, you need a positive report from your therapist. ASAP."

He didn't answer, and she said, "Can I give you the name of my naturopath? You're carrying a lot of weight right now."

"I'm fine."

"I just don't understand how they found out," the chief said.

Preach remembered the misplaced desk chair and thought about the calendar on his desktop. The appointments with his aunt were clearly marked.

He understood just fine. And he told her.

Her eyes narrowed. "This stays between us. Until we know more."

He nodded. "I learned something last night you need to know about."

A knock came at the door. Preach turned; it was Kirby. The chief caught Preach's eye, and he gave a quick nod. She waved in the junior officer. Preach told them about Elliott and the mayor, and Kirby whistled.

"I don't know if this means anything," the chief said, shaking her head, "but we keep it to ourselves for now." She turned to Preach. "Let's hope there were no security cameras on the property."

"There weren't."

It was Kirby's turn to talk, and Preach could tell his partner was leaving out a few details about his discussion with Tram and Kim Vu. That was okay. Such things were never clean.

"Good work," Preach said, causing Kirby's eyes to spark with pride.

"Damian's toxicology came back positive for Rohypnol," the chief said. "So did the dogs', just like you guessed. There's something else. You haven't logged in yet, have you? Damian's bank records came in, and the withdrawals only added up to half the amount in Farley's office. Fifteen grand."

"Maybe he has cash in the house," Kirby said. "He's rich."

"Then why withdraw any at all?" the chief asked. "And for exactly half the amount?"

The facts of the case popped like quarks in Preach's head, jumping in and out of neural pathways, making connections. He leaned forward, locking eyes with the chief. "Farley was blackmailing Damian and Elliott both," he said softly. "He got addicted and turned on his friends."

He was not surprised. He had seen fathers betray their sons when craving a hit, mothers watch their children go hungry. "What do you bet we find photos of Elliott and the mayor in whatever lockbox Farley's key opens?" He crossed his arms, the wheels still spinning. "Maybe Elliott and Damian hired Mac to get rid of Farley, to stop the blackmail. It would explain why Mac doesn't want us digging."

"Why take out the author?" the chief asked.

"Damian was getting nervous," Preach said. "I saw it in his eyes. He was terrified of going to jail and ruining his reputation."

"You think Elliott had a hand in his death?"

"I doubt it. But you never know."

The chief frowned and reached for her stress ball. Her red hair sat heavily on the collar of her blouse. "Belker? The novels?"

"A frame," Preach said. "Or a subcontract."

"What if the mayor knows, too?" Kirby asked, his words soaked with excitement.

"It could explain why she's so hot to crucify Belker," Preach said.

"What's his status?"

"His pill box was full of Oxycodone. We can hold him on prescription charges alone."

Chief Higgins tapped a slender finger on her desk as the phone rang. She looked down. "Terry," she said, then put the phone on speaker. "This better be important."

"I just took a call from dispatch." Officer Haskins's voice was raw with nervous energy. "There's another body."

The tension in the room was a tangible thing. Preach could feel it buzzing in the air, thrumming in his bones. Kirby put his elbows on his knees and pressed his hands together.

The chief picked up the phone, listened to the details, and slowly replaced the receiver. Preach and Kirby exchanged an uneasy glance just before she told them the name of the deceased.

Elliott Fenton.

38

"How did he die?" Preach asked the forensics expert as soon as he and Kirby arrived at Elliott's renovated Craftsman bungalow.

He hated the tension in his own voice. He had watched Elliott through a window just a few hours ago. Did Rebecca Worthington have something to do with this? Or had Elliott returned home late, drunk and off his guard, to find a murderer in his home?

The forensics expert was compact, Latina, brainy. Dark bangs cupped a cherubic face. Her name was Lela Jimenez, and she and Dax worked opposite shifts. "We'll do a toxicology report," she said, "but my guess is poison."

She led the officers through a side gate and into a park-like backyard. Elliott's corpse was lying on a clipped circle of lawn next to an oval pool situated between the main house and a guest cottage. Beside the body was a lounge chair and a glass table.

The air reeked of bile, and Preach noticed a dried heap of vomit a few feet from the corpse. On the side table was a beer bottle with the label torn off, and an empty draught glass.

Preach leaned over the body. Elliott was sprawled facedown, fingers clutching the ground like talons. No ligature marks on the neck, which meant strangulation was unlikely. "Why poison?" Preach asked. "Besides the glass and the vomit?"

"The bloodshot eyes and the bite marks on the tongue," Lela said.

Kirby looked slightly queasy. "Could he have overdosed on something?"

Lela shrugged. "Of course."

Preach rose. "How long will the toxicology take?"

"Days, maybe a week. Depends on the backlog in Chapel Hill."

"Expedite it."

Preach took pictures on his phone and then combed the house, which was a larger version of Elliott's office in town. Law books, law papers, law journals, law coffee mugs. A sizeable fiction collection, mostly Southern literature and signed copies of Damian's books. There was an unusual number of condoms in the bathroom closet, and a giant stack of German pornography, but no underage photos or other incriminating evidence.

Which was no surprise. Elliott had been a careful man, an attorney who would know what to hide in case of a search.

There were no signs of forced entry. Preach found an intact security system, a loaded gun in Elliott's bedroom, and a second handgun on the kitchen table. Had Elliott known something? Was he expecting trouble?

In a bedroom drawer, they discovered a small, unmarked, empty glass bottle that smelled vaguely of flowers. It was probably nothing, but Preach found it odd. He dropped it in an evidence bag.

The detached cottage was a dumping ground for golf clubs and fishing poles. Preach and Kirby walked the maze of garden paths and found a small pile of broken glass, shattered as if by a heel. Again, it seemed strange. Incongruous.

Purposeful.

"Maybe a pair of glasses?" Kirby suggested.

Preach stared at the shards on the ground. "Maybe."

They pointed out the pile of glass to evidence. News vans started arriving, clawing for information. When the reporters saw Preach on the other side of the yellow tape, they reacted like kids on sugar.

"You think it's another book murder?" Kirby asked. He was watching the reporters with hooded eyes, wary of their presence. More like a real cop, Preach thought.

"I don't know. But I'm going to find out. Why don't you talk to the neighbors, finish up here?"

Kirby preened. "Sure thing. You going to see another literature expert?" he asked, as Preach ducked away.

"Yeah."

Half an hour later, Preach knelt in a grassy strip between two graves. The pressure of the case and the reporters, this moment he didn't have time to take, pressed down on him with the weight of a collapsed mine.

To his left was his father's headstone. His mother had fought hard for cremation, but Preach had insisted on burying his father in his family's Creekville plot, which was attached to a hundred-year-old Baptist church. He wanted to be able to visit his father. He wanted him part of the earth, in a place of God.

To his right was Ricky. Even before the burn, Ricky's life had been hard. He was pimply and obese, struggled in school, had never fit in with the world. He loved his Mustang and his infamous blond relative, who had always been his protector. Ricky would have walked into a volcano for his cousin Joey.

Preach put one hand on the ground, another to his forehead. He had to decide whether to continue the investigation or step aside, and he was going to do it right now, right here. Between these two.

Ricky's internal organs had failed a week after the burn. Preach didn't attend the funeral, and it had caused quite a stir. His parents were furious. Everyone assumed he had regressed, but the truth was that he couldn't face his emotions. Not in public. He had gone alone to the lake and wept his body dry.

Then he graduated, left town, and never looked back.

He knew he had very little chance of solving the murders within the next few days. And that if someone else died on his watch, or if he was forcibly removed, then the chief was right. He was finished.

After paying his respects, he blew out a deep breath and rose. A grim smile parted his lips; he knew he had come to the right place. His father had brought him into this insane world, to this random speck on the map Preach called home, and his cousin's death had flung him away, into the great big world.

Preach's job was to protect and serve, not step aside and leave a junior officer to the wolves. But it was more than that. He wasn't here for the chief, for Kirby, or even himself.

He was here for the potential victims. For Ari. For the people living in fear in the town of Creekville.

He had run away once before, from this town and from himself.

He wasn't doing it again. Not while he still had a choice.

Preach strode into the bookstore. Customers gawked as he stood at the front door, scanning the crowd until he spotted Ari talking to a customer. She was wearing a white V-neck shirt with a teal and orange headscarf. Eyes red and shadowed.

When she saw him, she broke off the conversation and rushed over to him, her black leather boots clicking on the wood.

"I need you," he said, pushing away his attraction for her. "Right now."

She swallowed. "Where are we going?"

"Nowhere. I need your mind."

Ari turned to Nate, who was manning the register. "I'll be in the back for a while."

Nate's dreadlocks bobbed as he swiveled to take in the line at the counter, the mass of customers roaming the stacks. "Uh, how long?"

"*Nate.*"

He lowered his eyes with the deference of a still-hopeful suitor. Ari led Preach to Farley's office, and he closed the door.

She nervously twisted her thumb ring. "I saw the news. About Elliott Fenton and—" she bit her lip "—about you."

"Then you understand how serious it is that this conversation stays between us."

She nodded.

He showed her the crime scene photos. "Can you help?"

She bent over the images. "I don't recognize anything offhand," she said slowly, and Preach sagged. He'd have to try to find another professor, but that would take time he didn't have. And he didn't even know where to start.

She hugged her arms. "If this is a novel, even if it's a poisoning, there could be hundreds of similar passages. Thousands."

Preach looked away. He knew that already; he was hoping for a miracle.

She went to the computer and researched the elements of the crime on Google. He had already done that, but he watched her scan the results, hoping she would uncover something new.

Five minutes passed, and then ten.

Nothing.

He clenched his fists. It felt as if he had made no progress in the case. How many more bodies would there be?

"What if Elliott's death was unrelated to the other two?" she asked in a small voice. "A suicide or a natural cause? Or what if it's related and there's no novel this time? What if the first two were red herrings?"

Preach didn't need to think about his response, because he was no longer dealing with logic. He was dealing with instinct. "There's a book involved. Bank on it."

"I'll start researching right away, if you want," she said.

He felt the relief manifest on his face. "Thank you," he said, already moving to leave. "As soon you find something, even a suspicion, let me know."

"I will."

He paused at the door. He couldn't leave her alone anymore. Not after three murders, not after the pot he was about to stir. "I'll send a car for you tonight, or come myself. Okay?"

She looked as if she was going to protest, then gave a reluctant nod. Despite her attempt to hide it, her eyes crawled with fear.

Preach raced downtown at the tail end of rush hour, all too aware of the lateness of the hour. The traffic and streetlamps were a blur, a tunnel of muted colors and sounds.

Think.

Belker was incarcerated at the time of Elliott's murder. The author could have paid someone beforehand to kill Elliott—but why? As far as Preach could tell, there was no motive. One theory: Mac had killed all three, using Belker as a hired gun on the first two and then deciding to silence Elliott as well. Close the loop.

Preach needed the toxicology report. He needed for Ari to be brilliant. Until then, there had to be a way to shake things up.

He stopped at a red light. It jogged something in his memory, something he had read about pattern recognition. How it was an evolutionary advantage.

Three people murdered in a matter of days. All friends, or at least former friends. Good friends. *Childhood* friends.

Terry had gotten his hands on copies of the school paper and a Creekville High yearbook, from the victims' senior year. Nothing he had read had given Preach pause. As his mother had said, a sophomore named Deirdre Hollings had committed suicide, and one of the younger teachers had died from a heart attack. But none of the players in the present, besides the three deceased friends, appeared anywhere in the past.

While Preach didn't understand Mac's or Belker's involvement, the pattern of victims was clear.

Explore the ties that bind. Find the link.

The rainbow flag hanging over Town Hall came into view, flapping in the breeze like the plumage of some exotic bird.

It was time to confront the mayor.

Preach's cell rang. It was Terry. Preach took the call.

Officer Haskins told him that he had found someone, a retired

English teacher named Elvis Klein, who remembered the Byronic Wilderness Society. Preach remembered him from his own days at Creekville High: tall, broad shoulders, kept his long hair in a ponytail. He was gruff and a little weird, but likable. Ran the drama club and the chess club.

Good. Klein had left his number, and Preach would try him tonight, after he talked to the mayor. If the former teacher didn't pan out, he would try the names his aunt had given him. At least he had a few options.

He parked his car and braced for the storm.

39

Mayor Worthington sat primly behind a mahogany desk overlooking a tract of forest that included the byway leading to Ari's apartment. A fact that did not escape Preach's notice.

She checked her watch. "It's late. What does Chief Higgins want?"

Rebecca Worthington's compressed lips suggested power, ambition, and a willingness to let the ends justify the means. He supposed some men would find that attractive. Obviously Elliott Fenton had.

"The chief didn't send me," he said.

She drew back, eyes flickering.

"I'm here on my own." He dropped into the chair in front of her desk. This was his hunch, his fallout. "Investigating the murder of Elliott Fenton."

A look of regret passed across her face, quickly smothered. "And?" she said. "Is it connected to the other two murders you've failed to solve?"

"Do you have any information concerning Elliott's activities last night?"

"Why would I know anything about that?"

"Because you're his lover."

Her mouth quivered as she worked to regain control. She interlocked her jeweled fingers on the desk. "Don't be smart, Detective."

"That's not an accusation of which I'm typically on the receiving end."

"I don't know what you're playing at, but the chief will hear about this in the morning. And we both know how thin the ice you're standing on is."

He kept his tone commiserative. The woman had just lost her lover. "If you loved Elliott, if you even *liked* him, then help me. When did he leave your house? Was anyone supposed to visit him? Who might want Elliott Fenton, Damian Black, and Farley Robertson murdered?" He leaned in. "I swear to you, if you accept my confidence, I'll take your affair to my grave."

She hesitated. It was the briefest of pauses, but long enough to confirm his suspicion.

She knew something.

When she spoke, her voice was laced with venom. "Leave my office. Now."

If the mayor was withholding information, it meant one of two things. Either she cared about the potential fallout from the affair more than she cared about catching a murderer—or that whatever had gotten Elliott killed involved her.

She pointed at the door. "I won't ask again."

"Okay," Preach said. "But I should tell you—not as a threat, but as a courtesy—that if I discover material information has been withheld, I will do everything in my power to insure this information comes to light."

Her aquiline face tightened with fury. "And I will do everything in my power to ensure you're looking for a new job by Monday."

After she shut the door behind him, Preach took a few steps down the hallway and then paused. From where he was standing, in the window opposite her door, he could just barely see her reflection through a pane of glass.

The mayor had returned to her chair, hands balled into fists on top of her desk. After a moment of contemplation, she reached for the phone.

He couldn't hear the conversation, but if his hunch was correct it wasn't Chief Higgins she was calling.

An hour later, after shoveling down a bowl of soba noodles, Preach pulled up to the Island Gold Café on the edge of downtown. Elvis Klein had agreed to talk, and Preach didn't want to waste another moment. He had asked his former teacher where he was and gone to meet him.

The café was housed in an old working-class cottage, set back off the road and wedged between a dry cleaner and a thrift shop. Preach parked and waited for Kirby. Two bums idled on the sidewalk outside the thrift shop, sharing a cigarette. The whole block was scruffy.

When Kirby pulled up two minutes later, he said he'd uncovered nothing further at Elliott's house. "You know what this place is, right?" Kirby asked.

Preach swiveled to take in the café. "A place to get coffee? Grubby and hip?"

"It's a kava bar."

Preach frowned. "I have to confess my ignorance."

"Kava's a plant from the South Pacific. They use the root to make an herbal beverage that's supposed to have a calming effect. It tastes like dirt, but it's a stimulant, and it also helps you relax. Weird combo, right? This is a hangout for gamer types, D&D burnouts who like a little ganja with their elves and half-orcs. They say Kava and weed is a marriage made in heaven. The high without the paranoia."

"D&D?"

"Dungeons & Dragons." Kirby looked embarrassed. "I was into it as a kid."

"Okay," Preach said with a chuckle, then started for the door. Kirby grabbed his arm. "You know Mac owns this place, right? It's a front."

Preach stopped walking. He did not know.

"You think your guy's part of Mac's crew?" Kirby asked.

"He's a retired English teacher, has to be seventy-five by now. Though I guess you never know." Preach started for the door again, this time with his right hand hovering near his holster.

As they entered, the detective's eyes swept the café. The dark, narrow front room was one long tiki bar, complete with thatch fringe hanging from the ceiling. The floor, low ceiling, and cement walls were all painted purple, giving the place a weightless, psychedelic feel. Flat-screen monitors displayed a continuous loop of waves crashing on a tropical beach.

Near the entrance, a pair of tattooed men dressed in jeans and worn surfer T-shirts, baseball caps pulled low, turned when Preach and Kirby entered. One was clean-shaven with scarred and muscled forearms, the other sported a bushy goatee. Both had what Preach called gutter eyes. Lightless orbs that reflected the soiled environment in which they lived.

Two grizzled men and a much younger woman huddled over a card game at the other end of the bar. The place smelled like sassafras-scented antiseptic. A sign above the bar displayed the menu: seven and ten dollar shots of kava, single and double. And nothing else.

Definitely a front.

The two thugs ran their eyes over Preach and Kirby. There was no sign of a weapon, so Preach brushed past them. He waved off the bartender and approached the trio at the far end of the bar, recognizing one of the older men as Elvis Klein. The former teacher's shoulders were still broad, his chin still firm, but the long ponytail had grayed, and wrinkles crisscrossed his craggy face.

Elvis looked up from his hand of cards, which contained an assortment of wizards, warriors, and mythical beasts. The painfully thin younger woman, who had dyed green hair, scowled at the interruption.

"Whoa, Joe Everson." Elvis Klein said, with a firm handshake. He had always spoken like an erudite surfer, even in class.

The whole scene seemed surreal to Preach, a stop in wonderland during a murder investigation. But even Carroll's Wonderland, for all its quirks and childhood magic, was a dark, dark place.

"Thanks for meeting," Preach said. "I won't take up much of your time. Can we speak outside?"

Elvis set down his cards. "Let's use the back room. No one's ever there, and I won't be tempted to smoke."

He led them through a beaded curtain to a small room at the rear of the establishment. It was empty except for two couches facing a projector screen displaying the same hypnotic wave patterns as the monitors out front.

Elvis sprawled on one of the couches. "The Byronic Wilderness Society, huh? That's a blast from the past." He gave a nervous chuckle. "The officer who called implied it might have something to do with those crazy literary murders, but I didn't think he was . . ."

He trailed off when Preach grimaced. "I can't disclose details, but it's potentially germane to the investigation."

Elvis swung to an upright position. "No shit? How can I help?"

"What can you tell me about the Society?"

His former teacher's eyes went distant. "For about two years, they published an anonymous piece for each edition of the school paper. It showed up in my office every quarter the night before we went to press, slid underneath the door. Sometimes it was a poem, sometimes it was a short story, sometimes it was more experimental. But it was always excellent, and always packed with veiled gossip on the social scene. Who was sleeping with who, whose parents were divorcing, who had smoked dope for the first time. We teachers didn't realize this until later, of course. No one ever knew for sure who was in the club, but all the kids seemed to want to be. It was an unusual class—lots of really bright kids."

"Do you think Damian Black and Farley Robertson were members?"

"That's what the other students seemed to think, and I have to say, they were the best candidates. Both very good writers. Farley was better than Damian—ironic that. Both were also precocious enough to pull it off. Farley in particular, because he was snarky. Whoa, was he ever. Could strip another kid to his skivvies with a few words."

"Damian, too?"

"Not so much," he said slowly. "He was a likeable kid, seemed to be everybody's friend. But he was thick as thieves with Farley, and you know what they say about that. He was also . . . you remember I ran the drama club?"

"I do."

"Let's just say that Damian Black—Evan Shanks at the time—well, he was one helluva actor."

Preach and Kirby exchanged a glance.

"If you had to guess," Preach said, "Who else might have been in the Society?"

Elvis scratched at his scalp. "There was Lisa Fonce—pretty as a peach and clever as a hungry raccoon. Though I'm not sure she cared about, well, anything enough to put in the extra work. Bryce Yaw, Delia Hernandez, maybe Ryan Whiteman." He wagged a finger. "You know which two I'd bet on, now that I think about it? One was—"

He cut off, his face slowly draining of color. "Elliott Fenton."

Preach heard a cell phone go off in the front room. The ring tone had the deep, distorted chords of a death metal riff. "Is that one of your friend's phones?" he asked quietly.

"Don't think so," Elvis said.

Preach unsnapped his holster with his thumb, shifting so he was facing the beaded doorway. He motioned with his eyes for Kirby to watch the fire exit.

"You mentioned a second candidate for the Society," Preach said.

"She wasn't literary—whip-smart but not artistic—but Becky Farmer was mixed up with the other three, and was definitely into everyone's business. Which makes sense for a politician."

"A politician?" Preach echoed, growing cold at what he sensed was coming.

Becky. Rebecca.

"Farmer was her maiden name. It's Worthington now, of course. Creekville's illustrious mayor."

Preach's hands clenched against his sides. Her maiden name—that's why he hadn't noticed her in the yearbook.

"She was the hottest thing in town back then. Still a looker." Elvis shook his head. "Mean as a snake, though. She and Farley had a thing for a while."

"Isn't Farley gay?" Preach asked.

"He probably was, but back then that was still taboo around here. Maybe he slept with her to save face. But it didn't last, and she turned her attentions to Damian. For whatever reason, he wasn't interested, and she pined for him like nothing you've ever seen. That's a sight to behold, isn't it? A beautiful woman denied what she wants."

A beautiful woman denied what she wants.

"What about Elliott?" Preach asked. "Did he ever date Rebecca?"

"Only in his dreams. Elliott pined after Becky Farmer as bad as she pined after Evan."

I guess Elliott finally got what he wanted, Preach thought. *Except for the part where he got murdered.*

"So the four of them were friends, even with all the jealousy and unrequited love?" Kirby asked.

Elvis scoffed. "You know how kids are. High school is a blender full of ingredients that don't go together." His eyes visited the past again. "I seem to remember something different about their senior year. At least the second semester. They didn't seem as close . . ." He snapped his fingers. "The last submission we received from the Byronic Wilderness Society was just before Christmas break that year."

"Just before things changed," Preach said grimly.

"Whoa."

"This stays between us."

Elvis nodded as Preach eyed the beaded doorway. The sound of chatter from the front had ceased. Surely, he thought, Mac's thugs wouldn't attack a cop in broad daylight—even if they were getting orders from the mayor.

"Last question," he said, slipping his fingers around the hilt of his weapon. "*Crime and Punishment, The Murders in the Rue Morgue*—do those two books mean anything to you? Together?"

He shook his head. "I saw them on the news and thought about it already. Couldn't come up with anything."

Preach swallowed his disappointment, then took Elvis by the arm. "Let's use the back door. I think your friends might have left."

Elvis looked nervous, out of his depth. Kirby had picked up on the danger vibe and led the way to the fire exit.

Locked.

Preach swore and gripped the butt of his weapon. "I'll go first," he said, then turned to Kirby. "If something goes down, keep him safe and radio for help."

"You don't want to call it in now?" Kirby said.

"Call in what? Two unarmed men at a bar? They're already ready to crucify me."

Kirby's nostrils flared, and his eyes went hard. Preach bent to check underneath the beaded curtain. No sign of shoes. He stood and pushed through, ready to draw.

The breath he was holding seeped out when he saw Mac's men still sitting at the bar. Elvis's friends had gone silent because they were bent over the woman's cell phone. Preach could hear the synthesized sound of a video game.

He let his hands unclench. He was too on edge.

Elvis rejoined his friends. Just before Preach reached the front door, one of Mac's men, the one with the goatee and a Charlotte Hornets cap, dropped his mug at Preach's feet. It shattered, spraying Preach's pants with kava.

"Oops," the man said. Tattoos covered him like hieroglyphs. "My bad."

Kirby's hand flew to his holster. Preach stepped away from the shards and put a hand on his partner's shoulder. "Let's go. We have bigger fish to fry."

The man with the goatee jumped off his stool, blocking their path. "That's right, Ace," he said to Kirby. "Walk away."

Before Preach and Kirby could draw their weapons, the other man jumped off his stool as if lunging for Preach. The detective abandoned his gun and caught his assailant in a headlock. "Stand down!" he yelled.

Kirby tackled the goateed man, driving him into a row of bar stools that came crashing down. Preach wrestled the man in the Hornets cap to the ground. He didn't resist. The girl screamed in the background.

Preach disentangled himself from the man who had rushed him. The thug was on his stomach, and the detective put a foot on his back and drew his gun. The other man was also on the ground. Kirby kicked him in the ribs and drew his weapon.

"Kirby! It's under control."

"I'm cool," he said, breathing hard as he spoke.

"Get these two in cuffs."

Neither of the thugs resisted, and Preach called in the incident as Kirby secured the men. Elvis and his friends were gaping from their bar stools, and the bartender had shrunk against the back wall.

As Preach started walking the goateed man to the police car, he saw a strange look in his eye, a gleam that looked an awful lot to Preach like satisfaction.

He thought about it for about half a second, the pointless, weaponless assault and the time it would take him to haul them in and fill out the paperwork.

He thought about it, and then he went cold.

Ari.

40

Preach fumbled with his phone as he sped away from the café, leaving Kirby to arrest the men when more help arrived. He dialed Ari's number and then accelerated through a red light, siren blaring.

Straight to voicemail.

He made a fist over the phone and slammed it into the console. *Stupid. He was so stupid.*

There was a line of cars up ahead, unmoving. Preach strained for a glimpse of the delay, prepared to whip into the other lane. It was too dark; he couldn't see the end of the line.

He swerved to pass the first few cars, realizing where he was at the same time a long, abrasive moan pierced the night, overpowering the siren.

A train whistle.

He cursed and thumped the dash again, then pulled right up to the crossing gate, helpless before the giant blur of the locomotive. He called the station and had them send backup to the bookstore, instructing them to take the bridge on Grumley Street that passed above the tracks. It was a crap shoot as to who would arrive first.

The gate finally lifted, and Preach passed so close to the metal arm it scraped the hood of his car. He gunned past the vehicles on the other side, took a sharp left onto Second, an even sharper left through an alley, and then he was parked on Millburn and sprinting to the bookstore. Incoming sirens pierced the night.

The door was locked. He banged on the glass for a good three seconds, then stepped back and prepared to kick the door in. As his foot swung forward, he saw a man running to the door.

Hands waving. Dreadlocks swinging.

Nate.

Behind the counter, Preach saw Ari hurrying to the front, watching the scene unfold with a worried, perplexed look. Three officers sprinted up the sidewalk as Nate unlocked the door.

"Are you okay?" Preach asked Ari. She was standing near the register, arms tense at her sides.

"I'm fine." Her eyes flicked to the cops pouring through the door. "What's going on?"

"No one's threatened you?"

Her mouth gave an ironic twist. "Not this evening."

Preach put his fingers to his temple, took a deep breath, then sent the other cops away with his apologies. He didn't miss the grumbles and sidelong glances.

What was Mac playing at?

"I'm sorry if I scared you," he said. "I thought ... it was a false alarm. Why is your phone off?"

"It must have died," she said. "I've been so absorbed I didn't even realize. Funny, because I was about to call you."

"You were?"

Her eyes sparked, and she laid a hand on his arm. "I found the literary reference."

A frisson of excitement coursed through him. She was still holding his arm, and their eyes lingered before she pulled away. He realized she was carrying a slim paperback in her other hand, and that Nate was still watching them. "Let's go to the back," Preach said.

When they were alone, she unveiled the book she was holding. *Five Little Pigs* by Agatha Christie.

"It took me a while," she said, "but this is my best guess—if one thing fits. Have you read it?"

He eyed the paintbrush and the swath of blood on the cover. "No."

He leaned over her shoulder as she opened the novel to the first bookmarked page. She said, "The victim in the novel was a painter named Amyas Crale. He was found dead in his garden with no visible wounds. The only clues near the body were a bottle of beer and his drinking glass. Both were empty. Sound right so far?"

"Yeah. It does."

"I don't suppose you found an empty bottle in a bedroom drawer?"

Preach had been staring at the novel. He jerked his head up. "And if we did?"

"Then it should have had a floral scent. Jasmine."

He gave a slow nod, mouth tight. "It fits, but the evidence is still pretty sparse, compared to the others."

"Which is what made me think of Agatha Christie in the first place. Especially her novels featuring Hercules Poirot, who was fond of proclaiming that a murder could be solved solely by analyzing the testimony of the witnesses—without even looking at the crime scene. *Five Little Pigs* is a prime example. But there were a few clues in the novel. The body, the empty glass and bottle at the scene of the murder, the bottle in the drawer. There was one more thing—if it fits, and your toxicology report comes back positive for coniine, I think we've got our book."

"What's the final clue?"

"A crushed pipette was found on a garden path near the body."

"A pipette—you mean like a test tube?" he asked, remembering the small pile of broken glass he had found in the garden.

"It's the glass dropper used to *fill* a test tube. In this case, the pipette was used as a fountain pen filler." Ari flipped to a page in the novel, then showed him the portion of underlined text where the shattered pipette was found. "Well?"

Preach was staring in grim disbelief at the passage, which had an unnerving correlation to the crime scene in Elliott Fenton's garden. "You're an excellent literary detective."

Ari closed the novel. "So what now?"

"We go to my place while I figure out what the hell is going on."

41

P reach followed Ari to her place again to grab her things, and then drove her in silence to his rental. His mind was buzzing with the discovery of the third novel, working furiously to fit the pieces together.

When they entered his house, he understood at once why Mac had sent two of his flunkies to jail merely to delay Preach at the Island Gold Café.

The house was trashed. Furniture overturned, papers strewn on the floor, cabinets emptied.

Ari stopped in the doorway, gaping at the destruction. Then, without a word, she dropped her bag and began cleaning up. The first thing Preach did, after taking a few deep breaths to control his rage, was to balance the tiny Jesus figurine on its pedestal. Then he used his emergency fingerprint kit to lift a few prints. He didn't feel like having an evidence team invade his house only to tell him that, as with the prints from his desk, they had only found his own.

He put on a blues CD and helped Ari finish cleaning. "Bourbon or beer?" he asked, after they had swept the last broken dish into the dustbin.

"Both."

He fixed the same for himself. She reclined in the hammock with her copy of *Five Little Pigs* while he made a fire.

With her black sweater and the beige knit cap covering her hair, he thought her face looked even thinner than usual, almost gaunt. But still beautiful. The ambient light from the flames gave her skin a golden hue, and her green eyes blazed with intelligence.

Preach pulled up a chair next to the hammock, realizing someone had given him a clue by trashing his house. The search was too orderly, too thorough.

They were looking for something specific. His guess was one or more of the victims had possessed something incriminating, a document or a photo. And that someone thought Preach might have it in his custody.

"I don't know when I'll have time to read *Five Little Pigs*," he said. "I may not have a job by Monday. You'll have to be my expert; what's the storyline?"

"As I said, the novel concerns the murder of a famous painter, Amyas Crale. His wife, Caroline, was convicted of the crime, but sixteen years later, convinced of her mother's innocence, the Crales' daughter hires Hercule Poirot to revisit the case. He interviews everyone who was present on the day of the murder—the five little pigs. They all had dirty secrets."

"That fits with the theme of the questionable morality of the victims." Preach rolled his empty shot glass between thumb and forefinger. "How does the physical evidence relate?"

"After learning of the affair, Caroline Crale put some coniine—presumably to commit suicide—in a bottle that once contained oil of jasmine. She hid the coniine in a bedroom dresser."

Just like at Elliott's house.

"The final reveal is complicated, but to boil it down: Amyas's lover, Elsa, found the coniine and put it in Amyas's glass of beer. However, when the body was found, Caroline *thought* her younger sister Angela had committed the crime, so she wiped all the prints away and replaced them with Amyas's prints, to make it look like a suicide. However, Caroline put the prints on the *bottle* and not the glass. This is key because Poirot realizes Caroline didn't actually know how the poison had been delivered."

"So the lover did it," he murmured, rising for a refill while the fire crackled. "Is there anything unusual about the novel? Something you think might have bearing?"

"The book was notable for Poirot's use of logic alone to solve the crime," she said after a moment, as if thinking out loud. "There's also a brilliant red herring. You think it's the sister all along—the evidence against her is so subtle, so devious, you're sure you've figured out the killer." She shook her head. "But Agatha's too clever for that. She springs an even more devious surprise at the end, revealing the lover as the murderer."

Preach tilted back in his chair, absorbing the information. "So how does it fit with the other two novels? If at all?"

Ari propped her arms on her knees. "All three books are focused on exploring the complexities of human nature—guilt and innocence, darkness and light, violence and retribution. In terms of craft, there was lineage: Christie admitted she drew heavily from the Sherlock Holmes tradition, which in turn was influenced by Poe's Auguste Dupin. Poe, as we discussed, leaned on Dostoevsky. So there's a progression there."

There was also a message, Preach knew. Something loud and clear—if only he could read the language. He stood and paced the porch. "This is all too speculative."

"Don't give up," she said. "We can do this."

"Can we? We've lost three people already. You're a law student, and I'm a detective who was suspended from his last job."

He stopped pacing. She put an arm around his waist, drawing him into the hammock. He lay next to her, so close he could feel the warmth of her breath and see the shadows under the curves of her cheekbones. A current of desire crackled through him, and the air around them felt dense, more alive.

She leaned in to kiss him, but he sat up with an effort of will. "We can't do this," he said. "Not right now."

She stared straight ahead, her face flushed. "Okay."

He returned to his seat, within easy reach of his gun. "It makes us vulnerable."

"Okay," she said again.

He wanted to say something else, to explain, but he didn't want to make false promises. There was a reason cops didn't do well in relationships.

Instead he squeezed her hand and took a swallow of bourbon. His phone buzzed with a new email. He pulled it up and noticed the oversize signature block first: Deborah Kingfisher, Director of the Nondenominational Center for Social Services. Belker's homeless shelter.

Detective Everson,

I found someone at the center who recognized J. T. Belker. I think it's best if we discuss in person. Please contact me at your convenience. I will be in the office tomorrow morning after nine.

"What is it?" Ari asked.

He closed out of the email. "The little pig who had none."

42

Preach fueled up at Jimmy's Corner Store the next morning, restlessly skimming *Five Little Pigs* while waiting for Deborah Kingfisher to arrive at work.

He had dropped Ari at the law library, and she promised to take an Uber to the bookstore for her evening shift. He lectured her again about staying in a crowd, and asked Officer Haskins to watch the bookstore.

His stomach roiled from trying to figure out the angles in the case. Three cups of coffee didn't help, ratcheting up his tension to another level.

He checked the time as he inhaled the aroma of fresh pastries and watched two new people enter the café, a greasy-haired rocker and a young Asian woman with a scroll tattoo running down her back. That was the tedious part of being a cop. Watching the exits and the people around him at all times. Observing, never at rest.

8:45.

He downed his coffee and reached to close the novel. His gaze lingered on a passage of text Ari had starred and underlined. Elsa, the lover, was relating a conversation with Amyas Crale about divorcing his wife, Caroline. Elsa said she was sorry Caroline was going to be upset, and Amyas replied:

"Very nice and reasonable, Elsa. But Caroline isn't reasonable, never has been reasonable, and certainly isn't going to feel reasonable. She loves me, you know."

I said I understood that, but if she loved him, she'd put his happiness first, and at any rate she wouldn't want to keep him if he wanted to be free.

He said: "Life can't really be solved by admirable maxims out of modern literature. Nature's red in tooth and claw, remember."

I said: "Surely we are all civilized people nowadays?" and Amyas laughed. He said: "Civilized people my foot! Caroline would probably like to take a hatchet to you. She might do it too."

Preach tucked the book under his arm as he rose. Agatha Christie got it, he thought. She understood the way the world works.

And so did Ari.

The smell of ammonium and unwashed bodies assaulted Preach in the hallway of the shelter. He braced for the worst as he entered Deborah Kingfisher's office, expecting to learn that an ex-con saw Belker talking to a hit man for hire, or overheard him mumbling in his sleep about killing his publishers.

Dressed in slacks and a denim jacket, Deborah shook his hand in greeting, her eagle medallion dangling against the hollow of her throat.

"Thank you for emailing me," Preach said.

"I'm not sure how much help this is, but I found someone who remembered him. An ex-employee of the center who moved to Florida."

"Can you give me the contact information?"

"She prefers to remain anonymous." Deborah's voice was hard, unapologetic.

Preach let her stew. Surely she knew he could make her divulge the name.

She lifted a sticky note off the desk. "According to my friend, she was working the night shift this last August when Belker walked in close to midnight."

Preach tensed. August 23 was the date in Belker's journal when he had written that he had "Taken that first all-important step."

Deborah continued, "She said he looked jittery, almost giddy. She thought he was on drugs. She was about to call the cops when he asked her who she thought needed the most help at the shelter."

"Come again?"

She shrugged. "That's what she said. He insisted on an answer, and she told him there were proper channels for that sort of thing. He flashed a wad of cash and said he wasn't interested in proper channels. He wanted to help someone in need, that night, right that very moment."

Preach stared at her, unsure what to think. "And she gave him a name?"

"She introduced him to a woman who needed help. Isn't that what we're here for?"

"And what happened?"

"She doesn't know. Belker and the woman met briefly in a conference room—less than a minute—and then Belker walked out. The woman left the center an hour later, and never came back."

Preach folded his arms. "I have to know who he met with. You understand this is a murder investigation, and that I can subpoena your contact?"

She handed him the sticky note. The name Angie Simpson was written in blue ink. "That's why she gave me this."

Preach drove straight to the Creekville address that a quick records search on Angie Simpson had produced. He prayed he wasn't about to uncover a body rotting in a cellar.

The street was firmly on the poor side of town, but it was working-class poor: tidy strips of lawn fronting matchbox houses, flowers in the windowsills, pride in owning a few square feet of the American Dream.

A woman in her late thirties answered the door, dark hair pulled into a bun. The tendons of her forearms were ropy, her nails short and unpainted. An abundance of glossy lipstick made her mouth look greasy.

"Good morning, ma'am," Preach said, squinting against the sun. The day was crisp and still. "I'm looking for Angie Simpson."

Her eyes were wary but not unkind. "That would be me," she said, in a strong rural accent. "Can I help you?"

Preach flashed his identification, and she took a step back. He spoke quickly, trying to soothe her. "I'm looking for information on a man named J. T. Belker. It concerns an ongoing investigation. Do you know him?"

"Nope."

Preach noticed the hallway behind the woman was covered in photos of a girl who looked just like her, without the hardscrabble mouth and prematurely aged skin. The photos ranged from baby years to the prom.

"You've never heard that name?" he asked.

"Like I said." Her eyes narrowed further. "Why would I?"

Preach studied her face; she didn't appear to be lying.

Another false lead.

Just in case, he took out a photo of Belker and showed it to her. "I need you to be sure."

As soon as Angie saw the photo, her hand flew to her mouth, and she hiccupped with a spontaneous sob. At first Preach thought the emotion was grief or terror, but then he realized she had broken into a shocked, disbelieving smile, jabbing her finger at the photo."

"That's—that's him!!"

"I take it you do know him," Preach said dryly. "When did you first meet?"

Her gaze lingered on the photo, as if she couldn't bear to look away. "There was no first. There was only the one time." Her eyes teared up, and she began speaking in choppy, emotion-filled sentences. "A year ago I had a factory job that paid fifteen dollars an hour. My daughter and me, we were doing okay. Surviving. But then I got a leg infection, so bad I almost died. I lost my job. No disability or insurance. Medical bills took what savings I had." She dug out a cigarette and lit it with a shaky hand. "Things got bad. I was living in a homeless shelter, with my daughter. Can you imagine?"

She took a deep drag on the cigarette. Preach got a mental image of filthy bed sheets, drunks leering at her daughter all day, her friends at school treating her like a leper. His voice was thick when he spoke. "No, I can't."

"It damn near killed me. I survived because I had to, for her. But I had no job, no credit, no hope." Angie started to choke up again, ashing her cigarette while she pulled herself together. Preach could tell she was a tough woman. "One night—August 23—one of the workers at the center told me I had a visitor. I'm from Alabama; I don't got any family here. I went downstairs and a man—" she pointed at the photo—"that man, was waiting to talk to me. He looked nervous, then asked me why I was at the center. I told him." Her jaw worked back and forth. "He handed me a bag, told me it was mine, and walked away. I never saw him again. I asked around, but no one at the center had any idea who he was. Until today, I never knew his name."

Preach's face felt hot as he asked the question. "What was in the bag?"

Tears streamed down Angie's cheeks as she smiled up at him. "Twenty thousand dollars."

Preach marched down the hallway of the holding chamber and stopped in front of J. T. Belker's cell. The author was sitting on his cot and reading a novel, his back against the wall. His hair hung in oily strands, and he smelled as if he hadn't washed in weeks.

"I found Angie Simpson."

Belker's eyes moved lazily to meet his.

"The woman from the shelter. The one you gave the money to."

"Is that her name? Excellent work. Be honest, Detective: would you have believed me if I'd just told you the truth? Kept me out of jail and gone the extra mile to secure my innocence? I think not. Oh, and I heard about Elliott Fenton. It's a little hard to commit a murder from jail, don't you think?"

"You could have paid someone beforehand. Set it up so you were locked in here when Elliott was murdered."

Belker cackled. "Honestly, Detective, you give me a lot of credit."

"Yes," Preach said, looking Belker in the eye, "I do. And if you're working with Mac Dobbins, you might have wanted to be inside for your own safety. Mac could have hired you to kill Damian and Farley, then had Elliott killed. Why not you next?"

"So which is it? This Mac person convinced me to do his dirty work for some undisclosed reason, or I had another twenty grand tucked away to hire a killer who would stage literary crime scenes for me? You're delving into the realm of the fantastical."

"Then *help me understand*. Why give Angie Simpson your life savings?"

"What else should I have done? Bought a boat? It wasn't the Rockefeller fortune."

"It was to you. You want my help? Start by telling me the truth."

"The truth?" Belker gave a bitter, self-defeated grin. "The truth, Detective, is that I decided to test a theory and reverse engineer Dostoevsky."

Preach stared at him.

"If one can become a Napoleon through a random act of evil, why not through an act of good? It's a lot less risky than committing a murder, after all."

Preach barked a laugh, then reached out with a hand and gripped the bars of the cell. "Are you serious?"

"I'm afraid so."

Preach gave a disbelieving shake of his head. "Maybe you gave her the money to ease your conscience. Balance out the murders you were about to commit."

Belker cackled again.

Preach watched him long enough to decide that the writer was, indeed, serious. "So what did you find out?" Preach asked. "About yourself?"

Belker smirked and returned to his cot.

Preach sensed that line of questioning was a lost cause, maybe even to Belker himself. He had never met anyone who both worshipped and loathed himself as much as this man.

"You had nothing to do with the murders?"

"No, Detective, I did not."

Preach ran a hand through his hair and started walking down the hallway. He planned to drop the prescription drug charges and release Belker, but he could draw out the processing. He could waste some-one's time, too.

"Get me out of here, Detective! You can't hold me any longer!"

Belker kept shouting; Preach kept walking. His cell buzzed with an email, and he looked down.

Elliott's forensic results were in.

43

Preach hurried to the Chapel Hill Evidence and Forensics Services Unit to meet Dax. The forensics expert was working in the lab, his bony frame clad in blue scrubs and bent over a microscope.

Dax peeled off his latex gloves to greet him. "I'm sorry about the leak," he said. Preach knew he was talking about his psychiatric visits.

"Thanks."

He swept a hand across the crime lab. "All of us need therapy to deal with this shit. Whether we go in or not."

Preach pressed his lips together. "What do you have?"

"Autopsy results are back from SBI. Your third vic was poisoned, all right. Coniine was found in his system, in the empty glass, and in the bottle in the drawer—but not in the bottle by the body. Just like you said." He cocked his head. "How'd you know?"

"I'm very well read," Preach said. "What about the shards of glass?"

"That will take longer to verify, but it looks like a crushed pipette."

Preach blew out a breath. "Can we trace the coniine?"

"Maybe, if it was obtained online. The problem is that both the yellow pitcher plant and poison hemlock—plants from which coniine is derived—are all over North Carolina. And the recipe for extracting coniine is all over the Internet. It takes less than a tenth of a gram to induce respiratory paralysis, you know. The toxin is a nasty one; the central nervous system is unaffected, so the victim remains conscious during the process. It can take up to a few hours to die."

Preach pictured the killer squatting next to Elliott while he was lying paralyzed beside his pool. Gazing into his eyes, watching as his life ebbed away.

But why?

"Anything else?" Preach asked.

Dax opened a folder. "We found latex residue on the glass and the bottles. The same type found on Damian Black's neck. Rubber gloves, of course. Oh—we also found Rohypnol in Elliott's system, and in the glass beside the body."

"Probably used as a backup," Preach said.

Dax nodded. "Coniine tastes terrible. If Elliott was sipping his beer, he might have noticed it before he consumed a fatal amount."

"Our killer's thorough. But we knew that already."

Dax flipped through the pages and closed the folder. "That's it, except for an area of intradermal hemorrhaging on the thoracic spine. Given the color, it likely occurred at the same time as the murder."

"English, please."

"There was bruising in the middle of the victim's back. My guess? The killer stepped on his back to hold him down while the poison was taking effect."

Preach mulled over the physical evidence as he drove back to the station. Again, there were no signs of forced entry. No fingerprints besides the victims' own, no neighbors who had witnessed anything unusual, no further leads on the myriad of bizarre objects found at the crime scenes.

Basically, they had nothing—except for Preach's hunches about the Byronic Wilderness Society and the mayor.

When he returned to the station, the chief told him the mayor had demanded he be removed from the case. That public pressure was too high.

He stilled. "And?"

"I told her that might be possible if she'd given me the help I'd requested."

"How much time do I have?"

"She's calling a special budget meeting tomorrow, and she made me put in a request to Raleigh."

"Days, then."

"I'm sorry."

Kirby was huddled in his cubicle, unusually quiet. Over the next few hours, Preach enlisted him and Rance to help him dig into Rebecca Worthington's world. Using all the research capabilities of the department, he began to paint a portrait of a woman with huge ambitions who had never escaped the confines of her small town.

Rebecca Farmer had graduated valedictorian of her high school class, then turned down an offer to attend Cornell. Her family owned a small diner that had closed her senior year of high school, leaving her parents to scramble for work. Rebecca had three siblings, and Preach's guess was that she chose UNC so she could save money and help out at home.

The future mayor studied political science and minored in English Literature, which caused a tingling to spread along his arms. She was president of her sorority, a star for the debate team, and she had met Craig Worthington, her future husband, at a fraternity party. Craig was attending UNC on a golf scholarship.

Craig and Becky had a lavish wedding at the Grove Park Inn, a storied hotel in Asheville. Two children and a cocker spaniel followed, then a starter home and the upgrade to their current house. After that, a weekend cabin near Boone. The American dream.

Preach dug deeper.

Craig was currently a sales associate at a local car dealership, a position which Rebecca probably viewed as a failure. It certainly didn't pay the mortgage at Mediterranean Village. And while Rebecca had risen to become mayor of Creekville, Preach uncovered three failed political bids, one to Congress and two to the state senate.

Rebecca's parents had both passed, and Craig's father was a pharmacist, which caused more alarm bells to go off in Preach's head. Rebecca could have had knowledge of, or even easier access to, both Rohypnol and coniine.

A year ago, Rebecca had filed for divorce and then retracted the petition. The reason: marital infidelity. He also discovered that the Worthingtons were underwater on their mortgage, and that a year ago they had traded their Porsche Cayenne for a Nissan Leaf. Thinking of the environment, no doubt.

Deeper still. To the massive credit card debt Rebecca had accrued, a *six-figure* debt, most likely to send her children to private school and finance her campaigns. To the collection suits filed by three different banks and defended by Elliott Fenton. To the donations from Damian and Elliott to fund her run for mayor.

Yet Elliott and Damian were not her largest donors, a quick search revealed. A corporation named Vector Agricultural Products had contributed the staggering sum of fifty thousand dollars to Rebecca's mayoral campaign, an amount that was more appropriate for a town the size of Chapel Hill or even Durham. Preach had wondered before how white-bread Rebecca Worthington had come to be the mayor of a town that prized its diversity and counterculture.

There was something else: soon after she became mayor, the collection lawsuits were dropped, and the consumer debt went away. A hundred and forty grand, paid in full.

Preach researched Vector Agricultural Products and found nothing other than a listing on the Secretary of State website. Vector was an LLC in Columbus County, North Carolina, that had formed for the generic purpose of bringing local agricultural products to market.

He scrolled down to check the principals. The registered agent of process was—Preach's hand froze above the keyboard—Elliott Fenton. The only listed principal was Radley Jeremiah Barlow, the CEO.

Preach searched the Internet and law enforcement databases for information on Radley Barlow. Nothing. Unfortunately, no proof of identity was required to form an LLC. A random alias could be used.

But just like passwords, most people did not use random aliases.

Preach started thinking. Columbus County was in the southeastern part of the state, on the border with South Carolina. A shockingly poor part of the country.

Rural poverty. Elliott Fenton and the mayor. What connected them all?

"Kirby!" Preach called. The junior officer hurried over. Preach swiveled in his chair. "You said Mac Dobbins was from a trailer park close to South Carolina—you know which one?"

"Somewhere near Tabor City, I heard. Just a patch of dirt near the border."

"Tabor City—which county is that?"

"Hell if I know."

"Okay. Thanks."

"What gives?"

"I'll let you know."

When Kirby left, Preach looked up Tabor City, North Carolina, a dying tobacco town near a large state prison. Billed itself as the "Yam Capital of the World."

And it was in Columbus County.

A tingle of excitement spread through him. Either Rebecca Worthington had befriended a rich yam farmer who cared about Creekville politics—or Big Mac Dobbins had funded her campaign and paid off her debts.

His fingers tapped a rapid tempo on the desk. This was the reason Mac was involved, the missing link. He was protecting his political investment.

But *from what*?

Preach did another quick search in Columbus County, this time under Mac's own name. Zilch. But he did find two cash purchases in Tabor City by Radley Barlow, both within the last five years. A three hundred thousand dollar house and a Cadillac XTS. He checked into those. The cable bill at the house was in the name of Martha Dobbins, the same person who was listed on the insurance as the principal driver of the Cadillac.

Another search uncovered that Martha Wilma Dobbins was the birth mother of seven children, one of whom was Malcolm Willard Dobbins.

Mac was taking care of his mother.

While Preach processed it all, a clerk dropped off a stack of mail from Farley's townhouse. Farley's sister had given Preach permission to forward it to the station. He couldn't open anything until the executor of Farley's estate—formerly Elliott Fenton—signed off, but he could hold it.

He flipped through the usual assortment of advertisements, bills, and manila envelopes from authors. Near the bottom of the stack was a thin envelope from an insurance company Preach had never heard of. He checked Google; the company was local to Dare County, North Carolina. They specialized in property insurance.

Dare County, he knew, was in the Outer Banks.

Beach house territory.

He hunched over the envelope and started to tear it open, then stopped. Property records were easy to check. Maybe he didn't have to break the chain of evidence.

He searched under Farley's name and came up empty. He did the same for Farley's father and drew another blank. After drumming his fingers on the keyboard, he looked up Farley's mother's maiden name—Darden, a quick search revealed.

He searched under that name and located a property in Dare County, North Carolina. He mapped the address, his skin feeling flushed. The property was located on one of the long slivers of land that comprised the Outer Banks. From the map, it looked like the property backed right onto the Atlantic Ocean.

A family beach house that was four hours out of town, not listed under Farley's surname, and which might contain a shed, a safe, or a trunk.

Which, Preach was betting, would be unlocked by the key Farley had hidden inside a Dickens novel.

44

Kirby watched from his cubicle as Preach grabbed his coat with one hand and took off down the hallway like he was late for a funeral. The detective had muttered something about having to go somewhere, then left without an explanation.

He knows, Kirby thought.

He knows and he no longer trusts me.

So why hasn't he ratted me out?

Because he's good people, that's why.

Wherever the detective was going, Kirby did not think it was a social call, or even a visit to his therapist. No, the detective was pursuing a lead—and he was doing it alone.

If Preach broke the case without him, then Kirby's plan would have misfired in a very big way. And what if something happened to the detective, while he was out there alone? Kirby slumped into his chair, his hands trembling from nerves.

Or what if Preach was waiting for the right time to turn him in, maybe after the case was over and the department was under less scrutiny?

Kirby didn't know which was worse, the guilt or the stress of knowing someone else knew and might decide to ruin him.

He put his head in his hands. He needed to talk to Preach. Confess and let him know it would never happen again. No matter what.

Decision made. As soon as he got the detective alone, Kirby would come clean. Well, almost clean. Preach would probably give him a pass on Monica, but the other thing . . . that was more personal.

Kirby felt like he was able to breathe again. As if a stone had just been rolled off his back. He could still have it both ways, keep his job and smile for the cameras.

Help his family.

As he reached for his wheatgrass smoothie, an email popped up. The sender was crawfordlyons@BMDMedia. Weird. He clicked on it.

Dear Officer Kirby,

I hope this email finds you well. I'm an agent with BMD Media in Hollywood, and I have a director client interested in speaking with you about your work on the Literary Killer case. More specifically, potentially advising on a script based on your knowledge of these tragic events. A literary tie-in is also a possibility. If you could spare fifteen minutes, perhaps we could touch base? I'm in town for a few days and would be happy to meet.

Best,
Crawford Lyons

An involuntary laugh, a cackle of disbelieving excitement, bubbled out of Kirby. He stifled it, then glanced nervously behind him.

He knew what this was about. The case was national news, and Crawford Lyons was in town to lock down the inside scoop. Secure the rights. Kirby was surprised Hollywood had waited this long. Those vultures had no shame.

His stomach lurching with possibilities, he realized Crawford Lyons had probably contacted Preach as well. If Kirby hurried, maybe he could stipulate that his point of view was the one that got told. Or that he at least got equal credit. Preach was lead detective, after all. And the guy deserved a break.

Feeling giddy, he emailed back that he would love to meet.

The old state highway stretched before Preach like a worn-out conveyor belt. Driving to the ocean with the sun beaming down felt surreal, as if he were in a daydream and about to wake at his desk with drool on his chin.

He pushed it to eighty-five, ninety. Huge squares of farmland indented the endless forest. He had told the chief alone where he was going, convinced the station had eyes and ears.

He considered the fact that Kirby might be dirty, and again discarded it. Preach knew how much Kirby's reputation and his family meant to him. There were some things men would do, and some things they wouldn't. He had left Kirby behind because he might have to break some rules, and he wanted the junior officer to have plausible deniability.

Preach had arranged for Officer Haskins to escort Ari home from the bookstore, and watch her apartment until Preach returned. He needed Kirby to keep following leads, and Terry had a forthright nature—almost a naiveté—that made Preach trust him.

The forest finally broke, and the salt marshes began, a haunting, primeval landscape of brackish water, vultures perched on driftwood, and cypress trees twisting out of the swamp. Preach crossed the Croatan Sound and another long bridge at Manteo to reach the Outer Banks, one of the longest chain of barrier islands in the world. On the map, they resembled a series of green beans strung off the coast.

Preach was twitchy with anticipation. Now he understood why the mayor had been stonewalling the chief's request for help, and it was impossible not to speculate on what Farley's key might unlock. Was it a manila folder with photos of Rebecca Worthington and Elliott Fenton in flagrante? Hard evidence of the mayor taking a bribe from Mac?

The campaign fund and the debt payments might be the tip of the iceberg. What else had Mac done for the mayor, in exchange for debt payment and turning a blind eye to his activities?

The address was a weather-beaten, clapboard house on stilts, squatting right on the ocean. Scrub and wild grass comprised the front yard. The gray paint was flaking, the roof warped by the sun, but the crashing surf and sea oats waving in the breeze provided a surfeit of charm.

No sign of activity, no cars in the drive. Preach approached the front door under a shimmery blue sky. Earlier in the day, Farley's sister, who now controlled the property, had agreed to a search. Chief Higgins had also procured a warrant for whatever container the key might unlock.

Preach found the spare house key under a flowerpot, just as Farley's sister had said. The front door opened onto a kitchen that spilled into a shotgun-style dining area and living room. Sliding doors in the rear of the house led to a screen porch with wooden floorboards and a pair of hammocks. A sandy path cut through a line of waist-high dunes to the beach.

Preach did a thorough walk-through. Doors off the living room led to three bedrooms and a single bath. The décor was rustic and alligator-themed. He drew a breath when he found an old key safe in a bedroom closet, but it was the wrong fit.

Damn.

After searching the interior, he stepped outside and probed the ground beneath the stilts on hands and knees. He found nothing but cold sand, old beams, and slugs.

He walked down to the beach, viewing the house from the rear. There was no shed or garage. No place left to look.

Ghost crabs scurried underfoot as the heavy surf crashed at his back. The wind carried the salty tang of the ocean. Twenty yards away, a heron was poised in the shallows, so still it looked petrified.

Maybe the beach house was too obvious. After all, Elliott and Damian were childhood friends of Farley, and they surely knew about it. On the other hand, it was hours outside of Creekville, and if Mac and the mayor had already found what they were looking for, why had the murders continued?

Thoughts of Atlanta came unbidden. Flashes of a decorated career, of closed cases and a drawer full of medals. Of a moonlit night in the woods that had stripped him bare and flayed him alive, left him with a greasy residue no shower could remove.

He had thought he could do this job again, yet here he was, standing helplessly on a beach in the middle of nowhere, days before his removal from the case.

Three murders and one misguided arrest. He was being outwitted. The chief was right. This wasn't just about him. He should have let her remove him.

He went back inside and searched the house again, leaving no inch undisturbed, no floorboard unchecked. It was time to admit defeat. Just before he left, he emptied the quarter-full kitchen trash into the yard and picked through it. An old trick, and a final desperate act.

It was mostly wadded up paper, dusty refuse from a vacuum cleaner, and a few bits of rotting food. Given the season, he guessed no one had been to the house in weeks. He stubbornly unwadded each piece of paper, finding receipts and a few bills. One of the receipts made him pause, a two hundred dollar charge from a marina.

What did one buy for two hundred dollars at a marina? The date was right, but there was no way to tell if the receipt was Farley's.

Preach grew excited at the thought of a boat. Boats had locked compartments. Cabins that could hide a safe.

He searched for the marina on his phone. It was only a few miles away, so he locked up and sped over.

Easily spotted by the thicket of white, needle-like masts poking skyward, the marina was set beneath a bridge spanning the Intracoastal Waterway. Preach walked up to the deeply tanned man working the front desk. He looked to be in his fifties and was wearing a beige polo shirt.

Preach didn't bother with an explanation. He could tell by the man's wide eyes that the guy recognized him from the news. "I'm sorry to bother you, but do you know if anyone by the surnames of Darden or Robertson docks a boat at this marina?"

The man hacked a smoker's cough and took a sip of Fanta. "Gus never owned a boat. He cast off the pier."

Gus was Farley's father, Preach knew. "What about anyone else in the family?"

"Nope."

Preach deflated. Lips compressed, his eyes swept the marina and noticed a tiki bar, a screened-in shack where a group of fisherman were cleaning their catch, and a concrete walkway leading to the boats.

"Is there something else I can help you with, Detective?"

Just before Preach turned back to the attendant, he noticed a flash of metal across the canal where the boats were docked.

"What's over there?" Preach asked. "By the sign for the restroom?"

"Boat lockers."

His chest tightened. "You knew Farley Robertson?"

He gave a somber nod. "Since he was a boy. Terrible what happened."

"Did he have a locker here?"

"Not that I know about. I can check, though."

"Please do."

It seemed as if the man took three hours to get on his computer and pull up the records for locker rentals. Preach's nerves were strung as tight as a violin.

"Well, I'll be. Must have been someone else signed him up." He looked up, respectful but uncertain. "I'm not sure I should—"

"I have a key. And a warrant." Preach produced them both, working hard to stay calm.

The attendant shrugged. "Number thirty-seven. It's paid up for half the year."

Preach put his palms on the counter. "Have you had any burglaries in the last three weeks?"

The man looked confused, and then he got it. "I—oh. No, no we haven't."

Preach strode to the wall of lockers, his heartbeat fast against his chest. Brackish water lapped against the boats, and the greasy odor of gasoline undercut the fresh air.

He found the correct row. Locker number thirty-seven loomed in the middle like the mouth of a canyon. He sucked in a breath and tried the key.

It fit.

45

Officer Terry Haskins entered the Wandering Muse at closing time and told Ari he was there to escort her home.

"Where's Detective Everson?" she asked.

"Out on assignment. He asked me to keep an eye on you until he returns."

"Where on assignment?"

"I ... I'm not sure, ma'am."

Ari gave him a frigid smile. Anyone could impersonate a cop, and this guy looked more like an accountant than someone trained to protect and serve.

On the other hand, he didn't look very dangerous.

The last customer had just left the store, making her nervous. She sent a text to Preach to verify Officer Haskins's identity. The detective sent a return text within seconds, confirming the story.

Ari locked up and let the officer drive her home, a soft rain drumming the windshield. She shivered and asked him to turn up the heat.

Back at her apartment, she locked her doors and windows, wolfed down a bowl of Ramen noodles, and then curled on the couch with her wine. The stack of law books in front of her caused a sinking feeling in her stomach. Finals were imminent, but all she could think about was where Preach had gone and whether he was in danger. She picked up the phone to call him and then let it drop, not wanting to disturb him. He had made it clear he didn't want to mix business with pleasure.

She understood the exigencies of the job and didn't blame him, though his reticence made her question his true intentions.

Two hours later, restless and sick of forcing herself to study, she rose to glance out the window. Officer Haskins's car was still parked near the road, with a clear view of her front door.

She forced herself to grind through her notes on Trusts and Estates. Revocable and irrevocable trusts, intestacy, restrictions on the right to devise, the abominable rule against perpetuities. She decided she would rather have her eyes pecked out by crows than churn out wills for rich people for the rest of her life.

Near midnight, the legal concepts blurring together, she heard a faint scratching at the door. It sounded like a dog or a cat, asking to be let in.

It was probably nothing. A stray or a noise from someone else's door. The apartment complex was a refurbished roach motel, the walls pizza box–thin.

Just to be safe, she rose and checked the window again. Officer Haskins's car was still outside.

Another scratching sound. It made her nervous. She grabbed her phone and padded toward the door, leaning in to check the peephole. At first she thought something was blocking her view, but then the darkness shifted and she got an eyeful of lank brown hair spilling out from a ski mask.

She heard a loud click at the same time the man outside the door straightened, providing a glimpse of a cleft lip scar and latex-covered hands.

The doorknob started to twist.

Ari turned and fled.

Kirby fingered Crawford Lyons's business card as he knocked on the door of the penthouse suite. He had checked out BMD Media before the meeting. It was legit, one of those über-exclusive agencies whose Internet presence was designed to convey an aura of rarified mystery. Website spare as winter, built with clean lines and generic links. You didn't contact them; they contacted you.

Crawford Lyons had a few executive producer credits to his name, nothing major, just a few slasher flicks. Kirby didn't care. The man made *movies*.

He knew the whole thing might never go anywhere. But he believed most people never rose above their circumstances because they failed to recognize those rare moments the universe threw at you. They came once or twice per lifetime, and you had to be ready.

And if this was his shot, then Scotty the Body was going to pour every ounce of white-toothed, smooth-skinned charm he had into this meeting.

A large man in a black suit opened the door. He had a fluffy hipster beard, as did everyone these days. Silver studs in each ear, slicked back hair, a nose that had been broken a few times.

"Mr. Lyons will be right in," the man said, moving aside to let Kirby in. "He's on the phone."

Kirby spread his hands and smiled. "Sure."

Late-night meeting. A personal-attendant-slash-bodyguard. The penthouse suite.

How very Hollywood.

Kirby surveyed the room. The posh hotel was in downtown Chapel Hill and overlooked the arboreal hush of campus. He bit down on his cheek to calm his jitters. He had no idea where Preach had gone all day, but it had worked out for the best, since Kirby wouldn't have to explain where he was. For all he knew, the meeting with Lyons would involve bottles of champagne and contracts signed in blood and an after party that would last all night.

Kirby rocked slowly on the balls of his feet, trying to look as if he belonged. The bearded attendant stood near the wet bar with his arms folded. Maybe he was nervous about offering a cop a drink. A few minutes later, the door to the bedroom flew open, and Kirby prepared to greet a suave film agent with a Rolex and a Hollywood tan.

Instead, he got a barrel-chested brute in motorcycle leathers, black beard creasing as his nicotine-stained teeth broke into a grin. Mac's eyes stabbed through Kirby like needles, reflecting none of the light of his smile.

Kirby opened his mouth to speak, but his voice was lost in a wilderness of shame, anger, and disappointment.

"Cat got your tongue, Officer?" Mac shook his head as he laughed, his beard waving like a black bear stomping through the forest. "You're a gullible fellow, ain't you? Literary tie-in from a traffic cop. My white ass!" He jerked his head toward the bodyguard. "Bring us a couple of brews. Hollywood and me, we got some business to discuss."

"The hell we do," Kirby said, turning to leave. His face felt bright red.

Mac's voice turned low and menacing. "Stick around, Officer. I got something you might want to hear."

Kirby stopped with his hand on the doorknob.

"A filly name of Monica ring a bell? Happens to be on the national news now and again?"

Kirby wanted nothing more than to open the door and run out of that hotel and pretend as if that night, the entire last month, had never happened.

"Your partner's much better at watching out for tails than you are. It's a skill you might want to improve upon as a police officer, especially when you're selling state secrets." Kirby could feel the crime boss smirking behind his back. "Now turn on around and take your medicine."

The floor felt viscous, thick and unsteady, as he turned and saw Mac holding up a photograph of Kirby and Monica entering a local hotel.

The bodyguard took out a small CD player and set it down beside the two beers. He touched the screen and Kirby heard his own voice coming through, conversing with Monica about the details of the case.

"That hotel your girl likes?" Mac said. "The manager happens to be a client of mine. Can you believe that?" He shook his head and stroked a handful of beard. "So now, do we have some business to discuss?"

"You bastard."

"If you knew my daddy, you'd know that was a compliment."

Kirby desperately wanted to do the right thing. Walk out the door and drive down to the station and turn himself in. Take his medicine and end this.

But he could only think of Jalene and Kayla and Jared, of their lack of options if he lost his job. What would happen to them if he went to jail.

"I ain't gonna wait all night. Your choice, Hollywood. Deal with the devil or bear the cross."

Kirby felt shivery, like a cold front had swept through. The ape in the black suit was smirking. Mac was drinking his beer and looking at Kirby like he owned him.

Feeling as if the hourglass marking the passage of his life had just cracked, Kirby walked slowly to the window and stared outside. His voice was hollow when he asked Mac what he wanted him to do.

The door of the marina locker concealed a narrow, rectangular space. At first Preach thought there was nothing inside, but then he saw the legal envelope stuck into the cubby at the top.

His eyes swept the marina.

No one was watching.

Inside the envelope was a stack of 5 x 7 photos. He knelt as he went through them, his chest tight with anticipation.

The first few photos depicted Damian and Elliott having sex with different women, often two or three at a time and in different positions. The photos had been taken in Damian's basement. After that came the incriminating snapshots of Elliott and Rebecca Worthington he had expected to find, confirming the blackmail theory. There were also photos of the mayor and Elliott in a ménage a trois with another woman, and sometimes with another man. One was a close-up of the mayor having sex with Tram Vu.

The positions and equipment got more complicated as the photos progressed. Toward the end of the stack he came across a woman he thought looked familiar. A light-skinned black woman, lithe and beautiful, with an oval face and a mischievous mouth. She possessed an innocence that the other participants had lost, and though she was smiling in the photo, the smile was forced, and Preach detected a well of sadness behind her almond-shaped eyes.

Whoever she was, she didn't want to be there. Had they somehow forced her?

He flipped through a few more photos of that same woman having sex, first with Damian, then Elliott, then with the mayor. They moved on to the various contraptions in the basement, using them in increasingly novel ways.

Then he came to the last photo, which depicted the woman on all fours on the carpet, wearing nothing except a pair of fake canine ears, a large dog bowl positioned underneath her head. Damian was penetrating her from behind, Elliott was underneath her. Rebecca was also in the photo, sprawled naked on the bed while she watched the spectacle with hungry eyes.

The unknown woman had turned her head toward the photographer, whom Preach assumed was Farley. Her eyes had gone from sad to lifeless.

Good God. Preach had the gut feeling the woman in the photo was no prostitute, but some poor desperate woman they had paid to demean herself for their pleasure. *Sushi*, they were called on the street. One-offs. The perverted thrill derived from the loss of innocence.

He stood and, just before he stuffed the obscene photo back into the envelope, took one more look at the woman's face. He knew her from somewhere, he was sure of it. Where had he seen her? Something was different; she was wearing more makeup and maybe the hair had been straightened . . . that curve in the nose . . . he finally realized who it was and took a step backward, stomach caving, a wave of nauseating heat flushing his skin.

God, oh God, not her. Please let me be wrong.

But he knew he wasn't. He had never met the woman before, but he had seen a photo of her. At the police station. Sitting in a frame on his partner's desk.

She was Kirby's sister.

46

Ari heard the door open as she sprinted into the living room. Fear swallowed her whole. There was no time to fumble with her phone, no time to do anything but run for her life.

"Hello, gorgeous," a familiar voice rasped behind her.

The primal part of her brain took over, ordering her to run as far and as fast as she could. She spun around the wall and past the couch. Threw a lamp to the floor as she careened past the kitchen and into the main hallway. No time to grab the mace.

Adrenaline amplified her hearing. Footsteps crunched on glass behind her, the man's coat swishing as he ran.

Two doorways to pick from. The bedroom and the bathroom. Ari sensed she had one slim chance at escape: diving out a window before the man caught her and dragged to the ground, then gave her a scar like he had promised.

She chose the bedroom because the windows were larger. She had the presence of mind to fling open the bathroom door to try to fool him. When she raced into the bedroom she wasn't sure whether he had seen her.

"No place to run," he yelled. "I told you I'm coming for you."

She stumbled from the surge of terrified adrenaline his words produced, clutching the bedspread to right herself as she lurched to the window. Her hands were shaky as she flipped the latch and shoved it open.

"There you are," he said from behind her.

She dove right through the screen, ending up with her stomach straddling the sill. Footsteps pounded toward her as she scrambled to get through. She heard the rasp of his breath as he approached, and he grabbed her sweatpants before she could pull herself over.

She kicked as hard as she could, twice in a row. Her foot connected with something soft. He grunted and released her long enough for her to finish crawling through.

A clump of azaleas broke her fall, scratching her cheeks and arms. She pushed to her feet and stumbled out of the bushes. From the corner of her eye, she saw Officer Haskins lying prone on the ground behind a tree.

Her assailant was climbing out of the window behind her. "Help!" she screamed, then turned and fled toward the street.

Before she had taken three steps, two more figures stepped out of the shadows near the front of the complex. One was a burly man in a vest holding a canvas bag. The other was leaner, with a red beard and studded leather wristbands.

As terrified as she was, Ari wasn't about to willingly let them stuff a canvas bag over her head and drag her away. Still gripping her cell phone, she veered to the left, toward the parking lot. The smaller man was closest. He was grinning as he came for her. When he was five feet away, she reared back and threw her phone straight into his face, as hard as she could.

He wasn't expecting the maneuver, and didn't have time to put his hands up. The phone caught him square in the nose. Blood sprayed outward, and he clutched his face, bellowing in pain.

She had a small opening to reach the street. "Help!" she screamed again, as the boots of the other men thudded behind her. There were no cars, no pedestrians. She cursed the lack of nightlife in Creekville. She had thought she was living in a safe place, a provincial little town, but now she was trapped in a nightmare.

"Stop, bitch, or I swear it'll be worse!"

She risked a glance backward. They were gaining ground. Ari could run, but these men were faster.

When she turned back to the street, she saw her stalker standing twenty feet down the road in the direction she was trying to flee, blocking her escape. He was wearing the same outfit as always, bowler hat and overcoat, and this time he was holding a gun.

Ari's scream never left her throat. Her fear choked it off. She couldn't think, couldn't breathe. Somehow she realized the greenway was to her right, and she fled down it, knowing she was about to get shot in the back or tackled by one of the men. The leaves covering the blacktop glowed orange in the moonlight, transforming the narrow walkway into the tongue of some monstrous beast.

Two gunshots shattered the quiet of the night, so loud and close they reverberated in her ears. She flinched but hadn't been hit. She kept running, forcing her legs to churn faster, her body electric from adrenaline, the darkness cold and full, her breath leaping out of her in terrified gasps.

47

It was well after midnight by the time Preach returned to Creekville. He had just texted Ari but she hadn't answered. He assumed she was asleep. Just as he pulled onto her street, ready to relieve Officer Haskins, he heard the *crack crack* of two gunshots.

The sound was incongruous in Creekville, not a nightly occurrence like on the mean streets of Atlanta. But it was unmistakable.

And he was on Ari's street.

His foot slammed the accelerator down, jerking the car forward. The vehicle's high beams swallowed the blacktop. As he reached for the siren, he saw two men in dark jackets sprinting out of the darkness toward his car, less than a hundred feet away.

Preach screeched to a stop just before Ari's parking lot. He jumped out of the car, both hands squeezing the grip of his gun. "Stand down!" he shouted at the two men. "Police!"

The men were caught in the headlights. The burly one with the vest he recognized from the back room of the Rabbit Hole, and from the Gorgon.

The other had a cleft-lip scar.

Preach felt a surge of rage, and then panic for Ari. He had no idea why these men were running, but he had to assume the worst.

The two men slowed and then stopped, breathing hard and glaring at Preach.

"Hands behind your head! Now!"

They exchanged a glance but complied. Preach advanced, switching to a one-handed grip on his gun so he could call the station and demand immediate backup and an ambulance. His plan was to march these men to Ari's apartment. He had to know if she was okay.

He pulled his phone out of his pocket, managed to speed-dial the station, and then caught a glimpse, in the periphery of his vision, of someone with a bloody face rushing toward him.

Preach whirled to his right, but the man tackled him before he could get a shot off. The gun went flying. His attacker was much smaller, and Preach managed to keep his footing by throwing his legs back in a wrestling stance. His assailant tried to pull away, and Preach kneed him hard in the face, shattering whatever semblance of a nose the man had left. The attacker screamed and dropped.

The other two thugs sprinted for the gun. Preach dove onto the pavement for the weapon, crashing into the man with the scar. Preach's hand reached the gun and gripped it. A hand closed on his wrist. He threw an elbow into his opponent's jaw, feeling bone crunch when he connected. The man with the scar bellowed in pain. Preach threw two more elbows in rapid succession, fast and hard as a jackhammer. One connected with the smaller man's temple, and he slumped.

Preach tried to rise, but the third man kicked him in the hand, sending the gun flying and snapping his wrist back. Preach rose with a grunt and threw an uppercut straight into the burly man's solar plexus. His opponent doubled over, his breath leaving him with a *whoosh*.

Sirens whirred in the distance. Preach scrambled to retrieve his gun as blue lights rounded the corner, flashing in his eyes. Emergency vehicles pulled onto the street, disgorging police officers and medics.

As the other officers dealt with Mac's men, Preach dashed toward Ari's apartment. Just before he arrived, Terry stumbled into view, holding his head and looking panicked.

Preach barked as he ran. "Where's Ari?"

"I don't know. Someone jumped me while I was taking a piss. I—"

From behind, another voice shouted, "Detective Everson!"

Preach kept racing toward Ari's door. Those men had been running *away* from her apartment.

"*Detective!*" The shouting voice belonged to Officer Wright. Preach finally turned.

"Ari just called the station," Wright continued. "She's down the street at Philip's Tavern."

Preach put his hands on hips, breathing hard. All three assailants were in handcuffs, and the man with the cleft-lip scar was unconscious, his face so bloody and swollen it was almost unrecognizable. Mac was smart. He relied on intimidation and sent his men out without guns, to lessen the potential charges.

But this time they'd gone way, way too far.

"Read them their rights," Preach said, striding toward his cruiser, "and get them out of my sight."

He caught up with Ari as she was leaving the tavern in the company of two officers that Preach barely knew. Damp leaves littered the parking lot. Cold moist air filled his nostrils. The bar was next door to the Wandering Muse, and he noticed that it was the closest establishment to the greenway that led to Ari's apartment.

"I'll take it from here," he said to the two officers. They nodded and peeled away, and he turned to Ari, forcing himself not to embrace her. The tavern had emptied to observe the spectacle. "I'm sorry I wasn't here," he said.

She flashed a brave but guarded smile. "You can't be my babysitter."

Her face was still flushed with shock and fear, but there was heat in her eyes. Anger.

He felt a rush of respect for her bravery. He also realized, now that the adrenaline had faded, that his left wrist was purple, throbbing, and swollen. A jolt of pain shot through him when he tried to make a fist.

"Come with me downtown," he said. "After I wrap up, we'll stay at my place."

"No one chased me," she said.

"What?"

"When I got away from those men and ran into the road, my

stalker appeared out of nowhere, right in front of me. He had a gun. I ran into the greenway and heard shots, but I wasn't hit. They could have easily caught or shot me, but when I reached the street and looked back . . . there was no one coming."

She turned toward the entrance to the greenway, shivering in the night air. In the shadow of a streetlight, a family of deer, sleek and gray, slipped into the forest with their fluid rocking motion.

When Ari turned back there was confusion, as well as a dawning awareness, in her eyes. "I think my stalker saved my life," she said.

48

The medics told Preach he had a severely sprained wrist, gave him a handful of ibuprofen, and set it with a splint. It was four a.m. by the time he took Ari back to his house. She collapsed on the couch, and he covered her with a blanket.

She took his hand and said, hesitantly, "Can I ask you something about your therapy?"

He looked away.

"Did something happen to someone you love? A wife or a girlfriend?"

He shook his head, eyes sad and distant. "No," he said. "Nothing like that."

Her head relaxed on the pillow. She had just wanted to know if there had been someone else, and if so how deep the wound went.

"If you really want to know, I'll tell you someday."

"It can wait," she said. "As long as it doesn't involve a woman you can't get over."

He managed a faint smile. Just before she fell asleep, she whispered, "Don't you dare back down from them."

His good hand curled into a fist at his side.

The next morning, Preach took Ari to Jimmy's Corner Store. She perched over a law book with her cappuccino while he drummed his thumbs on his coffee mug, turning the case over in his mind. He hadn't decided what to do about her long-term safety, and he couldn't explain what had happened with her stalker. His immediate solution was to finish his coffee.

Every time he thought about the photos with Kirby's sister, a rush of empathy overwhelmed him. He knew he had to tell Kirby, but he didn't know how. Not yet, was all he knew. Not right now.

Damn this world.

He pushed his other thoughts aside and focused on the observer in the photos who was still alive, and who clearly didn't want anyone else to bear witness to her participation.

Rebecca Worthington.

The picture was getting clearer. The mayor had hired Mac Dobbins to murder Farley and keep her secrets safe. But they hadn't found the blackmail stash. That explained Mac's brazen behavior. He had to ensure that the mayor, who was indebted to Mac for an untold sum and greased the wheels for his growing business empire, stayed in office.

So Farley's murder Preach understood. But why Damian and Elliott?

Preach had to figure out the final angle. His goal wasn't to force Rebecca Worthington to resign in disgrace—he wanted her for murder.

His eyes roved the café, noticing the usual assortment of college students and hipsters. But he also saw a nervous young mother dressed in thrift-shop clothes, a trio of unwashed musicians who had rolled up in a rusted-out camper van, and a fresh-faced country kid wearing an old porkpie hat and scanning the message board for a room to rent. These were the people, he knew, who had moved to Creekville to find work, because it was the closest town of any size. The sons and daughters of tobacco workers and struggling artists and gas station attendants, the people from poverty-stricken homes and forgotten towns with no stop lights, hidden deep in the forests of the Piedmont. Sometimes they came to Creekville and made a life, sometimes they returned home, sometimes they moved on to bigger and better things.

And sometimes they ended up like Kirby's sister.

"Joe," Ari said.

"Yeah?"

"You've been staring at the wall for the last five minutes."

"Just thinking," he said.

"It's not adding up, is it? The murders and the books?"

Preach ran his uninjured hand through his hair. He had showered, but he felt stale, worn out by his failures in life. "No."

She closed her book. "I don't know all the details, but it sounds like you need a fresh angle."

She was right, of course she was right, but easier said than done. He had turned everything around a hundred times and kept reaching the same limited conclusions.

What was he missing?

He kept coming back to the novels. The crime scenes were so deliberate, so thematic. So *literary*.

He remembered a line he had read in *Five Little Pigs*, talking about the five suspects:

> Until you see what sort of people they were, you cannot begin to see clearly.

It was the embodiment of his own philosophy. When a case stalled, often the best way to move forward was to peer through the eyes of the victims. He'd been doing that on an individual basis, but what if he did it collectively?

Three victims, all from Creekville. All friends since high school and reputedly members of a secret literary society. All three complicit in modern-day perversions.

The voices in the café faded out. What if this wasn't about blackmail at all, or if the blackmail had sparked an old feud? Something terrible in the past that had spilled into the present? What if the three victims had wronged the mayor in some way . . . or even someone else?

He blinked and turned to Ari. "Maybe each book represents a piece of the puzzle. *Five Little Pigs* gives us the framework: a past crime that's never been brought to light."

She twisted one of her thumb rings and continued his theme.

"*Crime and Punishment* could represent the cleverness and mindset of the murderer," she said, "*The Murders in the Rue Morgue* the animalistic nature of the crime and those who committed it."

He rose and swept his coffee cup off the table. He was probably grasping, but he was desperate for a solution.

"Let's go. I need to pick up something at the house."

"What?"

"An old yearbook."

When they arrived at his house, he strode into the living room and grabbed the yearbook from the victims' senior year. He sat on the couch, Ari hovering beside him.

If something in the past had led to three murders in the present, then it had to be something powerful. He found the dedication to Deirdre Hollings, the student who had committed suicide. She was an elfin girl with long dark hair, innocent eyes, and elegant bone structure. In fact, except for the purple birthmark on her neck and the more rounded nose, she looked a lot like—Preach swallowed and stared down at the photo of the girl.

She looked a lot like Ari.

He hadn't looked closely at her face before. A chill coursed down his spine, and by the uneasy expression on Ari's face, he knew she had come to the same conclusion.

Ari pointed at the dedication. "Look at the date."

Preach read aloud: "On November 7th, a terrible tragedy struck Creekville High when Deirdre Hollings took her own life."

He looked up and met Ari's eyes. It was November 6.

Tomorrow was the thirty-fifth anniversary of Deirdre's death.

He did a quick online check. According to the property records, Deirdre's family still owned the house in which she had grown up on Georgia Street, a few blocks off Hillsdale. Preach knew where it was.

He took a deep breath. There was no time for a wild goose chase. He had to get to the mayor before she got to him. Interview the three men he had just locked up.

But first he was going to follow his gut.

He stood and paced the living room, trying to decide what to do with Ari. He couldn't leave her alone. Mac Dobbins was an angry hornet whose nest he had just kicked. After mulling over a few options, he decided to call Ray Logan, who agreed to stay with her.

"Your old wrestling coach?" Ari said.

"He lives in the woods with a pack of Dobermans. I trust him with my life."

"I thought he was religious?"

"He is. He believes in the Lord, wind sprints until you puke, and the Second Amendment."

Ari nodded, and he was thankful she didn't make him explain further. He grabbed the yearbook, and they jumped into his car.

After dropping Ari off with his old coach and giving enough of an explanation for him to grab his shotgun, Preach headed to the station and found Deirdre's old case file. It was tragic and sparse. Young Deirdre had killed herself with a cocktail of alcohol and her mother's prescription drugs. No suicide note, no evidence of foul play.

The chief was on the phone, which was a relief. Preach deflected Kirby's questions and told him to start interviewing their three prisoners.

Preach gave himself two hours to investigate the Deirdre Hollings angle. On the way to her old house, he called someone he thought might be able to help.

49

"What a pleasant surprise," Preach's mother said when she answered the phone.

He was driving through the narrow, forested lanes of West Creekville. Deirdre's house was five minutes away.

"Maybe not so pleasant," he said. "I need to ask you a few more questions about high school."

"Okaay." She drew the word out in confusion.

"You remember that suicide you told me about? Deirdre Hollings?"

"Of course. What a tragedy."

His mother spoke the words in a monotone, as if a tragedy were a theoretical thing.

"I can't go into detail, but what can you tell me about her?"

"I . . . that was a long time ago, Joey. I think she had a sister, and I remember her father leaving town soon after the suicide. Deirdre used her mother's sleeping pills, you know."

"What about the mother? What happened to her?"

"I've no idea."

"What was Deirdre like? What kind of person?"

The line quieted. He could sense his mother reaching into the past, trying to form a mental image. "She was very shy and quiet. Awkward even. Beautiful, mind you—but not in that All-American way boys were into at the time." *Not like you and I were beautiful*, his mother's slightly smug tone implied. "She was a writer, I remember. Her poems were in the school paper."

A writer. "Who were her friends?"

"To be honest, I don't remember her having any. She was always carrying around a novel, and she just seemed so . . . lonely. And intense. When you passed her in the hall she would look right through you, as if she were living this vibrant life, but it was all happening inside her mind. Do you know what I mean?"

"I do," Preach said quietly. "Do you remember seeing her with Farley Robertson, Damian Black, or Elliott Fenton?"

A pause. "The three victims."

"Yes."

"Maybe once or twice," she said. "But I don't really remember."

"What about Rebecca Farmer? The mayor."

"Hmm . . . again, I seem to remember Deirdre following her around—Becky was far more popular—but it's just been so long."

"If you think of anything else, anything at all, you'll let me know?"

"Of course," his mother said. "I don't want to know what this is about, do I?"

"Probably not."

"Joey . . ." A longer pause, one that Preach knew would end in a mundane question. "Dinner on Sunday?"

"I'll try."

The house where Deirdre Hollings had lived was a somber brick federal with black trim and four small windows facing the street. It resembled a piece of granite more than a house, a residence that kept its secrets and denizens sealed tightly inside. A lonely house that whispered to Preach that, no matter what else had occurred within its walls, birthdays and graduations and lifetimes full of love and tiny kindnesses, a single tragedy now defined its existence, the permanent stain of a child's suicide.

Preach parked behind a burgundy Camry in the driveway. The scent of pine drifted on the breeze. Solar-paneled neighbors, boulders and wood chips filling the lawns, the stamp of middle-class Creekville.

As he approached the door, Preach received a text from Chief Higgins that made him grimace.

-Come see me as soon as you can-

The chief's cryptic text meant the mayor was turning the screws even harder. He had to hurry. And if he left with nothing...

A trim woman in her fifties answered his knock. She was wearing a gold necklace and a knitted blue sweater. Most of her bangs had gone grey, and she peered at him above a nose that was a shade too big and a smile of greeting that stopped halfway.

Preach flashed his ID and said he was looking for the family of Deirdre Hollings.

"I'm Carrie Hollings," the woman said, hesitant. "Deirdre's younger sister."

"Do you mind if I come inside?"

"I wasn't prepared for visitors, but I, yes, of course."

"No preparation necessary," Preach said, as Carrie ushered him into a living room just off the entrance hall. "I just have a few questions. Are there any other siblings?"

"It's just mother and me." Carrie glanced at a wheelchair-bound woman on the far side of the room whose gaze was locked onto a garden filled with azaleas and hydrangeas turned brittle for the fall.

Preach waited for an introduction that never came.

"She doesn't speak," Carrie said finally. "Stroke."

Preach wondered whether Deirdre's mother couldn't hear as well, or whether Carrie was just rude.

He absorbed the room as he sat on a sectional gray sofa. A side table was laden with issues of *Vogue*, *Entertainment Weekly*, and *Southern Living*. Two armchairs, a sleek metal lamp, and a leatherette footrest. The requisite flat-screen TV. A bookshelf filled with trite curios purchased from department stores.

Not a single book.

"I'd like to ask you a few questions about Deirdre's death," he said.

Carrie frowned as if the question inconvenienced her. Out of the corner of his eye, Preach saw the mother's pinky twitch on the armrest of her wheelchair.

"Why?" Carrie asked bluntly.

"It's possible—unlikely, but possible—that something about her death concerns an ongoing investigation."

Carrie's mouth curled in disbelief. "The literary murders?"

Preach tipped his head in acknowledgment. "The three victims were close in high school."

"Well, I certainly don't know what that has to do with Deirdre. She wished she were acquainted with the victims, but that wasn't the case."

"Because they were popular?" he asked.

"That, and because my poor sister was convinced they were part of some secret literary society, which she desperately wanted to join. If there was one thing my sister cared about, it was literature."

He was put off by Carrie's callousness, but suicide could be a selfish act, and often destroyed the lives of those left behind.

"You're talking about the Byronic Wilderness Society?" Preach asked.

"Silly name, isn't it? She talked about it incessantly whenever a new issue of the school paper came out. Everyone knew how desperate she was, and then they made her into a saint. I know what you're thinking, but I spent all of my emotion ages ago. Now we're just left with the pieces. My father left soon after she died, and my mother," her voice turned scornful, "well, she never recovered."

Preach read between the lines: her mother had never recovered enough to care about *her*.

"You said your sister wished she was acquainted with the victims—are you saying she wasn't?"

"Oh, God, no. She was absolutely in love with Evan Shanks, or should I say Damian Black. Of course, Deirdre didn't stand a chance with him. And what a horrid teenager Becky Farmer was. She and Farley were two devils incarnate."

"What about Elliott Fenton?"

She waved a hand. "He did whatever Becky wanted."

"So, as far as you know, Deirdre had no contact with any of the victims outside of school?"

"She worked on the school paper with Evan. Shortly before her death, she'd started making up ridiculous stories about having a relationship with him."

Preach's gaze had wandered to the old woman, and he glanced sharply back at Carrie. "What do you mean?"

"Oh, she bragged that she and Evan would be going out soon. Whenever I asked for proof she gave a secretive smile and changed the subject. To books, of course. That was all she ever talked about, Evan Shanks and literature. And homemade cherry ice cream," she said, with the first hint of affection or regret Preach had heard. "My sister loved ice cream."

"When did she start discussing a potential relationship with Evan?"

Carrie pressed her lips together. "A month or so before her death, I suppose."

"Was there a public rebuff?"

"As I said, it was all in Deirdre's head."

"You told this to the authorities?"

"Probably. I don't really remember."

"Why do you think your sister committed suicide?" Preach asked quietly.

Carrie's mouth twisted. "My sister was always so ... emotional. Mentally fragile." She pressed her lips together as she shook her head. "I just don't know why she went so far."

"But if you had to guess?" Preach asked. "I'm sorry to dredge up the past."

He thought he saw another twitch of a pinky from Deirdre's mother. Then again, a hummingbird had just alighted on a bush near the window.

"Oh, something probably happened with a boy or at school that tipped the scales. Maybe Evan snubbed her. The smallest thing would set her off."

He lowered his voice out of respect. "What about at home?"

"My mother doted on her. Our father traveled constantly."

"I have to ask—was there any abuse?"

"Absolutely not."

"A rumor going around the school?"

Deirdre's sister smirked, shaking her head as if she had considered it a million times. "As I said, there was nothing any of us knew about."

Preach let out a wispy breath. The case, his career, was slipping through his fingers. "Can I see her bedroom?"

"Sure." She held up her palms. "But it won't do you any good."

The mother turned her head as Carrie led them upstairs. Preach smiled and greeted her, feeling uncomfortable, but the older woman merely blinked.

Deirdre's room was the first doorway on the left. As he had seen with many families struck by tragedy, Preach expected to find an eerily anachronistic bedroom unchanged from the day Deirdre had died, a memory trapped in amber.

Instead he found a room with a fresh coat of beige paint, empty except for an aging Steinway piano. He got a whiff of lemon-scented aerosol.

"We had a garage sale this summer," Carrie said. "Finally got rid of Deirdre's things. Sometimes you have to let go." She gave a nervous glance at the stairs, as if her mother hadn't approved of the decision.

Preach's shoulders slumped in disappointment. Any evidence that might have called out to him from the past, however remote, had drifted out of reach. "Are any of Deirdre's possessions left?"

"I'm afraid not. A woman came in and bought everything of Deidre's we had."

He blinked. "Do you know who this woman was?"

"She never gave her name. She was fixing up a room for a visiting niece and offered a good price for the whole kit and caboodle. I play the piano, so we kept that. I was glad to see it all go, to be honest. It was like living with a ghost."

"Was this woman from Creekville?"

She shrugged. "I assume so."

"Can you describe her? Please think hard."

"Oh." Carrie leaned on the piano with sudden seriousness. "I see. Well, she seemed about my age, maybe a little older. Medium height. Stocky."

Not even close to Rebecca Worthington's description, he thought, and Carrie would have recognized the mayor. "What about her face?"

She considered the question. "I didn't pay that much attention. I remember it was a bitterly cold day, very windy. She wore an overcoat and a hat pulled low."

Preach's heart started beating faster. "Was it a beige overcoat? With a bowler hat?"

"Yes. Yes, it was! In fact, I thought she was a man at first, but when she spoke, I realized she was a woman." She stared at him, her face twitching. "How did you know what she was wearing?"

"Would you be willing to describe this woman to a sketch artist?" Preach asked. "I'll send one over right away."

"I—of course. What I can remember."

"Did she say or do anything unusual?"

"She just took everything that might be a good fit for her niece. It seemed very natural. Since my old things were sold ages ago, it was all Deirdre's. You know, if the room itself is important, we have a photo of it from before the sale. I . . . took it for mother."

"I'd like to see it."

Preach's mind was spinning as Deirdre's sister left the room. Ari's stalker was a *woman*?

Carrie returned holding a 5 x 7 photo. It portrayed the same room in which they were standing, except the walls had flowery teal-and-mustard wallpaper. Framed photographs sat atop a dresser, a pair of bookshelves took up the wall opposite the bed, and a pair of old ballet shoes hung next to a vintage Degas poster.

Sitting on a nightstand was an alarm clock, a small stack of books, and a pink jewelry box shaped like a lotus flower. Above the bed, a Japanese woodblock displayed an ethereal scene of cherry blossoms sprinkling a sidewalk.

Preach peered closer, but he couldn't make out any of the people in the photos. "Do you have a magnifier?" he asked Carrie.

She left and returned with a handheld magnifying glass. Preach held it up to the image, eager to see if one of Deirdre's photos harbored a clue. After scanning the pictures, he straightened in disappointment. Besides Carrie, no one close to Deirdre's age was depicted in the photographs.

"It's just family," Carrie said, sensing his unvoiced question.

Preach examined the rest of the room with the magnifier, just in case. He found nothing else of interest until he peered closer at the stack of books on the nightstand, trying to read the titles.

There were four books, spines aligned and facing the photographer. He could just make out the titles, and the shock of what he was seeing pulsed over him, rocking him back on his heels.

Crime and Punishment.

The Works of Edgar Allan Poe.

Five Little Pigs.

Lolita.

50

The quartet of titles stared back at Preach like the mouth of a cave. They were even arranged in order of the murders, starting with *Crime and Punishment* on the bottom, and he was forced to make the ominous assumption that the novel on top, *Lolita*, would become the same emissary of death as the other three.

Carrie leaned over to see what he had focused on, then took a step back and clamped a hand to her mouth. "Dear Jesus. The books from the murders."

Preach scoured the photo a final time. "Did those books have any particular meaning to your sister?"

"If they were on her nightstand, they were probably her favorite novels at the time. They tended to rotate, though Poe and Agatha Christie were two of her favorites. And Jane Austen, of course. She worshipped her."

Preach lowered the photo, thinking of the halved Jane Austen tattoo on the inside of Ari's wrists—another connection between the two.

Except Deirdre Hollings had been full of agony, and short on hope.

"Was *The Murders in the Rue Morgue* a favorite of your sister's?" he asked, since the Poe volume was the only compilation among the four. If Deirdre hadn't chosen that particular short story, then someone else had.

"Not that she ever told me."

"I hate to ask," he said quietly, "but did you ever have any doubt as to whether your sister committed suicide?"

"No, and neither did the police."

He reached for one of his business cards. "If you think of anything else unusual, either around the time of your sister's death or in the weeks surrounding the garage sale, please call."

Carrie started to shake her head, then stopped. "There was one thing, though I'm sure it's unrelated. My sister had a secret admirer."

Preach tightened his grip on the business card.

"Someone sent her gifts, once a week for two months. Flowers, candy, even that jewelry box you saw in the photo."

"Deidre never told you who it was?"

"I don't think she knew." She gave him a knowing look. "Mother thought Deirdre was seeing someone behind our back, but I always thought it was a prank. One of her classmates getting his kicks, maybe even that horrid Byronic Society."

"Why would they do that?"

"Why are kids cruel the world over?"

Preach thought about his own days as a teenager, the ugly and callous behavior that had plagued his past. "Good question. Was there ever a note attached to the gifts?"

"Not that I know of."

"I don't suppose you still have any of them?" he asked, thinking of a potential DNA sample.

She chuckled. "Goodness, no."

"Did you tell the police about the gifts when she died?" He had seen no mention of any of this in the file.

"Probably not. They had stopped months earlier."

"Which is why you think they were unrelated?"

"That, and because they were just harmless gifts."

Preach gave Carrie his card and thanked her for her time. Nothing about this case was harmless, he thought, as he walked to his car under a hazy, whitewashed sky that resembled an overcooked fried egg.

Nothing at all.

He swung over to Ray's to get Ari, avoiding the police station and the chief's texts while he tried to get a handle on what was going on. The streets were a blur of sound and movement, amorphous forms in the forest of madness his hometown had become.

Somehow Deirdre Hollings's decades-old suicide was connected to the murders. More than connected: it was the star attraction.

Deirdre had been obsessed with joining the Byronic Wilderness Society. An unidentified person had sent a string of gifts to Deirdre a few months before her death.

Ari was almost Deirdre's doppelganger, and they both loved Jane Austen. Ari's stalker had purchased all of Deirdre's belongings at a garage sale. Ari's stalker was a woman.

He had to recalibrate.

"Have you read *Lolita*?" Preach asked.

Ari was staring out of the dash and furiously twisting her thumb ring. He knew she wanted to ask what he had found. "It's been a few years, but it's not a book you forget."

"I imagine not."

"It's the story of an aging child molester's doomed love affair with a nymphet. The book that launched his career. Apparently no one cared about Nabokov's transcendent prose until he wrote about a monster."

Preach gripped the wheel. He had always had a hard time with the fact that God allowed pedophilia to exist. After seeing the dying light in that child's eyes in the treehouse, two glass trinkets ground to dust, he could barely hear the word without an uncontrollable rage blurring his vision. "What do I need to know?"

"At the end of the book, Humbert Humbert—the protagonist—murdered Clare Quilty, the man who stole Lolita from him. Quilty was also a pedophile, though unlike Humbert, who truly loved Lolita, Quilty just wanted her to star in his pornographic films. Good stuff, huh? But Lolita worshipped Clare Quilty and chose to run away with him. Her portrayal as an instigator is my main beef with the novel—I mean, *c'mon*. Then again, it was Humbert's story, and he's an unreliable narrator."

"How did the murder go down?"

"Humbert tracked Quilty to his house and shot him to death. It was messy."

"Were there any other distinctive characteristics or physical clues?"

"I'd have to read it again. Swing by the bookstore and I'll pick up a copy. I can point you to the right pages."

Preach turned left at the next intersection, toward town. "Anything else that strikes you about the novel?"

Ari pressed her lips together and propped one of her sleek black boots on the dash. "The book's a no-holds-barred description of Humbert's obsession with a young girl, but it's also a book about the overwhelming power of love to transform, save, and destroy. Humbert is a man who can't control his passions but who is more alive because of them."

Preach's cell phone buzzed again. Another message from Chief Higgins. She was getting angry. He texted back that he was with a witness.

They picked up a copy of *Lolita* at the Wandering Muse, then swung by a food truck for dinner. Trios of carnitas tacos to go.

"I don't know if your stalker and the murderer are the same person," Preach said, as they ate out of disposable containers in his living room, "though it's looking likely. But if the stalker is obsessed with you because you look like Deirdre, doesn't your current age ring false? If Lolita is the model?"

"Toward the end of *Lolita*, Humbert realized he was truly in love with his muse, even after she was no longer a nymphet. Maybe the same thing happened to our killer. She never got over Deirdre, and for some reason, I"—she looked uncomfortable saying the words—"spark her killer's memory."

Preach loaded his tacos with hot sauce, then shoved them down as he skimmed the part of the novel describing the murder. Besides the location—the victim's house—nothing else caught his eye.

But for the first time, he might be a step ahead of the murderer. He was excited until an uncomfortable thought hit him. What if the murderer had been watching Deirdre's house? What if she had seen him leave?

Even if she had, she wouldn't have known about the photo.

So the question remained: *What had happened to Deirdre Hollings?*

Something had been done to her, he felt sure of it. Something terrible. And he guessed Ari's stalker, whether the murderer or not, knew about it.

He didn't know yet why retribution was being exacted after so much time, but he thought he had a very good idea as to the identity of the fourth victim. Ever since the conversation with Elvis Klein, he'd harbored a suspicion that one of the members of the Byronic Wilderness Society had started murdering the others. But now he saw a different angle: the members of the Society might have conspired to commit some awful crime against Deirdre. And someone else, an unknown member or an outsider, was taking matters into her own hands.

He turned to Ari, sitting on the couch with her feet tucked under her legs. "I don't think the mayor is the murderer," he said. "I think she's the fourth target."

Ari glanced outside, at the rising moon, then met Preach's gaze. "Tomorrow's the anniversary of Deirdre's death. Didn't the other murders take place during the night, early in the a.m.?"

In response, he grabbed his keys and shrugged into his coat, then tossed Ari's leather jacket to her as she jumped off the couch.

Preach raced through his hometown. Memories of his own childhood collided with the secrets that lurked beneath Creekville like debris on the bottom of an algae-choked lake.

Youth possessed no perspective, he thought, the fatal flaw to all of its extraordinary advantages. The young are able to take bold action because they don't fully grasp the consequences a wrong choice can entail. The late teen years were a mad dash up the mountain of knowledge, dodging bullets of self-doubt with thousand-foot drops looming on either side.

And at some point everyone stumbles. Enters the world by plunging off the cliff, like Icarus falling from the sky.

After Ricky was burned, Preach had felt as if he would never regain his equilibrium. He had once been so arrogant, so sure, but then he had learned about suffering, about God, and then he had descended into hell on earth in the prisons and returned with a soul blistered from the lake of fire.

He didn't understand the world. He couldn't reconcile.

He could only try to help.

They parked at the station. Reporters flowed into his wake as he swept into the station with Ari.

"Wait here," he said, grabbing a manila folder when they reached his cubicle. "I need to talk to the chief."

Ari gripped his arm and then sank into his chair. Again he admired her coolness under fire.

Preach noticed Kirby's head above the line of cubicles, walking down the hall toward them. Preach took a firm grip on the folder containing the photos of Kirby's sister. He still hadn't figured out how to tell him. The chief should probably decide.

"Chief's been looking for you all day. I did my best, but . . ."

Kirby's shrug implied that he could only do so much to hold off Chief Higgins, since partners on such a high-profile case should be accountable and know where each other were when needed.

"I'll catch you up later," Preach said, cordial but firm. Not only because of Jalene, but because a leak at this stage could ruin everything. The chief was the only person he could trust with the dynamite he had.

"The mayor stopped by again, too," Kirby said. "She looked like she wanted to chew on some iron."

"Gotcha," Preach said, then dismissed him with a nod.

Just before he reached the chief's office, the station's administrative assistant, Sandy McCorkle, called his name. Her cubicle was right next to Chief Higgins's office.

"Fax came in for you from Chapel Hill," Sandy said, holding out a sheet of paper. "Looks like a sketch."

The chief had already spotted him. Preach grabbed the piece of paper, flipping it over to view the artist's rendering of the woman who had purchased Deirdre Hollings's possessions.

The sketch was far from definitive, which only made sense. Unless Carrie Hollings had a photographic memory, she wouldn't have been able to provide perfect recall on someone she had briefly met a few months earlier. Especially since she had barely seen her face.

But there was some detail, more than he expected, and the longer Preach stared down at the image, the faster his heart started to beat.

The woman in the photo had a midsection like an apple, rounded but firm. The height was estimated at 5′8″ or 5′9″. A large, powerful woman. A woman with enough strength to crush Farley Robertson's skull with a hatchet and stuff Damian Black upside down in a fireplace.

Her face was middle-aged, vigorous, rawboned. Wide flat cheeks and a hat pulled low. Small eyes of an indeterminate color. A thick neck, and a jaw whose rigidity suggested an almost military force of will.

Certainly a woman who could pass for a male from a distance.

It was also, judging by the sketch, a woman he thought he knew.

There was a stocky, middle-aged woman with a strong jaw sitting not ten feet from that very spot, waiting to speak with him in her office—and just like the woman in the sketch, where a single strand of curls was poking out from underneath the bowler hat, Chief Higgins had blazing red hair.

51

Preach stood in the hallway, reeling, working to conceal his shock.

Who had easy access to an illegal substance like Rohypnol?

A police chief in charge of an evidence room.

Who would know how to use a variety of weapons with deadly precision, stage a crime scene and leave no clues?

Who was the only other person who knew about Preach's psychiatric visits and could have leaked the details to the media? Who had asked him to consider stepping down from the case and leave a void at the station?

Was it all an act, he wondered, or did Chief Higgins calm herself with yoga and peace bracelets and herbal teas to try to stave off the darkness, keep the demons at bay?

The only thing missing was the connection to Deirdre. Chief Higgins was around the same age as the players involved, and she might have lived in Creekville at some point during her youth. Because of her seeming obsession with Ari, Preach had to assume the chief had had some kind of relationship or similar obsession with Deirdre. Chief Higgins had never mentioned her sexual orientation, but she had also never mentioned seeing another man after her husband had died. Or maybe there was another angle that Preach was missing.

The chief waved impatiently for him to enter. He scrambled for something to say. He had been about to tell her everything.

Forcing himself to appear calm, he eased the door open and managed a sheepish expression. He couldn't go over her head without harder evidence. He had to throw her off her guard.

"Well?" she said, when he entered. "Where've you been?"

"Following up on a few leads."

The chief glanced in Ari's direction. Preach wondered what was going through her head, with the object of her fixation sitting twenty feet away.

"And her?"

"I'm keeping her in sight until I figure something out."

"What was so important you couldn't call me back?"

A note of commiseration softened the anger in her voice. She was such a good liar. She had fooled him from the start, fooled them all.

"The pest control company finally got back to us," he said. "One of their workers thought he saw someone lurking around the parking lot the day before Farley died. I tracked him down and got a description."

She leaned forward, eyes intense. "And?"

"It was just Wade Fee."

She eased into her seat and reached for the stress ball. He smacked a hand against the desk. "I'm sick and tired of being in the dark. If someone else dies . . ."

"We have other worries. The mayor is incensed with you. Claims you paid her an after-hours visit."

"I did."

"Care to elaborate?"

To keep the chief's attention diverted, he gave her the manila folder with the photos he had found at the marina. He had copies hidden safely at his house.

Her eyes grew wider and wider as she flipped through the photos, and she put a fist to her mouth. "Good God. Does Kirby know?"

"Not yet. I'm waiting for the right time."

"There'll never be a right time for that," she said.

"I know."

He could see genuine empathy tightening the chief's features. She exhaled a weary sigh and reached for her tea. "The mayor said she'd fire us both if you go anywhere near her again."

Preach held up the manila folder in disbelief. "Even with these?"

"What's the crime?"

He opened his mouth, then slowly closed it.

"Maybe if Kirby's sister comes forward and says she was paid by the mayor—but who's going to ask her to do that? Do we ruin her life for a slap on the mayor's wrist?"

"Losing a political career is hardly a slap on the wrist," Preach said. "Plus there's far more to it. You know that."

"So show me. We need concrete evidence linking the mayor and Mac to the murders. Emails, phone calls, eyewitness testimony. *Something*."

Preach started to speak, then looked away, hands clenching at his sides. *He could act, too.*

"I have faith in you," she said. "But you're under scrutiny, and she's still the mayor. I don't want you within a mile of her or her house."

Preach kept up the pretense of finishing the conversation, but Chief Higgins's last words kept ringing inside his head.

I don't want you within a mile of her.

The chief was clearing the path.

Preach found Kirby at his cubicle. "Take a walk with me," he said quietly. Then, more loudly, "Grab a slice across the street?"

Kirby consented with a wary nod, and Preach grabbed Ari—he couldn't leave her alone near the chief—and herded them both through the reporters, down the street to the Creekville Pizza Pub.

Preach ordered takeout to make it look real. He led Kirby to a table in the corner, asked Ari to wait a few tables over, and told his partner about everything except the photos of his sister.

"The *chief*?" Kirby said, his face slack with disbelief. He kept swallowing over and over, as if something were stuck in his throat. "Why?"

"I don't know yet."

"What do we do?"

"I'll get to the mayor and warn her. Then we catch Chief Higgins in the act."

"Should we get Chapel Hill involved?"

Preach shook his head. "Even if I send you, they're going to ask where you got all of this, and you'll have to tell them. With what we've got, a few hours isn't enough time to convince them to listen to a cop with issues who's been warned to stay away. Maybe they'd send a car to watch her, maybe they wouldn't, but they'd tie me up for the rest of the night. We'd be hamstrung. The mayor would die."

"What if you're wrong?"

"Then I'm wrong." Preach checked his watch. Eight-thirty p.m. "This is going down in a few hours. It might be our only shot. I need you to keep an eye on the chief for me."

Kirby's hand was tapping against his leg. "At the station, you mean?"

"Let me know when she leaves, then stay with her. Keep me posted on where she goes. Can you do that?"

"She'll make my car."

"Take an unmarked one and stay out of sight. Assume she's going to her house and heading out sometime after midnight. I just need to know when she leaves."

Kirby balled and unballed his fists. He looked nervous, out of his depth. Preach put a hand on his shoulder. "You've got this."

Kirby looked up, slowly meeting his gaze. "Then what?"

Preach wrote an address down on a napkin. "As soon as the chief leaves her house, let me know and get to the mayor's house as fast as you can. Tell Terry and Bill to be on call tonight, but don't tell them why."

As Preach rose to leave, he said, "I'm sorry for doubting you. I thought you might have been the leak."

Kirby clapped him on the shoulder, his eyes wounded but forgiving. "Don't sweat it," he said, after a moment.

Preach looked over at Ari and shook his head in disgust; he didn't like any of his choices when it came to her. But he had already made his decision.

Kirby returned to the station, and Preach walked Ari to his car. "I'm taking you to Ray's house again."

She bit her lip as he pulled into the street.

Just one night, he thought, *and this will all be over.*
Just one night.

After Preach left the station with Ari, Kirby slunk back to his cubicle. He was lower than the lowest of life-forms, he knew. Lower than a maggot wriggling in the month-old corpse of a rat.

You've got this, Preach had said.

Something Kirby had always wanted to hear.

Yet still he made the call.

"What ya got for me?" Mac said, after he answered.

"Preach is headed the mayor's way tonight."

Mac chuckled. "Crazy bastard. He won't have a job in the morning. He must think he has an offer she can't refuse."

"What?"

"Don't you worry about that. I've got eyes on him, so I hope you're playing me straight."

Kirby swallowed. "Just call the station if he gets close. Don't try anything yourself."

"Now why would I do that? What's he got on the mayor?"

"I don't know." Kirby gripped the phone. Explaining everything Preach had discovered wasn't part of the agreement, and he didn't want the mayor's blood on his hands, too. "You might want to put a few guys on her, just in case."

"You don't know? Not buying it."

"Trust me, he doesn't tell me everything. Not after the leak."

Mac's chuckle was dark and throaty. "I don't trust my own mother, bucko. Not even after I bought her a house."

The decades-old suicide haunted Preach as he and Ari sped down the long gravel road. What had so devastated Deirdre Hollings that she felt it necessary to take her own life? Preach had seen her photo, the hopeful young eyes. The terrible pain the teenager must have felt, the loss of hope, swelled inside him.

What had happened all those years ago?

He focused on the deserted road snaking through the pines. Ray's house was five minutes away, and he could feel Ari's tension radiating out from the passenger seat. A gentle fog coated the night, an ephemeral veil that made everything outside the car seem unformed, as if Preach and Ari were moving inside a soap bubble of reality, creating the world as they moved.

He pressed his lips together. Maybe the mayor hadn't murdered anyone, but she still hated his guts, and he felt sure she had given the order for Mac's goons to come after him and Kirby.

Nevertheless, it was his job to protect her.

Headlights appeared in the rearview, the first vehicle they had seen since turning off the main road. Preach tensed; Ray had chosen his house for its isolation.

The lights grew brighter, rushing toward them at a much faster clip than they were traveling. Preach slowed and squeezed the wheel, straining for a glimpse of the vehicle in the mirror. It wasn't a motorcycle, he was sure of that.

The headlights drew closer, and he realized they belonged to a battered pickup truck with a covered bed. He prayed it was just some redneck kids on a joyride. Just in case, he gripped his gun in his lap and told Ari to get low in her seat. She complied but tilted her head to watch the truck go by. As it passed, she drew a sharp breath. "That's the same—"

Her words cut off with a scream as the tailgate popped down and something large and brown flew out of the bed, crashing into Preach's windshield. An animal of some sort. The impact caused him to jerk to the right, into a steep ditch hidden in the darkness. Preach's head struck the window when the car flipped on its side, and colored spots filled his vision.

The pickup truck screeched to a stop.

52

Kirby sat in his cubicle at the station, lifeless as a wooden doll.

Mac hadn't had to set him up in the hotel like that. Humiliate him. He'd done it because he knew it would break Kirby down, hit him where it hurt the most. Worst of all, Kirby knew he had enjoyed it.

Now Kirby was in so deep he didn't know how to get out. Which was Mac's intention all along, he knew.

Another faithful servant.

He started to slam his fist down, then controlled himself. He couldn't fail Preach and tip the chief off by making a scene. He had to finish this task, get through the night. When this insane case was over, he would salvage what remained of his career and come clean with Preach. If anyone would understand, it was the detective.

He snorted at his own naiveté. *Get a grip, Kirby. You just sabotaged an ongoing police investigation by tipping off a criminal. Not even Preach will forgive you for that.*

No, Kirby had dug his own grave. He was a living corpse, covered in dirt and stripped of his future, dragging his family down with him.

Chief Higgins finally gathered her things and closed her door for the night. She had stayed late; it was a few minutes after ten.

Kirby texted Preach to let him know, then slumped in his chair again. How long should he wait before heading to her house? Two more officers left in rapid succession, now that the chief was gone. Kirby was the last man standing, except for dispatch.

He rose to pace the station. A cup of water did nothing to ease the dryness in his mouth. He decided to wait five more minutes, and in the meantime he sidled into the chief's office, still barely able to believe she had murdered three people and deceived them all so thoroughly. How could she go to work every day and look them in the face?

Probably just like I'm doing.

He didn't know what he expected to find in her office. A diary detailing her deception? A picture of Deirdre Hollings taped to the underside of her chair? Serial killer action figures?

Just before he left, he slapped on a pair of evidence gloves and riffled through her desk. In the middle drawer, he found the manila folder Preach had been holding when he entered her office. He knew the detective had been keeping things from him, and he couldn't help taking a peek. Thinking it through, it was odd that the detective had shown new evidence to the chief and not Kirby, when it was the chief who Preach no longer trusted. Maybe the detective was keeping up appearances by pretending to confide.

Kirby opened the folder and flipped through the photos, his eyebrows rising at the increasingly graphic subject matter. The detective had told Kirby about the photos at the Pizza Pub, but he was confused as to why Preach hadn't just showed them to him earlier, with the chief.

He leafed through the final few, about to put the photos back in the desk when he saw her.

Jalene.

A shiver whisked through him, numbing his limbs and stealing his breath, scooping out a hole in his stomach. He imagined it was the sort of shudder people felt just before they died, a last gasp of mortality as their soul slipped into the ether and left the body to fall away, a discarded husk.

His throat constricted as he pawed through the rest of the photos, separating the ones of his sister and ripping them to shreds. He let the rest of the photos fall to the floor, and then stood in a daze, out of body, his arms slack at his sides.

Jared didn't have a scholarship, and his sister didn't have a hernia. Oh no, not at all.

Thank goodness!

She was just a little bit tender.

His displaced energy bounced back, hitting him like a drug. He started to overturn the chief's desk in a fit of rage but stopped with his hands gripping its edge. Not from fear of reprisal but because he realized how futile it was. How *useless*.

And why bother with useless acts when he could do something that would actually address the situation? He had never felt so logical in his life. Yes, there was something he could do.

Something that would restore his sister's honor, and speak for voices unheard.

Something that would matter.

After the initial shock of the crash, Preach felt a rush of cold air and heard the sounds of shattering glass, followed by heavy footsteps on the pavement, and an engine idling somewhere off to the side. He smelled cigarettes, a foul and musty barnyard odor, the metallic scent of spilled blood, and charred rubber from the truck's sudden stop.

Then came the pain, focused in the side of his head and in his sprained wrist, spreading across his body in nauseating waves.

Sight returned last. His eyes blinked open, and he realized he was nearly upside down, his car stuck at the bottom of a wide ditch. A dead deer was sprawled on the ground in front of the car. Ari was slumped in the passenger seat, eyes closed, blood trickling across her forehead and covering her face and arms. He couldn't even tell if she was alive.

A familiar black beard appeared in a jagged hole in the driver's side window. Preach saw the shadowy outlines of more figures in the background.

"Howdy, Detective," Mac said, squatting down to talk. "Pity 'bout that deer. Must have come up out of nowhere."

"Ari," Preach managed to croak. He reached for his weapon with one hand and the seatbelt buckle with his other. If he could only get free, he could scramble out of the window.

Mac stuck a black handgun in his face. "Huh-uh."

Preach looked up, gasping through the pain. "Call an ambulance. She could die."

"You best be worrying about yourself."

Mina strode out of the gloom in a calfskin jacket, leaned halfway through the window, and, with Mac's gun in Preach's face the entire time, plucked the detective's gun and cell phone out of the car. After she managed to yank the passenger door halfway open, Mina rummaged through Ari's pockets and felt all around her seat. "No phone," she said.

Mac grunted. "Good enough. She ain't coming to, and there's no one around if she did."

"You've got it all wrong," Preach said, in desperation. "The mayor's life is in danger! Leave us here and go help her. I know you need her."

"It's gone a little far for that, don't ya think?"

"This isn't about us!"

Mac cocked the hammer. "Everything you represent is about you and me, pretty boy. Fuck you and the privileged horse you rode in on."

"Are you insane? Call an ambulance! I'm a *police officer*."

"Can't argue with that. If you survived, I'd be in a big old heap of trouble. Tell you what. I'm here because I'm guessing you found those blackmail pictures. Give me any copies you made, and I'll let the girl live. Lie to me, and I'll come back for her."

Preach thought fast. Mac must be depending on an accomplice at the police station to snatch the originals out of evidence. He glanced at Ari and balled his fists. He didn't have a choice. "They're inside the stove on my porch."

Mac made a call on his cell, Preach guessed to someone on standby at his house. Mac looked satisfied when he hung up the phone. "Just the one set?"

"I didn't have time for anything else."

He shoved the gun in Preach's face. "If you're lying—"

"That's it. I swear. Now drag her out."

Mac clicked his tongue, then winked at Mina. "Burn it down, girl."

"You promised!" Preach roared. "Let her go!"

Mina popped the gas tank, lifted a plastic jug off the ground, and started dousing the car and the grass around it. The stench of gasoline was unmistakable, and it brought him back to Ricky's garage, all those years ago. The screams, the flames, Ricky beating himself in vain.

Preach reached for the seat buckle but couldn't get it to release. The sudden movement made him dizzy, and Mac chuckled at the effort.

Mina dropped the jug and flicked her thumb against her cigarette lighter, eyes eager as they studied the flame.

"I'm begging you to take her out of here," Preach said. He couldn't watch Ari burn. Not her. Not again. "She hasn't seen a thing."

"That's real sweet-like," Mac said. "But she's had her chances, too."

Mina dropped the match, igniting a sizzling flame in a wide swath along the ground. Preach bellowed and made a grab for the gun, but Mac swatted his hand away and struck him in the temple with the butt of the weapon. Preach lost consciousness as the fire roared to life.

53

Kirby parked outside the mayor's house, right next to a Ford pickup with two of Mac's men inside. They nodded as Kirby passed, assuming he was acting on Mac's orders from the boss.

Dark patches encroached on the edges of Kirby's vision. He parked the car with a rancid taste in his mouth, trying to shake off the roar in his head. Swallowing over and over, he walked down the driveway and rang the doorbell, somehow keeping it together until Rebecca Worthington opened the door, her eyes on his badge. "Can I help you?" she asked.

"Do you have a minute, Ma'am?" Kirby's eyes flicked to the truck. "I'm Officer Kirby. Mac sends his regards."

She frowned and let him inside, closing the door behind him.

"Where's your family?" he asked. Speaking took effort, as if a vulture were perched inside his chest, squeezing his heart with its talons.

"At the lake house for the weekend." Her eyes narrowed. "What's this about? I wasn't told you were coming."

Kirby almost laughed out loud. *What's this about*, he found himself muttering.

"Officer Kirby! What are you doing at my house at eleven p.m.?"

He looked down at the floor, felt the muscles along the sides of his neck start to twitch. When he looked up, his hands had balled into fists, and the tone of his voice was pleading, begging her to tell him the pictures were fake, that none of it was real. "You turned her into an animal," he whispered.

"E*xcuse* me?"

It took her a few seconds, but he knew the instant she figured it out. Her eyes pinched at the corners and then widened, recognized the narrow face and chestnut-colored skin.

And in that moment, he knew it was true, all of it, and his last shred of hope for a different future slipped away.

She tried to conceal her surprise. "I have no idea what you're talking about. You'd better start explaining—"

He backhanded her across the face. "I saw the photos."

She stumbled, blood seeping from the edges of her mouth. She looked at him with almost comical surprise, then drew up straight. With icy calm, she said, "So how much do you want? I'll be paying for her twice, I suppose."

He stalked toward her, slowly, and she took a step back. "We didn't force her, you know," she said. "We made her an offer and she accepted."

"Shut up!" he screamed, whipping out his gun and raising it to eye level. "She had no choice. She did it to save her son. My *nephew*." He shook the gun at her, spittle flying out of his mouth. "So you *shut up*!"

The mayor swallowed. She was backed against a wall. "I committed no crime," she said, her voice a near-whisper. "You can't release those photos."

He took another step forward. "Release them?" he said, in disbelief. "I destroyed them."

"I don't understand. So why are you . . ." She trailed off as she looked in his eyes and understood. Sudden terror distorted her face. "You're a police officer," she said, trying to firm her voice. "If you don't leave my house this very instant you'll be relieved of your duties. Stripped of your pension. Then where will your sister be?"

If Kirby hadn't sold out to Mac, maybe a call to reason would have prevailed. But it was all too much. He had no future. Not only that, but he heard something in the mayor's voice when she mentioned his sister, a lack of empathy even when staring down a gun, that told him Jalene was nothing to her but a thing to be exploited.

Kirby had become a police officer because he needed to pay his bills and the department was hiring. While he had never believed in the system, he did share a deep-seated interest in one principle with his fellow boys in blue.

Justice.

An image from the photo of his sister dressed as a dog flashed through his mind, the one with the mayor laughing into her hand as his sister was violated by two men. Jalene's eyes flat and barren, stripped of humanity.

"I don't think I'll be getting a pension," Kirby said, in a thick-tongued voice.

He felt giddy, almost drunk, when he pulled the trigger.

54

Preach woke in a hospital bed with bleached November rays peeking through the blinds. He was lying on his side, facing a clock on the wall beside the window. 8:47 a.m.

Why was he still alive?

The events of the night before were still vivid, as if no time had passed and he was still trapped in the car. He shuddered and rubbed sleep out of his eyes, then shifted to his back and saw Chief Higgins sitting beside the bed.

His hands tensed under the sheet. He scrambled to a sitting position. A stabbing pain shot through his wrist, and his head felt as if someone was drilling a hole into it.

The chief's hands were clasped in her lap. "Good morning, sleepyhead."

"Where's Ari," he croaked. His throat was as dry and rough as a cat's tongue.

The chief twisted the lid off a bottle of water and handed it to him. He wouldn't have accepted anything unopened, but he drank half the bottle and repeated the question. The chief's eyebrows lifted in approval. "She's a brave one, isn't she?"

Is, not *was*. His heart leapt. "She's alive?"

The chief looked confused, then her face softened. "You poor thing. Of course you don't know, do you?"

The chief's demeanor, the whole Zenner-than-thou attitude, infuriated him. He wanted to twist her arm behind her back and march her through the streets, expose her for what she was. But she didn't know that he knew, and he had to keep it that way for at least a few more hours, until he could contact Internal Affairs and set things in motion.

Unless the chief did know, and she'd come to the hospital to take matters into her own hands. The thought chilled him. She probably wouldn't kill him in the hospital, but maybe she planned to take him out of there, then drug him on the way to the station.

That, he thought grimly, wasn't going to happen.

He uncovered his hands in case he needed to move quickly. His senses on high alert, he decided to find out what he could about the night before.

"Tell me," he said.

"Would you like some coffee first? Tea?"

"No."

She lifted her own tea off the bedside table. "Ari was conscious the whole time. After the crash, she said you didn't answer when she called your name, and when she saw Mac approaching the car and you finally woke up, she decided to play dead."

"I must have blacked out when my head hit the window," he murmured. "Go on."

"Before you came to, she turned her phone off and shoved it in her underwear. Once Mac left, she managed to drag you out of the car and call 911."

"Mac was sloppy," he said.

"That, and Ari was fast. Mina knew what she was doing. The gas tank exploded seconds after Ari dragged you out."

Preach exhaled with the thought of how close to death they had come. He looked back to the chief and saw a shadow crouching behind her gaze.

"What aren't you telling me?" Preach said. "Did something else happen to her?"

The chief was having trouble meeting his gaze. "No, no. She was released hours after the accident and stayed by your bed all night. I relieved her thirty minutes ago. The nurse assured us you were fine despite the head wound—you took quite a knock, buster—so Ari left to open the bookstore."

It suddenly dawned on him. "The mayor," he said quietly, with the full realization that the murderer was sitting right beside him.

The chief gave a slow nod, her expression grave. She deserved an Oscar. "Dead. Kirby killed her."

His next question fell away, dropped to the bottom of the abyss. "*What*?"

"He found the photos." Her lips compressed. "In my desk."

"Oh God."

"He's already turned himself in."

They were both quiet for a moment, and Preach had the sudden knowledge that the chief was laughing on the inside, cackling with glee that Kirby had done her work for her.

No, he thought, that's not right. She wasn't a monster in that way—just an instrument of revenge. Still, her actions had set all of this in motion, and he blamed her for every single thing that had happened. Including Kirby.

"Mac and Mina?" he asked grimly.

"In jail. Ari told us everything." The chief rose. "I've got to head in, and there's someone waiting to see you. We'll talk about the rest when you're well. Take your time coming back."

She reached over to pat his hand, and he forced himself not to recoil. She held his gaze for an uncomfortable amount of time, then said, "It's all over now."

After the chief left, before he could start to process what had happened and form a plan of action, the last person he expected to see entered the room.

"You look like hell, Joe," Wade said with a grunt. He was looking at his old friend with guarded relief.

"So do you. And I'm the one in the hospital."

Wade chuckled as he approached the bed, easing the tension. "Yeah, well, I don't have any flowers. Just wanted to make sure you're okay."

"Thanks. I mean it."

Wade's face tightened. "I came to say that Mac crossed the line with you. I also heard you told him to back off me. Listen, if you need anything, any testimony . . . you can count on me."

It was a brave gesture. Mac still had plenty of cronies.

Wade stuck out his hand. Preach looked down at it and thought about how easy it was to be childhood friends. Did you live next door to one another? Check. Play on the same sports team, share the same homeroom? Instant bond.

But then we age and formulate our responses to the challenges of life, to politics and taxes and religion, develop our *agenda*. We grow apart, sometimes to polar extremes, wondering where our old friends went so wrong without stopping to think how we might have, too.

Preach rejected Wade's attempt to shake his hand, instead pulling the grip tight, forearm to forearm.

Just like in the old days.

Preach left the hospital an hour later. He called his mother to let her know he was okay, then called Ari and got her voicemail. He would swing by the bookstore as soon as he took care of a few pressing matters.

First he returned to the station, where the number of reporters seemed to have metastasized. They gawked as he pushed through them without a word, bypassed the main entrance, and strode to the jail. He caught a glimpse of himself in one of the glass doors: unshaven, hair disheveled, wrist in a splint, bruised neck, a huge bandage covering the left side of his head.

He paced the long hallway and stopped in front of Kirby's cell, two cells down from where Belker had been. His partner was sitting in his cot with his back against the wall, arms slumped at his sides, chin tucked into his chest. He barely lifted his head as Preach approached.

A shudder of sadness rolled through him at the despair smothering his partner's face. "I'm sorry," he said.

"For what?" Kirby asked, in a voice that sounded like his soul had been vacuumed right out of it.

"For not handling it better. The photos."

"Trust me, it wouldn't have mattered."

Preach wasn't so sure.

They regarded each other in silence, and then Kirby's head slowly bent forward, as if he didn't have the will to hold it up.

"Is there anything else I should know?" Preach said quietly. "About the chief? Something you discussed with the mayor that might help with an arrest?"

"We didn't talk about that," Kirby said in monotone. "And you should change your email password; I watched you type it in one day and told Monica. I was the rat."

Preach stood there for a few more moments. His weight had sunk into his heels. "Hang in there, Kirby," he said finally. "We'll get you a good lawyer."

No response.

"And I'll do everything I can to help your family."

Kirby's eyes slowly lifted. "Don't let them fall, Preach," he whispered. "Don't let them fall."

Preach didn't go into the station. Instead, he got in his car and, while the reporters clamored for his attention, mentally prepared for a call with Internal Affairs. He had to convince them to detain Chief Higgins while he searched her house, pored over her phone and laptop, while the evidence was still fresh. It wouldn't be easy, and maybe she had covered her tracks too well, but he had to try. Kirby admitting he was the leak didn't help matters, but there was plenty of circumstantial evidence against the chief, and Preach was banking on Carrie Hollings to provide an eyewitness ID.

Yet there was a loose end to resolve before he went into battle with the chief of police. When he made his stand, a stand he knew would be very contentious and very public, he needed to have a clean record.

There could be no appearance of impropriety, no lingering doubt as to his mental state.

He needed that certificate of release from his aunt.

55

Preach hugged his aunt tight when she opened the door. She was the one person he needed to see, besides Ari, who might help wash the filth away.

The mayor and three other citizens dead on his watch. Kirby rotting in jail. Chief Higgins still a free woman, sitting behind her desk with her Girl Scout smiles.

Aunt Janice looped an arm through his. "Rough day," she said, the compassion in her eyes telling him she had seen the news.

He gave a tired nod. "I can't really discuss anything, but there's something very important I need to do today. And I need a certificate of sound mental health to do it. I understand you might not give it to me, but . . . do you think we can finish?"

Without a word, she walked him into her office and sat behind her desk, motioning for him to take the couch. She had assumed her professional demeanor, and he couldn't read her expression. It was childish, but he almost felt as if his aunt was betraying him by observing him in such a clinical manner after all that had happened.

Hopefully, after today, he would never have to visit her here again.

"We've talked enough about the past," she said, surprising him.

"We have?"

She folded her hands on the desk. "We should discuss the present."

"Oh."

"How would you characterize your current emotional state?"

Preach lowered his eyes. "Devastated. Four people have died. My partner is a good man, and he's in jail for murder. But I feel one hundred percent in control of my emotions. Able to carry out my duties."

"At any time during the course of the investigation, have you experienced a state of mind similar to what occurred in Atlanta?"

"No," he said, truthfully.

"Why do you think that is?"

"As I said before, I don't think anything else will hit me like that again. I think I've—" his eyes flicked away—"seen the worst."

"And if you haven't?"

"Then God help us all."

She was quiet for a moment, studying him.

"Look," he said. "I won't sit here and tell you there's nothing out there that could shock me again, because that's an impossible statement. But I can tell you that in all my years as a homicide officer, that was the only incident that caused me to stumble."

She kept looking at him as if making a physiognomic evaluation, judging the truth of his words by his face. Finally she relaxed her stare. "Joey, I've already prepared your certificate. I'll sign it for you now."

"What? You have? I . . ."

He trailed off, stunned, knowing he should accept the gift and walk out of there. Yet he couldn't bring himself to leave without knowing more. "What do you think happened?" he asked. "In Atlanta? By Ricky's bedside?"

"My assessment of you is that you are a functioning human being. A highly empathetic person who didn't know how to handle the depth of your emotions when you were young, so you pushed them away until they exploded. A person who has chosen a profession that is at times . . . challenging for that level of sensitivity. But I truly believe you have it under control, or you would not have been able to perform your duties so effectively over the years. You had one incident as a police officer. *One.* True, it bore an unfortunate result, but I'd wager we need a detective with your compassion working the streets far more than we need a callous officer with no possibility of a mental lapse."

It took him a moment to process her words. "I don't know what to say."

She stood and smiled. "I'll get the certificate. What about a glass of water? You look like you could use one."

WRITTEN IN BLOOD

"And some Tylenol, if you have any. I left mine in the car."

"I think I can find some."

After she left, he put his hands on his knees and released a deep sigh of relief that seemed to reach back through the decades. It was over. Truly over. He had screwed up, he felt certain things on a deep and visceral level, and his pent-up emotions had gotten the better of him a few times. But he was normal. He could start his life again.

Right after he put Chief Higgins away.

He stood to stretch his legs, and found his eyes once again drawn to the painting of the girl with the ibises. He found it so evocative. She was clutching her teal shawl to her throat, almost protectively, and when he looked closer he noticed that, in contrast to her smooth right hand, the girl's left hand was curved and frail, almost as if it had aged prematurely.

The girl's head was turned to the right, one eye hidden but the other facing the viewer. As if the girl knew a secret and had turned back, wondering if the observer knew as well. And there was something else . . . with a start, he realized that the girl, with her delicate features and smooth white skin, her dark hair and eyes, bore a strong resemblance to Deirdre and Ari.

He had to know who the artist was. He searched for "girl with two ibises painting" on his cell phone as a train whistled outside the window.

It was a Degas, which surprised him. He thought Degas painted only ballet dancers, like the one in Deirdre's room. The painting in his aunt's office was called, appropriately, *Young Woman with Ibis*.

The train whistled again, and Preach's eyes drifted to the other framed print, a Monet depicting a dreamy blue-green pond filled with pink lotus flowers.

The Monet seemed to spark another memory, and he kept staring at it until he figured out what it was: the lotus flowers in the painting bore a close resemblance to Deirdre's pink, lotus-shaped jewelry box.

Preach's eyes snapped back to the first painting.

Those strange, blood-red birds seemed to be both protecting the girl and trumpeting something to the sky. As if the girl harbored a secret, and her guardians wanted the world to know—and someone to pay.

Beauty and blood, the birds screamed. Sadness. Mystery. Pain. Retribution.

The train whistled a third time, long and keening. A train whose tracks dissected the woods that stretched behind his aunt's building—the same woods that began near J. T. Belker's house and ran right past Farley's Robertson's condo.

A prickling began along his forearms, spreading to the rest of his body in a shuddering wave of gooseflesh.

He berated himself. This was absurdity of the highest order. Sure, his aunt's and the chief's faces were somewhat similar, if you disregarded the chief's hair color and oily skin. The sketch artist's rendering was vague enough to apply to both. His aunt was the right age and had the same height and stocky build as the woman described by Deirdre's sister—but so was Chief Higgins.

It was the chief who had access to Rohypnol, who knew how to stage a crime scene.

Aunt Janice is a psychologist, is brilliant and always has been. She has access to drugs and could easily figure out a crime scene.

Everything I have against the chief is circumstantial.

And those same circumstances apply to Aunt Janice.

Good God, this was ridiculous! He stood and laughed at himself. There was one glaring detail, he thought triumphantly, that exonerated his aunt: the strand of red hair in the sketch, the feature that had cemented his suspicion of the chief.

Preach thought about it further and felt his face grow hot. *Aunt Janice keeps a red clown wig in her car. For the kids at the cancer ward.*

He tried feverishly to rule out his aunt. Unfortunately, her clown wig was fairly lifelike and made for a woman, as opposed to the garish Ronald McDonald variety. A quick glance, with only a bit of hair sticking out from underneath a bowler hat, could cause confusion.

He whipped his head around, desperate for answers, and saw the huge piano squatting a few feet to his left. An instrument his aunt didn't even play.

He remembered the one object still remaining in Deirdre's bedroom, and his hands started to tremble.

A Steinway piano.

He kept looking and noticed the bonsai calendar. Deirdre had owned a Japanese woodblock. Altogether, his aunt's office contained a Degas painting, a pink lotus flower, Japanese art, and a piano.

Just like Deirdre's room.

Madness. This is madness.

He cast a furtive glance through the open doorway where his aunt had disappeared. The hallway led to a communal kitchen where she was rummaging for Tylenol. Feeling feverish, he shot off a text to his mother.

-Do you know if Deirdre Hollings ever sought counseling at school?-

The response came within seconds.

-I think so. Not sure. Why?-

Preach swallowed. Not the negative reply he was praying for. He took a deep breath and sent one more text, a stab in the dark, not expecting his mother to reply.

-Has Aunt Janice ever stalked anyone?-

The response was delayed this time, but when it came, his throat constricted and he kept blinking his eyes, as if he could change his reality if he only tried hard enough.

-How do you know about that?? Talk in person-

Preach let the phone go limp in his hand.

His aunt had met Deirdre Hollings during her internship at the high school.

Janice had counseled her, maybe even learned about whatever had happened, and developed a bond.

Then she had become obsessed with her.

"Found some," his aunt said, as she pushed through the door. She approached with a glass of water and two white pills but stopped when she saw his face. She moved behind the desk and set the glass down. "Joey?"

"Tell me it wasn't you," he whispered. He felt as if an earthquake had split the ground beneath his feet, and he was teetering on the edge of oblivion. "Tell me you didn't recreate this office in her image."

"Honey, what are you talking about?"

She had dropped the professional demeanor, approaching him with a hand extended and palm up, a concerned aunt. He wanted to embrace her, let her soothe him as she always did, but he had to know.

He looked her in the eye. "Did you kill Farley Robertson, Damian Black, and Elliott Fenton?"

"What in the world are you—?"

Her other hand whipped out from behind her back, gripping a syringe. He tried to step away, but she was fast, and he had not been expecting the maneuver.

Because, of course, she was his aunt.

Because he loved her.

She injected him. He shoved her away, but a numbing sensation was already spreading.

"I knew if anyone figured it out, it would be you. I always felt you were meant to be my son and not your mother's." She glanced down at the syringe. "You came here to arrest me, didn't you?"

"No," he whispered as he tried to stumble toward her. Instead he toppled to the floor, managing a weak cry for help.

"Everyone else has gone home," she said, almost sadly. "No one's going to hear you." She dragged him behind the desk, next to a suitcase. He tried to fight her but could barely move his limbs. She brushed a hand through his hair. "I'm sorry, Joey. I really am. We can't keep this between us, can we?"

"No," he croaked.

"But they were monsters. All of them."

"So are you," he said.

"I'm sorry you feel that way. This doesn't change my feelings for you. But I understand."

"What did you give me?"

"It's just something to keep you sedated while I catch a plane. I'll send someone for you once I land. I won't, of course, be coming back."

"Why?" he gasped. "What did they do?"

She regarded him with a somber expression, poised above him with the needle still gripped in her hand. The somberness turned to sadness, and then pain, and then a white-hot anger so intense it caused her veins to raise like welts along her neck.

"What did they *do*?" She reached into a desk drawer and pulled out an aging jewelry box shaped like a lotus flower. It was the same box from the photo of Deirdre's room.

His aunt turned the box over, popped something with her finger, and a secret compartment opened. She extracted a pile of aging, folded notebook paper.

"I gave her that box, and she left these behind. For me to find."

Now he understood why his aunt had waited so long to act. She hadn't known the truth until she'd bought Deirdre's belongings and found the notes.

"Did she tell you to kill those people, too?"

"She's the only person I've ever truly loved, Joey. In that way, at least. She was perfect. Agatha Christie wrote that, over time, the mind retains what is essential and rejects all else. Deirdre Hollings, even the memory of her, is what is essential to me. I want you to understand that killing those bastards in the way that I did . . . I needed to honor her memory. It wasn't enough—it will never be enough—but it was something."

Preach bit down on his lip to force himself to stay awake. "What did they do to her that could possibly justify murder?"

"Murder? What about justice? Isn't that the purpose of your profession?" She laid a rigid hand atop the notes, her face as taut as a steel cable. "They lured her in with promises of joining the Byronic Wilderness Society. Evan seduced her over a period of months."

"He slept with her and then dumped her?"

Even now, the pain in her grimace was hard for him to bear. "They took her to a cabin in the woods that was owned by Elliott's family. He told her it was a ritual to get in the Society, that they had all done it. She didn't want to. It wasn't her. But she agreed because she wanted so badly to be loved, accepted. Don't we all at that age?"

"What happened?" he said thickly, feeling as if weights were attached to his eyelids. He had to keep her talking, at least find out the truth.

Aunt Janice replaced the letters in the jewelry box. "They stood and watched her masturbate. She thought that was the end of it, but they'd slipped something in her drink to make her compliant. They had sex with her one by one, over her protests, and then they all joined in."

"She was their first."

"Was she? Who knows? Who cares? They took pictures of her and said if she told anyone they would distribute them to the whole school. Then they dropped her off at her house, never spoke to her again, and wrote a veiled poem about what happened in the next issue of the school paper. She killed herself a week later. *They* killed her."

Good God, he thought. He managed a weak cry for help again, though it seemed as if he were an actor in a play, calling out for assistance. It didn't seem real.

She was stroking his hair. "I'm the same person you've always known. You just didn't know that side of me."

He tried to move but only managed to roll onto his side in an ineffective position. "Of all people," he whispered, "I thought I knew you."

"I believe Nabokov said it best. 'Years of secret suffering had taught me superhuman self-control.'"

He looked at his aunt and saw her in a new light, a young woman in love, perhaps confused or ashamed of her desires, perhaps not, perhaps just struck dumb by the beauty and sensitive soul of young Deirdre Hollings.

Struck so dumb she would avenge her death with murder.

"Didn't you read the end of *Five Little Pigs*?" He was grasping, his voice barely above a whisper, but he had to try something. "The murderess admits that she was the one who died because of what she did—not the person she murdered."

"Of course I read it," she said quietly. "And there are some things worth dying for. Deirdre was so much more alive than any of them."

"You got your revenge. Turn yourself in. I'll do everything I can for you."

She cupped his face, her eyes full of love, and then rose. He could feel himself fading.

"Goodbye, Joey. You'll always be in my heart."

"Please. Let me help, I'm begging you."

She tucked the jewelry box under her arm, grabbed the suitcase and her coat, and headed for the door. Preach flopped on the floor like a dying fish. His attempt at a yell for help came out as a croak.

With every step she took, his spirit churned within him, pain and grief and rage, a tornado of helpless emotion. He thought of the lifelong trust his aunt had betrayed and how it made him feel; the terrible shame Deirdre must have felt at the hands of her peers when she lay before them naked and defiled; the torture his cousin had suffered, his body and spirit a puddle of melted wax in that hospital bed. Preach went even deeper, jerking from his memory an image of the candy-colored tree house in Atlanta. This time he didn't turn away. Instead of fighting against it, he gave in and unlocked whatever it was that writhed in horror inside him. He gazed into that child's ruined eyes so close he felt the shattered innocence as his own, the pedophile dirt crusting his body, the bone-deep shame that would never go away.

Bloated with pain and loathing, a burst of emotion-fueled adrenaline shuddered through him, a burst of power, and he managed to drag himself to his elbows, high enough to reach the desk. His aunt heard him and turned, but not before Preach had fumbled for a paperweight and chucked it through the window. His bellow for help followed the sound of breaking glass.

His aunt dashed toward him, but he was already toppling over, unable to sustain his outburst. He fell to the floor as she stared at him in astonishment, then reached into a coat pocket and retrieved the syringe.

She injected him in the arm again, though when she finished a camera flashed behind her, and then another.

The last thing Preach saw before he slipped away was the shocked faces of two reporters crowding the broken window, one of them jabbing at a cell phone while the other worked furiously to photograph the scene.

56

P reach woke in a hospital bed for the second time in two days. The sedative had worn off, and he was released within the hour. As his aunt had promised, she had given him nothing deadly.

Aunt Janice. He still couldn't process it. A quick call to the station confirmed that she was in custody, but before he faced the blizzard of paperwork there was something he needed to do.

He left the hospital and drove straight to his mother's house. She opened the door before he could knock, gently probed his various injuries, and buried her face in her hands. She didn't cry, but when she looked up, shadows of grief and worry darkened her face, along with the same quicksand of disbelief in which Preach was mired.

It was the most emotional he had ever seen her.

"Is it true?" she said. "Did Janice . . ."

"I'm afraid so."

His mother looked away, shuddering as she fought for control. They moved inside and sat on the couch. The forest was brown and still outside the window.

"I have to know," Preach said, "if there were any indications. When I asked if she had ever stalked anyone, you said to talk to you later."

What he really wanted to know, he thought, was whether it was all his fault. Whether he had turned a blind eye for love, whether he could have prevented any of the murders.

His mother hesitated. Preach said, "I've never pressed you about the source of the animosity between you and Aunt Janice. But if there was ever a time for disclosure . . ."

The stiffness returned to his mother's posture, but after a resigned sigh she looked at him with eyes that spoke of a lifetime of hurt and restraint. "The trigger was an old boyfriend, before your father. It was someone I loved very much. Your aunt . . . stole him from me."

"Aunt Janice is gay."

His mother's stare bored into him. "Exactly."

Preach looked down and shuffled his feet.

"Your aunt is someone who gets what she wants in life. She didn't want my boyfriend, of course. But we were arguing about something else, money I'd been given by our parents for college, and she wanted me to suffer."

"Did you know about Deirdre?"

A slow shake of the head. "I knew she had stalked a different girl who spurned her advances. Come to think of it, the girl looked a lot like Deirdre. It was quite the scandal. We weren't speaking, but I know Janice left town because of it."

Preach inhaled deeply through his nose. His mother's house smelled of rose water. "I just don't . . . was she using me all those years? To get to you?"

"Oh, I don't think that at all," she said quickly. "From the first time she saw you, at the hospital, I could see in her eyes how much she loved you. She would have done anything for you."

They both fell silent as they realized the unintended gravity of his mother's words. *Would have done anything for you.*

Preach had heard it said that you only truly love one thing in life. He wasn't sure about that, but what he did know, from his years of experience as a chaplain and a detective, was that even monsters could love.

His mother's hands fluttered and then settled in her lap, as if she was trying to express something that was too much for her, beyond her powers of communication. "I've always known how much you loved her," she said, in a near-whisper. "I never wanted to take that from you."

Preach thought of all those years his mother must have suffered, watching her sister enjoy a closer relationship with her son than she had. His voice was husky when he spoke. "Thank you. And I'm sorry."

Her hand cupped his cheek. "I love you so much, son. I know I'm not very good at showing it." She smiled a sad, self-deprecating smile. "Where do you think you got it from?"

The waitress set the tray on the edge of the table, then deposited two plates full of barbecue ribs, coleslaw, hushpuppies, and fried okra in front of Preach and Ari. The tablecloths were red-and-white checkered cloth, the floor scuffed linoleum, the cement-block walls painted seawater green. Two daily specials were written in magic marker on a whiteboard propped on a table. Men in overalls and grease-stained work shirts waited in line to order.

A hard rain pockmarked the surface of an algae-choked pond outside the window. Preach and Ari had driven less than five miles, but they were worlds away from the vegan grocers and Prius-choked streets of downtown Creekville.

"Are you trying to kill me?" Ari said, staring down at the massive plate of food. "Or is this where you tell me this is the 'real Carolina,' and I'm supposed to get all gooey inside at the fact that you're a modern man who's dialed in to the common folk?"

Her comment was teasingly given, but it made him think about Creekville old and new, hipsters and locals, those on the "inside" and those trapped on the other side of the mirror. Everyone, he thought, was just trying to fit in somewhere.

Just like Deirdre Hollings.

He pushed those thoughts away, savoring the aroma of slow-cooked pork marinating in a mixture of ketchup, vinegar, and pepper. He returned Ari's smirk with one of his own. "Take a bite."

She eyed him in mock seduction as she brought a rib to her lips. As soon as she bit down, her expression started to morph, and by the time she finished chewing her eyes shone with the devotion of a zealot. "Oh my God. I think that's the best barbecue I've ever tasted. Maybe the best anything."

"It's called *cue* around here, Ari. And laws have been introduced to preserve its authenticity. Are you all gooey inside yet?"

She lingered over a few more bites, then wiped her mouth and took a drink of tea. "Everything's delicious, I admit. But you said you'd give me details once we got here."

She already knew about his aunt—everybody knew, thanks to the live broadcast from the team of reporters who'd rescued Preach in his aunt's office.

He told her about the sketch the police artist had rendered, the significance of the items in his aunt's office, and how he had put it all together. Somehow the retelling didn't affect him like he thought it would. It pained him, but it wasn't the rabbit punch of emotion he had expected.

When he finished, Ari couldn't conceal her shock. Eyes wide, she asked, "Where did the reporters come from?"

"They followed me from the station. They were in the parking lot of my aunt's office the whole time, ready to ambush me when I left."

"And instead they got the story of a lifetime."

"Lucky them," he said tonelessly.

She forked a piece of okra. "When you fought against the injection . . . was that real? Can emotions physically affect you like that?"

He had done his research after the fact, but only out of curiosity. He didn't need to verify what he already knew. "What do you think?"

She pressed her lips together, and then her head bobbed slowly up and down.

There wasn't much else to say. He still loved his aunt, and she had saved Ari's life, but she had also committed three acts of premeditated murder. She might never see another city sidewalk.

Due to Preach and Ari's eyewitness testimony, Mac and Mina were going away for a long time, too. Preach planned to do everything in his power to round up the rest of Mac's crew.

Belker was a free man, or at least free of prison. Preach suspected that the troubled author would never truly escape himself.

As for Kirby, his lawyer thought he had a very good chance at a diminished capacity plea, due to the minimal time that passed between Kirby's viewing the photos and killing the mayor. He might very well be looking at a few years for manslaughter instead of life in prison. The nature of the photos and the mayor's other crimes would help his cause, too. Preach could only pray that whatever sentence was handed down, his friend would find the strength to endure.

And that he would finish that book about the case he had started, the one whose name Kirby told him had been changed to *Written in Blood*.

Preach's mother had promised to help Jalene find an administrative position at the university, and he was working on finding her an apartment in a better school district. If he had to, he'd supplement the rent himself until she got on her feet.

By the time Preach and Ari finished eating, their moods had improved. So had the weather. The rain turned light and dreamy, and when a customer opened the door, a mild breeze drifted into the barbecue shack.

Ari was wearing a lacy shirt under an olive-green bomber jacket. Though her face was wan from the stress of the last few weeks, he found her as attractive as ever.

"So what's next on the to-be-read pile?" she asked. "Where does a clever detective turn for escape after a case like that?"

"Shel Silverstein? Dr. Seuss?"

Her eyes crinkled as she laughed.

"I don't know," he said. "I may never read a book in the same way. During the investigation, it felt as if those four novels almost took on a life of their own."

They shared a moment of silence, and the corners of her lips curled upward. "I've already picked out my next book."

"Is that right?"

She put her hands on the table, palms up and inviting him to join. "I'm thinking *Pride and Prejudice* would fit the bill."

He looked down at her tattoos. "I confess you don't seem like the Jane Austen type."

"What if I told you the book was about the errors in judgment that can occur when people first meet, and how those judgments can change over time?"

He took her hands in his, and they interlocked fingers. "Then I'd say the author was a wise woman."

"Is this where we talk about what happens next?" she asked.

"Didn't we agree that words were cheap?"

She looked at him from across the table, her eyes warm but challenging. "Then why don't you show me?"

He met her gaze, then slapped a pair of twenties on the table. They didn't wait for the change.

Acknowledgments

A cknowledgments are getting harder and harder for me to write. So many people have touched my career in positive ways over the years and contributed to the calculus of the final product. I am forever indebted to all of them and scoff at the myth of the solitary author. A few special thanks for this novel: as always, I am scarily dependent on my old friends and early readers Rusty Dalferes and John Strout. Maria Morris and Ryan McLemore are beacons of support, too. Special thanks to Marcus Hill for his input on local law and all things North Carolina. Dan Ozdowski made sure the Creekville IT team actually knew what they were talking about. Duke University Law Professors Jamie Boyle and Jennifer Jenkins watched my back on IP issues. Richard Marek and Judy Sternlight provided preliminary edits that really helped shape the book. Ayesha Pande, my wonderful agent, deserves a ton of credit for helping convince me to write the novel, and for shepherding it through with such expert hands. Dan Mayer has been a fantastic editor and supporter, as has the entire team at Seventh Street. Wife and family: it's all for you, as always.

About the Author

Layton Green is a former attorney who writes across multiple genres. His novels have been nominated for several awards (including a finalist for an International Thriller Writers award), optioned for film, and have reached number 1 on numerous genre lists in the United States, the United Kingdom, and Germany.

Please visit Layton on Goodreads, Facebook, and at www.layton green.com for additional information on the author, his works, and more.

If you have not joined Layton Green's VIP Reader's Group, go to laytongreenauthor.subscribemenow.com for notification of new releases, special promotions, and more.